Queens of Romance

*A collection of bestselling novels by
the world's leading romance writers*

**Three novels from international
bestselling author**

PENNY JORDAN

"Penny Jordan's latest is intense, passionate,
fun and volatile. The characters share a powerful
connection that is spellbinding."
—*Romantic Times BOOKreviews* on
Bedding His Virgin Mistress

"Penny Jordan's *Expecting the Playboy's Heir* is a
charming romance, with two lovely characters"
—*Romantic Times BOOKreviews*

"The story charms with romance,
passion and drama."
—*Romantic Times BOOKreviews* on
Blackmailing the Society Bride

MILLS & BOON

100 YEARS

of pure reading pleasure

100 Reasons to Celebrate

We invite you to join us in celebrating Mills & Boon's centenary. Gerald Mills and Charles Boon founded Mills & Boon Limited in 1908 and opened offices in London's Covent Garden. Since then, Mills & Boon has become a hallmark for romantic fiction, recognised around the world.

We're proud of our 100 years of publishing excellence, which wouldn't have been achieved without the loyalty and enthusiasm of our authors and readers.

Thank you!

Each month throughout the year there will be something new and exciting to mark the centenary, so watch for your favourite authors, captivating new stories, special limited edition collections…and more!

PENNY JORDAN

Jet Set Wives

Containing

**Bedding His Virgin Mistress,
Expecting the Playboy's Heir
& Blackmailing the Society Bride**

*M&B™ and M&B™ with the Rose Device
are trademarks of the publisher.
Harlequin Mills & Boon Limited, Eton House,
18-24 Paradise Road,
Richmond, Surrey TW9 1SR*

Jet Set Wives © by Harlequin Books S.A. 2008

Bedding His Virgin Mistress, Expecting the Playboy's Heir and
Blackmailing the Society Bride were first published in Great
Britain by Harlequin Mills & Boon Limited in separate,
single volumes.

Bedding His Virgin Mistress © Penny Jordan 2005
Expecting the Playboy's Heir © Penny Jordan 2005
Blackmailing the Society Bride © Penny Jordan 2005

ISBN: 978 0 263 86689 6

025-0908

*Printed and bound in Spain
by Litografia Rosés S.A., Barcelona*

Bedding His Virgin Mistress

PENNY JORDAN

The
Queens of Romance
Collection

February 2008
Their Wedding Deal Helen Bianchin

March 2008
Engaged to be Married? Jessica Steele

April 2008
A Passionate Bargain Michelle Reid

May 2008
Marriage Vows Sara Craven

June 2008
Rogues and Rakes Paula Marshall

July 2008
Summer Delights Nora Roberts

August 2008
Summer Engagements Betty Neels

September 2008
Jet Set Wives Penny Jordan

October 2008
At His Mercy Linda Howard

November 2008
Baby Bonds Caroline Anderson

Dear Readers,

What a wonderful year this centenary year for Mills & Boon is going to be for romance readers and writers alike. I can't claim to have been reading and writing Mills & Boon® books for one hundred years of course, but I can say that one hundred years would not be long enough for me to write and read all the Mills & Boon books I would like to write and read.

I am thrilled that my *Jet Set Wives* books are going to be issued in a special collection for this centenary year. I loved the heroines of these books and I really enjoyed bringing the glamour of the Jet Set life into them. What better year in which to read about the champagne lifestyle of my heroines than the year in which as readers and writers we can "toast" the centenary of our favourite publisher – even if that "toast" is in the form of a cup of coffee. May this year be a year in which we celebrate together the pleasure that comes from a "good read."

Hurrah for Mills & Boon and its family of writers, those who get the books onto the bookshelves, and its readers – a perfect match – may it continue for another hundred years and more.

I wish you this year and many years of the happiest of happy reading.

Penny Jordan

Penny Jordan has been writing for more than twenty years and has an outstanding record: over one hundred and sixty-five novels published, including the phenomenally successful *A Perfect Family, To Love, Honour & Betray, The Perfect Sinner* and *Power Play,* which hit *The Sunday Times* and *New York Times* bestseller lists. Penny Jordan was born in Preston, Lancashire, and now lives in rural Cheshire.

CHAPTER ONE

CARLY glanced discreetly at the small mixed party she was minding in her role as partner in one of the country's most prestigious and exclusive event-organising businesses, and wondered how long it would be before she could leave. The event was a fortieth birthday party for a banker and he'd chosen to have it at *the* London Nightclub CoralPink. It would not have been the venue she would have chosen but in a business where ultimately the customer was always right that was not her decision to make.

Already, though, she could see that their client's wife was beginning to look less than pleased at the amount of attention her husband was giving the upmarket eye candy on view. There were already half a dozen empty bottles of Cristal champagne on their table, and another of the men was chatting up a girl who had been walking past, inviting her to join them. Male libidos and wifely tempers were both beginning to rise ominously in the club's hormone-drenched heat, Carly realised dispiritedly.

She had balked at this assignment all along, knowing it wasn't her cup of tea. She preferred the kind of event she had supervised over the weekend—a jolly surprise eightieth birthday party held for a sharp-witted grandmother by her large family. It had taken some delicate finessing of finances on Carly's part to ensure that everything they had wanted was achievable within their modest budget, and she had been justifiably proud of the end result.

Mike Lucas's wife was going to explode in a minute if he didn't stop flirting with the young girl he had grabbed. Carly swiftly got up and made her way towards him, intent on defusing the situation before it got out of hand.

Ricardo didn't know why the hell he had allowed himself to be persuaded to come here. His appetite for the proposed business deal that had brought him here had already soured. The whole set-up was everything he loathed, and could best be summed up as rich, immoral men being pursued by greedy, amoral women, he decided cynically.

His attention was caught by the occupants of a table several feet away. A group of forty-something men, paunchy and sweating from a combination of the club's heat and the effect of the skimpily dressed young women thronging the room. Their wives and partners might be younger than they, but they were nowhere near as young as the girls the men were watching—apart from one. She was younger than the rest but still a woman and not a girl, and as Ricardo watched her she got up from her seat and walked round to the other side the table, where one of the men had started to paw a giggling leggy brunette for whom he had just ordered a bottle of champagne.

'Mike.' Carly smiled as she leaned towards him, strategically placing herself between him and the unknown girl.

'Hello, sexy. Want some champagne?'

Mike Lucas made a grab for her, pulling her down onto his knee and putting his hand on her breast.

Immediately Carly froze, warning anger zig-zagging

through the glance she gave him, but Mike was too drunk to notice. Still grinning, he pulled the other girl towards him as well. Unlike Carly, she made it plain that she was enjoying the attention.

'Look what I've got,' Mike called out to his friends, one hand on Carly's breast and the other on the other girl's. He jiggled them inexpertly and boasted drunkenly, 'Hey, what about this for a threesome, guys?'

Ricardo's hooded gaze monitored the small unsavoury scene. The sight of women selling their bodies was nothing new to him. He had grown up in the slums of Naples, and these women—these spoiled, pampered, lazy society women, with their designer clothes and their Cartier jewellery—were, as far as he was concerned, far more to be despised than the prostitutes of the Naples alleys.

He pushed back his chair and stood up, throwing a pile of banknotes down onto the table. The man who had invited him to the club was talking to someone at the bar, but Ricardo did not bother to go over and take any formal leave of him before quitting the club.

As a billionaire he had no need to observe the niceties that governed the behaviour of other, less wealthy men.

Ricardo studied the newspapers the most senior of his quartet of male PAs had left on his desk for him. He read them as he drank the second of his ritual two cups of thick, strong black coffee. Some tastes could be acquired, but others could never totally be destroyed or denied. He frowned, a look that was a formidable blend of anger and pride forking like lightning in the almost basalt darkness of his eyes.

He was not a prettily handsome man, but he was a man who commanded and indeed demanded the visual attention of others—especially women, who were aware immediately of the aura of raw, challenging male sexuality he exuded.

He reached for the first newspaper, flicking dismissively and contemptuously through its pages until he found what he wanted. A smile, in reality no more than cynically bared white teeth against the warmth of the skin tone that proclaimed his Italian heritage, curled his mouth without reaching his eyes as he glanced swiftly down the newspaper's much trumpeted, newly revised 'Rich List'.

He didn't have to look very far to find his own name. Indeed he could count on the fingers of one hand the names that came above his.

Ricardo Salvatore, billionaire. Estimated fortune... Ricardo gave a short, grim laugh as he looked at a figure that fell well short of his actual wealth.

Beneath his name there were also a couple of lines describing him truthfully as single and thirty-two years old, and untruthfully as having founded his fortune on an inheritance from his uncle. A further line offered the information that, in recognition of his charitable donations to a variety of good causes, it was rumoured that Ricardo Salvatore was to be given a knighthood.

Now Ricardo did smile.

A knighthood! Not a bad achievement for someone who had been orphaned by the deaths of his young Italian mother and British father in a rail accident, and who, because of that, had ended up growing up virtually alone in the worst of Naples' slums. It had been a tough and sometimes brutal way to grow up, but occasionally Ricardo felt that he had more respect and admiration for the companions of his youth than he did for the people he now mixed with.

Family ties and close friendships were not things that had ever formed a part of the fabric of his life, but he did not feel their absence. In fact, he actively liked his solitariness, and his corresponding freedom from other people's demands. He had learned young how to survive—by listening and observing—and how to make his own rules for the way he lived his life. He drew his strength from what existed within him rather than what other people thought of him. He had been just eighteen, fiercely competitive and ambitious, when he had gambled for and won the money that had enabled him to buy his first container ship.

He dropped the newspaper onto his desk, picked up the file adjacent to it marked 'Potential Acquisitions' and started to speed-read through its contents. Ricardo was always on the look out for promising new acquisitions to add to his portfolio, and Prêt a Party would fit into it very neatly.

The first time he had heard of the organisation had been when a business acquaintance had mentioned it in passing, commenting that he was a family friend of its young owner. In fact, knowing Marcus Canning as he did, he was rather surprised that a man as financially astute as Marcus hadn't seen the potential of the business for himself.

He gave a small shrug. Marcus's reasons for not acting on the potential of Prêt a Party were of relatively little interest to him. By nature Ricardo was a hunter, and, like all hunters, he enjoyed the adrenalin-boosting thrill of the chase almost as much as he enjoyed the ultimate and inevitable kill at the end of it.

Prêt a Party might only represent a small 'kill,' but Ricardo's preparations for the chase would still be carefully planned.

The normal avenue of obtaining detailed industry reports was not one he favoured; for one thing it tended to alert every other hunter to his interest, and for another he preferred his own methods and his own instincts.

The first thing he wanted to do was find out a good deal more about how the business worked—how efficient it was, how profitable it was, and how vulnerable to a takeover that would be profitable to him. The best person to tell him that was, of course, the owner, Lucy Blayne, but she was hardly likely to equip a potential and predatory buyer with such information. Which was why he had decided to pose as a potential client. The kind of fussy client who wanted to know every single in and out of how things worked and how his commission would be handled before he gave it. The kind of client who insisted on seeing Prêt a Party's organisational capabilities at first hand.

Of course in order to have these 'eccentricities' catered for, he in turn would have to dangle a very large and very juicy carrot in front of Lucy Blayne.

And that was exactly what he was going to do.

'Carly! Thank God you're back! It's absolute chaos here!'

Walking into Prêt a Party's smart but chaotic office in Sloane Street, one of the most upmarket areas of London, Carly acknowledged ruefully that things must indeed be chaotic for her once schoolfriend and now employer—kind-hearted and sweet-natured Lucy Blayne—to be in too much of a rush to ask Carly how things had gone last night.

One pretty but terrified-looking young girl who was new was rushing around trying to cope with the non-stop ringing of the telephone, whilst a couple more, who weren't new, were earnestly reassuring clients that, yes, everything was in hand for their big event.

'We're just sooo amazingly busy—that launch party we did for you-know-who, the It Girl of the moment's new jewellery range, got a mensh in *Vogue*. Nick's bringing us in so much new business,' Lucy enthused.

Carly said nothing. She had done her best not to let Lucy see how much she disliked Nick, and of course there was no way she could tell her friend why. Lucy was deeply in love with her new husband, and Carly knew how much it would hurt her to learn that Nick had actually come on to Carly herself within days of Lucy introducing him into the business.

'Oh!' The pretty young girl looked shocked and almost dropped the telephone receiver.

'It's the Duke of Ryle,' she told Lucy theatrically, in a cut-glass upper-class English voice. 'And he wants to speak to you.'

Lucy rolled her eyes. 'Don't disappear, there's something important I need to discuss with you,' she told Carly quickly, before saying cheerfully, 'Uncle Charles— how lovely. How is Aunt Jane?'

Smiling reassuringly at the flustered and flushed-faced young girl, Carly edged her way past the overflowing desks in the outer office and into her small private office, exhaling in relief as she stepped into her own circle of peace.

A note on her desk caught her eye and she grinned as she read it.

BEWARE—Lucy is in major panic mode—Jules

The three of them—Lucy, Julia and Carly—herself, had been at school together, and Carly knew that Jules, like her, had been extremely dubious at first when Lucy had told them she intended to set up an event organisation company.

But Lucy could be very persuasive when she wanted to be, and since—as Jules had pointed out—neither of them had any other job to go to, and Lucy, thanks to her large trust fund, could afford to both set up the business and pay them a respectable salary, they simply could not refuse.

Now, three years later and much to her own astonishment, Carly had been forced to admit that Lucy's business was beginning to look as though it had the potential to become a really big success. Just so long as she continued to insist that they kept a firm grip both on reality and their costings.

'Come back!'

'Jules!'

'So, how did last night go?'

Carly grimaced expressively. 'Well, let's just say that the tabloid journalist who snapped Mike Lucas with one hand down the front of the Honourable Seraphina Ordley's Matthew Williamson frock and the other gripping my far less worthy, five-year-old second-hand Armani silk-clad breast will by now have realised his mistake. ''Thou shalt not photograph the niece of one's rag's major shareholder in a pose more suited to a failed contestant from *Big Brother*''.'

'Ordley?' Jules mused. 'So she's a Harlowe, then.' As she was an earl's granddaughter, Julia knew *Burke's Peerage* inside out. 'It has said that the Harlowes' motto should be ''As in name, so in action''. It's a Charles II title,' Jules explained. 'He handed them out like sweets to his cast-off mistresses. You aren't smiling,' she accused Carly.

'Neither would you be if you had been there last night.'

'Oh. As bad as that, was it?'

When Carly made no verbal response, but instead simply looked at her, Jules grinned. 'Okay, okay, I apologise. I should have been the one to go with them, I know, and I backed out and left you to do it for me... Did he really grab your boob, Carly? What did you do?'

'I reminded myself that the evening was making us a profit of £6,000.'

'Ah.'

'And then I dropped a full bottle of Cristal on his balls.'

'Oh!'

'It wasn't funny, Jules,' she protested, when her friend started to laugh. 'I love Lucy to bits and most of the time I'm grateful to her for including me in her plans—like when she decided to set up this business. But when it comes to events like last night's...'

'It was one of Nick's, wasn't it?'

'Yes,' Carly agreed tersely.

'And the weekend—did you manage to get time to see...them?'

Carly frowned. The three of them were so close that there were no secrets between them, but even so the habit of loyalty was ingrained deeply within her.

Jules—or the Honourable Julia Fellowes, to give her her correct title—touched her gently on the arm, and Carly shook away her own reticence.

'It was dreadful,' she told her simply. 'Even now I don't think they've really taken it in. I felt so so sorry for them. They've lost so much—the estate and everything that went with it—and the prestige living there gave them was very important to them. And now this.'

'Well, at least thanks to you they've got a roof over their heads.'

'The Dower House.' Carly pulled a face. 'They hate living there.'

'What? When I think of how you've beggared yourself to get a mortgage and buy it from the estate for them—oh, honestly, Carly.'

'I might not be able to afford a designer lifestyle, but I've hardly beggared myself. Thanks to you I'm living rent-free in one of the poshest parts of London. I've got a job I love, all the travel I could possibly want...'

She had balked initially at Jules's generous offer that the three of them should share her flat—the three of them being Jules, Carly, and Jules's notorious 'I'm having a bad day and I need to shop' habit. Other people ate chocolate, or rowed with their mother; Jules bought shoes.

But who was she to mock other people's security blanket habits? Ever since she could remember she had saved: pennies, and then her allowance...comfort money. Not that it was bringing her much comfort now. Thanks to the needs of her adopted parents, her bank account was permanently empty.

'...and a weight round your neck that no one should have,' she heard Jules telling her protectively.

Ignoring her comment, Carly said, 'I wish I could have stayed for a bit longer. I felt guilty leaving them.'

'*You* felt guilty? That's crazy. Carly, you don't owe them anything. When I think of what they did to you!'

'You mean like giving me a first-class education?' Carly offered her quietly.

It was at times like this that she recognised the huge gap that existed between herself and the other two.

Despite their shared education, they had been born worlds apart.

'You've had to pay for it,' Julia told her protectively.

Carly made no response. After all it was true—but not in the way that Julia had meant. The payment she found unbearable was the knowledge that she was destined always to be an outsider, someone who did not quite fit in—anywhere.

Julia gave her another hug.

Pretty, brunette Julia, and gentle, tender-hearted blonde Lucy—Carly had envied them both, just as she had envied all the other girls at school: girls who knew beyond any kind of doubt that they were taking their rightful place in their own world. Unlike her. She had known she had no right to be there in that alien, wealthy environment. Everything about her had screamed out that she did not and could not fit in. She had felt so out of place—a fraud, a pauper, a charity case, someone whose life had been bought! And, of course, very quickly everyone had known just why she had come to be there.

'Sometimes I wonder what on earth I'm doing in this business.' Lucy exhaled as she came to join them.

'Only sometimes?' Carly teased her.

Lucy grinned.

'We've got a major client scenario about to take place. Nick is on his way over with him right now.'

Carly looked away discreetly as she saw a small shadow touch Julia's eyes. It had been Julia who had introduced Nick to Lucy, and sometimes Carly wondered if Nick, with his flashy pseudo-charm which she found so unappealing, hadn't perhaps made Julia as vulnerable to him as Lucy had been. Was she being overly cynical in worrying that Nick had married Lucy more for her trust fund and her family's social position and wealth than because he had genuinely fallen in love with her? For Lucy's sake she hoped it was the latter, but it had all happened so quickly—too quickly, Carly felt. And now here was Nick, a man she didn't like or trust, taking a very prominent role in the business.

'How major?' Carly asked.

'Jules, call over one of the girls, will you?' Lucy begged. 'I'm dying for an espresso! Absolutely huge. Apparently he knows Marcus—and you can imagine how I feel about that!'

Marcus Canning was Lucy's *bête noir*: a family friend who was also one of her trustees and who, against Lucy's wishes, had insisted on being kept fully informed of every aspect of the business before he would agree to Lucy investing her trust fund money in it. Personally, Carly thought that Marcus Canning, with his well-known reputation for astute financial dealings, was a good person for them to have on board, and she had felt both proud and pleased when he had praised her at their last financial meeting for the way she was running the administrative and financial side of the business.

'And, of course, if he does commission us then we're going to make a bomb!' she heard Lucy announcing enthusiastically.

'Who is he, and what does he want?' Julia chimed in.

'He's Ricardo Salvatore. He's mega-wealthy, and his story is real rags to riches stuff. There was an article in one of the Sunday supplements about him a couple of months ago. He grew up in Naples and he was orphaned very young. But he ran away from the orphanage when he was ten years old and ran wild with a group of children who existed by stealing and begging, generally blagging a living. He's a billionaire now, and he owns—amongst other things—three top-of-the-market exclusive luxury cruise liners. What he wants is for us to organise private parties and that kind of thing for people on these cruises at several villa venues throughout the world. He also owns the villas—and in one case the island it's on.

'He rang earlier, at a very bad moment. In fact, while we were still in bed at home.' She pulled a face and then giggled. 'Poor Nick was…well… Anyway, Nick's just phoned to warn me that they're on their way over here. Ricardo's told him that before he makes a decision he wants to observe a variety of our already planned events, as a sort of unofficial extra guest.'

'What? You're going to let him gatecrash other people's parties?' Carly demanded, shocked. 'Are you sure that's wise?'

'I can't imagine many of our clients would refuse to have a billionaire as an extra guest!' Lucy told her defensively. 'Anyway, Nick has already told him it's okay, and the thing is, Carly, it makes sense if you are the one to accompany him.'

'Me?'

'One of us has to go with him,' Lucy pointed out. 'And besides…' She bit her lip. 'Look, don't take this the wrong way, but I think you'd have more in common with him than either of us, and he'll feel more comfortable with you…'

It took Carly several seconds to catch on, and when she did she her face burned.

'I see.' She knew her voice was tense and edgy but she couldn't help herself. 'So what you're saying is that he's a self-made man, not out of the top drawer and not—'

'Oh, rats. I knew you'd take it the wrong way.' Lucy groaned. 'Yes, he *is* a self-made man, Carly—and a billionaire self-made man at that—but that wasn't what I meant! It isn't anything to do with class! I want *you* to escort and accompany him because I know you'll make a better impression on him than anyone else. Apparently he likes all that stuff you like—reading, museums, galleries. And it is desperately important that we do make a good him impression on him and secure his business.' She paused, and then told them both, 'I didn't want to tell you about this, but the truth is that things haven't being going as well as they were. We had that warehouse fire earlier in the year, which destroyed loads of our stuff…'

'But we were insured!' Carly protested.

Lucy shook her head.

'No, we weren't. Nick felt that the quotes you'd got were too high, and he asked me to hold off paying the premium until he'd checked out some other insurers,' she told her unhappily. 'I thought Nick had gone ahead and insured us with new insurers, but I'd got it wrong, and of course, unfortunately, the existing insurance lapsed.'

Carly frowned. Lucy looked and sounded strained and uncomfortable. She couldn't help wondering if Lucy was trying to protect Nick by taking the blame for his negligence.

She ought to be grateful to this as yet unknown potential client for giving her the opportunity to escape— if only for a while—from her growing discomfort about the way Nick was using the business's bank account as though it were his own private account. Since Lucy had made it clear that Nick was to have *carte blanche* to withdraw money from the account whenever he liked, there was no legitimate objection she could make. Nick had shrugged aside her concern about their growing overdraft by telling her that the deficit would be made good from Lucy's trust fund, but to Carly it seemed shockingly unbusinesslike to waste money paying interest on an overdraft.

'They'll be here in a few minutes. God, I hope we get his business.' Lucy yawned. 'I am sooo tired—and we've got dinner with the folks tonight. How about you? Have you got anything on?'

'Only my writing class,' Carly answered.

'I don't know why you're still going to that,' Julia told her ruefully.

Originally they had decided to attend the writing group together, at Julia's suggestion—mainly, Carly suspected, because Julia had been dating an up-and-coming literary novelist. But after a couple of weeks the romance had faded, and Julia had taken a period of extended leave to visit her sister in Australia, leaving Carly to attend the weekly meetings on her own.

'Mmm...'

'Well, it won't hurt to miss one class, surely? Unless, of course, it's Miss Pope's turn to read one of her poems?' Julia giggled.

Carly tried and failed to give her a quelling look.

'They are pretty awful,' she agreed, joining in her laughter.

'What project has the Professor given you all to write about this time?' Julia gave a small shudder. 'It's not litter again, is it?'

'No,' Carly confirmed carefully, 'it isn't litter. Actually it's *fantasy sex*!'

It was amazing what the word *sex* could do, she reflected ruefully as both her friends turned to stare at her.

'Fantasy sex?' Lucy demanded. 'What, you mean like…imagining sex with a fantasy man?' She started to laugh. 'Why?'

'Professor Elseworth wants us to stretch our imagination and take it into a new dimension.'

'Right now, any kind of sex is a fantasy for me,' Julia remarked gloomily, before adding, 'But I can't imagine *you* writing about fantasy sex, Carly. I mean, you don't actually do it at all, do you?'

Carly bared her teeth in a ferociously fake smile.

'No, I don't. And I won't until I find someone worth doing it with!'

'Well, okay—I mean, I don't have a problem with that—but how on earth are you going to write about fantasy sex when…?'

Carly gave her a withering look.

'I'm going to use my imagination. That is the whole point of the exercise,' she told her with awesome dignity.

'Rather you than me!'

'No talking about sex during working hours,' Lucy began mock primly, and then stopped as, to Carly's relief, their newest recruit arrived with Lucy's espresso.

In all honesty she would be only too happy to have an excuse to miss out on her writing class and its assignment. She certainly didn't want to write about fantasy sex—or indeed sex of any kind. She knew there was a barrier between her and the potential enjoyment of her sexuality. But how could she ever give herself freely and openly, to a man and to love, when she could never imagine being able to reveal her emotional scars to him? How could there be true intimacy when she herself was so afraid of it? So afraid of being judged and then rejected? Didn't events such as the one she had attended last night confirm all that she had always thought and feared? Giving yourself in and with love to another human being meant giving yourself over to being judged as not good enough, not acceptable, not worthy, and ultimately to rejection. And she had learned very young just how much that hurt.

Her game plan for her life involved focusing on emotional and financial security: building her career, enjoying the company of her friends, ultimately travelling—if she could afford to do so—but always ensuring that she never made the mistake of falling in love.

She had decided that she was only going to have a sexual relationship if she met a man she wanted physically with intense passion and hunger—a man with whom she knew she could share the heights of physical pleasure in a relationship that carried no health risks. A serial male sexual predator was not an option. And at the same time she would also have to feel one hundred per cent confident that she would never be at risk of becoming emotionally involved with him. Add to that the fact that she wasn't even actively looking for this paragon, and it seemed a pretty foregone conclusion that she was likely to remain a virgin indefinitely.

Not that the prospect bothered her.

CHAPTER TWO

'AND you're sure my requirements won't be a problem for you, Nick? I know you don't have a large staff,' Ricardo said blandly.

'Absolutely not. Lucy said that Carly jumped at the chance. In fact she begged for it.' Nick laughed. 'And I don't suppose anyone can blame her. After all, when you've been used to the best of everything all your life and suddenly it isn't available any more, and you're a decent-looking woman, I suppose you're bound to look forward to spending time with a rich man.'

'She's looking for a rich husband?'

Nick grinned.

'Who said anything about marriage? Anyway, come up to the office and I can introduce you to her.'

'I think you said earlier that she is your wife's partner?'

'Employee. The three of them—Lucy, Julia and Carly—were at school together. Neither Julia nor Carly have put any money into the business, though.'

'So financially the partnership is—'

'Just me and Lucy,' Nick informed him.

'Carly normally does all the financial and administrative stuff, but to be honest I don't think she's up to the job. You'd be doing me a favour by taking her off my hands for a week or two, so that I can get the financial side of things sorted out properly. Lucy's a loyal little soul, and devoted to her friends—you know the type, all breeding and no brains.' He shrugged. 'I don't

want to say too much to her. Anyway, having Carly
with you won't be too much of a hardship—she's a
good-looker, and obliging too, if you know what I
mean—especially if you treat her generously. Like I
said, Carly has her head screwed on.'

'Are you speaking from personal experience?'
Ricardo asked him dryly.

'What? Hell, no. I'm a married man. But let's just
say she let me know that it was available if I wanted
it,' Nick boasted.

He was well aware that Carly didn't like him, and it
amused him to think of what he was setting her up for.
Discrediting her wouldn't do him any harm in other
ways either, he congratulated himself. For one thing she
wouldn't be able to go tittle-tattling to Lucy.

'Carly is very good at getting other people to pay her
bills for her—as both Lucy and Julia already know.
She's even managed to blag a rent-free room in Julia's
flat. If she can't find a rich man to finance her, then the
lifestyle that working for Prêt a Party gives her is the
next best thing. All that first-class travel and accom-
modation provided by the clients, plus getting to mingle
with their guests.' He winked at Ricardo. 'Ideal for her
type of woman. Once I've introduced you, I'll get her
to go through the list of our upcoming events with you
so that you can cherry pick the ones you want to attend.'

'Excellent.' Inwardly, Ricardo decided that Nick
sounded more like a pimp than a businessman. Or in
this business did the two go hand in hand?

They had reached Prêt a Party's office, and Nick
pushed open the door for him.

'Ah, there's Carly,' he announced. 'I'll call her over.'

There was no way she could pretend not to be aware
of Nick's summons, Carly had to acknowledge reluc-

tantly, and she walked towards him. She was wearing her normal office uniform of jeans and a tee shirt—the jeans snugly encased the slender length of her legs but irritatingly, the tee shirt skimming the curves of her breasts had pulled free of the low waistband of her jeans. It was a familiar hazard when one was almost five foot ten tall, give or take one eighth of an inch, and it exposed the flat golden flesh of her taut stomach. Whenever she could, Carly ran—mostly on her own, but sometimes with a group of fellow amateur runners—and her body had a sensuous grace of which she herself was totally unaware.

Long thick hair, honey-brown, with natural highlights, swung past her shoulders as she walked calmly towards Nick—and then missed a step as she saw the man standing to one side of him.

If she were in the market for a man—sex-wise, that was, because she would not want one for any other reason—then this was definitely a man she would want. She could feel the power of his sexuality from here; she could breathe it in almost. And it was very heady stuff. Far more potent than any champagne, she thought dizzily.

A vulnerable woman—which, of course, she was not—would find it almost impossible to resist such a man. He was a living, breathing lure for the whole female sex. Except for her. She had exempted herself from such dangers.

Ricardo frowned in immediate recognition as he watched her walking towards them and coldly came to two very separate decisions.

The first was that he intended to have her in his bed, and the second was that she embodied everything he most disliked about her class and type.

She was stunningly beautiful and irritatingly confident. And he already knew from listening to Nick that she was a woman who judged a man by his wallet and how much she could extract from it. A gold-digger, in other words.

'Hello, gorgeous. Let me introduce you to Ricardo—oh, and by the way, Mike Lucas rang me to tell me how much he enjoyed your company last night,' Nick told Carly, as he put his arm round her shoulders and drew her close to his side.

Pulling herself free, Carly extended her hand to Ricardo and smiled at him with genuine pleasure. After all, he was going to be releasing her from the unpleasantness of Nick's unwanted company.

Well, she certainly didn't believe in wasting any time, Ricardo thought cynically as he took the hand Carly had extended and shook it firmly.

'Ricardo wants to have a look at our upcoming events so that he can decide which ones he wants to attend. You can use my office, Carly,' Nick told her benignly.

His office? Carly had to look away. 'His office', as he called it had, until he had come onto the scene, been her office. In fact it still was her office, she reflected, since she was the only one who did any work in it. Nick's only appearances in it were when he came in to ask her to countersign another cheque.

Carly smiled as she led the way to the small sectioned-off cubicle where she worked. Ricardo had lost count of the number of women who had smiled at him the way Carly was doing right now—with warmth and promise—especially women of Carly's type. Upmarket, privately educated pampered women, contemptuous of the very idea of supporting themselves, whose goal in life was to find a man to financially underwrite their desired lifestyle.

His gaze narrowed. Female predators were a familiar risk to any man to whom the press attached the label 'wealthy'; he had discovered that a long time ago. He had been twenty-two and merely a millionaire the first time he had encountered the type of well-bred young woman who believed that a man like him—a self-made man who had come up from nothing—would be delighted to spend lavishly on her in exchange for the social cachet of being connected with her.

She had been the sister of the thrusting young entrepreneur with whom he'd had business dealings. Initially he had thought he must be mistaken, and that she couldn't possibly be coming on to him as openly as she'd seemed to be. He had indeed been naïve. There had been an expensive lunch to which she had invited herself, he remembered, and an even more expensive afternoon's shopping, when she had pointed out to him the Rolex watch she wanted. Like a besotted fool he had gone back to the shop and bought it for her the moment she had left him to return to her brother. He had then, even more besottedly, booked himself out of his hotel room and into a huge suite, had ordered a magnum of champagne and the most luxurious meal he could think of, and then wasted more time than he cared to think about dreaming of the pleasure that lay in store for them both. He would make love to her as she had never been made love to her before, and then, in the morning, he would kiss her awake and surprise her with the watch...

He had very quickly been brought back to earth when, instead of relishing his tender caresses, the object of his adoration had told him peevishly to 'hurry up', and then pouted and sulked until he produced her watch. The final blow to his pride, though, had been unwittingly delivered by her brother, who had informed him that his sister was as good as engaged to an extremely wealthy older man. Fortunately, although his illusions had been shattered, his heart had been left intact, and the whole experience had taught him what he considered to be a valuable lesson: the only difference between spoilt, pampered society women and the prostitutes of Naples was that the prostitutes had no option other than to sell themselves if they wanted to feed their children.

He had yet to meet a woman whose desire for him did not go hand in hand with her desire for his money, no matter how much she might initially deny it. Indeed, if he hadn't been so fastidious he knew that he would have found it cheaper to hire the services of a professional than to satisfy the financial demands of the society women who had shared his bed. The discovery that the last one to do so had been contemplating being unfaithful to him with an elderly billionaire old enough to be her grandfather had confirmed his cynical belief that no woman was too beautiful or too well born to be above using her 'assets' to secure financial security.

He would take Carly to bed and he would ensure that both of them enjoyed the experience, and that would be that. Why shouldn't he take advantage of what she was? She was a beautiful woman, and it was a very long time since he had last had sex, but her social standing cut no ice with him, and nor was he impressed by it—quite the opposite, in fact.

'Here's a list of our upcoming events and their venues,' Carly announced a little breathlessly, after she had printed it off from the computer.

She hadn't expected to be so acutely aware of Ricardo's powerful and sensually invasive sexual aura. She wasn't used to this kind of man, and there was an unfamiliar flutter in her stomach and a hyped-up sensation of excitement in her head. She felt both excited and apprehensive, as though somehow her whole body had moved up into a higher gear, a more intense state of awareness. It was simply her hormones responding to his hormones, she told herself prosaically. Her office was way too small for the two of them.

Out of the corner of her eye she saw that he was removing his suit jacket, and she discovered that she was sucking in an unsteady breath of reluctant female appreciation. Beneath the fine cotton of his shirt she could see the muscular hardness of his body. She had recently read an article in a magazine about the new fashion for men to wax their chest hair. He obviously didn't subscribe to it.

The author of the article had propounded the theory that women found the abrasion of male body hair unwelcome against their own flesh. Carly's tongue-tip touched her lips. A fine mist of sensual heat had broken out on her skin. Beneath her tee shirt her bra-covered breasts suddenly ached, her nipples pushing against the restraining fabric.

How could she be having such intensely sexual thoughts about a man she had only just met? It must be because she had been talking about sex to Lucy and Jules. Yes, that was it; her mind was obviously more focused on sex than usual.

He was still studying the list she had given him, plainly oblivious to what she was experiencing, and of course she was glad about that—wasn't she? After all, she had never been the kind of woman who felt piqued because a man didn't show any interest in her.

Because until now she had not met the right kind of man?

'Perhaps if you were to tell me what kind of event you are thinking of having I might be able to pick out the best events for you to attend,' she suggested hastily.

'I haven't made up my mind as yet.'

Carly looked blankly at him. She had naturally assumed that, like their existing clients, he must have a specific event in mind.

Ricardo permitted himself a small cynical smile. If his plans went ahead as he expected, the first event Prêt a Party would be organising for him would be a party to celebrate his acquisition. But of course he wasn't going to tell Carly that. She, he had already decided, would be one of the first surplus-to-requirements 'assets' of the business to be offloaded.

'I understand you are responsible for the administration and accounts of the business?'

'Er, yes…'

'You must be very well organised if you can carry out those duties and still have time to accompany clients to their events.'

'I don't normally. That is, I stand in for the others sometimes.'

She was making it sound as though she had to be coerced into doing so, Ricardo thought cynically. Of course he knew better.

'Carly, your mother's telephoned. She wants you to ring her—Oh, I'm sorry.' The young girl who had burst into the office came to an abrupt halt, her face pink, as she realised that Carly wasn't on her own.

'It's all right, Izzie, I'll ring her later. Thank you.'

But as she thanked the younger girl Carly's heart was sinking beneath her professional smile. She already knew what her adoptive mother would want. More money.

Carly did her best, but the truth was that the woman had no real understanding of how to manage money. The fortune her adoptive father had once had was gone, swallowed up in lavish living and unwise investments. A stroke had made it impossible for him to do any kind of work, and so Carly found herself in the position of having to support them as best she could. But it wasn't easy. Her adoptive mother ran up bills and then wept because she couldn't pay them—like a small child rather than an adult. Their anguished unhappiness and despair made her feel so guilty—especially when...

She was so lucky to have friends like Lucy and Jules, Carly reflected emotionally. She might get on reasonably well with her adopted parents now, but that had not always been the case. Without Lucy and Jules what might she have done to escape from the misery and the wretchedness that had been her own childhood? Taken her own life? She had certainly thought about it.

Where had she gone? Ricardo wondered curiously, watching anxiety momentarily shadow her eyes before she blinked it away. He cleared his throat.

'Right. Here are the events I wish to attend.'

Pushing back her private thoughts, Carly leaned over the desk to study the list he had tossed towards her.

He had selected three events: a private party in St Tropez on board a newly acquired private yacht, to celebrate its acquisition; a media event in the Hamptons to launch a new glossy magazine, to which old money, new names and anyone who was anyone in the fashion world had been invited and a world-famous senior rock star's birthday bash at his French château.

Carly started to frown.

'What's wrong?'

'The St Tropez yacht party is next weekend, and only four days before the Hamptons do. It might be difficult co-ordinating flights and all the other travel arrangements.'

She kept a tight rein on expenses—or at least she had done until Nick had started to interfere. They always booked cheap, no frills flights to overseas events if they weren't being flown out by the clients.

Ricardo raised an eyebrow.

'That won't be a problem. We'll be using my private jet.' He gave a dismissive shrug of those powerful shoulders. 'One of my PAs can sort out all the details. Oh, and they'll need your passport, ASAP. I understand from Nick that your normal practice is to be *in situ* a day ahead of the actual event. That suits me, because that way I shall be able to see how things are organised.'

Too right he would, Ricardo decided.

He was standing up, and Carly followed suit. He was so tall—so big! She was suddenly aware of her reluctance to go through the doorway, because it would bring her too close to him. Too close to him? Get a grip, she mentally advised herself unsympathetically.

'My PA will be in touch with you regarding flight times.'

She walked determinedly towards the door. She was almost level with him now. In another few seconds she would be through the door and safe. Safe? From what? Him pouncing on her? No way would he do that, she told herself scornfully.

And then she made the mistake of looking up at him.

It was like stepping through a door into a previously unknown world.

Her heart whipped round inside her chest like a spinning barrel. Against her will her head turned, her lips parting as her gaze fastened on his mouth. His top lip was well shaped and firmly cut, his teeth white and just slightly uneven, and his bottom lip...

His bottom lip. A smoky sensuality darkened her normally crystal-clear grey eyes as she fed visually on the promise of its fullness. How would it feel to catch that fullness between her own lips? To nibble at it with small biting kisses, to...

'A word of warning—' Ricardo began.

She could feel guilty colour staining her skin as her mind grappled with inexplicable thoughts.

'It is imperative that full confidentiality as to the purpose of my attendance at these occasions is maintained at all times.'

He was cautioning her about the events—that was all! Carly exhaled in shaky relief.

'Yes—yes, of course,' she agreed quickly, as she finally made it through the doorway on legs that had developed a very suspicious weakness.

But she was unnervingly aware of him behind her.

'And one more thing.'

'Yes?' she offered politely, automatically turning round to face him.

'The next time you look at my mouth like that...' he said softly, with a mocking smile.

'Like what? I didn't look at it like anything!' Carly knew that her face was burning with guilt, but she had to defend herself.

'Liar. You looked at it, at *me*, as though you couldn't wait to feel it against your own. As though there was nothing you wanted more than for me to push you up against that doorframe and take you right here and now. As though you could already feel my hands on your skin, touching you intimately, and you were loving it. As though—'

'No!' Carly denied fiercely. And her denial was the truth—she hadn't got as far as thinking anything so intimate as that!

To her relief she could see Lucy hurrying towards them to introduce herself to him.

It was over an hour since Ricardo had gone, and Carly was still thinking about him. But a woman would surely have to be totally devoid of any kind of hormones to remain unaware of Ricardo as a fully functioning man.

And that was her sole excuse, was it? She pushed back her keyboard and stood up. She was shaking slightly. Her face was burning and her body ached. She felt shocked. Guilty. Horrified, in fact, by the door she had unwittingly opened in her own head, and—even worse—was uncomfortably aware that she was physically aroused. Physically, but of course not emotionally—that was impossible. After all, she had sworn never to fall in love, hadn't she? Never to fall in love; never to give herself emotionally to anyone; never to risk the emotional security she had given to herself.

She started to pace the small office. Her childhood had taught her all there was to know about the pain that came with being emotionally rejected. She had fought hard to give herself the protective air of calm self-confidence she projected to others, and for the right to claim their respect. The pathetic, needy child she had once been, desperate for approval and love, had been totally banished, and that was the way Carly intended it to stay.

So why was she thinking like this? No one was threatening her self-reliance, after all—least of all Ricardo Salvatore, who probably had the same loathing of emotional bondage as she did herself, if for very different reasons.

CHAPTER THREE

CARLY checked her watch—Lucy had given both Carly and Jules smart Cartier Tank Francaise watches for Christmas in the first year the business had made a profit—and then bent down and grabbed the handle of her case.

The car Ricardo Salvatore was sending to pick her up was due to arrive in exactly two minutes' time. It was time for her to leave.

She heaved her suitcase off the floor, grimacing a little ruefully as she did so, remembering how Lucy had burst into the office the previous Thursday morning announcing, 'Oh, my God, Carly—I've just realised! There won't be anything in the Wardrobe that will fit you!'

The 'Wardrobe' was a standing joke between them all, and was in actual fact a small room in Lucy's parents' London home which housed the glamorous outfits Lucy and Jules, who were very much the same height and build, wore when they were 'on duty' at events.

The clothes—all designer models—were second hand, surreptitiously trawled from a variety of sources, and the subject of amused speculation between them.

'Just look at this!' Lucy had marvelled after their last expedition, as she held up what looked like a sequin-covered handkerchief with halter neck straps. 'Who on earth would buy this?'

'You did,' Carly had pointed out, laughing.

'Yes, but *I* only paid fifty pounds for it—it cost over a thousand brand-new.'

'It's very sexy,' Jules had pronounced.

'It's repulsive,' Carly had criticised. 'Vulgar and tarty.'

'Mmm… Well, Nick spotted it.'

But the Wardrobe contained nothing that would fit Carly, and so, that Thursday, Lucy had announced firmly, 'Come on, Carly. We've got to go out on a trawl!'

Carly had tried to protest and resist, but Jules and Lucy had been insistent.

The result of their foray into the second-hand shops and market stalls of Lucy's favourite haunts—which had emptied the clothes budget Carly had so carefully worked out—had been collected from the dry cleaners this morning and were now packed in Carly's case, along with her own clothes.

Mentally Carly reviewed them—a white silk trouser suit which Lucy had cooed over, enraptured, pronouncing, 'Oh, this is so retro—Seventies rock wife! And you've got the boobs for it, Carly.'

Maybe she had, but she certainly wouldn't be wearing the jacket over bare skin and half open! There were also a couple of evening dresses, both of which were potentially so revealing that Carly had already decided she would be wearing a silk jacket over them.

She hadn't been very keen on the designer swimsuit Lucy had found either. It was cut away in so many places that Carly feared it threatened to reveal more of her than the skimpiest of bikinis, but at least it had matching culotte pants and a jacket.

Her own classic casuals—the simple linen separates she favoured for summer and some up-to-the-minute accessories they had found in the likes of Zara—had all passed Lucy's inspection and been declared perfect for the events she would be attending.

Dragging her suitcase behind her, Carly pushed open the door onto the street and stepped out into the late-morning sunshine.

Ricardo watched her from his vantage point in the back seat of the limo, as the driver moved the car out of the parking bay he had found further up the street.

Oh, yes, she was a typical example of her upmarket, 'no expense spared but someone else pays' lifestyle, Ricardo decided cynically as he watched her. Immaculate white tee shirt, perfectly fitting blue jeans, long shiny hair, minimal make-up, sunglasses, discreetly 'good' watch, penny loafers. The too-thin girl in designer clutter who was tottering past her on spindly heels, clutching a weird-looking handbag, couldn't hold a candle to her. Because Carly had *class*.

What would she be like in bed?

He didn't intend to let too much time elapse before he found out.

He thought of another society woman from his youth, one whom he had met when he was growing cynical but not yet completely hardened. Initially he had thought her pretty, but she hadn't looked very pretty at all when he had flatly refused to meet her escalating demands—especially when he'd discovered they included a wedding ring in exchange for the supposed benefit of marrying into a higher social bracket. He'd told her that he preferred an honest whore.

Women like her, like Carly, might not openly demand money in return for sex, but what they were looking for was the richest and highest status man they could find—their bodies in exchange for his name.

It was a trade-off that nauseated him, as did those who participated in it.

He had no illusions about women or sex. He had lived too long and seen too much for that. His wealth could buy him any woman he wanted, and that included Carly. She had made *that* plain enough already, with the way she had looked at his mouth.

She hadn't even tried to be subtle about it! She had stared openly and brazenly at him. If they hadn't been in her office it would have been an open invitation to him to push her tee shirt out of the way and free her breasts to spill into his hands so that he could accept their flaunting invitation.

It had told him that he could have yanked down her jeans and explored and enjoyed her and she would not have said a single word in denial.

And then in the morning she would no doubt expect to receive her payment—a piece of jewellery, a telephone call from an exclusive shop inviting her to choose herself something expensive…

That was the way things were done in her world.

He was wasting too much time on her, he warned himself. His primary reason for what he was doing was the potential acquisition of Prêt a Party, not the inevitable sexual acquisition of Carly Carlisle who, although she did not know it yet, would be one of the first in line to lose her job.

Carly frowned as the large, elegant steel-grey car drew up alongside her.

A limo, Lucy had said, and she had pictured a huge, shiny black ostentatious vehicle, not something so supremely understated. But the rear door was opening and Ricardo was getting out.

'Is this all your luggage?'

She gaped at him as he reached for her case, and then looked uncertainly towards the chauffeur.

'Charles is driving. I am perfectly capable of picking up a case,' Ricardo told her dryly, following her uncertain look.

'The...my case is heavy,' she told him, but he ignored her, picked it up and put it in to the boot of the car as if it was as light as a feather pillow.

He was wearing a black tee shirt and a pair of tan-coloured casual trousers, and the muscles in his arms were hardening as he lifted her case. He looked more like a man who worked outdoors than one who sat at a desk, she acknowledged, unwilling to admit to the response that the sight of him was eliciting from her own body.

After what had happened when she had given her imagination its head, she was now keeping it on a controlling diet of bread and water, and that meant no thinking about the effect Ricardo could have on her! So he had a good enough body to carry off the macho male thing—so what? she told herself dispassionately.

But the sight of his black-clad back, bent over the open boot, suddenly transformed by her rebellious thoughts into a totally naked back bent over her equally naked body, evoked such a powerful sensual image that she felt as though she were transfixed to the spot.

So it was true. You *could* go weak at the knees, Carly reflected several minutes later as she sat primly straight in the back seat of the powerful car, dizzily aware that her private thoughts were anything but prim. All those enforced deportment classes at school had definitely left her with an automatic 'sit up straight' reflex.

She was accomplished, Ricardo admitted to himself. That cool, remote pose she had adopted, that said *Pur-*

sue me would certainly work with most men. Unfortunately for her, he was not most men. He opened his briefcase and extracted some papers.

As soon as they were free of the city traffic the powerful car picked up speed. Carly was pleased that Ricardo was engrossed in his work, because that left her free to think about hers, instead of having to make polite conversation with him.

Since their clients were using their own yacht as the venue for their party there was no construction work in the shape of marquees on the like for her to oversee. The client's chef and kitchen staff were being augmented by a chef from the upmarket caterers she had sourced. They were already on the yacht. Menus had been agreed, floral arrangements decided on—she would be meeting with the florists, who had also been flown in from London.

The arrival and deployment of the hostess's hairdresser, make-up artist, and a dresser from the couture house she favoured were also Carly's responsibility, plus a hundred or more other small but vitally important arrangements.

She had an inch-thick pile of assorted coloured and coded lists in her briefcase, most of which she had actually memorised.

'You're so much better at this than me,' Lucy had told her ruefully before she left.

Carly had smiled, but she knew that it was true.

Carly shifted her body against the leather upholstery. It was ridiculous that she should be so acutely conscious of Ricardo's presence in the car with her—and even more ridiculous that she should be so acutely aware of the impact he was having on her physically. So much for the 'bread and water' regime, then!

The grand slam of his raw sensuality had sliced through her defences, leaving an alarming trail of female awareness in its wake. Her jeans, normally a comfortable easy fit, suddenly seemed to be uncomfortably tight, clinging to her flesh in a way she could only mentally describe as erotic, as though somehow she were being caressed by the lean, powerful male hands she couldn't resist looking towards.

She could feel the heat expanding inside her, dangerous little languorous curls of it thrusting against her sensitive flesh. She crossed her legs and then uncrossed them. Her arm accidentally brushed against her own breast and immediately she was aware of the hot pulsing of her nipples.

This was *crazy*. It felt as though somehow or other an unfamiliar and certainly unwanted very sexual alter ego had been released inside her. And, what was more, it seemed to be attempting to take her over! Or had it always been there and it had simply taken meeting Ricardo Salvatore to make her aware of it, just as her own senses were making her aware of him?

This was definitely crazy.

She realised with relief that they had reached the airport. The car slowed down and turned into an entrance marked 'Strictly Private'.

A uniformed customs officer stepped out of a nearby office and came over to the car.

'Your passport, please,' Ricardo demanded, turning to Carly.

Foolishly, she had not been ready for this formality, and it took her several seconds to open her bag, find her passport, and then hand it over to Ricardo.

As he took it from her, her open bag slipped from her hand, showering the immaculate leather and the car's floor with coins, her lipstick, her purse and several other small personal items.

Her face hot, she undid her seatbelt and tried to pick them up as fast as she could, but the lipstick rolled away out of her reach with the movement of the car as the driver set it in motion again.

To her dismay the lipstick had rolled along the leather and come to rest right next to Ricardo's thigh.

She couldn't retrieve it without touching him.

She moistened her lips with the tip of her tongue.

'Could I have my lipstick, please? It's… You're sitting on it,' she told Ricardo.

'What?'

The look he gave her was totally male and uncomprehending.

'My lipstick!' Carly repeated. 'It fell out of my bag and now it's…'

She looked meaningfully at the leather seat, somehow managing at the same time to keep her gaze off his thigh.

His sigh was definitely exasperated as he reached down and picked up the small slim tube.

It was a relief to release her own pent-up breath as he handed the lipstick to her. She reached out for it, too focused on what she was doing to be aware of a deep pothole in the tarmac, which the driver couldn't avoid because of an oncoming vehicle.

The violent movement of the car flung her bodily against Ricardo, sending her slamming into his side. The air was driven out of her lungs by the force of the impact, leaving her half lying against him, her face buried in his tee shirt, her hand ignominiously clutching at his arm.

A shock of unfamiliar sensation hit her all at once, like a hail of sharp-pointed arrows. His personal man-scent, the texture of his tee shirt, the hardness of his chest beneath her cheek, the softness of something that she realised must be his body hair. The slow, heavy thud of his heartbeat…

Somewhere inside her head unwanted images were forming. A man—Ricardo—carrying her in his arms, his torso bare, his flesh warm beneath her fingertips. She could feel the heat of her own desire for him. Her fingers tightened automatically on his arm, her nails digging into his flesh.

Abruptly Carly snapped back to reality, and to the humiliating awareness of what she was doing. Her face burning, she released Ricardo's arm and pulled away for him, refusing to look at him.

As she retreated to her side of the car Ricardo shifted his own position and turned away from her, to conceal the telltale thick ridge of flesh pressing against the fabric of his trousers.

He was beginning to realise that he had badly underestimated the effect Carly was going to have on him. It was one thing for him to acknowledge to himself that he was happy to have sex with her, but it was quite another to have to admit that his desire for her was far more urgent than he had planned for—and, even worse, that it was threatening to overwhelm his self-control. He simply did not want this fierce, thrusting surge of need, this urgent, compelling hunger to take hold of her and fill himself with the scent and the feel of her; the taste of her, to fill her *with* himself and to…

The ache in his body was intensifying instead of fading, and he had to resort to the subterfuge of opening his newspaper and busying himself re-reading it in order to conceal that fact.

*　　*　　*

'Thank you, Charles.'

Carly had no time to do more than smile her own gratitude at Ricardo's chauffeur before a smartly uniformed flight steward was escorting her up the steps to the waiting private jet, whilst Ricardo paused to speak with its captain—*his* captain, Carly realised.

She had often heard Lucy marvelling about the luxury of travelling in the private jets owned by some of their more wealthy clients, but this would be the first time she had experienced it for herself.

The interior of the jet had more resemblance to a modern apartment than to any aeroplane Carly had flown in. A colour scheme of off-white and cool grey set off the black leather upholstery of the sofas, and the steward discreetly indicated to her that both a bedroom and a separate shower room lay to the rear of the sitting area.

'The galley is behind the cockpit, and there is another lavatory there as well—' He broke off from his explanations, to say formally, 'Good morning, sir.'

Carly turned round to see Ricardo standing in the open doorway.

'Morning, Eddie. How are Sally and the new baby?'

There was a genuine warmth in his voice that touched a painful nerve within Carly's heart.

'They're both fine. Sally was over the moon that you flew her folks here for the birth. She was resigned to them not being able to be there.'

Ricardo shrugged, and changed the subject. 'Phil says that we're going to have a good flight, both to Nice and on to New York.' He turned to Carly. 'I've got some work I need to attend to, but feel free to ask Eddie for anything you need.'

'If you would like to sit down here, madam, until we've taken off?' Eddie suggested politely to her, indicating a space on one of the sofas.

Obediently, Carly went and sat down.

'Perhaps I could get you a glass of champagne?' the steward said, once he had shown Carly how to use her seatbelt, and explained to her how to access the power and telephone lines for her laptop should she wish to use it. 'We've got a very nice Cristal.'

Carly couldn't help it. She gave a small shudder. 'Water will be fine,' she told him emphatically.

From his own seat at a desk on the other side of the cabin, Ricardo frowned. Why had she refused champagne? She certainly hadn't been having any qualms about drinking it the night he had seen her in CoralPink.

Thanking Eddie for her water, Carly unzipped her own laptop. Ricardo wasn't the only one who had work to do. Five minutes later, as the jet taxied down the runway, Carly was deeply engrossed in reading her e-mails—but not so deeply that she wasn't acutely aware of Ricardo's presence.

She couldn't forget the disturbing effect those fleeting seconds of physical intimacy in the car had had on her. Her stomach muscles clenched immediately, as though in rejection of the response she had felt, her mouth going dry.

Eddie had said the jet had a fully equipped bedroom… The ache inside her sharpened and tightened and then started to spread.

The jet lifted off the tarmac and Carly held her breath, willing herself not to think about Ricardo.

'I'd like to ask you a few questions about certain aspects of the way Prêt a Party's business works.'

Dutifully Carly put aside the list she was studying. Ricardo was, after all, a potential client.

'Were I to commission Prêt a Party to organise an event for me, who would be responsible for establishing the cost of everything involved?'

'I would,' Carly answered him promptly.

'And would you do that by sourcing suppliers yourself? Or does someone else—Lucy, for instance—source suppliers?'

'Normally I would source them. We've been in business for long enough now to have established a core of suppliers we use on a regular basis. However, sometimes a client will specify that they want to use a specific caterer, or florist, or musician. When that happens we either negotiate with them on the client's behalf or, if the client prefers, they negotiate with them themselves. If they opt to do that then we ask that the clients also make themselves responsible for paying the supplier's bill. When we're in charge of suppliers' estimates and invoices we know exactly what their charges will be—that isn't always the case if the client has commissioned a supplier.'

'Presumably you obtain good discounts from your regular suppliers?'

'Of course, and we pass them on to our clients via our costings for their events. But discount isn't the main criteria we apply when selecting suppliers. Quality, reliability, exclusivity are often more important to our clients than cut-price deals.'

'What do you do when potential suppliers offer to make it worth your while to select them?'

Carly couldn't look at him, and she could feel her face starting to burn. Since Nick had joined the business she had received several such approaches from suppliers, who had insisted that Nick had promised them work. Nick himself had tried to pressure her into using them, but Carly had refused to do so. She knew that Lucy would never have authorised such dishonest business practices, but she hadn't felt able to tell her friend what her husband was doing because she didn't want to hurt her. And she certainly couldn't tell Ricardo—a potential client—about them.

'We…I…I make it plain to them that that we don't take bribes and that they are wasting their time,' she hedged, uncomfortably aware that she was not being totally honest.

Ricardo looked at her, but she was refusing to look back at him, her body language reflecting both her guilt and the lie she had just told him.

Backhanders from suppliers would add a very sizeable 'bonus' to Carly's salary, Ricardo thought grimly.

It surprised him that she wasn't making more use of the fact that they were alone and in the intimate surroundings of the jet in order to let him know that she was available. And did that disappoint him? He shrugged the thought aside. Hardly. He had simply assumed that she would want to showcase her skills for his benefit.

He recognised the discreet little come-ons that women like her were so adept at giving, such as leaning close to him whilst pretending to show him something, so that he could breathe in her perfume—which he had not as yet been able to identify other than to be aware that it suited her. A good quality signature perfume? Custom blended? Expensive! Blended exclusively for her? *Very* expensive! By one of the top three perfumiers? Very expensive—and paid for by a very rich and very doting man!

At least she had not had a boob job. He had been aware of that the moment she'd fallen against him. But she was wearing a bra, a plain, seamless, no-nonsense tee shirt bra. Unusual for a woman out to snare a man, surely? And unnecessary, in view of the excellence of the shape and firmness Mother Nature had generously given her.

Had she leaned over him now, he would have lifted his hand to caress her breast and even, had he felt so inclined, pushed aside her tee shirt and bra and explored the shape and texture of her naked breast, both with his fingers and his lips.

He found himself wondering idly if her grooming regime went as far as a Brazilian wax. He personally wasn't enamoured of the look, although he knew of men who insisted not just on a Brazilian but that their lovers go for the full Hollywood 'everything-off' wax. He personally preferred something a bit more natural, a bit more sensual. And she had such thick, luxuriant, clean and shiny hair—the kind that made him want to reach out and touch it. He moved uncomfortably as he tried to change the direction of his thoughts.

'We'll be landing in a few minutes.'

Carly smiled at the steward and put away her papers. She would be rather glad to get off the plane, although not because she was afraid of flying—at least not in the non-sexual sense. There she was again! Thinking about sex.

And all because… Because what? Because secretly she wanted to have sex with Ricardo? Chance would be a fine thing, she mocked herself. But if she were to be given the chance…

The first thing Carly noticed as they came out of the airport was the small group of beggars—children, not

adults—clustered pathetically together whilst people ignored them. Thin and dirty, wearing shabby torn
clothes, they stood out amongst the seething mass of
people to-ing and fro-ing, and yet everyone was acting
as though they simply did not exist. The smallest of
them was barely old enough to walk.

Ricardo had gone to collect his valet parked rental
car, telling her to wait where she was.

She had noticed a sandwich shop on her way out of
the airport, and now, impetuously, she came to a swift
decision. Wasn't the golden rule to give food rather than
money because money might be taken from them?
Dragging her case behind her, she hurried back to the
sandwich bar.

The children watched her approach without interest.
Their pinched faces and emotionally dead eyes
wrenched at her heart. When she handed them the food,
small claw-like hands snatched it from her.

'Euros,' the older children demanded sullenly, but
she shook her head.

She could see people looking disapprovingly at her,
no doubt thinking she was encouraging them to beg.

Her mobile was ringing. Carly felt a familiar sense
of anxiety and despair twist her stomach when she saw
that the caller was her adoptive mother—she could
never think of her as anything other than that, and she
was, she knew, bound to her adoptive parents by guilt
and duty rather than love. Guilt because she did not love
them, and because she was alive whilst their own flesh
and blood daughter was dead.

Fenella had made her life a misery when they were
growing up together, and her death from a drugs overdose had not been the shock to her that it had been to
her parents—how could it, in view of the number of

times Fenella had turned up at her flat either to beg or harangue her into giving her money to fund her habit? And of course when they were growing up Fenella had been the loved and valued one, whilst she... Automatically she clamped down on her thoughts. She was an adult now, not a child.

It took her several minutes to find out what was wrong. Her adoptive parents had run up a bill of several thousand pounds for which they were past the stage of final demands and warnings and which they could not now repay. How could they have spent so much? Carly felt slightly sick. She did some mental arithmetic and heaved a small sigh of relief. She had just about enough in her own accounts to cover it.

'Don't worry—I'll sort everything out,' she promised, fighting not to feel upset at the thought of such a large sum of money—to her—being wasted. Ending the call, she turned towards her case, her eyes widening as she stared in disbelief at the empty space where it should have been.

Carly was trying desperately not to give in to her panic as she saw Ricardo striding imperiously towards her.

'The car's this way.'

Somehow or other he had relieved her of both her laptop and her hand luggage.

'Where's your case?'

Her mouth went dry with panic.

'I...er... It's gone,' she told him uncomfortably, well aware that she probably only had herself to blame, and that her act of charity had badly backfired on her.

'Gone?'

'Yes. I think someone must have stolen it.'

Ricardo absorbed her none too subtle message cynically. Managing to 'lose' her luggage was certainly a dramatic start to setting him up to replenish her wardrobe. What *had* she done with it? Put it in a left luggage locker?

'So now you don't have any clothes to wear?' he offered helpfully. He would play along with her for now, if only to see her *modus operandi* in action.

Carly exhaled shakily, relieved that he was taking it so well.

'No—nothing apart from what I'm wearing.' And, thanks to that desperate phone call she had just received, she wouldn't be able to afford to replace what she had lost either, she realised with growing dismay.

'Annoying, I know. But at least you'll be able to claim on your insurance policy later,' he told her dispassionately, and then watched her. He had to admit that she was very good—that small indrawn breath, that tiny betraying flicker of her eyelashes, which demanded a response. 'You are insured, I trust?'

'I do have insurance,' Carly agreed.

But it was not the kind of insurance that would enable her to replace her carefully chosen designer wardrobe, she realised dispiritedly.

'So there isn't any problem, is there?' Ricardo offered smoothly. 'After all, you are in one of the best places in the world for female retail therapy, aren't you?'

'I'm sure it's certainly one of the most expensive,' Carly agreed wryly.

'I'd better find a police station and report it, I suppose.'

Ricardo listened appreciatively. She was *very* good.

'I doubt that would do any good. You can report it by phone later from the villa, if you wish.'

He was impatient to leave and she was holding him up, Carly realised at his crisp words. And he was a potential client.

So what did she do now? She couldn't keep her promise to her adoptive parents, to whom she needed to transfer the money quickly, *and* replenish her wardrobe. None of her small 'for her old age' investments could be realised quickly, and she was loath to put a further charge on the business by asking Lucy for money to replace clothes *she* was responsible for losing—especially since they had emptied the budget and cash flow was problematic.

This was not a good time to remember the lecture she had delivered to both Jules and Lucy about how they should follow her example and refuse to possess any credit cards.

She had a few hundred euros in cash—petty cash and personal spending money—probably about enough to buy herself some new knickers, she acknowledged derisively.

Which meant...

What? It was a Saturday; her bank would be closed. Attempting to arrange a temporary bank loan here, with her limited French? Not a good idea. Ringing Jules, explaining what had happened and asking her for a temporary loan? Better—if Jules was even there. But Jules would probably tell Lucy, and then Lucy would insist on sending her money from the business. Asking someone else if they could help her out? Like who? One of their contractors? Or... She looked uncertainly at Ricardo as she followed him to the car.

There was nothing she hated more than being beholden to someone, accepting a benefit she could neither repay nor return. It went against everything she believed in to ask anyone to even lend her money—and were the money for her own personal spending she would have starved rather than consider it. But it wasn't. It would just be temporary. And she had a duty to the business that surely overrode her own pride?

As they reached the car Ricardo looked at Carly. It was obvious to him that she was expecting him to do the gentlemanly thing and offer to replace her lost clothing. Poor girl—how on earth could she be expected to manage with just the contents of her hand luggage and the clothes she stood up in? She couldn't—and, since effectively she was here at least in part for his benefit, naturally he, as a very wealthy man should offer to provide her with a suitable new wardrobe.

And when he didn't respond as she obviously wanted him to, what, he mused, would be her next move?

Did St Tropez have second-hand clothes shops? Charity shops? Carly wondered worriedly as she thanked Ricardo when he politely held open the passenger door of the car for her. Surely it must. French women were known to be shrewd in such matters.

'Something wrong?' Ricardo asked her smoothly.

She was very tempted to admit just how much was wrong—although she doubted he would share her dismay at the thought of a £4,000 bill, she thought ruefully. She opted for discretion instead, and told him lightly, 'I didn't realise you'd be driving yourself. I was expecting a chauffeur-driven car.'

Of course she was. Women like her did.

'Even billionaires sometimes like to economise,' he told her dryly, before adding, more truthfully, 'I like driving, and I grew up in Naples. If you can drive there and live, you can drive anywhere.'

The car was plain and solidly built, but—blissfully—the air-conditioning was wonderfully effective.

They were stationary in a queue of traffic, and at the side of the road a young man was offering a stunningly pretty girl a peach. As Carly looked on, the girl, oblivious to everything and everyone other than the young man, leaned forward and cupped her hand round his. Then, without taking her gaze from his, she took a bite out of the ripe fruit whilst its juice ran from it onto their interlocked hands.

The small tableau was so intensely sensual and intimate that Carly immediately looked away—and found she was looking right into Ricardo's eyes.

Could he see in hers that she had watched the young couple, wondering how it would feel if *he* had been the one offering the peach to her? If its juice had run on *her* bare skin, would he have bent his head to savour its path with his tongue? Would he have…?

She started to tremble violently, small beads of sweat breaking out on her skin, and her body was suddenly thrown forward against her seatbelt as Ricardo depressed the accelerator savagely, causing the car to shoot forward.

What the hell was the matter with him? Ricardo berated himself silently. No way was he dumb enough to fall for something so obvious as the tired old come-on Carly had just tried out on him. *Look at my lips, watch my tongue, imagine…*

It was those damned eyes of hers that did it! How the hell did she manage to get them to turn so smoky and lustrous with desire on demand like that?

Hell—insanely, for a second, she'd almost had him

persuaded that the sight of those two kids with their peach had made her ache for him as if he was the only man on earth. Not that his body needed much persuading. It was all too eager to believe she wanted him.

CHAPTER FOUR

'WHERE exactly are we staying?' Carly asked Ricardo, hoping that it would be within easy walking distance of the town and the harbour. She would need easy access to both from early tomorrow morning, so that she could liaise properly with their contractors and get to the bank, as she had promised her parents, plus somehow find time to replenish her wardrobe.

'Villa Mimosa,' Ricardo answered her. 'It's outside St Tropez itself, up in the hills overlooking the sea. I'm not a particular fan of over-hyped, supposedly *in* places. Invariably, every minor celebrity that TV and magazines have ever created flock to them for maximum publicity exposure, destroying whatever charm the place may once have had. I like my privacy, and personally I prefer quality to quantity every time.'

'Oh, yes. Me too,' Carly agreed immediately. 'But I do need to be able to get into St Tropez quickly and easily.'

'Ah, you're thinking about replacing your missing clothes,' Ricardo said affably.

Carly couldn't help laughing. 'That, yes—but I was thinking more of liaising with our contractors.'

'Mmm. I thought the purpose of this trip was for you to liaise with me,' Ricardo told her softly.

Damn and double damn. He cursed himself mentally as he saw Carly absorbing the subtle flirtatiousness of his remark. Why the hell had he done that? Why hadn't he waited and let her come on to him? Now she knew he was receptive to her!

Ricardo had just flirted with her! A heady mixture of pleasure and excitement danced along her veins. Careful, she warned herself. Remember you don't want to get into a situation you can't afford. On the other hand, there was such a thing as being too cautious. After all, her common sense told her that a man like Ricardo would not be interested in anything more than the very briefest kind of relationship—a 'no commitment of any kind' type of relationship. The perfect kind of relationship, surely, for a woman like her, who did not want to fall in love but who secretly—even if this was the first time she had admitted it to herself—wondered what it would be like to have sex with a man all her instincts told her would be a once-in-a-lifetime lover. Why shouldn't she live a little recklessly for once?

'Well, I certainly want to do my best to please you.'

Carly could scarcely believe such words had come from her own lips. Words that, no matter how demurely she had spoken them, could surely only convey to Ricardo a very provocative message.

Ricardo turned his head to look at her. That was more like it!

The look in those dark eyes was quite unmistakable, Carly recognised, as her heart missed a beat and sweet, hot, sensual arousal poured through her body like warm honey.

'We're here.'

'What? Oh. Yes.'

She had actually blushed, Ricardo marvelled as he stopped the car. And her nipples were standing out beneath the fabric of her tee shirt in flagrant sexual arousal.

Ridiculously, suddenly he was as hot for her as though he were a mere youth and this was his first time.

She might as well ask for his help and get it out of the way now, Carly decided. Because once they got inside…

Once they got inside *what*? Once they got inside she hoped he would take her to bed?

Her thoughts were leaving her torn between shock and delight. And urgency! Suddenly she wanted very much to get the matter of her need for a short-term loan and her discomfort about mentioning it to him out of the way.

So that she could be free to encourage him to flirt with her and ultimately—maybe—take her to bed without it hanging over her?

The unfamiliar recklessness of her own thoughts took some getting used to. But she wasn't tempted to abandon them, was she?

So first things first, and then…

She cleared her throat and took a deep breath.

'Ricardo… I…er…'

The husky little catch in her voice was very effective, Ricardo thought, as he waited for her to continue.

'I feel very uncomfortable about this, but…'

'Yes?' he encouraged when she pretended to falter. After all, he reasoned cynically, the sooner he could get this farce over with, the sooner he could satisfy the itch to possess her that had now become an almighty, savage, unignorable ache.

Carly took heart from the kindness in Ricardo's patient encouragement.

'I need to replace some of the things that were in my suitcase. I don't want to worry Lucy—it's my job to deal with the accounts, after all—and… And I know this is…' Her face had started to burn. 'I was wondering if I could ask you to lend me some money—just temporarily, of course.'

Why had she ever thought this was a good idea? Carly wondered, feeling acutely embarrassed. Just listening to herself as she stumbled over her words made her go cold with horror at what she was doing. And if *she* found her request unacceptable, then what on earth must Ricardo be thinking?

'I feel dreadful about this,' she admitted honestly, 'but I can't think of what else I can do.'

Really? Didn't she possess a bank account of her own? A credit card? A debit card? The ability to walk into a bank?

'It would just be a loan. I would pay you back, of course…'

Indeed she would—and with interest.

Several different potential responses presented themselves to him, but in the end he decided that, since Carly was so patently thick-skinned, he might as well go for the oldest and least believable of all of them.

So he smiled at her, and then he took hold of her hand and patted it. And then he told her smoothly, 'I shall be delighted to help you. How much do you think you will need?'

She was gazing at him starry-eyed, her face slightly flushed, her lips slightly parted, as though she could hardly believe her good fortune.

Such a heroic effort deserved a generous reward, Ricardo decided cynically.

'Wait! I've had a better idea.' But she, of course, had no doubt already had the same idea before him. 'Why don't we go into St Tropez together tomorrow and you can choose whatever you think you may need?'

For some reason she didn't look as delighted as Ricardo had expected.

Ricardo had made her a wonderful offer, but she was not sure it was one she felt comfortable with, Carly reflected, as she thanked him.

'That's very generous of you.'

'I'm delighted to be able to help,' Ricardo assured her, before adding, 'Come on, let's go inside.'

Carly was used to staying in beautiful and magnificent properties, but the Villa Mimosa was truly breathtaking. Its setting alone—tucked into a hillside, overlooking the Mediterranean—provided a view that must surely always catch at the heart.

From the balcony of her bedroom she could look out over immaculate gardens and across a miraculous infinity pool to the horizon, and although it was a couple of hours now since they had arrived at the villa she still kept going to the balcony and gazing at the view.

The middle-aged Frenchwoman who had welcomed them had explained that she was the maid but that she did not live in. Cathy must have looked rather surprised at that, she realised, because after she had left them Ricardo had explained to her that he preferred to have his own personal staff on hand or do without.

'My own people know how I like things done, and they know too that I like my privacy. It's mid-afternoon now, and I have some business matters to attend to,' he had told her, 'so why don't we agree to meet up on the terrace at, say, six? My choice would be for us to eat in,' he had added suavely. 'I can arrange to have something delivered.'

Carly had felt her heart miss a couple of beats at the potential implications of dining alone with him.

'That sounds perfect,' she had answered, and then worried when she had seen the gleam in his eyes that she had sounded naïvely over-enthusiastic.

Six o'clock, he had said. And it was five now. She might not have anything to change in to, but she certainly intended to shower and tidy herself up.

Half an hour later, showered and still wearing the thick towelling robe she had found hanging up in the bathroom, she was just brushing her hair when she heard a soft tap on her bedroom door. It opened and Ricardo walked in, carrying two well filled champagne glasses.

'I've mixed you a Bellini. I hope you like them.'

'Oh, yes. Yes, I do,' she agreed.

Unlike her, he was fully dressed, in dark linen trousers and a white linen shirt, his bare brown feet thrust into soft plain leather sandals.

He came over to where she was sitting and put one glass down on the glass-topped dressing table, then held the other out to her.

'Try it first,' he urged her.

Sipping from a glass whilst he held it surely shouldn't be such a sensually intimate experience, should it? And why couldn't she stop looking at the long brown fingers curled round the stem of the glass? She tried to focus on something else, but discovered that the only other thing to focus on was his body, and that the place where the line of his trousers was broken by a telltale bulge was exactly on her eye line. And, what was worse, she couldn't seem to stop herself from gazing appreciatively at it.

'It's lovely,' she assured him hurriedly, taking a sip and then turning away. 'I hadn't realised that was the time. I'd better hurry up and get dressed.'

He gave a small shrug.

'You might as well stay as you are. I hope you like lobster by the way.'

'I love it,' she told him truthfully.

'And I also hope that the gourmet meals-on-wheels outfit who brought the food are as good they are supposed to be. I thought we'd eat outside on the terrace.'

He was obviously expecting her to go with him, Carly realised. A bathrobe wouldn't normally have been her first choice of dinner outfit, but on this occasion it seemed she had no alternative.

'I really am grateful to you for being so kind about the money,' she told him.

'Good. Maybe later you might find a way of showing me how much, mmm?'

Ricardo watched cynically as somehow or other she managed to summon a look of shocked bemusement quickly followed by hot excitement into the smoky darkness of her eyes. But his cynicism wasn't stopping him from wanting her, was it? he reminded himself. In fact he had spent the last three hours thinking about very little other than satisfying that want. Which was why, in the end, he had given in to it and gone to her room.

Was Ricardo saying what she thought he was saying? Carly wondered dizzily. Or was she letting her own erotic imagination run away with her?

At least Lucy and Jules would be pleased to learn she was about to abandon her virgin status. Abandon…it was such an emotive word, such a sensual word. And, recklessly, she was already eager to abandon herself to the physical pleasure of Ricardo's possession.

'Or would you prefer to make a start now?'

Carly's eyes widened as he came to within a few

inches of her and bent his head toward hers, his hand resting lightly on the side of her face.

She had never been kissed like this before. There was no physical contact other than that of their lips and his fingers lightly caressing her face. His mouth moved more fiercely on hers and Carly responded instinctively, moving closer to him, leaning into him as his tongue drove deeper into the soft recesses of her mouth to take possession of it.

She started to raise her arms, wanting to hold him, but to her confusion he stopped her, gripping her shoulders and releasing her mouth to step back from her.

Whilst she looked up at him in confusion he untied the belt of her robe and then pushed it off her shoulders in one swift easy movement that left her totally naked in front of him. Her only covering was the hot wave of colour that beat up under her skin. His gaze dropped to her body with the swift descent of an eagle to its prey. It stalked slowly over creamy slender shoulders, down to ripely rounded breasts, softly heavy with sensual promise, silky pale skin contrasting with the darker aureoles from which her rose nipples thrust so eagerly.

Her ribcage curved into a narrow waist, below which her hips flared out again, and her legs were, as he had already known they would be, unbelievably long and perfectly shaped. A soft cap of downy dark curls formed a neat little triangle just above the delicately shaped outer lips of her sex, curled protectively over it.

A dozen—no, a hundred different sensations and desires struck him, which in the end were only one need, one desire, and that the most ancient and powerful of all male needs and desires.

His gaze was fixed on her as though her body was a visual magnet from which he could not look away.

He wanted her. He wanted her right here and right now. He wanted her as he had never wanted any woman before. His own flesh was so immediately and intensely aroused that it was almost painful.

He wanted to take her quickly, fiercely, hotly plunging his flesh within hers and filling her, as though in taking her he would somehow drive out his own need for her.

And yet at the same time he wanted to savour the experience of having her, to relish it and wait for it.

Carly felt like a…a houri in front of a sultan—aware of her own nakedness before him and in some weird way actually physically excited by the fact that he was seeing her like that. Because she knew that he desired her, and his desire for her gave her power over him? The telltale bulge had now become a definite and openly defined ridge of flesh she badly wanted to reach out to and caress. Carly touched her tongue-tip to her lips.

No man had looked at her in the way Ricardo just had. With such a blazing heat of desire that she could have sworn she'd actually felt its burn against her skin.

But then no man had ever seen her like this—stripped bare, vulnerable, the whole of herself revealed.

She could feel a small, excited pulse beating inside her body.

Ricardo was picking up her Bellini and handing it to her. Uncertainly she took it from him. 'You have a beautiful body,' he told her emotionlessly. 'I'm tempted to tell you to stay like this, so that I can continue to have the pleasure of looking at it, but I'm not sure my self-control could go the distance.'

He bent down to pick up her robe and handed it to her.

When she learned forward to take it from him, he

lowered his head and took one taut nipple into his mouth. Could those fierce pangs she felt deep inside her body really be caused by the fierce tugging of his mouth on her nipple? She heard herself moan and was afraid she might collapse. Her legs felt so weak. And yet when his mouth was no longer there she ached for its return, she realised, as he pulled her robe back on for her as unceremoniously and as swiftly as he had removed it.

'More wine?'

Should she? Carly stared into her empty glass. 'No. No more,' she told him firmly, aware of how quickly what she had already had to drink had gone to her head.

It had been heaven eating out here on the secluded patio. The night air was soft and scented, the smallest of warm breezes was caressing her skin, and the moon was a fat yellow disc up above them.

She gave a small sensual shiver, acknowledging that the memory of those few minutes in her bedroom had left a very erotic imprint on her body.

'More lobster?'

Carly shook her head.

'No?' Ricardo questioned softly. 'You're satisfied, then, in every single way?'

He reached across the table and took hold of her hand, caressing it lightly.

How on earth could Ricardo touching her hand cause her throat to constrict? Carly wondered helplessly as she gazed at him, unable to speak.

She was extremely clever, Ricardo acknowledged. She obviously knew from past experience that men liked to do their own hunting. She had let him know she was available, and now she was sitting back and letting him set the pace.

He released her hand and stood up. Carly looked up uncertainly. Ricardo smiled back at her and held out his hand. A little breathlessly, she pushed back her chair and stood up herself. Holding her hand, he drew her towards the low wall that separated the terrace from the rest of the garden.

'Wait,' Carly protested, just before they reached it.

He watched her as she wriggled swiftly out of the robe. She had been aching to do it all through the meal, unable to stop thinking about how she had felt and how he had looked at her earlier on. She had never previously given any thought to her own nakedness in terms of its erotic appeal, but now she was acutely aware of the warm touch of the night air on her skin, and the gloriously wanton feeling that knowing Ricardo couldn't stop looking at her was giving her.

Ricardo felt as though the air was being ripped out of his lungs, whilst at the same time the darkest kind of male pleasure was exploding inside him.

He took hold of her, imprisoning her between his own body and a thick mass of geraniums tumbling over the wall, his hands at the curve of her waist, his mouth fastening on hers.

Carly melted into him, her lips parting eagerly in invitation, her arms winding round his neck. His tongue, deliberately pointed and hard, thrust against her own, its stabbing movement making her moan and shake with pleasure. She wanted him to give her more of it, to fill the hot, wet cavity he was pleasuring until she could take no more of him.

She whimpered in pleasure and arched her body into his, removing one hand from his neck to unfasten his shirt buttons.

She was just as he had known she would be! Just like

every other woman who had looked at him and seen an easy future for herself, Ricardo told himself. But his hands were still sliding up over her ribcage to mould the warm weight of her breasts; his fingers were seeking the eager hardness of nipples as swollen and firm as small thimbles.

She moaned against his tongue as he played with them, caressing and rubbing them, and her own fingers struggled with his zip before she finally managed to slide it down.

He had expected her immediately to touch him intimately, but instead she moved closer to him, rubbing herself sensuously against him with a soft sound of pleasure.

Her height meant that she fitted him as perfectly as though they had been made for one another. He released her breasts and allowed her to rub their sensitive tips against his flesh, his hands supporting her back and then massaging it, shaping her spine and going lower, to cup the rounded curves of her buttocks, hold the bones of her hips. His hand slipped lower, his fingers finding the cleft between her legs. He might not be able to see the ripe readiness of her desire-swollen lips, but he could feel it. His fingers dipped seductively into the wetness of her sex.

She made a sound deep in her throat and moved eagerly against him, the movement of her body against him in time with the thrust of his tongue within the soft, dark cave of her mouth.

His body was straining against her, and the moment he moved she looked down, her gaze fastening on the swollen, darkly veined head of his sex.

His fingers stroked the length of her wetness, caressing her more intimately with each stroke until she felt hot and open, her eager moans inviting him to plunge deeper. Her fingertips were just skimming the hard outline of his penis, almost as though she was afraid to touch it. Or was she simply enjoying tormenting him because she knew how much he wanted her?

Perhaps he should punish her a little for doing that to him?

Punish her and please himself, he thought hotly, as his fingertip massaged the slick wetness of her clitoris and he felt her whole body jump and then shudder wantonly.

Her fingers were circling him, holding him, exploring him, her touch cool against his own heat.

He had to have her.

Carly made a small mewling sound of pleasure deep in her throat and reached out for him, cupping his face with her hands and pressing her mouth passionately against his. All she wanted—all she would want for the rest of her life—was this, and him.

Abruptly she pulled back from him.

Her heart was thudding unevenly with the shock of her thoughts and feelings. Her emotional thoughts, and her equally emotional feelings. She felt sick and shaky as reaction set in and she recognised her own danger. How had this happened? How had she gone from wanting to have sex with to him to wanting *him*?

'What's wrong?'

She was too engrossed in her own thoughts to hear the sharp warning of male frustration in Ricardo's voice.

'I'm sorry… I…I don't think this is a good idea…'

Ricardo could taste the raw savagery of his own furious disbelief. How could he have been such a fool as to let her play him so cleverly? To let her arouse him to the point where nothing mattered more than him having her?

'So what would make it a good idea?' Ricardo demanded bitingly, gripping her arms and swinging her round so hard that she almost stumbled. 'Or should I say how much would make it a good idea? Five thousand? Ten? *Carte blanche* on a credit card?'

Carly stared at him in bewildered shock.

'And you can cut that out,' Ricardo told her. 'I've known what you are from the start. Nick Blayne made it plain enough—not that he needed to. It was obvious what you were from the night I saw you in that damned club, letting someone else's husband paw you.'

A slow, achingly painful form of semi-numbness was creeping up over her body, paralysing her ability to move.

'Well? Come on—answer me. Obviously the promise of a "loan" wasn't enough. So what else are you after? A new designer wardrobe? A Cartier diamond? Nick told me that you were good at recognising how to get the maximum amount of financial benefit out of a relationship.'

Belated anger seared through her. 'I'm certainly good at recognising what he's doing to the business—and ultimately to Lucy,' Carly told him hotly. Humiliation was scorching her skin as she absorbed what Ricardo had said to her—what he had said *about* her.

'Well?' Ricardo demanded again, ignoring her furious outburst. 'How much?'

'Nothing,' Carly told him proudly. 'You could have had me for nothing, Ricardo. For no other reason than that I wanted you, for nothing other than the benefit to me of having sex with you.'

'What?' He gave her a derisively cynical look. 'We

both know that that's a lie, and it's not even a good one. You are the one who called a halt.'

Yes, she had. But not for the reasons he was so insultingly suggesting. And she certainly couldn't tell him now why she had wanted to stop.

'You are so wrong about me. I would never—have never—' She stopped as she saw the contemptuous look in his eyes.

'What about the money you asked me for?'

The money she had wanted to borrow from him? Of course—in his eyes that had damned her.

'You don't understand—that *was* just a loan. I *will* pay you back,' she told him quietly.

Ricardo was in no mood to be placated.

'Oh, I think I do understand. Let's see. You pretend to lose your suitcase, then you come on to me, expecting that I will take the bait. Then when I do you immediately back off, thinking that I'm going to ache so damned much for you I'll do anything to have you. How complicated to understand is that?' His mouth twisted in open contempt.

She had thought she knew what it was like to have her pride ripped from her, leaving her exposed to people's contempt, but she had been wrong, she recognised through the blur of her shocked, anguished, furious humiliation. But what was even worse was that she now knew exactly what he had really been thinking about her.

Automatically she tried to defend herself, protesting emotionally, 'You're wrong!'

But he stopped her immediately, challenging her. 'About what? You coming on to me?' He shook his head. 'I don't think so. Not that you didn't get something out of it yourself, so don't bother trying to pretend you didn't. No woman gets as hot and wet as you did and—'

It was too much. Carly reacted immediately and instinctively, her pride driving her to react in a way that was pure, instinctive, emotionally wounded female.

She raised her hand, but before she could do any more Ricardo was gripping her wrist in a bruisingly painful hold.

'If you want to fight dirty that's fine,' he told her softly. 'But remember I grew up on the streets. If you hit me, then I promise you I shall retaliate in kind.'

When he saw her face he laughed. 'No, I don't hit women. But there are other ways of administering punishment!'

'You are a barbarian!' Carly whispered shakily. 'And you have no right... You are totally wrong!' Tears of reaction were stinging her eyes now, but no way was she going to let him see that. 'I only asked to borrow the money because I didn't want to worry Lucy.'

'Yes, of course. Blame someone else. Women like you are very good at that.'

Carly had had enough. 'You don't know the first thing about a woman like me!'

'On the contrary, I know a very great deal.' Ricardo stopped her sharply. 'I know, for instance, that you are the product of generations of so-called good breeding, that your parents are wealthy and well connected, but that you yourself do not have any independent means. You also went to one of the country's top schools. In short, you believe you have an automatic right to the very best of everything and an even more deeply ingrained belief that because of what you are you are superior to those people who have not had your advantages. You expect to be granted a first-class passage through life, preferably paid for by someone else. You are a taker, a user—a gold-digger.'

Something—a bubble of either pain or hysterical laughter—was tightening her chest and then her throat.

'And I know that *you* are a prejudiced, ill-informed misogynist. And—as I've already said—you know nothing about me,' she told him shakily, before turning on her heel and walking away from him.

Alone in the safety of her room she gave in to the tremors of aftershock racking her body, holding onto the back of a chair to steady herself. One day—maybe—she would look back on this, on *him*, and what he had said to her, with irony and perhaps even amusement. Because he was so breathtakingly, hugely wrong about her.

But for now… For now she would be grateful to him for showing her how easily she could have slipped into the emotional danger she had always feared and for going on to destroy every single tendril of those tentative feelings. At least now she was safe from feeling anything for him other than furious outrage.

Were it possible for her to do so, she would leave the villa immediately. But she had Lucy and the business to think of, and Carly had been taught from a very young age to carry a dual burden of gratitude and responsibility.

She would have to stay, and she would have to remember why she was here and why he was here, and behave towards him with all the professional courtesy she could muster.

For the rest, she would rather go naked than ask him for so much as a rag to cover her—would rather starve than accept a crust from his table, rather die than let him see how very much he had hurt her and in how many different ways.

'I know what you are,' he had said.

But the truth was he did not know her at all.

The truth was… The truth was a secret, and so painful that she could not bear to share it with anyone.

CHAPTER FIVE

CARLY stood on the harbourside, her eyes shaded by dark glasses, as she and the chefs ticked off the items being delivered.

It was eleven o'clock in the morning and she had been up since half past five. Luckily she had managed to persuade a taxi driver to pick her up from the villa, despite the earliness of the hour, initially to go to the flower market with the florist, Jeff, and his team to ensure that the freshest and most perfect blooms were purchased for the party, and then to accompany the two chefs when they bought the fresh produce they needed.

She was trying very hard not to keep looking at the strip of pale flesh where her Cartier watch had been. She had loved it so much—not because of its monetary value but because of what it represented. The owner of the small shop she had found tucked down a narrow alley had expressed neither curiosity nor surprise when she had handed over her watch in return for a wad of euros and a pawn ticket. Once she got home she intended to speak with her bank and arrange to either take out a loan or realise some of her assets so that she could both buy it back and give herself a small cash reserve. She hated the idea of being in debt, but there was nothing else she could do.

As soon as she could snatch an hour she intended to replace the lost clothes as best she could. Which wasn't going to be easy. True, she had seen a wide variety of trendy shops and boutiques on her way to and from the market, but the clothes at the cheaper end of the market were really only suitable for the very young, whilst those she would have considered suitable were way, way out of her price range.

Luckily, on her way back from the flower market she had spotted a stall selling casual holiday wear and had been able to buy a pair of three-quarter capri pants and a couple of tee shirts. Buying new underwear had proved a little more difficult, but eventually she had found the small shop she had been recommended to try, tucked down a side street off Rue Georges, and had been able to buy a pack of plain white briefs and a simple flesh-coloured bra.

Behind them the harbour was filled with the huge white luxury yachts of wealthy visitors, but the yacht belonging to Prêt a Party's client surely had to be the most expensive and glamorous looking of all.

Carly had been given a tour of it earlier by Mariella D'Argent's PA, Sarah, who had also generously offered Carly the use of her own small cabin to change in, and had then insisted on taking her travel-worn clothes to the yacht's laundry, promising that Carly would have them back before evening.

'It's a pity we aren't the same size, otherwise I could have loaned you something,' she had commiserated when Carly had told her what had happened with her luggage. 'Mariella is, though,' she had added thoughtfully. 'Okay, she may be a bit taller...'

'And at least two sizes thinner,' Carly had tacked on, laughing.

Mariella D'Argent, their client, had been one of the fashion world's best known and best paid top models before her marriage to her financier husband, and even now, at close to forty, she was still an exceptionally stunning and beautiful woman. And an even more exceptionally spoiled one, Carly had decided, after listening politely to her fretful demands.

'Mmm, and guess how she stays that way.' Sarah had grimaced. 'I swear to heaven one of these days she's going to get it wrong—sniff Botox up the new nose her surgeon has had to construct for her and inject cocaine into her wrinkles. And then, of course, there's always the danger that she might take his Viagra whilst he takes her Prozac—or at least there would be if they still shared a bed.'

Carly had tried not to laugh.

'Anyway, what about one of those fab silky floaty cotton kaftans that are all the rage? A short one, worn over some slinky cream or white pants, and perhaps a stunning belt—that would look terrific. Or a sarong tied round them, perhaps? That's a very cool look now,' Sarah had suggested helpfully.

Carly had nodded her head and smiled, even whilst knowing that the type of oh, so casual but oh, so expensive items Sarah was referring to were completely outside her budget. She had seen the kaftans Sarah had described on her way down to the harbour this morning. Gorgeous, silky fine floaty wisps of cotton, with wonderful embroidery and a price tag of well over a whole month's salary!

The party was due to start at ten o'clock in the evening, prior to which the D'Argents were holding a 'small' dinner party for fifty of their guests onshore.

'So, what do you think of this?'

Dutifully Carly gave her attention to the clever arrangement of greenery and mirrors the florist had used to create a magical effect, making the small reception area appear far larger than it actually was.

'Very impressive, Jeff,' she told him truthfully.

Their own construction crew were speedily finishing erecting a framework for the tenting fabric, which was cream with a design on it in black to complement Mariella D'Argent's theme for the evening: cream, black and grey.

Currently a redhead, she, of course, would look stunning in any combination of such colours!

Looking at the fabric, Carly thought briefly of persuading the man in charge of the construction crew to give her a piece. Wrapped around plain black trousers it would look stunning—but perhaps just a bit too obvious? On the other hand, wearing it, she should be able to melt into her surroundings!

A rueful, mischievous smile illuminated her face— and that was how Ricardo saw her as he drove into the harbour area.

He had thought at first when he got up that she was still sleeping, and it had been nearly midday when he had finally decided to go and check on her.

The discovery that she had left the villa without him knowing had caused him a quixotic mix of emotions, the most dangerous and unwanted of which had been a shaft of pure male possessiveness and jealousy.

Because she had aroused him? She was far from the first woman to have done that, and he certainly hadn't felt possessive about any of the others!

Deep down inside himself Ricardo was aware of the insistent and powerful effect she had on his emotions. She made him feel incredibly, furiously, savagely angry, for one thing. For another, she was making him spend far too much time thinking about her.

He was still several yards away from her when Carly suddenly became aware of his presence, alerted to it by a sudden tingling physical awareness that had her turning round apprehensively.

Dressed in natural-coloured linen trousers and a white linen shirt, dark glasses shielding his eyes from the brilliant glare of the sun, he looked utterly at home against the moneyed backdrop of St. Tropez, and Carly was not surprised to see several women stop to look appreciatively at him as he strode towards her.

'How did you get down here?'

The peremptory demand was curt and to the point.

'I called a cab.'

He was frowning.

'You could have asked me to drive you.'

She gave him a bitterly angry look and started to turn away from him without responding.

Immediately he placed a restraining hand on her arm.

'I said—'

'I heard what you said.' Carly stopped him. 'And for your information I would have walked here—barefoot, if necessary—rather than ask you for help.'

A cautionary inner voice tried to remind her that she had decided to behave towards him with cool professionalism.

'The wounded pride effect won't cut any ice with me, Carly,' he told her. 'I see you've managed to acquire a change of clothes,' he added dryly.

No way was she going to tell him that the cost of the taxi plus these clothes had taken all but a few of her small store of euros, and that without the money she had got from pawning her watch right now she would have had less than the cost of a cup of coffee and a sandwich in her bag. She pulled away from him instead.

A small commotion on the yacht's walkway had her turning round to watch Mariella D'Argent, flanked by sundry members of her personal staff, walking towards them.

The ex-model looked stunning. She was wearing close-fitting Capri pants low on the hips to reveal an enviably taut flat stomach and hipbones. A contrasting halter-necked top skimmed the perfect, if somewhat suspiciously unmoving shape of her breasts, which were obviously bare beneath it. A large straw hat and a pair of huge dark sunglasses shielded her face from the sunlight, and on her feet she was wearing a pair of impossibly flimsy high-heeled sandals.

She ignored Carly, smiling warmly at Ricardo instead and exclaiming excitedly, 'Ricardo, darling—how wonderful. I didn't know you were in St Tropez. You must join us tonight. We're having a small party to launch the new yacht.'

Carly watched as Ricardo smiled his acceptance without saying that he had already intended to be present.

'And you must come to the dinner we're having first—just a select few of us.'

Behind Mariella's back Sarah caught Carly's eye and pulled a face.

'What are you doing now?' Mariella was asking. 'We're all on our way to Nikki Beach. Why don't you come with us?'

'I don't think so, Mariella,' Carly heard Ricardo reply firmly. 'I'm afraid I've outgrown the appeal of paying a hugely inflated sum of money to buy a bottle of champagne to spray all over some so-called model's equally hugely inflated chest.'

Mariella gave a small trill of laughter—which was quite an impressive feat, since not a single muscle in her face moved as she did so, Carly reflected, then pulled herself up mentally for being a bitch.

'That won't please her,' Sarah muttered to Carly as she came to stand next to her. 'And she's already in a strop because *Hello!* magazine has pulled out of giving the party a double-page spread. It's doing one on some film star's new nursery instead. Who's the hunk, by the way?' she whispered, looking at Ricardo.

'A potential new client,' Carly answered her. 'He wants to see the way we work.'

'Mmm, well, he's certainly brightened Mariella's day for her. What's the betting she's already planning how to lure him down to her stateroom and which Agent Provocateur underwear she's going to be wearing when she does?'

'I don't think she'll have to try very hard,' Carly answered lightly. 'They seem very much two of a kind.'

So why was she suffering such a wrenching pain at the thought of them together?

It was physical frustration, that was all, she reassured herself as she continued to ignore Ricardo, keeping her back turned towards him. Because after the pang of longing that had come through her when she had seen him striding towards her she didn't trust herself to be able to look directly at him.

From the table where he was sitting at a café opposite the harbour, Ricardo had an uninterrupted view of the D'Argents' yacht and the activity around it being orchestrated by Carly.

It was true that last night he had been too enraged and frustrated to think analytically about the way she was likely to react to his denunciation of her, and it was also true that, had he done so, it certainly wouldn't have occurred to him that she would retreat behind a screen of icy politeness and professionalism. On the one hand meticulously making sure that he was provided with ample opportunity to witness every aspect of the preparations for the upcoming event and ask whatever questions he wished, and yet on the other managing to convey to him very clearly that she loathed and resented every second she had to spend in his company.

As a portrayal of an affronted woman whose morals were beyond reproach it was very impressive, he admitted. Unfortunately for her, though, he knew she was no such thing. So she was wasting her time.

It was irritating that Prêt a Party's financial year-end meant that the only figures available for his inspection were virtually a year out of date. He had given instructions that he wanted more up to date financial information, but that, of course, would take time as it would have to be acquired discreetly. He certainly did not want anyone else alerted to the fact that he was considering it as an acquisition.

He picked up the local newspaper a previous occupant of the table had left and opened it. Italian was his first language, but he was fluent in several others, including French. He was idly flicking through the pages when a sentimentally captioned photograph on one of them caught his eye. Frowning, he studied it in disbelief.

An 'angel of mercy', the paper fancifully described a young woman holding out sandwiches to a group of beggar children. The photo accompanied a piece on the best ways to help street children, and the woman was quite definitely Carly, even if she had been photographed with her back to the camera. He also recognised the airport location, and the suitcase on the ground behind her—although not the outstretched male hand that was just in the shot, grasping it.

He closed the paper, his mouth grim.

Okay, so maybe—just maybe—her suitcase had genuinely been stolen. As for her act of charity... He hadn't missed the way she had reached out to the smallest and weakest of the children, making sure that he received his fair share of the food she was handing out. As a boy he had had first-hand experience of what it was like to have to beg for food.

A large limousine drew up in front of Carly and several people got out and started to walk towards her. One of them she recognised as the current 'in' classical violinist who had been hired to play as the guests came on board.

Immediately she went to greet him and introduce herself to him and his entourage. The violinist, unlike the catering staff and the florist, had been invited to mingle with the guests later in the evening, and had been given a room in a St Tropez luxurious boutique hotel, paid for by the D'Argents.

Naturally he wanted to know where he would be playing, and dutifully Carly set about answering his manager's questions.

Inside she was still feeling sick with shock and misery over Ricardo's accusations, but she was here to do a job, not indulge her own feelings. And besides, she had a long history of having to hide what she was feeling and the pain and humiliation others had inflicted on her.

Her adoptive parents might turn to her for financial assistance, but it had been their own daughter to whom they had given their love, not Carly.

Ricardo got up and came towards Carly.

'I'm going back to the villa shortly. Presumably you

will wish to go back yourself at some stage, in order to get ready for this evening. Should you want a lift—'

'I don't,' Carly told him curtly, without looking up from checking one of the invoices in front of her.

'Cut out the hard-done-by act, Carly,' Ricardo snapped, equally curtly. 'I'm not taken in by it.'

'I don't wish to discuss it.'

'You thought you'd fooled me and you don't like the fact that I caught you out.'

'No. What I don't like is the fact that I was stupid enough to think there was anything remotely desirable about you.'

'But you did desire me, didn't you?'

'You must excuse me, Mr Salvatore. I've got work to do.'

She didn't turn to watch him as he walked away from her, but nevertheless she knew immediately when he had gone.

'How's it going?'

Carly gave Sarah, the PA, a slightly harassed smile.

'Okay! So far there's only been one major fall-out between the chefs.'

Sarah laughed. 'You're lucky,' she announced, 'You can add a zero to that so far as the D'Argent's are concerned. Not that *they* fall out so much as *she* falls out with *him*! Did you manage to find something to wear for later?'

Carly shook her head. 'I haven't had time,' she told her truthfully.

'Would these be any use, then?' Sarah asked her, pointing to the overstuffed bin liner she had just put down.

'It's some stuff Mariella told me to get rid of ages

ago. Look at this—it would be perfect for you for to-night,' she announced, whipping a mass of silk black fabric out of the top of the bin liner. 'It's a sort of top and palazzo pants thing, all in one.'

The fine silk floated mouthwateringly through Carly's fingers. 'Are you sure that Mariella won't mind?' she asked Sarah worriedly.

'I doubt she'll even notice. Not once she hits the champagne and cocaine,' Sarah answered bluntly.

'It's very sheer…' Carly hesitated.

'You can wear a body underneath it—although Mariella didn't. Oh, and you'll need a pair of high heels—you should be able to pick something up at the market whilst they're having dinner. And if you can't get away you can use my cabin to shower and get changed in.'

Carly gave her a grateful look of relief. 'I was wondering how one earth I was going to manage to make time for that,' she admitted. 'I daren't leave the chefs alone together for too long, and I've promised Jeff I'll make sure no one touches his box trees!'

Sarah laughed and shook her head. 'When is my prince going to come and take me away from all this?' She sighed.

CHAPTER SIX

'HERE they come...'

Carly gave Sarah a slightly distracted smile as they both watched the long line of limousines queuing up to disgorge the D'Argents' guests.

Carly had changed into the black outfit Sarah had given her, and was self-consciously aware of how very suggestively revealing it was. Not even the flesh-coloured body she was wearing beneath it could totally offset the effect of the layers of sheer black fabric floating around her body, revealing with every movement the sensual gleam of her skin beneath the silk.

If she had had something else to wear she would have done so. Sarah had intended to be kind, Carly knew, but no way was this outfit, with its tight-fitting top and hip-hugging palazzo pants bottom, suitable as discreet 'work wear'. But the other outfits had been just as bad.

Already as people approached the gangway they were looking at her—especially the men, some of whom were giving her openly lascivious glances.

Two over-chunky and businesslike dinner-suited bouncer types were checking the invitations before allowing guests to step forward into the open-fronted enclosure, where uniformed staff were waiting to offer welcome glasses of champagne cocktail. The glasses were arranged on white trays, whilst the cocktails were a steel-grey colour.

'What on earth is in them?' Carly had whispered to their own *maître d'*.

'Champagne, liqueur and colouring,' he had told her dryly. 'Mariella D'Argent was insistent that they had to be grey!'

Prior to the D'Argents' return Carly had made a swift inspection of the yacht's receptions areas, to check that everything was as it should be. Privately she felt that the glass floor over thousands of small white lights was a bit OTT, but she had been assured that it was nothing compared with what some people asked for.

The violinist had begun to play, the dinner guests had returned, and Mariella had gone to her suite to get changed into her specially commissioned outfit.

A posse of older men and their too-young arm candy were arriving, the girls all wearing similar teeny-weenie, heavily embroidered clinging dresses and tottering on too-high heels. They were all obviously bleached blondes. Carly suppressed a small sigh.

More guests were arriving, and Carly recognised amongst them some very A-list celebrities—a famous actress, the daughter of a pop icon, a couple of ex-models—all of them accompanied by good-looking men.

But Ricardo hadn't arrived as yet. Not that she was looking for him!

'I'd better go in and be on hand, just in case Mariella wants me for anything,' Sarah whispered to her.

Nodding her head, Carly continued to keep a discreet watch on the arrivals.

'We're going to run short of cocktails any minute,' the *maître d'* muttered warningly.

It took over an hour for all the guests to arrive, by which time Carly was downstairs in the main salon, keeping an eye on the proceedings there and trying to avoid

getting too close to Mariella—just in case she should
object to Carly wearing her discarded outfit!

Drugs were being passed round openly, and the sound
of laughter was growing louder as they began to take
effect.

Already some of the guests had started to behave
recklessly. A well-known media mogul had grabbed a
girl almost in front of Carly and now proceeded to caress her intimately whilst the girl herself encouraged
him.

This was just not a lifestyle with which she felt comfortable, Carly reflected with revulsion. She couldn't
understand how anyone could find any pleasure in
something that ultimately was so very destructive.
Drugs were anathema to her. Her eyes shadowed as she
remembered how she had seen the misery that they
could cause.

She felt a tug on her arm and turned to see one of
the older men leering at her. She'd realised from over-
hearing them talking earlier that they were Russian.

'You come with me,' he demanded drunkenly.

'I'm sorry, I'm not a guest. I'm working,' Carly told
him politely, trying to disengage herself.

'Good, then you work for me…in bed,' he responded
coarsely. 'I pay you good, eh?'

Carly felt nauseated. Was that how all men saw
women—as someone, *something* they could buy? A
commodity they could use? Or did she attract that type
because somehow instinctively they could sense what
she had come from?

Trash! She winced as though she had been knifed,
hearing again the contemptuous word that had been
thrown at her so often during her childhood.

'You are trash, do you know that? Garbage. In fact,

that's where they found you—lying in the rubbish, un-wanted—and that's where you should have stayed.'

Abruptly she realised that she could feel the man's hot breath on her bare skin.

She turned to demand that he release her, and then tensed. Ricardo was standing on the other side of the salon, watching her.

He knew what she was, Ricardo reminded himself savagely, so why did the sight of Carly allowing another man to hold her arm so intimately fill him with jealousy instead of contempt? And why the hell was he now pushing his way through the crowd milling through the salon, in the wake of the D'Argents, in order to get to her? After all, he had already seen the proprietorial way her male companion had reached for her. And what was driving him through the crowd certainly wasn't rooted in some kind of male solidarity, or an altruistic desire to warn her latest victim of just what she was, was it? He derided himself cynically. The truth was, he pre-ferred not to analyse just what the sight of another man holding on to her was doing to him—or why.

Instead he channelled his anger into deciding that her escort's taste in clothes—for obviously he must have bought her the abomination she was wearing—was about as good as Carly's was in men. The pair of them deserved one another, and Carly deserved everything she would get from selling herself to a man who might just as well have had what he was tattooed across his forehead.

But Carly wasn't here to have a relationship with another man, and he intended to remind her in no un-certain terms that *he* was supposed to be her prime con-cern. How dared she reject him and then let that over-weight, sweaty nobody put his greasy hands all over her? Where was her pride? Her self-respect? Didn't it ever occur to her that she was intelligent enough to earn her own living and support herself, instead of debasing herself by offering herself to any man who would give her the price of a few designer rags?

'You! Here!'

Carly stared at the man who had spoken to her so arrogantly as he approached, and then realised that he was with the man who was holding her.

'How much do you want?'

He was already opening his wallet and starting to remove money from it.

Another man had joined the other two, taller and leaner, and with an unmistakable air of authority about him. He spoke sharply to them, and to Carly's relief she was immediately released.

'I apologise for my countrymen—I hope you will not condemn all Russian men as unmannerly oafs because of them?'

He was charming, and very good-looking, Carly acknowledged.

'Of course not,' she assured him.

'You are here alone?'

Someone pushed past and he reached out a protective arm to shield her. Unexpectedly Carly suddenly felt very femininely weak and vulnerable. She wasn't used to men behaving protectively towards her.

'I'm with the event planning organisation,' she explained.

'Ah, so you are responsible for this magnificent party we are enjoying?'

He was flattering as well as charming, Carly recognised.

'In part,' she agreed.

'And you are staying here, on board the yacht?'

'No, I'm—' Carly broke off as she saw both Sarah and the *maître d'* edging towards her. 'Please excuse me,' she apologised to him. 'But I must get back to work.'

'Mmm, I see Igor was chatting you up. Mariella won't like that,' Sarah warned Carly, when she joined her, having dealt with the *maître d'*. 'She's already got him marked down as husband number four. Mind you, she'll have her work cut out, because she certainly isn't the only woman who's hoping for a legal right to his billions. God, I hate these dos,' Sarah complained. 'Sometimes I wonder why the hell I don't just give in my notice and go home.'

'Why don't you?' Carly asked her

'Let's just say there's a man there who I can't have,' Sarah told her bleakly. 'I need another drink. I'll be back in a minute…'

Carly was standing with her back to him, watching Sarah hurry away from her, when Ricardo finally managed to reach her.

'Lost your new admirer?'

Carly stiffened, and then turned round reluctantly to face him.

Before she could defend herself, he continued savagely, 'What the hell possessed you to let him buy you that? You look like a tart,' he told her mercilessly. 'Or was that the idea? It certainly looked as though he was doing a brisk business in selling you on to his friends.'

Carly's face burned. 'You are despicable,' she told him. 'And for your information—'

'Ricardo, darling—there you are!'

Although she was delighted to have Ricardo's attention removed from her, Carly couldn't help wishing that the woman claiming it was not Mariella—especially when she saw the way Mariella was staring at her outfit.

Fortunately, though, before she could say anything Sarah returned. Equally fortunately, she immediately realised what was happening and adroitly came to Carly's rescue, exclaiming, 'Mariella! Carly hasn't been able to stop singing your praises for being so kind to her and saving her so much embarrassment. I told her that it is typical of you to be so generous, and that you'd understand immediately how she felt about having her suitcase stolen. I knew you wouldn't mind if I let her borrow those old things you told me to put to one side for the charity shop. Remember? You said they were too big for you...'

Was it the weight of false sentiment and sugar in Sarah's paean of praise that miraculously squashed the hostility in Mariella's gaze? Carly wondered cynically. Suddenly she became all gracious smiles.

'Of course. I love helping other people—everyone knows that. Although I must say you are rather too big to fit into my things, my dear. Of course I am very slim,' she added smugly, before ignoring Carly to turn to Ricardo and say prettily, 'Ricardo, why don't I introduce you to a few more people...?'

As Mariella drew Ricardo away Sarah exhaled and apologised to Carly.

'I hope you didn't mind me saying that—only she looked as though she was about to create a bit of a scene...'

'No, I didn't mind at all,' Carly assured her truthfully. But she would have loved to see Ricardo's face if Mariella had claimed ownership of her outfit when he had been in the middle of insulting it. Although he hadn't merely insulted the outfit, had he? He'd insulted her as well.

She didn't care what he thought about her, Carly assured herself. After all, she knew the truth and she knew that he was wrong. At least this way, even if she couldn't deny or ignore the physical, sexual effect he had on her, she knew she would be safe from any risk of becoming emotionally attracted to him.

Not, of course, that she *had* been in any danger of that.

It seemed as if the evening was never going to end, Carly thought wearily. The last of the guests had finally gone, but she and the others were still cleaning up.

'Look, why don't you go? There's nothing more for you to do here,' Jeff the florist said in a kind voice.

'It's my responsibility to stay until everything is packed up,' Carly told him.

'You don't think that anyone else would stay around this long, do you?' He grinned at her and shook his head. 'We're perfectly capable of sorting what's left, and besides…' He was looking past her and she turned her head to see what he was looking at.

Her heart gave a sudden heavy thud as the door of the car which had drawn up a few yards away opened and Ricardo got out.

The last time she'd seen him he had been deep in conversation with a stunning redhead whom she was sure she had heard murmuring something about going back to her hotel suite with her. So what was he doing back here now?

Why should the fact that he was striding so purposefully towards her make her legs and her will-power quiver with weakness? He had insulted her in the most offensive way possible, and yet here she was letting his sexuality and, even worse, her own reaction to it, get to her.

Maybe she should adopt a different and more modern attitude. After all, she had heard plenty of women say openly and unashamedly that they were up for having sex with a man without wanting or needing any kind of emotional connection with him. Surely that kind of relationship was exactly what would suit her best?

'It's gone three a.m. and we leave for New York in the morning,' he told her curtly.

'You go, Carly,' Jeff repeated. 'We can easily finish up here now.'

It seemed that she didn't have any choice. Turning aside, Carly went to retrieve the canvas hold-all she had bought earlier to hold her modest new purchases.

She watched with a certain sense of grim satisfaction as Ricardo frowned and took it from her.

'Before you say anything,' she warned him coolly, when they were out of Jeff's hearing, 'I didn't have to sell my body to buy either the bag or its contents. What happened to the redhead, by the way?' she asked unkindly as they walked back to the car. The fact that Ricardo was a potential client had been overwhelmed by her still smarting pride. 'Didn't she come up to your expectations—or was it you who didn't come up to hers?'

'Neither. She left with the man with whom she arrived—and even if she hadn't *I* don't take those kinds of risks with my health,' Ricardo answered pointedly.

He was opening the car door for her, but Carly paused to turn round and demand angrily, 'Meaning what? That I do? Isn't the discovery that you've already made one offensive and insulting error of judgement about me enough?'

Without waiting for his response she got into the car, ignoring him as she reached for the seatbelt, and continuing to ignore him when he walked round the car, climbed into the driver's seat and started the car engine.

They reached the villa. Carly opened the car door and got out without waiting for Ricardo to help her.

The pink-washed building was bathed in a soft rose glow from the artfully placed nightscape lighting, which illuminated both the villa and its gardens. Rose-pink— the colour of romance. A small, painful smile twisted her lips.

'Carly.'

She stopped walking and turned to look as Ricardo caught up with her.

'Why didn't you tell me that the outfit you were wearing belonged to Mariella?'

'Perhaps I didn't want to spoil your fun. You were obviously enjoying thinking the worst of me,' she answered sharply.

'You can't blame me for making entirely logical assumptions. You're a woman in her twenties with a career, therefore logically you must have a bank account. Having a bank account means that you have access to credit cards, bank loans, a wide variety of different ways of borrowing money in an emergency—as this—' he indicated the bag he was now carrying '—proves. And yet you chose to ask me for a loan.'

'Logical assumptions? You've already as good as admitted that the assumptions you've made about me, far from being logical, are based entirely on your own preconceived ideas and personal hang-ups. The truth is that you know nothing whatsoever about my life or my circumstances. If the women you mix with are the type who are happy to exchange sex for a few gaudy trinkets and a wardrobe of designer clothes, then I'm afraid that so far as I'm concerned it says just as much about your judgement and morals as it does about theirs.'

'Really? Well, *my* judgement told me that you were more than ready to have sex with me until you found out that sex was all you would be getting. Miraculously, now that you know that, suddenly you have all the money you need to replace your stolen clothes. Oh, and a word of warning. That gang are notorious for wanting value for their money. They'll pass you round from hand to hand and have all they want of you. You may not find it worth the pay.'

No one had ever made her feel so furiously angry. She was so angry, in fact, that for once she forgot her normal caution and instead burst out, 'You are so wrong. The only reason I was ready to have sex with you was because I wanted you—but, luckily for me, I wanted to retain my self-respect more. And as for my bank account and my new clothes—I asked you for a loan because I have had to empty my bank account to…to make my parents a…a loan. I do not own a credit card, since I disapprove of their punitively high rates of interest, and there wasn't time for me to realise any of my assets.'

Ricardo frowned. Surely no one could manufacture the level of fury Carly was showing? But he wasn't simply going to give in.

'But obviously somehow you managed to find some money?'

'Yes, but not by selling my body, as you so obviously would like to think.'

'No? How, then?' The cynical disbelief in his voice infuriated her.

'If you must know—not that it is any of your business—I pawned my watch,' she told him flatly.

Ricardo discovered that a sensation akin to the slow, measured drip of ice being fed straight into his bloodstream was creeping up over him—a mental awareness that somehow he had got something very important spectacularly wrong.

He couldn't remember the last time anyone had wrongfooted him, and the knowledge that it should be Carly who had done so sparked off inside him a very dangerous cocktail of emotions. He looked down at her bare wrist and then back at her face.

'You said your parents needed a loan? Surely you could—'

'I don't want to talk about it.' Carly cut him off quickly.

Ricardo frowned. Surely the kind of woman he had assumed her to be would have been only too eager to make much of the glow of virtue accruing to her from such selflessness. But Carly was turning away from him, quite plainly agitated and anxious to change the subject.

Why? Ricardo wondered. What on earth could there be about something as generous as lending money to one's parents to spark off the hostility and fear he could see so plainly in her eyes?

She was starting to walk away from him. He looked down at her wrist again, and then back at her face.

He had always trusted his instincts, and right now those instincts were insisting that Carly had been telling him the truth. Therefore he was guilty of seriously misjudging her. And his body was telling him that, no matter what she was or what she had done or not done, he wanted her.

He strode towards her, catching hold of her arm.

Immediately her whole body tensed, and she demanded fiercely, 'Let go of me.'

'Not yet. You aren't the only one who takes their moral responsibilities seriously. I obviously owe you an apology.'

Ricardo was actually apologising to her? He certainly needed to, she reminded herself angrily. And she needed to apologise to herself, for being so stupid as to actually still want him.

'Yes, you do,' she agreed coolly. 'But I don't want it.'

She watched his stunned disbelief give way to male anger.

'No? But you do want me, don't you?' he taunted softly.

'No,' she began, but it was already too late. He pulled her hard against him and bent his head to take her mouth in a savagely intimate kiss before she could object. And, of course, the moment his mouth touched hers, her own helpless response betrayed her. She tried to pull away but he held on to her, and her eyes widened as she saw in his eyes the same hunger she knew was in her own.

She made a small helpless sound of denial and need, and then she gave in. His mouth moved urgently on hers and her lips parted eagerly, greedily for its possession, her nails digging into the hard muscles of his arms as her need roared through her.

It was last night all over again—only this time they were impeded by two sets of clothes. She had changed back into her own things before supervising the clearing up after the party. Now she was being driven wild by her longing to be as naked and open to him now as she had been the previous evening.

Her fingers clenched spasmodically on his arm, her body gripped by savage shudders of dark pleasure.

She wanted his hands on her breasts, on *all* of her—his fingers finding her, touching her as they had done last night. Just wanting him to touch her in that way made her go hot and limp with the desire she could feel pulsing inside her. She wanted him there…there—deep, deep inside her, thrusting hard and fast against the possessive hold of her muscles, taking her, satisfying her quickly and mercilessly.

She could feel the open heat of his mouth against her throat as he tipped her back over his arm, moonlight gleaming whitely on her skin as he tugged off her top to reveal her breast, darkly crowned in the night light.

His thumb-tip rubbed against the deep dark pink of her nipple and she cried out—a sharp, agonised sound of primitive female mating hunger.

She wanted him to take her now, here. As quickly and completely, as fiercely and thoroughly as a panting she-creature on heat. She wanted him to fill her, flood her with his own release, and to go on doing so until she was sated and complete.

She reached for the hardness she knew was waiting for her, running her fingers over and over the jutting ridge of his erection, quivering with anticipation. The head would be swollen and hot, the body thick and darkly veined, the flesh tightly drawn over the hard muscle, but still fluid and slick when she touched it.

In her imagination she could already feel the first rub of that engorged head between the lips of her sex, and then against the sensitive pleasure-pulse of her clitoris over and over again, faster and faster, until she was wet and hot with her pleasure. Until she could endure no more and Ricardo finally plunged deep inside her.

As though she had cried her desire out loud to him, she felt Ricardo tugging at her clothes, his hands hard and firm against her naked skin. His mouth found her nipple and drew fiercely on it. She cried out again in a mewling sound of intense arousal.

His mouth returned to hers. She felt as though she had been starving for it, for him, as though she had been waiting all their life to be with him. She felt...

Immediately she tensed, pushing him away, her voice tight with rejection and self-loathing as she told him fiercely, 'I don't want this.'

'Yes, you do. You want this and you want me, and you can't deny it!' Ricardo challenged her whilst he fought to control his breathing. And to rationalise what had happened—if he could rationalise it. It was something he had had no intention of allowing to happen at all. But from the moment he had touched her he had been out of control, unable to stop what was happening to him.

Carly drew in a deep, shaky breath.

'We mustn't.'

'We must not what?' Ricardo demanded. 'We must not want one another?'

Carly turned her head away from him and shook it in bewilderment. 'This can't happen again,' she told him quickly.

Baffled and frustrated, Ricardo reluctantly let her go. She wanted him, and he certainly damned well wanted her, so why was she behaving like this? One thing he did know was that he was determined that he would have her, sooner or later—and he would prefer it to be sooner.

Thank heavens Ricardo hadn't followed her to her room. Because if he had she knew that she would not have been able to resist him. And she had to resist him, because she wanted him far more than it was safe for her to do.

Why, though, did she feel like this about him? Why did she want him when she had never wanted any of the other men she had met?

Was it because subconsciously she knew he was different from them? Because the most intimate part of her recognised that, at some primal level, she felt a deep-rooted kinship with him?

Because, like him, she too had known and suffered childhood poverty and the withdrawal, the denial of the love and nurturing, the protection every child should be given as of right?

The wretched squalor and unhappiness of her own early childhood had marked her for ever, as she knew his must have marked him.

Not even Julia and Lucy, who thought they knew everything about her, knew the full truth of the beginning of her life—how she had been found dressed in rags, abandoned in the street beside some rubbish, her pitiful cries alerting a loitering tramp to her existence.

She had been a piece of unwanted humanity, left there to die. Unwanted and unloved, even by her own birth mother. No wonder, then, that her adopted mother had never been able to love her either.

CHAPTER SEVEN

'YOU mentioned last night that you didn't have any money in your bank account because you'd had to help your parents?'

Carly almost dropped the glass of water she had been drinking. A little unsteadily, she put it down. They had boarded Ricardo's jet several hours later than Ricardo had originally planned, although he had not give her any reason for the delay, and would soon be landing at JFK airport for their onward journey to the Hamptons.

She looked out of the window, telling herself that it was pointless now to berate herself for letting anger lead her into admitting that she had needed to help them.

'I…I shouldn't have said that,' she admitted uncomfortably. 'And I wouldn't have done if you hadn't made me so angry.'

'I misjudged you, and I've apologised for that. A man in my position becomes very cynical about other people's motives. Why did you have to give your parents money? Are you an only child?'

'I…I had a sister…'

Her mouth had gone dry, and she wanted desperately to bring their conversation to an end.

'Had?' Ricardo questioned, as she had known he would.

'Yes. She… Fenella died a…a few months ago,' she told him reluctantly.

Ricardo could almost feel her resistance to his questions as he registered her words and felt the shock of them, plus his own shock that she should be so composed.

'I'm sorry. That must have been dreadful for you.'

Carly looked at him.

'Fenella and I weren't really related. I…her parents adopted me when I was very young. They adored her, and they were naturally devastated by her death,' she told him in a guarded voice.

'But you weren't?' Ricardo guessed.

'We were very different. Fenella naturally was always the favoured child. Adoption doesn't always work out the way people hope it will.'

Carly looked away from him. It was obvious that she was withholding something from him, *withdrawing* herself from him, in fact—as though she didn't want to let him into the personal side of her life. To his own astonishment he discovered that he didn't like the fact that she was reluctant to talk openly about herself to him. What was it about her that caused him to have this compulsion to learn more? And was it more, or was it *everything* there was to learn?

His curiosity was merely that of a potential employer, he assured himself.

'What do you mean, adoption doesn't always work? Didn't it work for you? Weren't you happy with your adoptive parents?'

'Why are you asking me so many questions?'

Ricardo could almost feel her anxiety and panic.

'Perhaps because I want to know more about you.'

On the face of it he already knew all he needed to know. But it was what was beneath the surface that was arousing his curiosity. She was concealing something from him, something that changed her from a self-confident woman into someone who was far more vulnerable—and also very determined to deny that vulnerability. He had a fiercely honed instinct about such things, and he knew he wasn't wrong. So what was it? He intended to find out. But what would it take to break down her barriers?

He looked at her and watched in satisfaction as, under his deliberate scrutiny, the colour seeped up under her skin.

'You haven't answered my question,' he reminded her.

'No, I wasn't happy.' The terseness in her voice warned him that she didn't like his probing.

'What about your natural parents?'

Ricardo could see immediately that his question had had a very dramatic effect on her. Her face lost its colour and he could hear her audibly indrawn breath. He expected her to refuse to answer, but instead she spoke fiercely.

'My mother was probably a drug addict, who died in a house fire along with two other young women. No one knew who my father might have been. I was left to die amongst the rubbish outside a hospital. A tramp found me. I was only a few weeks old. I was ten years old and in foster care when Fenella's parents decided they wanted to adopt a sister for her, because they were concerned that she might be lonely.'

Ricardo was frowning.

'They adopted you for their daughter?'

'Yes. I imagine they felt I'd be easier to house-train than a puppy and less expensive to keep than a pony,' Carly told him lightly. 'Unfortunately, though, it didn't work out. Fenella, quite naturally, hated having to share her parents and her toys with an unwanted sibling, and demanded that her parents send me back. I think they wanted to, but of course it was too late. I wasn't allowed to touch anything of Fenella's, or even to eat in the same room with her at first. But then we were both sent to boarding school. That's when I met Jules and Lucy. Somehow or other my…my history, and the fact that I wasn't really Fenella's sister, became public knowledge.'

'You mean she told everyone?' Ricardo asked bluntly.

'She was a year older than me, so she'd already made her own circle of friends at the school before I went there. She was a very popular girl—she could be charming when she wanted to be—and I very quickly became ostracised.'

'You were bullied, you mean?'

'I was different and I didn't fit in,' Carly continued without answering him. 'But luckily for me, Jules and Lucy came to my rescue and gave me their friendship. Without that and them…' The shadows in her eyes caused Ricardo to experience a sudden fierce surge of protectiveness towards her, and anger towards those who had so obviously tormented her.

'What happened to Fenella?'

Carly shook her head. It disturbed her to realise how much she had told him about herself.

She wasn't going to tell him any more, Ricardo recognised, as he watched her turn away from him to focus on her laptop.

Carly frowned as she tried to study the figures on the company's bank statements on her screen. Answering Ricardo's questions had brought back so many painful memories.

She had truly believed when she had been adopted that she was going to be loved by her new parents and

sister, and she had given them her own love unstint-
ingly. It had confused her at first when she had been
rebuffed, but then she had seen her adoptive mother
hugging Fenella, fussing over her, and she had begun
to realise that there was a huge difference between the
way Fenella was given her parents' love and approval,
and the way she was refused it.

She had tried to make herself as like Fenella as possible, mirroring the other girl's behaviour as closely as
she could, assuming that this would gain her adoptive
parents' approval. Instead it had simply made Fenella
hate her even more. Now, as an adult, she could not
entirely blame them. Fenella had been their child, after
all. But her experience with her adoptive parents had
taught her the danger of giving her love to anyone.

The figures in front of her blurred, and she had to
blink fiercely in order to be able to concentrate on them.

Suddenly, when she saw them properly, she frowned,
firmly putting her own problems to one side as she
stared in shocked anxiety at the unfamiliarly large
cheques that had gone through the account, almost completely emptying it of cash.

It was unthinkable that this should have happened.
She prided herself on keeping a mental running total of
what was going in and out of the account, and according
to her own mental reckoning they should have been
several hundred thousand pounds in credit. In fact, they
needed to be several hundred thousand pounds in credit
to meet the bills their suppliers would be presenting at
the end of the month, and to leave sufficient working
capital to carry them until they received payment from
other clients.

So what were these cheques for? She couldn't remember signing them. A cold trickle of anxiety mixed

106 BEDDING HIS VIRGIN MISTRESS

with instinct iced down her spine. Her heart started to beat uncomfortably heavily. She needed to see those cheques.

Carly had quickly become totally engrossed in her work. Too quickly, Ricardo thought. Did she use it to block out emotional issues she found it difficult to handle? She had not said so, but he imagined that she must have suffered severe emotional trauma during her childhood.

That he should even have such a concern, never mind actively feel protective of her because of it, was such alien emotional territory to him that it took several seconds to recognise his own danger. Once he had done so he reminded himself firmly that that had been then and this was now, and now he wanted her in his bed.

Carly ordered photocopies of the cheques. Until they came she wouldn't be able to do anything else.

'Carly!'

She acknowledged Ricardo with a wary look.

'I hope you ached as much for me last night as I did for you.'

She could feel her face starting to burn.

'I'd really rather not talk about it. I've already said that I don't want to…to go there.'

Her voice was calm, but he could see that her hand was trembling.

He gave a small shrug.

'Why not? Why should we deny ourselves something it's obvious we both want? Sexually there's a chemistry between us that maybe neither of us would have wanted, given free choice, but I don't see any point in trying to pretend that it doesn't exist. And, given that it does exist, perhaps it would be better for both of us if we enjoyed it instead of trying to ignore or reject it.

That way at least we could get our sexual hunger for one another out of our systems.'

Our sexual hunger. Three simple words. But they had the power to change her life for ever. Had Adam felt what she was feeling now when Eve had handed him the apple and announced, 'Here, take a bite?' Had he thought then, just as she was thinking now, of all that he would be denying himself if he refused? If she had sex with Ricardo it wouldn't change the world, but it would change her. Was she brave enough to accept that? Or would she rather spend the rest of her life wishing and wondering?

'I don't want to have an affair with you,' she answered him. An affair would involve falling in love, putting herself in a situation where ultimately she would be rejected in favour of someone else. Every emotional experience she'd ever had had taught her that. In her foster homes, with her adoptive parents, and then at school. Even with her closest friends, Lucy and Jules, she was aware that they shared an extra special bond of birth and upbringing which excluded her.

'But you do want to have sex with me,' Ricardo guessed.

Her face was burning, but she managed to hold his gaze.

'I...I think so.'

The look he gave her was pure male power.

'Are you asking me to make the decision for you?'

'What would be the point? I'm sure a man with your experience could find someone else who wouldn't need to have a decision made for them.'

'I'm sure I could,' Ricardo agreed dryly. 'However, they would not be you, and it is you I want. But, since we're on the subject of relationships, how many relationships *have* there been for you?'

He had caught her unprepared, slipping the question under her guard.

'Er... I don't... I can't really remember,' she told him untruthfully. 'And besides, it isn't really any of your business, is it?'

'It would be if we slept together,' Ricardo told her.

How could she tell him the truth?

How could she say that he was different—special— that she had never felt the way she did about him with anyone else, and that that alone was enough to make her feel threatened and afraid? And if she couldn't tell him that, then how could she tell him that she had never done with anyone else what she so much wanted to do with him?

'What time do you think we will arrive at the Hamptons?' she asked instead.

The look he gave her made her feel as though he had set a match to her will-power and it was curling up into nothing inside her.

'We'll be there in plenty of time. We'll stay over in my New York apartment tonight and fly out tomorrow.'

'Wouldn't it make more sense to go straight there?'

'Not really. You're looking and sounding very agitated, Carly. Why?'

'No reason. I mean, I'm not. Why should I be?'

'Perhaps you don't feel you can trust yourself to be alone with me?' Ricardo suggested softly.

Carly had had enough.

'It isn't a matter of that! I just don't think we should put ourselves in a position where—'

'Where what? Where you might be tempted to offer

yourself to me and I might accept? Is that what you mean?'

'No! At least...' That was exactly what she had meant, she admitted to herself. Only in her mental scenario it had been Ricardo offering himself to her, not the other way around.

Something about the way he had phrased his statement touched a raw nerve. 'I don't like what you're implying,' she told him frankly. 'I appreciate that lots of women probably come on to you because...'

'Because I'm very rich?' he suggested smoothly, picking up her dropped sentence.

His voice might sound smooth, but beneath it he was angry, Carly recognised. He might not feel concerned about her sensitivities, but he obviously did not like her treading on his own!

'I wasn't going to say that.'

'Liar!' Ricardo told her, adding coolly,

'Besides, there are always several components to sexual desire, surely? For instance there are those which relate to our senses—sight, scent, taste...touch...'

Carly could feel herself beginning to respond to each word that rolled off his tongue.

Yes, the sight of him aroused her, and his scent certainly did, and as for his taste... She pulled in her stomach muscles to try and control the ache spreading through her. And touch... She pulled them in tighter, but it was already too late to halt what she was feeling. And, yes, the sound of his voice as well...

'And then there are those that relate to personality, status...lifestyle. For instance—' He broke off as the steward emerged from the crew's quarters and came towards them.

Carly could feel herself shaking slightly inside—the sensual effect on her body from just listening to him.

'We'll be landing in half an hour. Would you like another drink before we do? Or something to eat?'

Carly shook her head, unable to trust herself to speak. Ricardo had dragged from her confidences and admissions she would normally never have made to anyone, and right now emotional reaction was beginning to set in—much the same way as physical reaction would have set in if she had just had a tooth pulled without anaesthetic. She felt slightly sick, more than slightly shaky, and very much in shock.

Perhaps Ricardo was right, and the only way to overcome her physical ache for him was to satisfy it instead of trying to avoid it.

Ricardo watched her, shielding his scrutiny with a pretended concentration on his own papers. Over and over again she broke out of the stereotyped image he wanted to impose on her. No other woman had shown him—given him—*shared* with him—such an intensity of sexual desire. And no other woman had ever aroused him to such a point of compelling compulsive hunger either.

They were coming in to land, the jet descending through the thin cloud-cover.

Carly packed away her papers and fastened her seat-belt. She had always been the sort of person who took every precaution she could to protect herself. But she had not been able to protect herself from what was happening to her now—and wasn't it true that a part of her didn't want to be protected from it?

'Ah, Rafael, there you are…this is Ms Carlisle.'

The young Mexican gave Carly a grave smile.

'Carly, please,' she corrected Ricardo as she shook Rafael's hand.

'Rafael and his wife Dolores run my New York apartment. How is Dolores, Rafael?'

'She is very well, and she said to tell you that she is making a special meal for you tonight. It is Italian. She also said to tell you that the orphanage is very happy and the children think you should be called Saint Salvatore.'

Saint Salvatore? Carly questioned mentally, watching the way Ricardo frowned.

'You want me to fly the chopper to the apartment block?' Rafael asked.

Ricardo shook his head.

'No, I'll fly it myself.'

Ricardo had a pilot's licence? Carly tried not to look either awed or impressed as Rafael urged her to climb on board the golf-buggy-type vehicle he had waiting for them.

She'd never flown in a helicopter before, and she acknowledged that she felt slightly daunted at the prospect of doing so. But she had no intention of saying so to Ricardo.

'I'll go and fetch the luggage,' Rafael announced, once he had helped Carly out of the buggy.

'We'll use the chopper tomorrow to get to the Hamptons,' Ricardo said as he guided Carly towards it. 'It will be much quicker and easier. You will have an excellent overview of New York City if you sit beside me. Technically Rafael should take that seat, since he is my co-pilot, but—'

'Oh, then he must sit there,' Carly insisted quickly.

'You sound apprehensive. Don't you trust me?'

'I...'

'I can assure you, I take a keen interest in my own continued existence!'

Ricardo had been right about the view of New York, Carly acknowledged, and she held her breath instinctively as he flew them between two huge tower blocks.

Via the headphones she was wearing she could hear his running commentary on the city below them—the straight lines of the modern streets, and then the curve in Broadway where the new merged with the old.

'That's Wall Street down there,' Ricardo told her, and she looked, bemused to see how quaintly narrow and small it seemed. He turned the helicopter and announced, 'We'll be flying over Central Park soon. My apartment's way up on the east side.'

The streets on either side of the park were lined with what looked like nineteenth-century buildings, and Carly held her breath as Ricardo headed for one of them, not releasing it until she saw the helicopter landing area marked out on its roof.

'You don't leave the helicopter here, do you?' Carly asked once he had helped her out.

Ricardo shook his head. 'No. Rafael will fly it back to the airport and then drive back. I dare say he will take Dolores with him, and they will call on their family on the way back.'

He was obviously a fair and well-liked employer, Carly reflected as he guided her towards the building and in through a doorway to a small foyer and lift. Once they were inside Ricardo punched a code into the panel and the doors closed, enclosing them in what—for Carly—was a far too intimate bubble of seclusion. Immediately the thought filled her mind that if he should turn to her now and take her in his arms she would not want to resist him.

'Don't look at me like that,' Ricardo warned her
softly, so easily and immediately reading her thoughts
that she could only gape at him. 'I can't—not in here.
That's a camera up there,' he told her, pointing upwards
towards the ceiling.

The lift stopped silently and smoothly and the doors
opened onto another foyer. It was a large, coolly spa-
cious one this time, with only one door opening off it,
its walls painted a flat matt cream to highlight the paintings hanging on them.

'Lucien Freud?' Carly questioned, recognising the
style immediately.

'Yes. His work has a raw feel to it that I like.'

The posed nudes *were* compelling, Carly admitted.

The foyer's single door opened and Ricardo stood
back to allow her to precede him.

He had excellent manners, and they seemed to be a
natural part of him rather than something carefully
learned. But from the brief description she'd had of his
early life she doubted if standing back to allow others
to precede him was something he'd learned on the
streets of Naples.

A small, dark-haired woman with twinkling eyes was
standing in the inner hallway, waiting for them.

'Ah, Dolores. You got my message about Ms
Carlisle?'

'Yes, and I have prepared a guest suite for her. You
had a good journey, I hope, Ms Carlisle?'

'Yes, indeed—and do please call me Carly.'

'You go with Dolores; she will show you to your
suite,' Ricardo told Carly, before continuing, 'What
time is dinner planned for, Dolores?'

'Eight-thirty, if that is okay with you? And Rafael—

he said that you will want an early lunch tomorrow, before you fly to the Hamptons?'

'Yes, that's right. I'd better warn you that Ms Carlisle may not make it to the dinner table tonight. It may be three in the afternoon here, but for her it's eight in the evening.'

'Oh, my goodness! You would perhaps like something to eat now, then?' Dolores asked Carly.

'No, I'm fine,' Carly assured her.

She would have to make contact with the New York agency who were sharing the organisation of the Hamptons event with them, and she had hoped to have time to fit in a bit of sightseeing. She was also planning to ask Dolores if she could recommend somewhere Carly might find clothes that would be within her budget. Jeans might be the universal uniform, acceptable everywhere, but she could hardly turn up at the glitzy events she was overseeing wearing them. And unfortunately Mariella's cast-offs—designer label or not—were simply not the kind of clothes she would ever feel comfortable wearing.

'So, you will sleep here, in this guest suite, and you will have a lovely view over the park. Come and see, please.'

Dutifully Carly followed Dolores through the door she had just opened.

The room she walked into was huge, its windows, as Dolores had stated, overlooking the greenery of the park.

'Here there is a desk, and you can plug in your computer,' Dolores told her.

Carly nodded her head.

'And here there is a television.' She folded back what Carly had assumed was wall panelling to reveal a large flatscreen TV hidden behind it, along with shelves of DVDs and books. 'See—the TV, it pulls out so you can watch it from your bed,' Dolores told Carly, proudly displaying this extra function. 'The dressing room and your bathroom are through here. Mr Salvatore, he have everything ripped out when he moved in here, and it's all new. Even in our rooms as well.'

The dressing room was lined with mirror-fronted wardrobes and contained a small sofa, whilst the bathroom was almost a luxury mini-spa. Carly was unable to stop herself from comparing it with the rather more basic bathroom in the flat she shared with Jules.

'It's all wonderful,' she told Dolores truthfully.

'Yes. Mr Salvatore, he is a very good man. Very kind—especially to the children. When he hear that there is an orphanage in our old home town that has no money, he goes there to see it and then he writes one big cheque!' Dolores beamed.

Carly phoned Lucy and then the New York event organiser who was co-running the event. Everything seemed to be in hand, she thought as she stifled a yawn.

The bed looked very tempting, and she *was* tired. Perhaps an hour's sleep might do her good. It was only five o'clock New York time—more than three hours yet before dinner.

She was too tired to shower, and so, after removing her shoes and folding back the bedspread, she simply lay on top of the bed. Sleep claimed her the moment she closed her eyes.

CHAPTER EIGHT

IT WAS the small sound of a door clicking closed that woke her. At first she struggled to remember exactly where she was, reluctant to be dragged out of her sleeping fantasy of lying naked in Ricardo's arms whist he caressed her.

She sat up and then swung her feet onto the floor, all too aware of the pulsing ache in her lower body. She could hear someone moving about in the dressing room.

Ricardo? Her heart bumped against her ribs, excitement spiked with anticipation heating her body. If it was—if he wasn't going to give her the chance to say that she wanted him but intended instead to simply overwhelm her with the reality of her desire for him—there was no way she was going to be able to reject him, she admitted to herself, and she hurried across the room, pushing open the dressing room door.

Dolores was just closing one of the wardrobe doors. She turned towards Carly with a warm smile.

The deep-rooted sensual ache she had begun to learn to live with turned into a fierce pang of anguished need. How could just a few hours in his company have turned her body into this sexually eager collection of erotically aroused nerve endings and hotly responsive flesh? Her whole body ached, hungering for his touch and his possession. It was being consumed by a fever of longing and arousal. Virtually all she could think about was how long she would have to wait. The question driving her thoughts now wasn't 'if' but 'when'.

'I have hung everything up for you, so that they don't get too crushed. I can pack them again before you leave tomorrow. So you have any laundry you want me to do?'

Everything? What *everything*? What did Dolores mean?

There was an unfamiliar case on the dressing room floor—a Louis Vuitton case, Carly realised with horrified fascination—and a matching vanity case placed right next to it. And there was a mound of neatly folded tissue paper on the pretty daybed-cum-sofa, and some shoe boxes placed beneath it.

'Dolores, I think there must be some mistake,' she began faintly. 'Those cases aren't mine.'

Dolores looked confused.

'But, yes, they are. Rafael fetched them from the jet himself. Just as Mr Salvatore instructed him to do. So that they will not be lost.'

A horrible sense of disbelief mixed with anger was filling Carly. Unsteadily she went over to the nearest wardrobe and pulled back the door.

The clothes hanging in it were totally unfamiliar. She lifted down one of the skirts and checked the label, her hands trembling.

It was certainly her size, *and* her colour.

She put the skirt back and went over the sofa, kneeling on the floor as she opened one of the shoeboxes.

The delicate strappy sandals inside were her size too.

'There is something wrong?' Dolores asked her worriedly

Carly replaced the sandal in its box and stood up.

'No, Dolores. Everything is fine,' she told her.

But of course she was lying.

She went slowly through all the clothes hanging in

the wardrobes. Expensive, elegant, beautiful designer clothes, in wonderful fabrics and a palette of her favourite colours: creams, chocolate-browns, black. She touched the fringed hem of a jacket in Chanel's signature pastel tweed—warm cream threaded with tiny silky strands of brilliant jewel colours. She had seen exactly the same jacket in Chanel's Sloane Street store and had stood mutely gazing at it, almost transfixed by its beauty. It would go perfectly with the toning heavy silk satin trousers hanging next to it. She knew exactly how much the jacket would have cost because she had been foolish enough to go into the store and ask. More than she would ever spend on clothes in a whole year, never mind on one single item. She stepped back from the wardrobe and closed the door firmly.

Did he really think she would allow him to do this to her? After what he had said to her? After what he had thought of her? Oh, yes, he had claimed it was a mistake and he had apologised, but...

Inside her head, from another lifetime, she could hear a flustered nervous voice insisting, 'Say thank you to the nice lady for the lovely clothes she's bought for you, Carly. Aren't you a lucky, lucky girl? And such a very pretty dress. I'm sure she'll be ever so grateful once she realises how lucky she is...won't you, Carly?'

Grateful? She had sworn on her eighteenth birthday that never, ever again was she going to have to be grateful for someone else's charity. That she would support herself, by herself, and that was exactly what she had done.

She had financed her own way through university via a variety of low-paid, physically hard jobs—bar work, cleaning, working as a nursing aide in an old people's home—determinedly ignoring the allowance being paid into her bank account. The first thing she had done when her adoptive parents had broken the news to her of their financial ruin had been to give that money back to them.

'Dolores, I need to speak with Ricardo. Can you tell me where I will find him, please?'

'He is in his office. But he does not like to be disturbed when he is in there.'

He didn't like being disturbed? Well, he was about to discover that neither did she. And what he had done *had* disturbed her. It had disturbed her...and it had infuriated her—a very great deal!

Dolores didn't want to give her directions for the office, but Carly insisted. She knocked briefly on the door and then, without waiting, turned the handle and went in.

Ricardo was seated behind a desk on the opposite side of the room from the door. The evening sun light coming in from the two high windows behind dazzled her whilst leaving his face cloaked in shadow.

'Dolores has filled the wardrobes in my room with clothes which she believes are mine.'

'Ah. Yes, I'm glad you reminded me; I had almost forgotten. I've spoken to the manager at Barneys and arranged a temporary account there for you so that you can get something suitable for the French do. I didn't want to risk picking out something myself. You'll have time to go over there tomorrow morning. It's right behind the Pierre Hotel—'

'No!' Carly stopped him angrily.

'No what?' Ricardo demanded, pushing back his chair and standing up.

Carly had to take a steadying breath. Every sinuous movement of his body reminded her of how it had felt against her own, of how much she wanted it, ached for it, longed for it.

Ricardo had changed his own clothes at some stage, and was wearing a tee shirt and a pair of jeans. Some men could wear jeans and some could not. Ricardo was quite definitely one of the ones who could. Longing shot through her—pure, wanton, female liquid need.

'No. I won't wear clothes that you have paid for.'

'Why not?' he demanded. 'You eat food bought with my money, sleep in a bed paid for with it. Why should you refuse to wear clothes it has bought?'

'You know why. You accused me yourself of trying to force you to—'

'I was wrong about that and I apologised.'

His voice was terse, and Carly could see he did not like being reminded that he had been at fault.

'Yes, I know that,' Carly agreed reluctantly 'But—'

'But what? You object to the colours I chose? The styles?'

'*You* chose?' she breathed in disbelief. 'How could you have done that? You couldn't possibly have had time!'

He gave a small shrug.

'I made time.'

'How?' Carly challenged him.

'I went into St Tropez this morning, before we left.'

Carly stared at him. Was he making it up…making fun of her, perhaps?

'How did you know my size?'

'I'm a man,' he told her dryly. 'I've touched your body. Held it close to my own. You have full breasts, but a very narrow ribcage. I can span your waist with my hands, your hips curve as woman's hips should do—shall I continue?'

'No,' Carly told him in a choked voice. 'I won't wear them,' she added in the next breath. 'I won't take charity.'

'Charity!' Ricardo frowned, sharply aware of the anguish in her voice, and wondering about her use of the word *charity*. 'And I will not take a woman out with me who has nothing to wear other than a pair of jeans!'

'You are not taking me out with you. I am here to work.'

'Maybe, but it is not out of the question that we could be photographed together by someone who does not know the real situation.'

'You're a snob,' Carly accused him wildly.

'No. I am a realist! I believed that you were entirely professional in your attitude towards your work, but it seems that I was wrong.'

'What do you mean?'

'I should have thought it was obvious. Were you the professional I believed you to be you would accept the necessity of dressing suitably for your role instead of behaving like an outraged virgin. Especially since we both know that is something you most definitely are *not*!'

He might think he knew that, but she knew something very different indeed, Carly reflected. 'And that is the only reason you bought the clothes?'

'What other reason could there be?' he challenged her.

'You've already made it clear to me that you think sex is something you can buy,' she pointed out. 'But I won't and can't be bought, Ricardo.'

He was very angry, she recognised, his pride no doubt stinging in much the same way as hers had when she had opened those wardrobe doors. Good!

'You're making a mountain out of a molehill. I have simply provided you with the kind of clothes I expect the women I am seen with in public to wear. That is all. Had you not had your case stolen it would not have been necessary, but it was and it is. If it makes you feel any better, then perhaps you should think of the clothes merely as being on loan to you, to wear as a necessary uniform. As for paying for sex—I think I am capable of recognising when a woman wants me, Carly.'

There was nothing she could say to that.

'It's almost dinnertime. I hope you are hungry. Dolores is very proud of her cooking,' he announced coolly, changing the subject.

Carly looked down at her jeans.

'I'm really not hungry.'

Not for food, perhaps—but for him? Ah, that was a different story. She was hungry for him—starving for him, in fact. Starving for the feel and the scent of him, for the taste of him, the reality of him. She could feel her body aching heavily with the weight of that hunger.

A sense of desolation and pain filled her. She hadn't asked to feel like this. She didn't want to feel like this. Not for any man, and least of all for a man such as this one.

Ricardo studied her downbent head. She looked tired, somehow vulnerable, and he could feel a reluctant and unwanted compassion—a desire to protect her—stirring inside him.

His only interest in her—aside from the fact that he wanted her like hell—was because of her role in Prêt a Party, Ricardo reminded himself fiercely. Emotional entanglements and complications just weren't something he had any intention of factoring into his life. He was prepared to accept that one day he might want a child—

a son, an *heir*—but when that day came he intended to satisfy that need not via marriage, with all its potential financial risks, but instead by paying a carefully selected woman to have a child for him and then to hand over all rights to it to him. With modern medical procedures he wouldn't even need to meet her.

'If you wish, I am sure Dolores will be happy to serve you dinner in your room,' he told her brusquely.

Carly veiled her eyes with her lashes, not wanting him to see what she was feeling.

If last night she had not stopped him, tonight—this night—they would have been together, and food would have been the last thing on either of their minds. It could still happen. All she had to do was go to him and touch him, show him, give way to what she was feeling. Other women had no qualms about showing men that they wanted them, so why should she?

She gave a small shiver, already knowing the answer to her own question.

CHAPTER NINE

SHE was used to the motion of the helicopter now, and did not feel as apprehensive as she had done before. They had already left New York behind them. The traffic on the highway beneath them looked like a child's toys.

She was alone with Ricardo in the helicopter this time, but he wasn't giving her a running commentary on their surroundings as he had done before. She told herself that she was glad of his businesslike attitude towards her, and the distance it had put between them.

Had he come to any decision yet as to whether or not he intended to use Prêt a Party's services? If so, she hoped that he had decided in their favour. They certainly needed the business.

She had received the e-mailed copies of the cheques she had requested and her inspection of them had confirmed what she'd already suspected. All the cheques bore—as legally they had to, according to the terms of the business—two signatures. Her own and Nick's. Only she knew that she had not signed the cheques herself. Which meant that someone had forged her signature. Someone? It could only have been Nick. Lucy was the only other person beside herself who had keys for the cupboard in which she kept the chequebooks.

Even without checking her forward costings for the year Carly knew that, because of the huge amount Nick had withdrawn from the business, by the time they

reached their year-end they would be showing a loss of
nearly half a million pounds.

The terms of their bank account were that Lucy
would personally make up any overdraft from her trust
fund. They had been in business for three years so far,
and Carly had taken great pride in the fact that she had
managed the financial affairs of the company so well
that the bank had not had to invoke this condition. Until
now.

Half a million pounds. She had no idea how much
money there was in Lucy's trust fund, but she suspected
that Nick would know. And she suspected too that he
had made a deliberate and cold-blooded decision to help
himself to money from it via the business, because he
knew that Marcus would never agree to hand so much
money over to him.

But understanding the situation was one thing.
Knowing what to do about it was another. By rights she
should tell Lucy what she had discovered, because she
was sure that the *carte blanche* Lucy had given Nick to
draw money from the business did not include forging
Carly's signature in order to get even more. But Nick
was Lucy's husband. Lucy would be bound to feel humiliated and hurt if Carly told her that he had been
stealing from her. And what if Lucy refused to believe
her and Nick insisted that he had not signed Carly's
name? Would it be better if she got in touch with
Marcus and alerted him to what was happening? Carly
felt torn between her loyalty to Lucy and her fear for
her.

Mentally shelving the problem, she focused instead
on more immediate issues. She had spoken to her opposite number at the New York event organisers earlier,

and she had assured Carly that everything was going according to plan.

'It looked like there was going to be a problem with the caterers at one stage. The magazine told us they wanted only colour-co-ordinated vegan food, in their house colours, but then they rang up saying that they'd heard that a certain glossy magazine editor only ate Beluga caviar and they had to have some.'

Carly had sympathised with her. Everyone knew how that particular British editor dictated and directed what was 'in' in certain important New York fashion circles. Just having her attend the event would be a major achievement. Of course she'd agreed gravely with her counterpart—it was essential that the caviar was provided, even though it meant breaking the colour-co-ordinated theme.

'We're serving champagne cocktails on arrival— peach and rhubarb with pepper. We're using this new chef who's into mixing together different textures and tastes. He's very *avant garde*. Virginia wants everything exclusive but statement-making simple. That's why she's chosen the Hamptons as the venue.'

Carly had continued to listen sympathetically.

Only the very richest of the rich could afford to live the 'simple' life Hamptons-style. She had read up on the area and knew that it was the preserve of those with old money—or at least it had been, until the media and fashion set had discovered it.

The magazine had been insistent that they wanted a very stylish and upmarket event—which was, Carly suspected, why they had been commissioned.

Lucy might not be the type to boast that her great-grandfather had been a duke, but the fact remained that she was very well connected socially.

'We've got the silverware on loan from Cristoffle, and the stemware is Baccarat—but very plain, of course.'

'Of course,' Carly had agreed, mentally praying that everything was well insured.

She had thought she knew what luxury was, but she had been wrong, she now admitted. As her visit to Barneys this morning had shown her. The exclusive store far surpassed anything she had ever seen, and had made her wonder who on earth could afford to shop there.

An elegant sales assistant had offered to help her, and Carly had suffered being shown a variety of stunning but impossibly expensive gowns—they could not be called anything else—before finally escaping by announcing that she had run out of time.

Any one of the dresses she had been shown would have been perfect for the French château birthday ball, but one in particular had stood out from the rest—a column of palest green silk, layer after delicately fine layer of it, the fabric floating magically with every movement of the air.

Carly had hardly dared to try it on, but the sales assistant had insisted and she had had no option other than to give way.

'It is perfect for you,' she had told Carly, and Carly had mentally agreed with her. But she had shaken her head and taken it off.

The Hamptons event was due to commence at four in the afternoon and go on until eight in the evening. A private house had been hired for the occasion, with large lawns and its own beach, and Carly had dressed—she hoped—appropriately—both for the occasion and the fact that she was part of the 'hired help', plus the fact that she was representing Lucy.

To do so she had had to give in and wear one of the outfits Ricardo had paid for. A pair of plain white Chloe linen pants teamed with an almost but not quite off the shoulder knit in navy and white. She had teamed the trousers with simple but oh, so expensive beige leather flats, and in order to accommodate all the paperwork she had to carry around with her she had splashed out this morning in New York before leaving and bought herself a large and stylish dark red straw bag—not from Barneys, where she had sighed over the unbelievable display of bags, but from a regular department store, and a marked-down sale item at that.

A couple of 'of the moment' trendy Perspex bangles, her own small gold earrings, and her good (although several years old) Oliver Peoples sunglasses completed her outfit.

She had been curious to see what Ricardo would wear. She had heard that there was an unofficial casual 'uniform' for visitors to the island—a variation on the traditional faded red jeans which had become a Hamptons visitors trademark—and had been unexpectedly touched and impressed to see that he was wearing classic Italian casual—almost as though he wanted to underline his own nationality. It was a mix of white and beige in cotton and linen, and he managed to wear it without looking either crumpled or over-groomed—which was quite an achievement.

Bare brown feet thrust into soft leather open shoes were a raw and masculine touch that certainly made her very much aware of the fact that he was dangerously male—and very much aware of him as well, she admitted, as she ignored the temptation to turn her head and look at him.

The more time she spent with him, the more she was being forced to accept how much he aroused her physically.

Even now, just sitting here beside him in silence, she could feel the tormenting ache of her own need growing stronger with every pulse of her body.

She was out of her depth. Why didn't she admit it? If he were to turn to her now and tell her that tonight he wanted to take her to bed and make love to her until morning there was no way she would refuse.

And why should she? She could go through the rest of her life without ever again meeting a man who could make her feel like this.

And sex without love was surely like… Like what? Like whisky without water? Undiminished? Its strength and flavour heightened by the fact that it was not touched by anything else? Why shouldn't sex be like that? Why shouldn't it? Why couldn't it be a pure, intense, once-in-a-lifetime experience just as it was?

What she had to ask herself was, if she didn't have sex with Ricardo, in later years would she praise herself or would she berate herself? Would she feel that she had gained or lost? Would she yearn to have the opportunity back again or…?

What was she trying to do? Persuade herself into bed with him? Wasn't that Ricardo's role? Nothing about him suggested to her that he was the kind of man who wasn't capable of going in all-out pursuit of anything and everything he wanted, be it a woman or a business. Ricardo played to win. If he truly wanted her he would be the one doing the persuading—and he would surely have persuaded her into his bed by now! As if she actually needed persuading, she admitted wryly.

But why did she want him so much? It definitely wasn't because of his money! And equally definitely it wasn't because of love. Loving someone meant risking being hurt.

So it was the man himself, then? The tightening sensation within her own body told her she had found the truth.

All these years of believing she wasn't interested in sex—she had told herself that nothing would ever induce her to adopt the casual attitude towards sex of so many women she knew, which she found repugnant—had been washed away by the ferocity of her own desire, like a dam bursting its banks to flood a hitherto dried-out gully.

She had a terrible and terrifying urge to turn to Ricardo and ask him to turn the helicopter around. To take her back to New York and his apartment, his bed, so that she could discover for herself which was the more powerfully sensual and erotic—her fantasies or Ricardo's reality.

When had the balance, the scales themselves tipped? Ricardo wondered savagely as he tried to fight against the message his body's fierce hunger was sending him.

When had his hunger for Carly started to occupy his thoughts more than acquiring Prêt a Party? When had he somehow given way and abandoned the rule he'd thought he had set in stone never to allow himself to want any woman so much that the wanting overpowered him?

He didn't know! What he did know, though, was that he had looked at her earlier, when she had walked to-

wards him in his apartment, and had had to fight against
the madness of an overwhelming need to take hold of
her and kiss her until he could feel in her the same
passionate response he had felt in her before—until her
body was pliant and eagerly, erotically desirous of his
touch, and her breathing was signalling an arousal that
matched his own.

They had almost reached their destination; he could
see the helipad up ahead of him. It was too late to turn
back now.

East Hampton. New money and lots of it—or at least
that was what she had read, Carly thought as a uniformed hunk, wearing eye-wateringly canary-yellow
cut-offs and a bright blue logoed polo shirt—all muscles
and too-white teeth—tenderly handed her down from
the helicopter. What was it about such movie-perfect
men that was so antiseptic and unsexy? Carly mused as
she was asked for her name. And was it her imagination
or did the bright smile fade just a little once its owner
realised she was here as part of the workforce?

To the side of her, though, Ricardo was being greeted
almost effusively by a stunningly pretty girl also wearing a greeter's uniform.

So this was corporate entertaining New York style!
Certainly everything was well organised, very slick and
professional—right down to the small packs they were
being handed which she already knew included a map
of the layout of the house and its gardens, a timetable
of the afternoon's events, and a ticketed voucher so that
guests could collect their goodie bags as they left—no
cluttering the tables or, even worse, disgruntled guests
leaving rejected and unwanted gifts behind them.

Ricardo was certainly receiving the *de luxe* treatment,

Carly decided, as a further glance in his direction informed her that his greeter was still making him the focus of her attention whilst her own had mysteriously disappeared. He was nursing a half-empty glass of red wine, glancing away from his companion to stare down into its depths.

If Ricardo were a glass of full-bodied, richly flavoured red wine, Carly thought fancifully, she would want to drink deeply of him, not sip delicately at him. She would want to roll the glorious velvety texture of him around her tongue before allowing him to turn the whole of her body to liquid pleasure. She would want to breathe in the richness of him and savour his unique musky flavour. She would want to fill her senses with the richness of him and then...

Hot-faced, Carly struggled to call her thoughts to order. Ricardo wasn't a wine, he was a man. And just seeing the way he was smiling back at the girl who was so obviously flirting with him filled Carly with a fierce, painful surge of jealousy.

She was here to work, she reminded herself starkly, and she turned her back on Ricardo and made her way towards the main hospitality area.

They were, of course, virtually the first arrivals, and Carly wanted to check in with both the New York event organiser and the clients to make sure that everything was going to plan. Waiters and waitresses—their uniforms comprising retro Hawaiian-style shirts with a brilliantly patterned design made up of front covers of the magazine—were already circulating with trays of drinks, presumably serving the clients themselves.

When Carly reached the main pavilion a security guard on the door stopped her, and she showed him both her pass and her identity badge. Once inside, she found the magazine's PR team and Luella Klein, her opposite number from the New York event organiser, standing together, engaged in conversation.

'*Lurve* the shirts those guys out there are wearing!' Luella announced dramatically as soon as the introductions were over.

'That was Jules's idea.' Carly smiled.

'Yeah, great—and cool, too. We've had the goodie bags made out of the same fabric!'

Carly nodded her head. Using the magazine's past covers as a basis for the design theme of the event had been the result of a brainstorming session held between Lucy, Jules and herself when they had first been approached to pitch for this event.

Getting a canapé menu organised that would translate into plates of food put together in the magazine's house colours had proved to be a major headache, though, with several chefs refusing the commission before Carly had had the bright idea of getting one of the top catering colleges to take it on as a showcase for the talents of their students.

She was just keeping her fingers crossed that the results would be as impressive as the sample plates they had seen photographs of earlier in the year.

'And it may sound kinda silly, but I've always had a thing about Italian men—'

'I'm sorry—I have to go.'

The young woman, who had spent the best part of the last fifteen minutes congratulating herself on having got Ricardo's exclusive attention, just about managed not to stamp her expensive heel down into the turf as he cut through her breathless words and started to walk away. Her chagrin gave way to resentment as she saw that he had left her to go to someone else—a woman who was standing with a group of caterers, of all things. Grudgingly she acknowledged that the white linen trousers her competitor was wearing did do full justice to legs that, as the male sex would have it, went all the way up to her armpits.

Carly smiled her thanks at the team leaders of the hired catering staff. It was nearly nine in the evening and most of the guests had left. Most, but not all. Not, for instance, the baby blonde whom she had seen clinging fragilely to Ricardo's arm earlier in the afternoon, whilst she had been talking to a trio of famous British fashionista sisters whom she knew, in a roundabout sort of way, via mutual contacts in London.

The clients had just told her how pleased they were with the event, and her New York opposite number had said that she knew her agency would want to do business with Prêt a Party again.

All in all, a successful event. A successful event but not, so far she was concerned, a personally successful or mood-enhancing few hours. But then she was not here for her own benefit, was she? Carly reminded herself, as she dismissed the waiting staff and wondered how long it would be before she could reasonably suggest to Ricardo that they leave.

Two men—executives from a big New York PR agency to whom she had been introduced earlier—were approaching her. She forced her lips to widen in what she hoped looked like a genuine professional smile.

'Good event,' one of them told her approvingly. 'Harvey thought it was real neat—didn't you, Harv?'

'Yeah,' the second one agreed. 'Real neat!'

Ricardo increased the pace of his stride. Every time he gave in to his need to look for her Carly was surrounded by other men. And he didn't like it. He didn't like it one little bit!

'Sorry to break up the party,' he announced untruthfully now, as he reached the trio.

Immediately the two men fell back, leaving an empty space at Carly's side, which Ricardo promptly filled. As he did so he deliberately stood so that he was blocking out the other men—and anyone else who might have wanted to approach Carly.

'Have you seen everything you want to see?' Carly asked him brightly. All afternoon she had been reminding herself that she was supposed to be making sure that Ricardo was so impressed with Prêt a Party's skills that he offered them a contract.

Ricardo was tempted to tell her bluntly and in explicit detail that *she* was what he most wanted to see—preferably lying naked on his bed, with that look in her eyes that said she wanted him like crazy.

Instead he nodded his head tersely and asked, 'How soon can you be ready to leave?'

Her New York counterpart had already assured her that there was no need for her to stay, and she had spoken with the clients.

'I'm ready now.'

'Fine. Let's go, then.'

Carly didn't really want to move. Ricardo was standing right next to her, and if she turned towards him now they would be standing body to body...like lovers...

'What's wrong? Missing the attention of your new friends? Want me to call them back?'

Instead of turning towards him, Carly took a step back.

'No, I don't,' she told him quietly. 'And as for what's

wrong—I was just wishing that I didn't ache so much for you to take me to bed!'

She turned away from him and started to walk towards the helipad, trembling inside from the shock of actually having told him what she was thinking and how she felt. Her face and body both felt equally hot, but for very different reasons. Her face was burning because of her embarrassment, but her body was burning because what she had said to him was the truth.

Ricardo caught up with her before she had taken more than three steps, his hand on her arm halting her progress until he could stand four-square in front of her.

'Is that an admission or is it an invitation?' he asked silkily.

Carly forced herself to look up at him, and to hold his gaze as she responded calmly, 'Both!'

Ricardo couldn't even remember how many women had propositioned him over the years, never mind count them, but none of them had ever spoken to him like this—simply and directly, admitting and owning their need for him.

'That's quite a change of heart! Why?'

'I suddenly realised how much I would regret it if I went to my grave without knowing you.'

'*Knowing* me?'

His voice was cynically mocking as he moved aside so that they could continue to walk together to the helipad.

'Without having sex with you,' Carly corrected herself steadily. 'Obviously it goes without saying that it *is* only sex that we both want.'

'Less than twenty-four hours ago you were outraged because I'd paid for your clothes. Now you're offering to have sex with me?'

'I was furious because I felt what you'd done implied that I could be bought. Choosing freely to have sex with you is completely different.'

'Indeed. Didn't it occur to you that I might feel equally insulted by your suggestion that I would want a woman I had to bribe into bed with me?' he challenged her.

They had almost reached the helipad.

She had spoken to him, touched a deeply secret part of him, as no other woman had ever done, and instinctively he felt wary of his own emotional response to that. At the same time he also felt challenged by the fact that she was so obviously determined not to allow herself to become emotionally involved with him. A woman who wanted to give herself freely to him physically whilst refusing to become emotionally involved? Shouldn't that knowledge delight him instead of irking him? he taunted himself derisively. He certainly wasn't going to refuse her, was he?

Carly wondered what he was thinking. Was Ricardo shocked by what she had said? Turned off by it? Indifferent to it? Should she have been less direct, and instead created an artificial opportunity for him to come on to her if he wanted to do so?

Ricardo had gone to speak to the ground staff brought in to take care of the helicopters lined up away from the helipad. She could feel her stomach muscles clench as he walked back to her.

'I was watching you earlier on today,' he told her softly. 'Imagining just what it would be like to have those long legs of yours wrapped tightly around me whilst I took you. How do you like it best? Tell me!'

Shocked pleasure rushed through her, hot, sweet and

intoxicating. A dizzying, breathtaking sensation of open and responsive arousal.

Ricardo watched her, acknowledging that the look of dazzled, dazed anticipation in her eyes was doing more to arouse him than he would have thought possible.

'Time to go,' he said, nodding in the direction of the waiting helicopter.

'You've been very quiet. Second thoughts?' Ricardo challenged Carly as he piloted them towards the landing pad of his New York building.

'About what? Telling you that I want you? Or the fact that I do want you?'

Did she realise how the musical sound of her voice could play on a man's desire, heightening it and arousing him? Ricardo wondered as he looked directly at her.

'Either.'

Carly shook her head. She had spent most of the flight surreptitiously sneaking glances at Ricardo and then imagining herself touching him, learning him, allowing the fantasy that she hoped would soon become a reality to guide and slightly shock her thoughts. She'd touch first with her fingertips, tracing the bones that shaped him, and then with her hands as she absorbed the strength of his muscles and the taut smoothness of his flesh. And then finally with her lips and her tongue, as she explored every delicate hollow and plane of him.

The heat that constantly beat through her body was roaring now, pulse-points of urgency throbbing not just between her legs and in her breasts but everywhere— her fingertips, her toes, her lips—everywhere…

'I've said more than I should,' she admitted huskily.

'Yes,' Ricardo acknowledged coolly. 'You have.

Haven't the other men in your life preferred to do their own hunting and their own propositioning?'

There was a small jolt as the helicopter hit the ground.

She waited silently for Ricardo to climb out and then come round to help her. Above them, stars glittered in the darkness of the night sky, but it was impossible for them to compete with the brilliance and colour of the New York skyline.

His hands on her body felt hard but remote. Rejecting? Had she got it wrong? Had she misunderstood? Had he merely been pretending before that he wanted her?

He had set her free, and she had no option other than to walk ahead of him to the lift foyer door.

Ricardo followed her and activated the lift. Within seconds they were stepping out of it into his own private entrance foyer, and within seconds of that he was opening the door to his apartment.

'Dolores and Rafael are away for a family event,' he told her.

Carly nodded her head. Disappointment was a cold, sick, leaden lump weighing down her body. It struck her how ironic it was. Had someone previously suggested to her that she would find herself in this kind of situation, the feelings she would have expected would have been shame and humiliation, rather than the gut-wrenching sense of disappointment she actually did have.

All those years of silently, determinedly telling herself she had a right to her pride had obviously not made as big an impression on her psyche as she had believed.

They were in the large square hallway. It was nearly eleven o'clock. She turned away from Ricardo, intending to make her way to her suite and the sleepless night she suspected lay ahead of her.

'This way.'

His fingers closed round her bare forearm and immediately her flesh reacted in a burst of over-sensitivity and raised goosebumps.

This corridor was unfamiliar, its walls hung with what she suspected must be priceless pieces of modern art. At the end of it was a pair of double doors. Ricardo opened one of them without releasing her.

Silently she walked through it into the darkness that lay beyond. Ricardo let her go, and she heard the quiet snap of the door closing.

She could feel him standing behind her, and waited for him to switch on the lights, but instead he turned her round, his hands gripping her upper arms.

CHAPTER TEN

'Now. *Now* you can tell me that you want me.'

His voice was a raw sound of out-of-control male need.

A thrill of shocked delight exploded inside her. She could feel herself shaking with excitement as he pulled her into his own body and took her mouth with explicit sexual hunger.

Her response to him rolled over her like an eighty-foot wave, swamping her, picking her up and taking her bodily. She had no defence against it, nor did she want one.

His tongue, seeking and demanding, thrust hotly between her lips without any preliminaries. Her small sob of pleasure was submerged beneath his own sounds of overriding need. His hands were on her body, tugging down her top, pushing aside her bra.

Carly moaned as his hands grazed her nipples, and then moaned again more sharply when he took one between his thumb and forefinger and began to tease it into hard, tight, aching need. Without knowing she was doing it Carly ground her hips against him, mimicking the hard thrust of his tongue between her lips.

'Don't,' he cautioned her thickly. 'Do you want me to completely lose control and take you here?'

Getting her back here without touching her had strained his self control to its limits. And now...

'Yes,' Carly told him quickly, feeling the words catch against her throat. 'I want you to take me, wherever and

141

whenever you want—but most of all I want you to do it *now*. Now! Ricardo, now!'

Did she realise that she had just destroyed the last shreds of his control, what her hungry, half-moaned words were doing to him?

'Now?' he repeated.

His eyes, accustomed to the darkness, showed him the pale glimmer of her breasts. He stroked his forefinger round one nipple and watched her whole body surge with pleasure. He could feel the muscles locking in his throat. He bent his head and took the tight sexual flowering of her desire for him into his mouth, savouring the sensation of the smooth swell of her breast before running his tongue over her nipple, all the time trying to hold onto his sanity, to stop himself from pushing her up against the wall and tearing the clothes off her so that he could have the pleasure of sinking as deep inside her as he could get.

Carly could hear someone start to moan, but it took her several seconds to recognise that she was the one making the noise. She felt as though she were on a long slide, unable to stop herself from plunging into her own pleasure. Not wanting to stop herself.

Reluctantly Ricardo released her nipple, his fingers immediately returning to enjoy its arousal.

'How do you want it?' he demanded softly. 'Do you have a favourite position? Do you want to take care of the condom issue or shall I?'

Carly looked at him and took a deep breath. 'I think this is when I should tell that I don't have very much previous experience,' she announced carefully.

'What?'

She couldn't tell whether the harshness in his voice came from anger or disbelief.

'What does that mean?'

Carly swallowed, and then said in a small voice,

'Actually, I'm afraid it means that I haven't... There hasn't... I'm still a virgin.'

'*What?* You're joking, right?

Carly shook her head.

He released her abruptly and stood back from her, looking at her for what felt like for ever.

'I can't think of one single reason why the hell you would be a virgin.'

'Actually, there are several,' Carly responded with dignity. 'For one thing... Well, I don't suppose the opportunity has been there at the right time or with the right man,' she hedged.

Her revelation was the last thing Ricardo had expected. If she had kept to her virgin purity until now why was she, to put it crudely, offering it to him on a plate? Did she think he would feel some sort of moral responsibility towards her? Was that it? Was she setting some sort of trap for him? Would she try to use emotional blackmail to turn mere physical intimacy into something more?

If he had any sense he would send her back to her own room, right now, but somehow, in some way, a part of him was actually responding to what she had told him with a primitive surge of male possessiveness. It actively *liked* the thought of the sexual exclusivity of being her first lover, of knowing that the sensuality he would imprint on her would remain with her throughout her life, that if the experience he gave her was truly pleasurable then she would treasure it all her life. And she would not be comparing him to anyone else. Was he really that vain? That insecure? Ricardo grimaced to himself, knowing that he wasn't.

'You damn sure don't act like a virgin,' he told her grimly.

Probably because when she was around him she didn't think that she was. Mentally, in the privacy of her own thoughts, the intimacy she had with him had gone well beyond the bounds of virginity.

'Perhaps I shouldn't have told you?' Carly offered.

Ricardo looked at her with incredulity.

'Don't you think it would have been obvious? Especially given the kind of intimacy I'd planned to—'

He saw the excitement begin to burn in her eyes and he cursed himself for the way his body immediately responded to it.

'Are you sure this is what you want? An affair that—?'

Carly stopped him. 'I don't want an affair. I just want to have sex with you.'

'Just sex?' Ricardo questioned, not sure that he believed her.

'Yes. But of course if you'd rather not…' she added lightly.

No one gave that kind of challenge to Ricardo.

'You'll cry "enough" before I do,' he told her against her mouth.

He was barely brushing her lips with his own, a feather-light touch that, as Carly quickly discovered, made her hunger for more. Her own lips clung to his, willing him to part them with his tongue as he had done before, and a shudder of visible pleasure gripped her body when finally he did so, thrusting the seeking point of his tongue deep and hard within the warm softness of her mouth.

His hand cupped the back of her head and his tongue plunged deeper, twining with her own. She could feel the heavy slam of her heart as it banged against her ribs—or was it his?

He was holding her right up against him, so close that she could feel his erection. And she wanted to feel it. And not just to feel it—she wanted to see it, touch it…experience it deep inside her.

She felt weak and dizzy with arousal, her whole body shuddering with pleasure when Ricardo cupped her breast and then slowly circled his fingertip around her nipple. Lazy delicate circles that were driving her insane. She sucked in a deep breath and felt the corresponding tightening low down in her body. Unable to stop herself, she reached out and touched the hard ridge of male flesh, mimicking Ricardo's caress as she circled the head of it with her fingertip and then traced its whole shape through the fabric of his clothes. It felt thick and strong. Her fingers trembled and so did her body.

To her shock Ricardo immediately released her. She stared up at him through the darkness.

'I need a shower,' he told her thickly, 'and you are going to share it with me.'

He had taken hold of her hand. She could break free of him if she wanted to, but she knew that she didn't.

He guided her through the darkness past the shape of a huge bed and then into a dressing room, switching on the light as he did so.

'It's a wet room,' he told her. 'So we undress in here.'

Undress. Her mouth went dry. But Ricardo had turned away from her and was already stripping off his clothes.

Mesmerised, Carly watched him, her curiosity followed by an awe that darkened her eyes so that when

Ricardo looked at her he could see arousal shimmering in them, just as she could see his arousal, straining tautly from its thick mat of dark springy curls.

Her legs had suddenly gone weak.

Her fingers trembling, she started to tug off her own clothes, hesitating only when she got down to the silky sheer thong that barely concealed her sex.

Ricardo had turned away from her and was walking towards the door to the wet room. Carly took a deep breath and then followed him.

Ricardo touched a button, and immediately lusciously warm water sprang from hidden jets, soaking her.

'Do you really need this?' Ricardo was standing in front of her, hooking one lean finger under the narrow strap of her thong whilst the pad of his thumb stroked sensuously against her bare skin. Thrills of pleasure skittered over her.

He leaned forward and stroked his tongue-tip over her lips. Carly exhaled in a voluptuous sigh and closed her eyes, moving closer to him. The soft stroking touch of his fingertip traced the edge of her thong very slowly, and then traced it again.

'Mmm…'

She could feel the heat building up between her legs.

Ricardo's fingertip was tracing down the side of her thong. She could feel herself starting to shudder.

His hand moved back, easing her thong down…out of his way. Her legs had gone so weak she could barely stand to step out of it.

Half dazed, she started to soap herself, tensing when Ricardo took hold of her hands and told her softly, 'That's my job—and my pleasure.'

The silky suds made his hands glide sensuously over her flesh: her breasts, exquisitely sensitive now to his touch, her belly, where the spread of his fingers caused the heat inside her to turn her liquid with longing, her behind, which he soaped with a long slow movement that left one hand resting on the back of her thigh whilst the fingers of the other stroked between her legs, and then right up along the wet cleft between the swollen lips of her sex.

Helplessly Carly leaned into his caress, her body clenching on shudders of arousal. Driven by age-old instinct, she reached out and enclosed him with her hand, eagerly caressing the full length of him, and then released him again so that she could explore the swollen head of his erection. Now he was the one doing the shuddering, then subjecting them both to a sudden swift pounding of more water jets to rinse their bodies free of suds.

She had always believed that she was far too tall and heavy for any man to ever be able to pick her up bodily, but now, for a second time, Ricardo was proving her wrong, Carly thought, as Ricardo finished towelling her dry and then lifted her into his arms.

The bedroom was now bathed in soft lamplight, and the bedlinen was cool beneath her skin as Ricardo laid her on the bed and then bent his head towards her own.

'Still want this?' he whispered against her lips.

'Yes,' Carly whispered back. 'Do you?'

For the first time since she had known him she saw genuine humour in his eyes.

'My arousal and desire are quite plainly evident.'

'So are mine—to me,' Carly told him huskily.

His hand cupped her breast. 'You mean this—here?' he murmured, his thumb stroking lightly against her nipple. 'Or this—here?' His knowing stroke the full length of her sex made her moan with pleasure. Her arousal-swollen flesh housed a million nerve endings that were pleasure points, and it seemed to Carly that Ricardo's caress lingered over each one of them. And then he stroked her clitoris, rhythmically and deliberately.

Immediately her body arched in supplication, her gaze fixed on his. How could she ever have thought his eyes were cold? They burned now with dark fire.

His hand moved away. He kissed the side of her throat and then her collarbone, sliding his free hand into her hair and cradling the back of her head. Already she was anticipating—longing for the feel of his mouth against her.

Her throat tightened, shudders of pleasure running through her as his tongue-tip traced a lazy line down to her breasts and circled each nipple. A soft breath of longing bubbled in her throat. His lips closed over one nipple, his tongue working it. She gasped breathlessly, reaching out to hold his head against her body, her fingers locking into his hair as she arched up against him, unable to stop herself from wanting the wild surges of pleasure his mouth and fingers were creating inside her.

Of their own volition her legs fell open, her muscles contracting as she felt the warmth of Ricardo's hand skimming her body and then coming to rest against the small curls covering her sex.

Heat ran through her to gather beneath his hand. A pulse of need was beating where he touched her.

She had believed that she knew desire, but all she had known was its shadow. This, its reality, was overpowering, overwhelming her.

She felt Ricardo's thumb probing the cleft below the soft curls. A pleading, mewling sound broke from her lips and she lifted her body towards him.

The dark fire in his eyes burned even more hotly. But not as hot as the fire burning inside her.

Wild tremors seized her and she whimpered in helpless arousal as he parted the outer lips of her sex and then started to caress her.

The white heat of ravening need filled her, her head falling back against the pillows. Her hips writhed frantically against the movement of his fingertip as he rubbed it the full length of her, lingering deliberately on the hard swell of her clitoris.

No woman had ever abandoned herself, given herself to him and his pleasuring of her like this, Ricardo acknowledged. He didn't know how much longer he could keep his own arousal under control.

She felt hot and wet, the swollen lips beneath his fingers opening to him of their own volition to offer him the gift of her sex.

A wild surge of longing engulfed him. It wasn't enough that he could feel her; he wanted to see her as well.

Carly cried out in protest as she felt Ricardo move, but his hand was still resting reassuringly on the mound of her sex and his body was still openly aroused. Her eyes, though, still asked an anxious question, and as he sat up Ricardo answered it for her, telling her rawly, 'I want to see you. I want to watch your sex flush with pleasure and lie open and eager for my touch.'

Wild thoughts of urging him, begging him not to, fled, as she felt him caressing her again. But this time… This time, as her head dropped back and her body was gripped by intense surges of pleasure, she could feel him caressing her lips apart, exposing her swollen, glistening secret inner flesh to his gaze and his touch. Just the pressure of his fingertip against her clitoris made her cry out in frantic arousal. He bent his head and his tongue stroked along her silken folds. All the way along them, Carly recognised on a shudder of fierce delight, as the hard-pointed tip of his tongue probed and stroked into life sensations she had never imagined existing.

He couldn't hold out much longer, Ricardo realised, as he felt his body throb in reaction to the pleasure of tasting her and arousing her. He drove the tip of his tongue into her moist opening and heard her moan of pleasure He stroked her clitoris with quick rhythmic strokes of his tongue and eased a finger slowly into her.

Immediately her muscles closed round it, holding it, and his body responded with a savage thrust of male urgency.

He could feel his heart thudding, sweat beading his forehead, but he made himself go slowly. One finger, and then two, waiting for her body to accommodate him and then respond as he caressed her.

She was moving urgently against him now, her body aroused and eager as she thrust against him and moaned.

Frantically Carly reached out and touched Ricardo's body, her fingers closing round him, moving over him. He felt so hot and slick, the foreskin moving easily and fluidly over the swollen head of his erection. Her body tightened, and excitement locked the air into her lungs in expectation.

Still caressing her, Ricardo pulled her beneath him, easing himself slowly into her, his muscles aching with the punishing pressure he was exerting over them as he refused to give in to their demand for him to thrust deeply and fully.

Her muscles closed round him, making him shudder with violent need. He thrust deeper, and then deeper

still, whilst Carly dug her nails into his shoulder—not
in pain, but in urgent female need to have more of him.
Unable to stop herself, she gave voice to that need, the
words tumbling huskily from her lips as she pleaded
frantically, 'More... Ricardo. Deeper...' matching her
pleas to the eager movement of her body against his.

'Like this? How much more? This much?'

She gasped into his thrust, driven by her own need
to make him fill her and take her higher.

'Mmm. Yes. More...deeper...again.'

Her frantic litany of pleas and praise fell against
Ricardo's senses like a song sung in sensual counterpart
to their mingled breathing, underscored by the rise and
fall of its urgency and satisfaction, whilst her body's
response to him blew apart his intention of remaining
in control.

His own need to go deeper, harder, to know and possess all of her, overwhelmed him. His increasingly powerful thrusts took them both higher, and his own satisfaction was matched by the eager rhythmic movement
of Carly's hips, and the sounds of her rising pleasure.
She clung to him, kissing his throat and his shoulder,
then raking his arm with her nails in a sudden ecstasy
of physical delight as he drove them both closer to the
edge.

It was too much for his self-control. The muscles in
his neck corded as he fought to delay his own climax,
but it was too late. His body was already claiming its
final mindless driving surge of release.

Carly called out a jumble of helpless words of feverish pleasure as Ricardo's fierce pulsing thrusts of completion carried her with him over the edge of pleasure,
her body suddenly contorting in a burst of rhythmic
climactic contractions of release.

It was over.

Very carefully, Ricardo rolled Carly over onto her side and held her against him.

Carly lay there, trying to steady her breathing, her body still trembling with reaction. Tears blurred her vision, although she had no idea why she should want to cry. The pleasure had been so very much more than she had imagined.

Ricardo was lying facing her, his arm resting heavily but oh, so sweetly over her, holding her close to him.

'Are you okay?'

'I think so,' she answered shakily. 'I'm still trying to come back down to earth. I hadn't realised it would be so...' She stopped.

'So what?' Ricardo probed.

'So...so intense. Not when you ...when we don't... when this isn't about loving one another,' she finally managed to say.

She felt Ricardo moving, but before she could say anything he was holding her tightly in his arms and kissing her. Slowly and gently and...oh, so very sweetly.

It was six o'clock and the park was quiet. Ricardo had left Carly sleeping, easing himself away from her body and taking care not to wake her.

He had woken a dozen times during the night, silently listening to her breathing, watching her, and whilst he was doing so he had relived the intimacy they had shared, trying to analyse his own reaction to it.

He had had sex before, after all, and he had had good sex before. But never, ever anything that had come anywhere near to making him feel the way he had felt with Carly.

Her use of the word 'intense' had mirrored his own feelings.

Why, though? Why should her body, her flesh, her need be so very different? Not because she had been a virgin? No, definitely not because of that!

The second time they had made love, in the early hours of the morning, had to him been an even more intense experience than the first time. And Carly had made it plain to him that she had no regrets. Her virginity had been something he'd had to take account of in possessing her, yes, but it had not been the cause of that difference.

So what was it about her that lingered so strongly that he had needed to keep waking up to check that she was still there?

What was it about her that made his whole body compress with possessiveness at the thought of losing her?

Was it the intensity of the intimacy they had shared? The fact that, for some unfathomable reason, something in her humbled and softened something in him? He didn't know. But he did know that, whatever it was, it had somehow caused an abrupt turnaround inside his head, and that instead of mentally working out how fast he could get away from her and get on with the really exciting things in his life—like another business acquisition—he was actually wondering how he could prolong their time together.

He looked at his watch. Soon she would be waking up. And he wanted to be there when she did.

'Carly?'

Reluctantly she opened her eyes.

She had woken up an hour earlier, wondering where Ricardo had gone, and then, after showering and brushing her teeth, she had come back to bed and promptly fallen deeply asleep again.

Ricardo was sitting on the side of the bed next to her, and what was more he was fully dressed.

She struggled to sit up, and then realised self-consciously that she was naked.

'We need to leave for France this afternoon,' Ricardo reminded her.

'Oh, yes, of course. I—'

She gave a shallow gasp as Ricardo leaned forward and covered her mouth with his own. Automatically she clung to his shoulders, and then wrapped her arms around his neck when she felt his tongue demanding possession of her mouth. Already her body felt sweetly heavy with longing for him, drawn to him like a moth to a flame.

He lifted his mouth from hers and she stretched sensuously, watching the heat burn in his gaze as it feasted on her, relishing the hot glitter. His hand cupped her shoulder and then stroked slowly over her, ignoring the urgent, desiring peaking of her nipples and coming to rest on her hip, his thumb moving lazily over the indent of her belly. Feathery, frustrating little touches that had her arching up to him in silent demand.

'Undress me!'

The command sounded thick and slightly unsteady, rather like her own fingers as they curled round the hem of his tee shirt and then trembled wildly the minute they came into contact with the hard-muscled heat of his skin.

Her task might have been easier if Ricardo hadn't tormented her, occupying himself by kissing her and caressing her whilst she was trying to complete it, Carly decided, but she finally tugged off his tee shirt, to be rewarded with the hot fierce suckle of his mouth on her breast.

Sensation pierced her, sweet and shocking and achingly erotic, and the stroke of his tongue and the deliberate, delicate rasp of his teeth made her moan and beg for more.

In the end he had to finish undressing himself, shedding his clothes with unsteady urgency and then taking hold of Carly and lifting her to straddle his prone body.

He watched as her eyes widened, and kept on watching whilst he stroked his fingertip through her wetness.

She cried out immediately, her body tensing. Ricardo reached up and laved first one and then the other nipple with his tongue, feral male arousal gripping him as the morning sun highlighted for him the swollen wet crests. He found the sensitive heat of her clitoris and rubbed his fingertip rhythmically over it.

Carly arched tightly against his touch, her eagerness for him darkening her eyes as she reached for him and positioned herself over him, slowly sinking down on him, taking him into her.

Ricardo kept still, hardly daring to breathe, hardly able to endure the pleasure of the sensation of her body opening to him, her muscles slowly claiming him.

Experimentally Carly moved her body, gasping in shocked delight as she felt her own pleasure. She moved again, eagerly and demandingly. Exhaling, Ricardo responded to her need, grasping her hips as she took control, letting her take as much of him as she wanted, and then groaning in raw heat as she demanded more.

She came quickly, almost violently, just before Ricardo, in a series of intense spasms that left her too weak to even move. It was left to Ricardo to lift her from him and then hold her sweat-slick trembling body against his own, his arms wrapped securely around her.

CHAPTER ELEVEN

'I SHOULD really stay at the château, so that I can be on hand in case anything goes wrong.'

They had arrived in France two hours ago, and now Carly was seated next to Ricardo in the large Mercedes hire car that had been waiting for him at the airport. He had just informed her that he wanted her to stay with him at the house he was renting instead of at the château where the party was to be held.

'If anything does go wrong you can be there within minutes,' he told her.

She knew that he was right, and she knew too that she wanted to be with him. How, in such a short space of time, could she have become so physically addicted to him that she could hardly bear not to be close to him?

'How are you feeling? Are you okay?'

Both his question and the almost tender note in his voice startled her.

'I'm—I'm fine. I can't believe I didn't realise before how...how compulsive sex can be.'

Ricardo started to frown. Her answer wasn't the one he had been expecting. Or the one he had wanted?

'It wasn't just sex for you, though, was it?' he challenged her.

Carly couldn't look at him. Prickles of warning were burning their way into her head, triggering her defences.

'Why do you say that?'

'A woman doesn't get to your age still a virgin unless

she's either too traumatised to want sex or she's waiting to feel as drawn to a partner emotionally as she is sexually.'

'No, that isn't true. The reason I haven't had sex before now is because I *haven't* wanted any emotional involvement, not because I have.'

Ricardo could hear the panic in her voice. No matter how old-fashioned it might be, every instinct he possessed told him that she had to have very deep emotional feelings for him to have responded the way she had. His male logic couldn't accept that, given her virginity, it could be any other way.

'Human beings are allowed to have emotions, you know,' he told her wryly. 'But my guess is that you are afraid of emotional vulnerability because of what you experienced as a child. Your adoptive parents rejected you, gave their love to their own daughter whilst withholding it from you.'

Carly was too intelligent to try and deny what he was saying.

'I may have been an emotionally needy child, but I have no intention of allowing myself to become an emotionally needy woman.'

'There's a huge difference between being emotionally needy and loving someone.'

'Maybe. Or maybe, just as some people are genetically disposed to be more vulnerable to drug addiction, some people might be genetically disposed to emotional vulnerability. I prefer not to put my own resistance to the test.'

'How did your adopted sister die?'

His question caught her off guard.

'She...she was a drug addict. She died from an overdose of heroin. She started using drugs when we were at school. She was a year above me, and in a different crowd. I... It never appealed to me. I told you that my mother was one of three young women who died in a house fire. They were probably all drug addicts. I never... I couldn't... I know that, deep down inside, my adoptive parents blamed me for her addiction. My adoptive mother admitted as much. She said that she felt by bringing me into their lives they had brought in the evil of drug addiction.'

'Rubbish,' Ricardo announced briskly. 'It strikes me that they were looking for someone to blame and picked on you.'

'Maybe, but I still feel guilty. They loved her, not me, and now she's dead. All they've got left is me. I've tried to do what I can to help them, to repay them for everything they've given me.'

'Everything they've given you? Such as what?'

'A chance to live a normal life. My education. Without them I could have ended up making a living selling myself on the street, like my mother probably did.'

'No,' Ricardo told her firmly. 'No, you would never have done that. Somehow you would have found a way to set yourself free.'

Carly could feel emotional tears prickling her eyes. Emotional tears?

'I want you, Carly, and not just physically. You touch my emotions and delight my senses. When you aren't with me, I want you to be. You've become integral to my pleasure in life—to my happiness, if you like. I want to explore with you what's happening to us. I trust you enough to tell you that, and to tell you too that emotionally I am vulnerable to you. Is it really so hard for you to do the same?'

'I don't know what to say,' she admitted shakily.

'Then don't say anything,' Ricardo told her. 'Just allow yourself to feel instead. And when we're together you *do* feel, don't you, Carly?'

'I…I know that when we have sex it gives me a lot of pleasure.'

She answered him primly, but prim was the very opposite of what she felt. Just talking with him like this had made her body begin to pulse with sensual need. It seemed a lifetime since they had last had sex, though in fact it was less than twenty-four hours. Already she was longing for the opportunity to spend more time with him in intimate privacy. Her legs were weak, and she had to make a small denying movement in her seat to clamp down on the sensation pulsing inside her.

She could feel Ricardo looking at her. She turned her head and looked back at him. He knew! Somehow he knew what she was feeling. The car was an automatic, and he reached for her hand, placing it against his own body.

It wasn't the answer he wanted, but it would do—for now. If her sexual response to him was her area of vulnerability, then he would have to use that to try and break down her emotional barriers.

Ricardo was hard!

Carly tried to swallow, and for one wanton shocking moment she actually found herself wishing she were the kind of woman who felt comfortable abandoning her underwear, and that only the lightness of a thin summer skirt, instead of jeans and beneath them her thong, separated her from Ricardo's intimate touch.

'Don't,' she heard Ricardo growl thickly. 'Otherwise I'll have to stop. And the back of a car just doesn't have room for what I want to do with you right now…'

'What do you want to do?' Carly encouraged him huskily.

She felt his momentary hesitation mingling with her own shock that she could be so enticing.

'I want to spread you out in front of me, your body naked and eager…just like it was that first time. I want to start at your toes, touching every inch of you, tasting every inch of you. I want to bring you to orgasm with my hand and my mouth, and watch you take your pleasure from me…'

Carly let out a soft beseeching moan. 'Stop it,' she begged. 'I can't—'

'Wait?' he demanded softly. 'Do you think it's any different for me?'

Emotionless sex! Ricardo knew perfectly well that he was brooding too much and too betrayingly over Carly's attitude. She had no idea just what emotionless sex actually was, he told himself fiercely. She had already admitted to him that she was simply trying to protect herself from being hurt, as she had been hurt as a child. And because of that she was refusing to admit that her emotions were as dangerously involved with him as his were with her. After all, she had given herself to him totally and completely as his, and he had claimed her in exactly that same way.

The figures he had been working on for making a bid for Prêt a Party were in front of him on the table of the small café where they had stopped for drink. He glanced uncaringly at them whilst he waited for Carly to return from the lavatory. He no longer cared how profitable it was, or indeed whether or not he acquired it. In fact the only acquisition he was really interested in right now was the total and exclusive right to Carly herself—preferably by way of an unbreakable and permanent legally binding document.

Where was she? His muscles tensed, and then started to relax as he saw her hurrying towards him. Two men at another table were also looking at her, and immediately he wanted to get up, lay claim to her.

'We need to stop at a chemist,' he told her as he signalled for their bill. When she looked at him in concern, he explained succinctly, 'Condoms.'

'Oh!' Carly could feel her face going pink.

'Not that I think there's any risk to either of us from a health issue point of view, but I assume you aren't protected from pregnancy?'

'Yes. I mean, no. I mean, no—I'm not protected,' Carly confirmed guiltily. How could she have overlooked something as basic and important as that?

The château owned by a famous rock star and his stunningly attractive American wife was in the Loire valley, home to some of France's famous wine-growing districts. Carly had seen photographs of the château in a magazine article about the star and his family, and she knew that his well-born wife had scoured Europe's antique dealers and employed the very best craftsmen in order to restore the building and turn it into a modern home. A mirrored ballroom similar to that at Versailles was the showpiece of the restoration work, along with the gardens.

This event was by far the largest of the three they had attended. Just about everyone who was anyone had been invited. Five hundred celebrity guests in all, mainly from the world of rock music, films, the upper classes and fashion.

In addition to a six-course dinner, the menu for which

had been organised by one of the world's leading chefs, and the regulation post-dinner dancing, the rock star's wife had chosen to have magicians moving amongst the tables, performing a variety of tricks. Cream, gold and black were the colours she had chosen, insisting that the flowers used for table decoration must not have any scent as she wanted to have the huge marquee scented only by the special candles she had ordered in her favourite room fragrance.

The marquee itself was to be black, ornamented with cream and gold, the dining chairs were cream with black rope ties, and the floor a dazzling gold that looked like crushed tissue paper beneath glass.

The house Ricardo had rented was in a small picturesque town a few kilometres away from the château on the bank of the River Loire, a tall, narrow honey-coloured stone building wedged in amongst its fellows on a dim, narrow, winding cobbled street, with its own private courtyard at the rear and a balcony on the second floor which overlooked the Loire itself.

It came complete with Madame Bouton, who was waiting to introduce herself and the house to them, explaining that she would come every morning to clean, and that she was willing to buy them whatever food they might require.

'What's that look for?' Ricardo demanded as soon as Madame had gone.

'I'm just so hungry for you,' Carly told him simply.

A sensation like a giant fist striking his chest hit him with a combination of unfamiliar emotions spiked with warnings. And then he looked into her eyes, at her mouth…

They didn't make it out of the kitchen. They didn't even make it out of their clothes. The sex was hot and immediate. Ricardo's hands cupped the bare cheeks of her bottom as he lifted her onto the table, and Carly wrapped her legs tightly round him.

She had been waiting for this and for him all day—thinking, fantasising about him, longing for him—and just the sensation of his mouth against her naked breast as he pushed aside her clothes took her to such a pitch of excitement that she thought she might actually orgasm there and then.

But, as she quickly discovered, she had more things to learn from Ricardo about the pleasure of sex. A lot more!

When he had delayed both their climaxes to the point where Carly was ready to scream with frustration, he finally complied with her urgent demands, and the intensity of orgasm that followed left her lying limply against him whilst her body shook with tremors of sensual aftershock.

Wearing her cropped jeans, a tee shirt, and a hat to protect her head from the heat of the sun, Carly stood listening to their clients as the three of them discussed the event.

'I really like the interior of the marquee, but I'm not sure now about the flowers. I think I want to change them,' Angelina Forrester informed her. 'I love the drama of having black. Perhaps if we changed things so that the tablecloths are just barely cream and the flowers black…you know, very heavy and oriental-looking. Sort of passionate and dangerous!'

Carly's heart began to sink as she recalled the trouble and the expense they had gone to in order to comply with Angelina's initial demand for scent-free blooms.

'Bloody hell, Angelina, does it matter what colour the bloody flowers are?'

The Famous Rock Star looked and sounded angrily impatient, and Carly could see the pink tinge of temper creeping up his wife's perfect complexion.

'Perhaps if we added one or two dramatic dark flowers to the table decorations?' Carly suggested calmingly, mentally deciding that if Angelina agreed to her suggestion the extra flowers would have to be artificial—or sprayed. No way was there time to source black-petalled flowers for tomorrow night! She would need to speak to the florist as well...

'Well... I'd have to see what you mean...' Angelina hesitated.

The Famous Rock Star swore crudely. 'All this because you've changed your mind about your bloody dress!'

The pink tinge had become distinctly darker.

Discreetly Carly excused herself, explaining that she needed to speak with the hired entertainers.

Arms folded over his black-clad chest, his long chino-covered legs stretched out in front of him, Ricardo propped himself up against a nearby wall and watched her.

She had good people-managing skills, and she was able to establish a genuine rapport with those she worked with. She treated them well, and with respect, and they in turn were obviously prepared to listen to what she had to say. But he didn't want her as an employee. He wanted her as a woman. He wanted her exclusively and permanently as his woman. He had, he admitted, fallen deeply and completely in love with her.

He heard a burst of laughter from the mainly male

group surrounding her and immediately his muscles contracted on a primitive surge of male jealousy.

He was halfway towards her before Carly became aware of his presence, alerted to the fact that something was happening by the sudden silence from those around her.

She turned round and saw Ricardo striding towards her, and her heart turned over inside her chest with need, her whole body going boneless with the pleasure of just looking at him.

'I thought you might be ready for some lunch.'

'Yes, I am. I think there's a sort of workers' canteen affair set up somewhere.'

Ricardo shook his head and then took hold of her arm, deliberately drawing her away from the others.

'No. Not here. I was thinking of somewhere more…private.'

She knew he could feel the betraying leap of her pulse because his thumb was resting on her wrist.

'Yes!' she told him unsteadily. 'Yes.'

Their clothes lay abandoned on the bedroom floor— Ricardo's tee shirt and her top, his chinos and her cut-offs, the smooth plain Calvins in which he could have posed as effectively and even more erotically than any male model—or so at least Carly considered—her bra, and finally the tiny side-bow-tied silky thong he had given her only yesterday. A gift for her that he would ensure brought pleasure to them both, he had told her seductively.

They lay skin to skin, Ricardo's hands slowly shaping her whilst she lay in the luxurious sensual aftermath of their earlier urgent coupling.

'You're quiet,' Ricardo murmured.

'I'm just thinking about how perfect this is and how happy I am,' Carly admitted.

Ricardo looked at her, and then cupped her face and kissed her.

'So you're ready to accept that we do have something special, that it isn't just sex, then?' he said softly.

He reached for her hand and twined his fingers through hers, holding it—and her—safely. She had fought so hard to deny what she felt, but today, lying here in the sun with him, she knew that she couldn't deny her love any longer.

'I… Ricardo, I…I do feel emotionally connected to you.'

'"Emotionally connected"?' Ricardo queried, shaking his head as he continued tenderly, 'Is the word "love" really so very hard to say? Or are you waiting for me to say it first?'

Without waiting for her to reply he kissed her gently, saying, 'I—love—you—Carly,' spacing out the words between kisses.

There could be no greater happiness than this—no greater sense of belonging, no deeper trust or awareness of being loved, Carly decided as she let him walk into her heart.

'Ricardo, we ought to get dressed.'

'Why?'

'I'm supposed to be working,' she reminded him, trying to sound as though she meant it.

'Mmm…'

Ricardo had slid his hand into her hair and was kissing the sensitive little spot just beneath her ear. But it was too late. Her own reminder to herself that she should be working had made her uncomfortably aware that she still had not dealt with the problem of Nick forging her signature.

'What's wrong?'

'Nothing's wrong. What makes you think that there is?'

'You're anxious and tense, and you're avoiding eye contact with me,' Ricardo told her wryly. 'So much for me hoping that you'd finally let me in past the barricades.'

'No, it isn't anything to do with that,' Carly assured him.

'Then what is it to do with?'

He had caught her neatly with that one. There was no point in her trying to pretend now that she wasn't worrying about anything.

'It's… It's something that doesn't only concern *me*, Ricardo.'

'The business?' he guessed.

Carly nodded her head.

'You're a potential client, and…'

He reached for her and looked into her eyes. 'I thought we'd gone way beyond that. What we have means that our personal bond with one another comes way, way before our loyalties to anything or anyone else. Surely you know that you can trust me?'

'Yes.'

'So what's the problem?'

Hesitantly, she started to explain.

'You mean to say that he's forged your signature so that he can steal from his own wife?' he said incredulously.

'I don't know that, but it does look that way. I'm just so worried about what I should do. If I tell Lucy she's going to be so hurt, and she may not even believe me.

I've been in touch with the bank and told them that no cheques are to be allowed through the account for the time being, so at least that should stop him from drawing any more.'

'How much has he taken?'

'A lot. In fact so much that the company just won't be viable by year-end unless Lucy makes up the shortfall from her trust fund.'

'So as of now the business is a sitting duck for any lurking predator?'

'Well, yes, I suppose it is. Although I hadn't thought of it in that way,' Carly admitted. 'My concern has been for Lucy and how this is going to affect her.'

'Well, you've done as much as you can do for the moment. If I were you I'd simply put it out of your mind until we get back to London.'

Strange how that one small word 'we' could mean so very much, Carly thought, as Ricardo drew her back down into his arms.

Ricardo felt the tight coiling of his own stomach muscles as Carly's nipple responded to the slow stroke of his thumb-pad. He could already see the betraying tightening of the muscles in her belly, and the now familiar way in which that threw into relief the mound of her sex.

Carly closed her eyes and gave in to what she was feeling, hoarding the pleasure to her like a child trying to hold a rainbow. She raised her head and kissed the column of Ricardo's throat, running the tip of her tongue along it, right up to his ear, then slowly and luxuriously exploring the hard whorls of flesh.

They had already made love once, but once wasn't going to be enough. She whispered to Ricardo what she wanted, her voice blurred with pleasure and longing, her body shuddering with expectation. The moment he placed his hand on her mound she spread her legs in eager anticipation and invitation, then murmured her appreciation when Ricardo parted the still-swollen lips of her sex with his fingers and started to caress her.

'What about this?' he asked thickly, rolling her over on top of him and holding her just off his own body, his mouth at the juncture of her thighs.

Carly's heart thumped excitedly against her ribs. She had wondered...been tempted...but hadn't liked to suggest such intimacy.

But now, with him holding her arched over him, his fingers exploring her wetness and then holding her open, so that his tongue could sweep the full length of her eager arousal, she could only shudder in mindless, wanton pleasure. His tongue pressed against her clitoris, caressing it into swollen heat, whilst his fingers stroked into her, finding a new pleasure spot she hadn't known existed.

Unable to stop herself she reached for him, circling the head with her own tongue, whilst her fingers worked busily on the shaft. Daringly, the fingers of her free hand moved a little lower.

She heard him groan, his whole body stiffening, and his response increased her own arousal. She could feel him lapping fiercely at her, the intimate stroke of his fingers bringing her so quickly to orgasm that she cried out in the immediacy and intensity of it.

Her body was still tingling, still quivering intensely, when he turned her over and entered her.

Immediately her muscles fastened around him, the small shallow ripples growing into violent shuddering contractions of almost unbearable pleasure.

'I love you so much,' Carly whispered, as she lay held fast in Ricardo's arms. 'I never, ever thought I could feel like this. So loved and loving, and so very, very happy.'

CHAPTER TWELVE

A SMALL tender smile curled Carly's mouth as she let herself into the house. It was lunchtime, and with the birthday ball taking place in a few hours' time by rights she should have been at the château, just in case she was needed, but instead she had given in to Ricardo's whispered suggestion that they snatch a couple of hours alone together.

Ricardo had dropped her off outside before going to park the car, promising her that he wouldn't be very long.

Any time spent apart from him right now was far, far too long, she reflected as she put the fresh bread they had stopped off to buy on the kitchen table and then, unable to stop herself, walked into the room Ricardo was using to work in.

What was it about loving someone that caused this compulsion to share their personal space, even when they weren't in it? She had become so sensitive to everything about him that she was sure she could actually feel his body warmth in the air. Half laughing at herself for her foolishness, she paused to smooth her fingers over the chair in which he normally sat. There were some papers on the desk. She glanced absently at them, and then more hungrily as she saw his handwriting.

And then, as she realised what she was looking at, she stiffened, picking up the papers so that she could study them more closely whilst her heart thudded out an uneven, anguished death knell to her love.

Ricardo frowned as the empty silence of the house surrounded him.

Carly heard him call her name, and then come down the hallway, but she waited until he had walked into the small room before she confronted him. The papers were still in her hand, and she held on to them as she might have done a shield as she accused him bitterly, 'You lied about wanting to give Prêt a Party your business. You don't want to give us anything. You want to take us over.'

'I was considering it, yes,' Ricardo agreed levelly.

'You used me! You deliberately tricked me with all those questions you asked!' Her voice was strained and accusatory, her eyes huge in the pale shape of her face.

'The only questions I asked you were exactly the same ones I, or anyone else, would have asked if they had been intending to give Prêt a Party their business.'

'You pretended to want me…to love me… because—'

'No! Carly, no—you mustn't think that.' As he stepped towards her she moved back from him. 'Yes, I had originally planned to find out from you as much as I could about the way the business is run—that's simple defensive business practice—but—'

'You accused me of being a gold-digger. But what you are, Ricardo, is far, far worse. You used me. You let me believe that you cared about me, that you loved me, when all the time what you really wanted was the business.'

'Carly, that is not true. My potential acquisition of Prêt a Party and my love for you are two completely separate issues. Yes, originally I did think I might get an insight into any vulnerabilities the business might have through you, but I promise you that was the last

thing on my mind when we became lovers. In fact be-
cause of that—because of *us*—I—'

'I don't believe you.' Carly cut him off flatly. 'I
thought I could trust you. Otherwise I would never have
told you what I did about Lucy and Nick. I've made it
all so easy for you, haven't I? Because of my stupidity
Lucy will lose the company. All the time I was letting
myself believe that you were genuine, that you cared
about me, what you really wanted was Prêt a Party.'

'It isn't like that. When you confided in me you were
confiding in me as your lover, and I can assure you *can*
trust me—'

'Trust you? Carly interrupted him furiously. 'What
with? You've taken all the trust I had, Ricardo, and
you've destroyed it. You knew how hard it was for me
to allow myself to admit that I loved you—but you
didn't care what you were doing to me, did you? Not
so long as it got you what you wanted. And you wanted
me vulnerable to you, didn't you? The only thing that
matters to you is making your next billion, nothing else
and no one else. I hate you for what you've done to
me, and I hate you even more for what you're going to
do to Lucy.'

'Carly, you've got it all wrong. I *did* think about acquiring Prêt a Party, but once I'd met you the only
acquisition I cared about was the acquisition of your
love.'

Her muscles ached from the tension inside her body,
and even though she knew he was lying to her, incredibly she actually wanted to believe him. No wonder she
had been so afraid of love if this was what it did to her.
How could she still ache for him, knowing what she
did?

'You're lying, Ricardo,' she told him. 'If you weren't

planning to go ahead with the acquisition why were the papers on your desk?

'I was considering the best way to stop you worrying about Lucy and her trust fund,' he told her quietly.

Carly gave him a mirthless smile. 'Of course. And no doubt you'd decided that the best way was for you to acquire the business. You may have taken me for a fool, Ricardo, but that doesn't mean I intend to go on being one.'

'You're getting this all wrong. I can see that right now you're too upset to listen to reason—'

'Reason? More lies, you mean! I trusted you, and you betrayed that trust!' Carly could feel the anguish of her pain leaking into her voice, betraying to him how badly he had hurt her and how much she loved him.

'Trust works both ways, Carly. I could say to you that I trusted *you*, to have faith in me and my love for you. Those papers were on my desk because I was trying to come up with a way of helping Lucy without benefiting that wretched husband of hers, and the reason I was doing that was because of you. Because I love you, and I knew how upset and worried you were.'

Carly stared at him in disbelief.

'You can't really expect me to believe that,' she told him contemptuously.

'Why not? It's the truth. And if you loved me you would trust me and accept it as such.'

Tears were burning the backs of her eyes and her throat had gone tight with pain. This was the worst kind of emotional blackmail and cold-blooded cynicism, and she wasn't going to fall for it a second time.

'Then obviously I don't love you,' she told him, too brightly. 'Because I don't trust you and I don't accept it. Why should any woman accept anything a man tells her? Look at the way Nick is cheating Lucy. It's over, Ricardo, and it would have been better for me if it had never started in the first place.'

Carly stared bleakly into the mirror. She hated the fact that the only suitable outfit she had to wear for the party was a dress that came from Barneys, which Ricardo had paid for. Well, after tonight he could keep it—and everything else as well.

Including her heart?

She was perilously close to losing control, she warned herself, and no way could she afford to do that. She still had a job to do, after all.

It had been a very long day. Fortunately she had finally managed to get Angelina's approval for the flowers, even if the florist had initially been furious at the change of plan.

Guests who had arrived early and were staying locally had started to appear at the château, wanting to look at the marquee and demanding to see the seating plan.

Privately Carly felt that Angelina, or one at least one of her PAs, should have been on hand to deal with them, but it seemed that several other members of the Famous Rock Star's original band had already arrived, with their entourages, and this had led to an impromptu pre-party party taking place.

'I bet it's all sex, drugs and rock and roll up there,' one of the entertainers had said to Carly dryly, nodding his head in the direction of the château.

Discreetly, Carly had not made any response. But she did know that some seriously businesslike heavies had been hired by the celeb magazine with exclusive rights to reporting the event to protect the guests and the event from any unwanted intrusion by rival members of the press.

Outwardly she was conducting herself professionally and calmly; inwardly she was in emotional turmoil.

Ricardo had lied to her and deceived her, used her, and yet unbelievably, despite all that, and despite what she knew she had to do for the sake of her own self-respect, she still ached for him. Given the choice, if she could have turned back time and not seen those damning papers she knew she would have chosen to do so. How could she still love him? She didn't know how she could; she just knew that she did.

She had removed her things to a spare bedroom, and would have moved out of the house itself if it had been practical to do so. As it was, she was going to have to travel to the château with Ricardo, because it had proved impossible to book a taxi. She didn't know how she was going to endure it, but somehow she must.

And she hadn't even thought properly yet about what she was going to say to Lucy.

Ricardo was waiting for Carly to come downstairs. Did she have any idea how he felt about what she had said to him? Did she really think all the vulnerability and pain was on her side? It tore him apart to think that he had hurt her in any kind of way, and he cursed the fact that he had left those papers on his desk. He also cursed the fact that she had stubbornly refused to accept his explanation.

He heard a door open upstairs and watched as Carly came down the stairs towards him. She looked so beautiful that the sight of her threatened to close his throat. Carly's face was pale and set, and she looked very much as though she had been crying. He wanted to go to her, take her in his arms and never let her go, but he knew if he did she would reject him.

The guests had finished eating, and the magicians had cleverly kept them entertained whilst the tables were cleared. Any minute now the dancing would start.

Carly's head ached, and she longed for the evening to be over. She couldn't bear to look at Ricardo. They were seated at a small table tucked away next to the entrance used by the waiting staff. She would not be able to dance, of course; she wasn't here as a guest. Not that she wanted to risk dancing with Ricardo—not in her present vulnerable state.

Her feelings were just the last dying throes of her love for him, she tried to reassure herself. She was only feeling like this because she knew that after tonight she would never see him again. She was going to miss having sex with him, that was all.

She got up and told Ricardo stiffly, 'I'd better go and check that the bar staff have everything they need.'

He inclined his head in acknowledgement, but didn't make any response. She delayed going back for as long as she could, hoping that when she returned to the table Ricardo might have gone, and yet as she approached the first thing she did was look anxiously for his familiar dark head, as though she dreaded him not being there rather than the opposite. How was she going to get through the rest of her life without him, lying alone in her bed at night longing for him?

'The fireworks are about to start,' Ricardo warned her before she could sit down.

As a special finale to the evening a firework display had been choreographed and timed to go with music from the Famous Rock Star's biggest hit, and to judge from the enthusiastic reception the display received from the assembled guests it had been well worth the time spent on its organisation.

Carly, though, watched the display through a haze of tears, standing stiffly at Ricardo's side, aching to reach out and touch him, but refusing to allow herself to do so.

Despite what he had done she still loved him, and because of that she was hurting herself just as much as he had hurt her.

It was almost four o'clock in the morning before she was finally able to leave. She wasn't returning to the house she had shared with Ricardo though; she had arranged with one of their suppliers to return direct with them to Paris, and from there she intended to fly home. She had her passport with her, and her clothes—her *own* clothes, paid for with her *own* money—were already stowed in the supplier's four-wheel drive.

A cowardly way to leave, perhaps, but she didn't trust herself to spend another night with him. She had some pride left still, she told herself fiercely, even if he had taken everything else from her.

CHAPTER THIRTEEN

SHE had been back in London for three days now, and still hadn't been able to persuade herself to go into the office. Officially at least, so far as Lucy was concerned, she was taking a few days' leave. The reality was that she had felt too sick with loss and misery to do anything other than retreat into herself and stay in her bedroom. Fortunately Jules was away, so she had the flat to herself, but today she had to go out—because today she had an appointment to see Marcus.

No matter how much she was suffering because of Ricardo's deceit and betrayal, she reminded herself that she still owed a duty to Lucy, both as a friend and an employee, and so she had screwed up her courage and got in touch with Marcus to tell him she had some concerns about the financial affairs of the business that she did not at this stage want to discuss with Lucy. Fortunately she'd had his e-mail address, and virtually immediately he had e-mailed her back to ask her to go and see him.

The first thing she noticed when she abandoned the comfort of her 'at home' joggers and top was how loosely her jeans fitted her. It was true that she had not felt much like eating, but the sight of her pale, drawn face and grief-shadowed eyes when she looked at herself in the mirror told her that it wasn't just lack of food that was responsible for her altered appearance. But there was nothing she could take to alleviate the devastating effect of lack of Ricardo, was there? At least only she knew how humiliatingly she longed for him, despite what he had done.

Love knew no sense of moral outrage, as she had now discovered. And, equally, once it had been given life it could not be easily destroyed. She had tried focusing on all the reasons she should not love Ricardo, but rebelliously her thoughts had lingered longingly instead on the happiness she had felt before she had discovered the truth. It might have been a false happiness, but her heart would not let go of it. Her heart longed and yearned to be back in that place of happiness, just as her body yearned to be back in Ricardo's embrace.

She took a taxi to the address Marcus had given her, and was surprised to discover that she had been set down not outside an office building, but outside an elegant house just off one of London's private garden squares.

Even more surprisingly it was Marcus himself who opened the door for her and showed her in to the comfort of a book-lined library-cum-study.

'You must think it rather odd that I've got in touch with you privately,' Carly began awkwardly, having refused his offer of a cup of coffee. She was so on edge that for once she did not feel the need for her regular caffeine fix.

'Not at all,' Marcus reassured her. 'In fact...' He paused, and then looked thoughtfully at her.

'I think I have a fair idea of why you want to see me, Carly.'

'You do?'

'Ricardo has been in touch with me. He told me that you would probably wish to talk to me.'

Carly could feel her face burning with the heat of her emotions.

She couldn't understand why Ricardo should have been in touch with Marcus, but just hearing Marcus say his name made her long for him so much she could hardly think, never mind speak. But of course she had to. She took a deep breath to steady herself, and began.

'Marcus, Ricardo is planning to acquire Prêt a Party, and I'm afraid I may have made it easier for him to get the business at a lower price. You see—'

'Carly, Ricardo has no intention of acquiring the business. In fact, when he telephoned me he made it plain that whilst he had at one stage contemplated doing so, his relationship with you had caused him to change his mind. He also said that you were concerned about Nick's role within the business, specifically when it came to the financial side of things, and that it might be a good idea for me, as Lucy's trustee, to look into it.'

Carly could hardly take in what he was saying.

'But that's not true,' she protested. 'He—'

'I can assure you that it is true. In fact, Ricardo also told me that, because of your concern for Lucy and the business, he wondered if there might be some way that, between us he and I could put together a discreet rescue package, potentially with him using the services of Prêt a Party in connection with his business whilst I deal with the side of things relating to Lucy's trust fund. We agreed that we would both give some thought to our options before making a final decision.

'At that time I rather gained the impression that you and he...' Marcus paused as Carly made a small shocked sound of distress, and then continued, 'However, when he called in to tell me that you were likely to want to see me, he made no mention of your relationship. But he did ask me to give you this.'

Carly was too busy struggling to take in everything Marcus had told her to do anything more than glance vaguely at the small, neatly wrapped box Marcus had handed to her. There was one question she had to ask.

'When...when exactly did Ricardo first telephone you?'

Marcus was frowning.

'Let me have a look in my diary.'

He opened a large leather-bound desk diary and flicked through it.

'Yes, here it is...'

Ricardo had spoken to Marcus *before* she had seen the papers on his desk. He had told Marcus then about her concern and his own decision not to go ahead with any acquisition because of his relationship with her. And she had accused him of lying to her, betraying her.

She was in the taxi Marcus had insisted on calling for her before she remembered the parcel he had given her. Shakily, she took it from her bag and opened it. Inside it was a cardboard box, and inside that was her Cartier watch.

Carly tried to focus on it through the tears blurring her vision, and then realised that beneath it was a note from Ricardo which read; 'You left before I could return this to you.'

Nothing else. Just that. No words of love. But on the card was a handwritten address in London and a telephone number.

Initially he had misjudged her, but that had not stopped her loving him. Then she had misjudged him. Was his love for her strong enough to withstand that?

There was only one way she could find out.

Carly rapped on the glass panel separating her from

the taxi driver. When he pulled it open, she told him she had changed her mind and gave him the address on Ricardo's note.

She had paid off the taxi and now she was standing uncertainly in front of the imposing Georgian terraced house, its gold-tipped black railings glinting in the sunshine, and trying to remember the words she had rehearsed in the taxi on her way here. Words that would tell him how much she loved him, how much she wished she had listened to him and trusted him.

Would he allow her to say them?

Trying not to give way to the mixture of anxiety, dread, and longing leavened with hope that was gripping her body, Carly walked up the stone steps to the imposing black gloss-painted door, and rang the bell.

Seconds ticked by with no response. The street was empty. Like the house? Had she let her own feelings allow her to put an interpretation on Ricardo's note he had never intended? Should she ring the bell again? It was a huge house and maybe no one had heard it the first time? Or maybe no one was there to hear it, she told herself. But she pressed the bell a second time and waited, whilst her heart thumped and the hope drained from her.

There was no point in her ringing a third time.

Carly walked back down the steps, oblivious to the fact that the reason she was struggling to see properly was because she was crying, oblivious too to the taxi turning into the street—until it screeched to a halt only feet away from her, causing her to freeze with shock.

'Carly!'

Her shock turned to disbelief as the passenger door

opened and Ricardo got out, immediately striding towards her.

The taxi driver was reversing and turning round, but Carly didn't notice. She was in Ricardo's arms and he was kissing her with all the passionate hunger and love she had been longing for since she had left him.

'Come on. Let's go inside,' he told her huskily, keeping his arm round her as he guided her back up the stone steps.

'Ricardo, I'm so sorry I refused to believe you. I—'

'Shush,' he told her tenderly as he unlocked the door and ushered her into the hallway.

Motes of dust danced in the sunlight coming through the fanlight, and an impressive staircase curled upwards from the black and white tiled floor. But Carly was oblivious to the elegance of her surroundings, feasting her gaze instead on Ricardo's face.

How could she ever have thought she could live without him?

'You bought my watch back for me,' she whispered emotionally. 'And you told Marcus you didn't want to acquire the business because of me.'

'I knew you would worry about Lucy if I did, and your happiness and peace of mind are far more important to me than any business acquisition. The reason those papers you found were on the desk was because I'd seen how upset you were about Nick and the cheques, and I know Marcus vaguely, and so I'd decided that maybe it was worth making contact with him, to see if between us we couldn't do something that would set your mind at rest. I reasoned that since he was Lucy's trustee he would want to protect her, just as I wanted to protect you.'

'And then I accused you of trying to use me. I'm surprised you even want to see me again.'

'Well, you shouldn't be. Real love, true love, the kind of love I feel for you and you feel for me, is far stronger than pride—as you have proved by coming here to find me. Now, did Marcus tell you that I'm going to give Prêt a Party some business?'

'What?' said Carly blankly. 'Well, yes…'

'I've got several events in mind I can use them for, but the first and most important of them all is going to be our wedding.'

Carly looked up at him. 'You want us to get married?'

Ricardo nodded his head.

'I want us to get married; I want you to be my wife; I want you to be the mother of my children. You are my soulmate, Carly, and my life is of no value to me without you in it, at my side… But this is not the way or the place in which I had intended to propose to you.'

'It isn't?'

'No. I wanted something far more romantic—something that would make up for all the unhappiness life has brought you and show you how much I love you. A room filled with roses, perhaps, or—'

Carly reached up and placed her finger against his lips.

'I don't need or want that, Ricardo. All I want is you, and your heart filled with love for me.'

'Always,' he told her softly, before bending his head to kiss her.

Expecting the Playboy's Heir

PENNY JORDAN

CHAPTER ONE

LIPS light as the touch of a butterfly's wings, but far more sensual, brushed the back of her neck, a male hand on her shoulder enclosing the small intimacy in protective secrecy, before he whispered in her ear.

'Back in a few minutes. Don't go away.'

She hadn't moved, not even to turn her head to look at him, and she didn't move now. Mainly because she couldn't, Jules realised shakily.

There were times when she would rather be anything other than one of the partners in an event planning organisation. And this was definitely one of them.

Everyone who was anyone in the celebrity world was here in Majorca, thronging the grounds of the exclusive holiday villa currently on loan to the most excitingly 'in' Hollywood superstar couple.

A-List Life, the magazine responsible for paying for this particular 'bash,' which was ostensibly being given to celebrate the couple's first wedding anniversary, had already described them as Hollywood Royalty.

Now their carefully selected celebrity 'friends' were 'celebrating,' whilst the magazine's flamboyant owner and editor, Dorland Chesterfield, interviewed the happy couple and its photographers mingled with the guests.

She was getting too cynical, Julia decided. Lucy, her friend and the owner of Prêt a Party, had been thrilled about this commission, and of course Julia could understand why.

Dorland was a millionaire and was *the* most influential

person on the upmarket social event scene. Being hired to organise any event the magazine was sponsoring—never mind being selected, as they had been, to organise Dorland's fabulous and high-profile end-of-summer celeb bash—was virtually a licence to print money, via future commissions, as Nick, Lucy's husband, had said.

A small frown pleated Julia's forehead as she remembered Nick's unkind comments about Dorland.

'The man's a fat, brainless star-sucker—if he is a man,' he had announced derisively when Dorland had first approached them.

'That's neither true nor fair, Nick.' Julia had immediately defended Dorland.

Yes, Dorland was slightly overweight, and it was true that there were rumours that prior to bursting onto the social scene and setting up his magazine he had undergone a sex-change operation, as well as equally unproven gossip and speculation about his sexual orientation. However, Julia privately suspected he might well be one of those people who genuinely were asexual. Although he was surrounded by eager wannabes of both sexes, thanks to the success of *A-List Life*, no one had ever been able to say categorically that he had had any sexual involvements or partnerships. It was Julia's belief that Dorland reserved all his passion for the great love in his life, which was fame and those who achieved it. Whatever his sexuality, Dorland could tap into the female psyche, and he also had the knack of massaging a vulnerable and famous ego to the point where even the most out-of-reach 'star' was prepared to let down their guard with him.

The truth was that Dorland genuinely liked and admired the famous, and they, sensing that, turned to him and his magazine with the kind of exclusive articles that had other editors gnashing their teeth with envy.

Nick affected to loathe and despise him, but Julia couldn't help wondering if secretly Nick was jealous of both his success and his wealth.

She, not Nick, was the one who had had the headache of organising and co-ordinating the two lavish events Dorland had hired them for. Including dealing with more mammoth egos than any sane person would ever want to know. Nick had cleverly managed to be away chasing up new business or interviewing potential new clients when all the really hard work had had to be done. Nick *was* here today, though.

A pang of pain mingled with guilt squeezed her heart.

There had been a time when in her heart, if not in public, she had begun to dream that she and Nick would become a pair. When he had dropped her for Lucy, shortly after she had introduced them, she had naturally done her best to conceal how she felt, assuring herself that hearts did not break, and that if hers was so very badly cracked that she felt it would never mend, then that was her own affair.

Her mental choice of the word *affair* made her grimace. Nick might have pursued and flattered her, but things had not got to the point where they had exchanged anything more than a few passionate kisses, and thankfully she had not had time to confide in her friends about how she'd felt about him.

But just recently Nick had started to complain to her that his marriage was in difficulties and he felt he had made a mistake. Lucy, too, whilst fiercely loyal to her husband and her marriage, had begun to look strained and unhappy.

After a thorough visual scan, to ensure that nothing

needed her attention, Julia was just about to go inside and check on the progress of the interview when Nick came up behind her and put his hand on her bare shoulder again, deliberately caressing the smooth, lightly tanned skin.

'Don't, Nick.' She warned him off.

He ignored her, murmuring tauntingly, 'Don't? Don't what? Don't stop? You know you want it every bit as much as I do.'

'That's not true,' she denied fiercely. 'Apart from anything else, you're married to Lucy.'

'Don't remind me.'

Automatically Julia felt herself recoil. These were words she just did not want to hear, just as this was a situation she did not want to be in, but Nick was still holding her, and closing the gap between them as he whispered thickly, 'Remember how good it was between us? What are you holding back for? Why shouldn't we enjoy one another when it's what we both want? I could come to your room later. No one need know, and—'

'No! It's over between us, Nick. I mean that. And I won't change my mind.'

'Oh, yes, you will,' he told her softly. 'You know that, and so do I.'

He was bending his head towards her and in another heartbeat he would be kissing her. Panic and guilt invaded her. The last time he had kissed her had been under a tropical moon in the garden of the luxury hotel where they had met, and where she had assumed they would become lovers. But by the end of the holiday Lucy had been the one Nick had declared he loved. Lucy had been the one he had married. Lucy was his *wife*. And one of her two closest friends. No way was she going to betray that friendship. Every marriage went through a bad patch.

Somehow she managed to wrench herself away from Nick, but she had barely taken a couple of steps when she felt hard male fingers gripping her arm.

'No, Nick. I meant what I said,' she said sharply, without bothering to turn her head.

'Did you? He certainly didn't seem to think so—and neither do I!'

'Silas!'

Her whole body went into shock as she stared up in consternation at the man holding on to her.

'How—?' she began, only to be cut off with ruthless efficiency.

'How much did I overhear? All of it,' he told her succinctly. 'How long has it been going on?'

'Nothing is going on!'

The look he gave her—ice-blue eyes narrowed, cynicism tightening his mouth, even the angle of his head as he turned it toward her—reflected his disbelief. She could feel the old familiar mix of anger and antipathy taking hold of her.

'It's true,' she insisted. 'I met Nick before he met Lucy, and the relationship he was referring to was that relationship—not that it's any of your business.'

'A relationship he obviously now believes you want to resume,' Silas said silkily.

'Well, he believes wrong. Because I don't.'

The way he was looking at her was driving up her own anger. They'd never got on, not really. She only tolerated him because of Gramps, whose title and land he would one day inherit.

In Gramps's shoes, she doubted that she would have been able to take to her heart so warmly this American outsider who, by virtue of being descended in the male line from Gramps's younger brother, would one day inherit his title and land. But then she did not possess her grandfather's sanguine outlook on life.

'But you do want *him*.'

It was a taunt rather than a question.

'No!' she said furiously. 'Nick is married to Lucy. And she is my best friend.'

'I know that. But I also know that if you want what you're saying you do, you'll make damn sure he knows that you aren't available.'

Julia had had enough. 'By doing what, exactly?' she demanded angrily.

Silas gave the kind of shrug that only very tall, very muscular, very *male* men could give. And, as always, being forced to recognise his maleness triggered a frisson of awareness inside her that hiked up her antipathy towards him. He had no right to be so damn sexy. It was somehow all wrong that a man who aggravated her as much as Silas did should possess the kind of physique and looks that made grown women react like hormone-controlled teenagers.

'By doing whatever it takes. Either by giving up your job—'

'I won't do that,' Julia interrupted him irritably. 'Especially as Lucy's already lost Carly, now that she's married to Ricardo and expecting a baby. I can't leave as well.'

'—or by making sure Blayne knows you aren't available.'

'I've already told him that I'm not.'

'But, as he can quite plainly see, you are. On the other hand, if there were another man in your life...'

'But there isn't.'

'So find one who's willing to pretend to be there for long enough to get Nick Blayne to back off.'

'What? Like who?'

'Like me.'

'What?' Julia shook her head in violent denial. 'You? No. No way! Ever. Absolutely not. Anyway, everyone knows that we loathe one another.'

'It isn't unheard of for couples to discover that what they thought was love is really loathing, so why shouldn't we have made the discovery the other way around?'

'I can't believe I'm hearing this. Do you really expect me to agree to pretend that you and I are in a relationship?'

'I thought you said you wanted to protect Lucy's marriage.'

'I do, but not by offering myself up as a sacrifice for you to devour.'

'Very bacchanalian imagery. Although I confess the thought of you offering yourself up...'

'I wouldn't. Not to you. Not ever.'

'But you would to Nick Blayne?'

'No!'

'So prove it.'

Julia glared at him.

'Just what is this all about, Silas? What's in it for you?' she demanded trenchantly. 'And what on earth are you doing here, anyway? You hate this kind of thing.'

'I'm here because you're here.' Another shrug, more lazily dismissive this time, and the movement of powerful shoulders beneath the linen suit jacket unbelievably and very much unwantedly conjured up images of just such a pair of male shoulders naked, and gleaming in the morning sunlight as their owner arched his equally naked and male body over her own.

Silas naked?

Such an image might not be legally or even morally taboo, but it was certainly not the way she was used to thinking about him. Was this the kind of thing that happened when you were in your mid-twenties and your sex life was an arid desert, refreshed only by watching reruns of *Sex and the City* and determinedly refusing to study the ads in the back of glossy magazines for purveyors of sex toys?

'Oh, yes. Of course,' she agreed wryly, hurriedly banishing her unexpectedly erotic mental images.

But before she could ask him why he was really there, he told her coolly, 'You should wear a hat in this heat. Your face is burning.'

Maybe it was, but the heat it was giving off hadn't been caused by the sun, Julia admitted to herself.

That was the trouble with Silas. Much as he filled her with wary dislike and suspicion, she still couldn't stop herself from being aware of him as a man. And not just any man, but a very dangerously sexy man.

'What is it you really want?' she demanded.

'Well, for one thing I want your grandfather's peace of mind and continued good health. We both know how much it would upset him if it got into the papers—as it more than likely would—that his beloved granddaughter was involved in a sordid love triangle. And for another... Let's just say that it would be convenient for me right now to be seen publicly as romantically involved.'

It might not, Silas had decided in his practical way, be in his own best interests to discuss Aimee DeTroite and the problems she was causing him with Julia. There was no need, after all, for her to have to know. And as for Aimee herself—since she continued to take such an unwanted and intrusive interest in his private life, hopefully the discovery that he was now 'coupled up' with Julia should send a very clear message to her that she was wasting her time.

Not that that was the only or even the most important reason he had for what he was doing.

'Well, at least you haven't claimed that you want me,' Julia told him.

'Would you like me to?'

Say it or mean it? Julia felt her heart ricochet from one side of her chest to the other.

'It might be worth it, just for the pleasure of calling your bluff,' she told him sweetly.

'Like Blayne was calling yours, you mean?' Silas challenged her.

'I meant what I said to him,' Julia told him hotly.

'Then prove it.'

'I don't have to prove anything to you.'

'Not to me, perhaps,' he agreed, in that mocking way of his that so infuriated her. 'But I rather think that you do have something to prove to Lucy. She was standing right next to me when Blayne was kissing your neck.'

Immediately, and anxiously, she looked beyond his shoulder to where she could see Lucy, talking to the magazine editor.

'She saw him?' she demanded, concern for her friend immediately pushing everything else she was feeling out of the way.

'Yes.'

Lucy, her lifelong friend. Lucy, who always somehow seemed to be struggling to conceal an inner fragility and vulnerability. Lucy, who would be broken and destroyed by the thought that her husband was cheating on her with her best friend. No way could she allow that to happen, no matter what temporary sacrifices she might have to make herself.

'Very well, then. I'll do it,' she told him impetuously. It would be worth it to protect her friend's marriage. And to assuage her own guilt?

CHAPTER TWO

'AH! HERE you are!'

Julia hoped that her expression hadn't betrayed how very unloverlike and ill at ease Silas's appearance had caused her to feel, coupled with his warm, husky greeting—somehow as sensually intimate as though he had addressed her in far more loverlike terms—and the weight of Silas's arm around her shoulders.

'Missed me?'

Two words and one look, focused on her eyes and then dropping to her mouth, one small touch of male fingers in her hair. Dammit, Silas should have been an actor. He was certainly putting on an Oscar-worthy performance. Even her own body had been taken in by it.

And as for either Lucy or Dorland Chesterfield guessing they were putting on an act—if their expressions of delighted astonishment were anything to go by they were far too excited to notice anything other than what Silas wanted them to see.

'Jules!' Lucy squeaked. 'Why on earth didn't you tell me?'

Dorland mopped his round sweating face with his handkerchief, and then breathed happily, 'Oh, my, what a potentially delectable feast of delicious gossip. Billions of dollars, a title, and the fact that the two of you are related. Perfect.'

'Dorland...' Julia began apprehensively, but her caution was lost in Silas's words.

'We haven't known for very long ourselves, have we?'

Automatically she turned towards him. He must have been right about the heat, because suddenly she felt distinctly odd, sort of dizzy and light-headed, whilst her heart fluttered in shallow little beats. How was he managing to look every bit as arrogant and potently male as he always did? He was focusing on her with a gaze of such sensual hunger that it actually made the colour rise up under her skin.

'Jules, you're blushing!' Lucy exclaimed, laughing.

This was ridiculous!

'We said that we were not going to go public yet— remember,' she told Silas, forcing herself to soften her voice to an unfelt sweetness whilst returning his look with one of her own that was not so much ardent as reproachful.

'I wasn't aware that we had,' Silas countered, causing Lucy to laugh.

'Just the way you're looking at Jules says it all, Silas. If ever a man's gaze said *I love you and I want you in bed*, yours just did.'

'Mmm… Well, it has been a while,' Silas answered shamelessly, and Julia longed for the privacy to tell him exactly what she thought of his enthusiasm for his new role.

'You'll have to take some time off from that Foundation of yours and spend it with Julia instead,' Dorland chipped in.

Julia looked at him in triumph and waited. No way would Silas do that. He was caught neatly in his own lies, and it served him right.

His hand had moved from her shoulder to her neck,

and his fingers were stroking into her hair. She had to fight against an instinctive desire to stretch luxuriously into his touch, demanding more of it.

'That's exactly what I intend to do. In fact, that's exactly what I am doing. From now on where Jules goes, I go.'

'You can't do that,' Julia objected, panicking. 'I'm working.'

The hard fingers weren't stroking now, but pressing warningly instead.

'Of course, but not twenty-four hours a day. And when you aren't working...'

'Silas, don't you dare take her away from me until the end of the year,' Lucy begged. 'We've got so much work on I couldn't manage without her—especially now that Dorland has asked us to organise his big summer party.'

'You've got her until the end of the year,' Silas agreed. 'But, as I've just said, where Jules goes, I go—and her off-duty time is mine.'

Lucy burst out laughing. 'Silas, you *must* be in love. I thought you hated parties and huge events.'

'I do, but I love Julia more than I loathe them.'

She had had enough, Julia decided—more than enough, and in spades.

'Darling, I can't possibly let you make such a sacrifice. Of course you mustn't do any such thing. You'd be bored to tears, hanging around waiting for me. And besides, we are going to spend the rest of our lives together.' She smiled sweetly and waited. She could see the 'I take no prisoners' glint in Silas's eyes, but no way was she going to back down.

'How could being with you ever be a sacrifice?' His

arm was round her waist and he had closed the distance between them, holding her against him, his free hand resting on her hip, which he was rubbing tenderly in a gesture of supposedly subtle intimacy.

'No, my mind is made up. Unless Lucy objects, where you go, I go.'

'Of course I don't object,' Lucy assured him.

'You've got the Silverwoods' combined silver wedding and eighteenth for their son coming up next, haven't you, Jules? That is going to be huge, I know.' She hesitated, and then said diffidently, 'Nick mentioned to me that you'd hinted that you'd like him to give you some support with it, and—'

'No! I mean, there's no need for him to do that.' She could hardly tell Lucy that she had said no such thing, and that Nick had lied to her. 'Nick must have misunderstood what I was saying.'

Lucy might be looking relieved and smiling, but Julia noticed that Silas certainly wasn't mirroring Lucy's response.

'And don't forget my end-of-summer bash,' Dorland broke in.

'Yes, you're doing that, Jules,' Lucy agreed. 'And I'll do all the smaller UK-based stuff—which will leave you with just the Sheikh's post-Ramadan party in Dubai.'

'Fine.' Did her voice and face sound and look as tight as they felt? 'But right now it's time for the buffet to be served, plus I've got to organise champagne for the toast and check that everything's set for the firework display. So if you'll all excuse me...'

She turned to walk away and then found that she couldn't. Silas had somehow taken her hand in his and entwined his fingers through her own in a pseudo-lover's clasp that effectively locked her to him like a prisoner.

Indignation flashed hotly in the irate glare Jules gave him, turning the normal amber of her eyes to a brilliant speckled gold.

But Silas ignored her outrage, just as he ignored the rejecting shake of her head and the resultant shiny disorder of her blonde hair, with its streaks of dark gold.

'Silas,' she began, through gritted teeth, but stopped as he raised their clasped hands to his lips and then opened her palm and pressed a very deliberate and very sensual kiss into it.

Shock, heat, and a surge of lust she would never in a thousand lifetimes have associated with her true feelings towards Silas rampaged through her, leaving her in possession of the unwanted discovery that knees *did* go weak and that desire *was* a shockingly unfathomable and treacherous thing.

When Silas released her, her body felt as giddy and unstable as though she had consumed a whole bottle of Cristal champagne. She made a valiant effort not to simply stand and stare at him.

Dorland's photographers were still swarming all over the place, chasing down celebrities for the photographs that the magazine's readers pored over so eagerly, and so too were the legions of PRs, make-up artists, hairdressers, personal trainers, dressers, astrologers... No right-thinking superstar would dream of being without his or her entourage.

The white powder so beloved amongst the foibles of the foolish and famous had also been very much in evidence during the big event, and Julia had lost count of the number of times she had refused offers of 'something'.

To those who loved reading celebrity magazines the lifestyle of those they read about might seem enviable and glamorous, but the reality was that beneath the glitter and excitement lay a deep and dark abyss into which today's star could all too easily disappear and be forgotten.

'Thank God Tiffany relented and allowed Martina to borrow that diamond necklace she'd set her heart on wearing,' she heard Dorland remark.

'Only thanks to you,' Julia pointed out, determinedly not looking at Silas.

'Well, like I told them, they'd be missing a terrific PR opportunity if they refused,' Dorland agreed happily.

'Perhaps they were more concerned about the possibility of missing a few million dollars' worthy of diamond necklace,' Silas pointed out dryly. 'After all, it would not be the first time a star has "lost" a valuable piece of jewellery she's only had on loan.'

'Oooh, Silas, that is so naughty of you.' Dorland pouted theatrically. 'What kind of ring are you going to give our Julia? Something new and shiny? Or is it going to be a family heirloom? I heard on the grapevine that you've hunted down most of the stuff your mutual great-great-grandfather gambled away—and paid enough to cover the national debt of a small country for it,' he added gleefully.

'Silas, you haven't?' Julia protested.

'The sapphire and diamond set presented to our great-great-grandmother on her betrothal is of considerable historical value, and as such reassembling it was a worthwhile project.'

Julia's eyes widened. '*All* of it?'

A certain Indian Maharajah had presented the jewellery to the bride, with whom, as rumour had it, he had fallen passionately in love. The household records her grandfather had shown her when he had told her the story had listed the gift as comprising not just the expected necklace, earrings, bracelets and tiara, but in addition matching jewelled combs and brushes, along with perfume bottles and a gem-studded carrying case. The necklace itself had contained seven sapphires unique in colour and size.

'All of it,' Silas agreed.

'Ah, Julia, my dear, you are so fortunate. Your very own billionaire. What fun!'

Fun? Silas? Julia didn't think so. No way could she ever envisage using such a lightweight word as *fun* in connection with a man who was predominantly and dangerously a heavyweight alpha male.

What would he be like in bed?

Her curiosity caught her unprepared with its small provocative question.

'I must go. I've got a meeting with the PR people,' she fibbed, cravenly making her escape.

Inside the villa, the 'happy couple' were still being interviewed, looking anything but happy.

Love! The older she got, the less she believed it actually existed, Jules reflected cynically as she went to warn the caterers that it was time to start serving the buffet.

The villa hired for the anniversary party had originally belonged to an eccentric art collector who had had it built early in the twentieth century to house his collection of Greek and Roman artefacts. It was built on a small promontory overlooking the sea, in a design vaguely reminiscent of a Roman villa, around an enclosed courtyard complete with marble columns and a sunken pool.

The plan was that as the sun set the celebrating celebrities would reaffirm their vows on the sea-facing terrace outside the villa, the light of the sun to be replaced by the light of the one thousand and one candles inside the villa and the inner courtyard.

They had had terrific problems getting the people who owned the villa to agree to the lit candles, and Julia was hoping that she had organised enough candle-lighters to get them all lit at the same time. The idea was that the first one in every ten would be lit first, then the second, and so on until they were all burning.

She just hoped it was going to work.

Her palm was still tingling where Silas had kissed it. *Kissed* it. He had done much more than that, she reminded herself indignantly, as she remembered the way his tongue-tip had stroked a fiery circle of erotic pleasure over her skin.

His expertise had suggested that he would be a very accomplished lover. But would he be sensual and passionate? Would he give himself to the need he aroused in his partner? Would he…?

Not that she was interested in knowing, of course. No way would she ever flutter her eyelashes and fawn over a man the way she had seen the girls he had brought down to Amberley do.

She had still been a schoolgirl then, resenting the fact that Silas's annual summer visit to Amberley coincided with her own time there. And aware too that whilst for now Amberley was *her* home, one day it would belong to Silas.

Now it was not the potential loss of Amberley that hurt, but rather the potential loss of her grandfather. Her mother was the child of his second marriage, and he was in his seventies now, his heart weakened by the serious heart attack he had suffered eighteen months ago.

He was so precious to her, and so loved. He had provided her with the male influence in her life after her parents' divorce, and at the same time he had given her and her mother a home.

Her mother had remarried three years ago, and, though Jules liked her stepfather, he could never take the place of her grandfather.

What exactly had Silas meant when he had said that it would suit him to be in a relationship? One day he would have to marry, if he wanted to provide an heir for Amberley—and Jules felt sure that he would want to do so. He was in his thirties now, and he was not the kind of man who would flinch from telling a woman that his relationship with her was over.

Like her, Silas had grown up without his father. Not because his parents had been divorced, as her own had been, but because his father had been killed in a freak sailing accident when Silas had only been a few months old.

She looked down at the floor, not wanting to think of Silas as a vulnerable fatherless baby, and then frowned as she studied her shoes. Shopping was her Achilles' heel and shoes were her downfall, and had been all her life. She still had, in their original shoe boxes, the pretty dancing shoes she had persuaded her mother to buy for her as a child, and tomorrow morning she was hoping to be able to slip away to visit a local shop, where she had heard it was possible to pick up exclusive samples of shoes from one of fashion's hottest new young designers.

The sun was beginning to set. The celebrity couple emerged on to the steps of the impressive portico to the villa, she with her head thrown back and her throat arched, to reveal the glitter of the Tiffany necklace as she leaned into her husband, and he gazing adoringly down at her. They were presenting a very different image from the one Jules had seen earlier in the day, when she had been screaming at him, accusing him of cheating on her, whilst he had snarled back that she was so self-obsessed he was surprised she had even noticed.

'It would have been hard not to, darling. Not when the little slut in question was supposed to be my manicurist. Except it wasn't a *nail* job she was giving you when I walked into the bedroom and found you with her, was it?'

Now the slender, supple female figure—kept that way, so rumour had it, by a rigorous regime of drugs reinforced by cosmetic surgery—was angled towards her husband's, whilst his hand rested possessively on her hip.

Jules heard Lucy, who was standing next to her, give a small sad sigh. Poor Lucy, married to a man who had no respect either for her or the vows he had made to her. And where was Nick anyway?

Automatically Julia turned her head to look for him, almost jumping out of her skin when she heard Silas demanding, 'Looking for someone?'

'Yes—you, of course, darling,' she responded with sugary sweetness.

'Girls, this is great,' Dorland enthused as he lumbered towards them, mopping the perspiration from his face with a large handkerchief.

The sun was setting, the photographers were busily snapping away as the celebs reaffirmed their vows, and in their tens, twenties and hundreds the lights of the candles glowed against the warm Mediterranean darkness.

Silas looked on, and murmured, 'What a total farce.'

'It's supposed to be very romantic and symbolic,' Julia pointed out crossly.

'I'm astonished that you managed to get insurance for something like this.' Silas grimaced.

'Nick dealt with the insurance,' Julia told him absently, before demanding, 'You didn't really mean what you said to Dorland and Lucy, did you?'

'Which bit?'

All of it, Julia was tempted to say, but instead she answered, 'The bit that went "Where Jules goes, I go". I mean, it's bad enough that you said anything to Dorland at all—'

'Why?'

'Why?' She stared at him in disbelief. 'Silas, Dorland owns *A-List Life*. He gets off on going public on personal stuff that people want to keep private.'

'Like Nick Blayne and you, you mean?'

Julia hissed in angry disbelief. 'There is no Nick Blayne and me.'

'Blayne doesn't seem to think that. Which would you rather have, Julia? Dorland publishing a coy announcement that you and I are an item, or Dorland hinting that you and Blayne are having an affair behind his wife's back?'

'Neither,' Julia told him shortly. 'Silas, you're going

to have to say something to Dorland and…and tell him that you don't want anyone else to know about us yet.'

'With the ego-driven photo fodder Dorland's assembled here, the last thing he's going to be interested in is us,' Silas told her derisively.

'Shush!' Julia hushed him warningly, looking round quickly to check that no one was standing close enough to him to have overheard him. 'Lucy's business is dependent on people like these, and, since I work for her, so is my job.'

She caught his derisive look and felt compelled to demand, 'What's your real motive for this, Silas? I refuse to believe that you really intend to spend virtually the whole of the next six months policing me just because you don't want to see Lucy hurt or because you disapprove of extra-marital affairs.'

'So you *have* been having an affair with Blayne, then?'

Julia exhaled noisily and fixed him with a furious amber glare.

'Oh, that's just so typical of you—trying to play catch-out by deliberately twisting what I'm saying to suit your own purposes. No, I'm not having an affair with Nick.'

'Okay, maybe describing it as an affair *is* going too far. You've had sex with him and you want to have sex with him again—is that better?'

'No, it is not. Just in case you've forgotten, Silas, I'm twenty-six—not sixteen.'

'Meaning?'

'Meaning that I'm plenty old enough to have lost my illusions about what sex is really like. A sixteen-year-old might—just might—be starry-eyed and hormone-driven enough to believe that wonderful, mind-blowing, transports-you-to-another-dimension sex actually exists, and to lust after it and the partner she thinks will supply it for her, but a twenty-six-year-old woman knows the truth.'

'Which is?'

Julia gave a small dismissive shrug.

'That the kind of sex we fantasise about as teenagers is just that—a fantasy. Sexual satisfaction isn't a life-changing experience that transports you to some kind of unique physical heaven, and it certainly isn't worth betraying a friendship like mine and Lucy's for. But of course no one wants to admit it. I'm not saying that sex isn't enjoyable. I'm just saying that after the fantasy sex girls build up inside their heads, the reality can be a bit of a let-down.'

'It's an interesting theory, but not one, I suspect, that is shared by the majority of your peers.'

'You'd be surprised,' Julia told him darkly. 'More and more women in their thirties who are in relationships are saying that sex just doesn't interest them any more.'

'Mmm, well, to judge by the antics being indulged in by the majority of the guests here this evening, they are not in agreement with you.'

'Most of them are out of their heads on drink or drugs—or both.'

'Habits you don't share?'

'I've seen too much of what they can do. I like a glass of wine with a meal and the occasional glass of champagne, but that's all. Besides, I couldn't do my job if I was out of my head on drink and drugs.'

The first of the fireworks exploded above their heads

in a shimmer of brilliant falling stars, quickly followed by several others.

'I understand from Dorland that you'll be leaving for Italy tomorrow?'

'Yes, I'm flying to Naples and going from there to Positano for my next job. Silas, there's no need for you to come with me. Lucy is bound to tell Nick about us, and seeing us together has certainly reassured her. I hate to think of her being hurt.'

'But ultimately I suspect that she will be, unfortunately,' Silas warned her. 'Her marriage to Blayne makes that inevitable.'

Another firework went off in an explosive crackle of noise that caught Julia off guard, and instinctively she took a step closer to Silas. Immediately he put his arm around her, causing her to turn her head to look up at him.

Silas was looking back at her, his head bent towards her own. A frisson of something unfamiliar and yet oddly instantly recognised by her senses gripped her emotions, causing her eyes to widen. She could feel the warmth of Silas's arm round her and smell the scent of his skin, warm, male, and luring her to move closer to him to breathe it into herself more deeply. A small, sharp spasm of physical shock shook through her. She could feel the rocky, unsteady thud of her own heartbeat. Why had she never noticed before how sexy Silas's mouth was? His lower lip was sensually full, whilst his top lip was so cleanly cut that she had to subdue a crazy impulse to reach out and trace it with her fingertip.

'Blayne's watching us.'

'What?'

It took several seconds for Silas's comment to penetrate the disconcerting confusion of her wandering thoughts, and then several more for her to translate it into an explanation of why Silas was continuing to hold her.

And a reason for the downward movement of his head now, at the same time as he drew her against his body and held her there, one hand in the hollow of her back, pressing her into him, the other splayed against the back of her head, supporting it as the lips she had been admiring brushed coolly against her own.

The temptation was too much for her to resist. Silas's mouth was now hers to explore more intimately. Slowly and carefully she traced their outline with the tip of her tongue. His lips felt cool, and smooth, and firm. A cascade of small quivering shots of delight tumbled down her spine, coupled with a desire for something more. Automatically she moved even closer, and then made a small sound of complaint when Silas stepped back from her.

'If you were doing that for Blayne's benefit,' he began in an almost harsh voice, 'then—'

'Nick's benefit?' Julia realised that she had completely forgotten about Lucy's husband. No way did she want Silas to know that, though.

'I don't know why you sound so disapproving,' she told him airily. 'This whole thing was your idea, after all—although why you should want to protect Lucy…' A sudden thought struck her. 'You aren't doing this for Lucy's sake at all, are you? So why…? Oh, I get it. You're using me to— What's she like, Silas, and why are you going to such lengths to get rid of her?'

'What?' He was frowning impatiently now.

'You heard me,' Julia persisted. 'What's she like, this

woman you want to shake off by pretending to be involved with me?'

'What makes you think there is any such woman?'

'What other reason could there be?' Julia answered him practically. 'Although I must admit you've never struck me as the kind of man who'd have any trouble leaving behind anything or anyone he didn't want any more.'

'Thanks.'

'Even Gramps admits that you can be single-minded,' Julia pointed out. 'And he dotes on you. Mind you, I would have thought that you'd be looking for commitment instead of trying to avoid it—or wasn't she the right type to become a countess and the mother of the next Amberley heir?'

'You're jealousy's showing,' Silas warned her.

'What?' Julia gave him an indignant look. 'No way am I jealous of your women.'

Through the darkness Julia could almost feel his quick, almost bruisingly hard visual inspection of her shadowed face in a silence that suddenly seemed to be packed tight with explosive tension.

'I meant your jealousy of the fact that ultimately I will inherit Amberley and not you.'

Julia felt her face start to burn. If she kept on like this Silas would probably start thinking that she was secretly in love with him. And she most certainly was not.

'That's ridiculous,' she defended herself. 'I've always known that you will inherit Amberley.'

'And you've always resented me because of it.'

He made it a fact rather than a question.

'No, I haven't,' Julia objected immediately.

'Liar. Even as a child you went to extraordinary lengths to make it clear to me that I was an outsider.'

Julia frowned. 'That wasn't because you'll inherit Amberley.'

'No?'

'No!' Reluctantly she admitted, 'Ma told me, when I was about six that if Gramps died then she and I would have to find somewhere else to live because Amberley would be yours. I suppose she just wanted to warn me what the situation was, but for a long time I was afraid that I would come back from school one day and Gramps would be dead. Ma always did her best, but sometimes not having a father hurts.'

'Tell me about it.'

Julia glanced at him and then said bleakly, 'Neither of us has had much luck in that department, have we? Your father died when you were only a few months old and landed you with those ancient trustees you inherited from him, and mine took one look at me and left Ma for someone else. Which do you think is worse? Your father being dead or your father being alive but not wanting you?'

To her own irritation, her voice had thickened with the tears blurring her eyes. She had thought she'd talked herself out of this kind of self-pity at junior school.

And even worse than self-pity was the thought of someone else's pity—especially if that someone else was Silas. To forestall any offer of it she pulled away from him, and was startled to discover how much her body resented its removal from the warmth of his.

'I'd better go and check that the candles are all put out properly.' The look he gave her made her point out defensively, 'I am supposed to be working.'

'Working?'

'My job might seem shallow and pointless to you, Silas, and I know that other people envy me because they think I spend all my time mixing with celebrities and partying, but the reality is that neither you nor they appreciate what a tough job this actually is. Lucy's worked very hard to build up this business, and I owe it to her to do my job as professionally as I can.'

'By schmoozing rich old men and their plastic-fantastic Stepford Wife women?' Silas taunted her.

'That's unfair. Corporate and event entertainment is big business—and don't tell me that you haven't hired event organisers yourself, because I won't believe you.'

Some of the billions of dollars Silas's grandmother's family had earned from oil had been used in his grand-father's time to set up a charitable arts foundation, which Silas now headed.

Silas gave a small dismissive gesture, his accent sud-denly very American as he drawled, 'Sure. We've done stuff—fundraisers at the Met, and in conjunction with the Getty. My mother generally organises them, since she's the head of our fund-raising committee.'

She saw the gleam in his eyes as he looked at her. 'She would have been happy to give you a job—you know that.'

Julia made no comment. Like everyone, apart from Silas himself, Julia was slightly in awe of Silas's charm-ing but formidably organised and successful mother.

'Lucy asked me first, and I couldn't let her down.'

'But you could allow her husband to proposition you?'

Julia's mouth compressed.

'Nick and Lucy are going through a bad patch.'

'And having sex with you was going to be a Band-Aid to hold their marriage together?'

Julia didn't bother to make any response, simply walking away from him instead, but his words were very much in her thoughts as she checked that all the candles were being doused properly.

She had felt so envious of Lucy when she and Nick had married, and so determined to make sure that no one guessed how she felt, but just lately she had begun to see Nick in a different light, and to feel sorry for Lucy instead of envying her.

In fact, refusing Nick's blandishments and often openly sexual hints that he wasn't happy in his marriage had proved to be surprisingly easy. Nick made no secret of the fact that he considered himself to be an accomplished lover, openly boasting to her of the pleasure he could give her, but some instinct told her that in bed he would not be in the same class as Silas.

Her face burned hotly with guilt as she recognised the path along which her thoughts were trespassing. Silas's sexual expertise or lack of it was not something she should be thinking about or interested in. After all, he had never shown any kind of sexual interest in her.

Until tonight.

Tonight? That passionless brush of his mouth against her own?

Passionless for him, maybe, but *she* had certainly felt a distinct kick of sexual curiosity galvanising her body.

Don't even think about going there, Julia muttered warningly to herself, and then jumped as Nick materialised at her side and demanded huskily, 'Missed me?'

'Have you been somewhere?' Julia riposted sweetly.

'I've been too busy to notice—although I expect Lucy will be wondering where you are.'

'Well, in the morning you can tell her that I spent the night in your bed, if you want to.'

He was standing in front of her, blocking her in, having placed one hand on the column behind her.

'I've already told you, Nick, I'm not interested.'

'Of course you are. You've been acting like a bitch on heat since I dropped you for Lucy.' He was smiling at her as though the words had been a compliment and not an insult, Julia saw, and a surge of angry contempt for him mixed with compassionate pity for Lucy gathered force inside her.

'Really?' She kept her voice deliberately light. 'I must tell Silas that. He'll be delighted to learn that other men are aware of how much I want him.'

Immediately Nick removed his hand from the column behind her.

'Silas?' he demanded. 'You mean Silas is shagging you?'

'We are lovers, yes,' Julia lied firmly. How could she ever have found anything attractive in Nick? Even the way he spoke revealed his contempt for women.

'Why?'

'The usual reasons. He's sexy, and I want him, and—'

'No, I meant why should he want to shag *you*?' Nick told her brutally. 'With his money he could have anyone he wants.'

Her original distaste for Nick's comments was rapidly turning into outright loathing for Nick himself.

'The "anyone" Silas wants is me. And the only man

I want is Silas. You, Nick, are married to Lucy. She's
my friend, and—'

Julia protested in shock as Nick suddenly grabbed
hold of her upper arms and forced her back against the
column, shaking her so hard that she only just avoided
banging her head on the hard stone.

'Are you sure you don't want it? I think you do. I
think you're gagging for it. And I think I should give it
to you hot and hard, right here and now. You owe me,
Jules, and I intend to collect—one way or another.'

All of a sudden Julia didn't just feel angry and re-
pulsed, but actually afraid. There was an ugly sound to
Nick's voice, a miasma of lust and contempt somehow
emanating from him. Instinctively she fought to break
free of him as he held on to her, twisting and turning,
the fragile fabric of her dress tearing beneath his grip.
Her furious panic gave her a fierce determination not to
give in to him, even though he was hurting her. But it
was only when she kicked out at him and her heel caught
his leg, that he yelled out in pain and let her go. She
could hear him cursing her as he held his calf, and she
pushed past him and started to run towards the building
and safety, too afraid of him coming after her to turn
round to look and see if he was following her.

She was still trembling almost fifteen minutes later in
the sanctuary of the ladies' room, where she pulled off
her torn dress and re-dressed in the jeans and tee shirt
she had been wearing earlier in the day, which she had
stuffed, rolled up, into a bag she had left with the caterers.

There would be bruises on her arms in the morning
from Nick's assault on her.

Assault. The word tasted gritty and unpleasant in her

mouth, but he *had* assaulted her. Would he have raped her if she hadn't broken free and escaped from him? Julia was not a naive teenager. She knew full well that there was a sordid underbelly to the glamourous celebrity lifestyle depicted in magazines such as *A-List Life*, but this was the first time its sleaziness had actively touched her. She had spoken the truth when she had told Silas that she neither drank to excess nor took drugs. In addition, she might not be sexually innocent, but she was very firm about maintaining a professional distancing manner when she was working, and she was most certainly not promiscuous. The drink- and drug-fuelled group sex sessions of the type that featured in the lives of many of their clients, as well as in the more down-market tabloids, held absolutely no appeal for her.

But she had not been aware of how dangerous Nick was. He was taking her refusal to have sex with him far more personally than she had expected, treating it as though it were a personal strike against him he had to avenge. Shuddering a little as she remembered the horrible way he had spoken to her, and how frightened he had made her feel, Julia bundled her torn dress into the bag that had held her jeans and top. Suddenly Silas's constant presence for the rest of the summer felt more comforting than burdensome. Not, of course, that she would ever tell Silas himself as much.

Along with Lucy and Nick, as well as the catering staff and virtually everyone else who had accompanied them to Majorca, Julia was staying at a small budget-priced hotel in one of the main holiday resorts. She had planned to get a lift back to the hotel with Lucy and Nick but now she knew that nothing would persuade her to do so. Instead she would have to blag a lift with one of the contractors.

'Jules, have you seen Nick anywhere?'

She tensed as she heard the anxiety in Lucy's voice as she came hurrying toward her.

'Not recently,' she answered truthfully.

'He might still be with Alexina Matalos, then,' Lucy sighed. 'She wants us to quote for her husband's fiftieth birthday party. Oh, and Silas was looking for you. I'm so pleased about the two of you.'

'Not as pleased as I am,' said a deep voice.

'Oh, Silas, good. You've found her.' Lucy laughed as he materialised beside them out of the darkness.

'What happened to the dress?' he asked Julia as he smiled in acknowledgment of Lucy's statement.

'I changed it. Jeans are more practical for putting out candles than chiffon.'

'How much longer will it be before you've finished here?'

'I'm virtually done, but there's no need for you to hang around waiting for me, Si...*darling*,' she emphasised, conscious that Lucy was listening to them.

'How are you planning to get back to the hotel?' he asked, ignoring her hint.

'Oh, I'll get a lift with one of the contractors,' Julia told him airily.

'Fine. I'll come with you.'

With her?

She knew they were supposed to be an item, but surely that was taking things too far? Especially when he would then have to make his way back to wherever it was he was staying, which she presumed must be the same ultra-exclusive boutique hotel in Palma as Dorland.

'Well, now that you two have made contact with one another, I'd better go and find Nick,' Lucy announced.

'There's really no need for you to come back to the hotel with me,' Julia repeated as soon as Lucy had gone.

'Julia, we're going now, if you're coming,' one of the contractors called out.

'Can you fit both of us in?' Silas asked him.

'Sure.'

Silas's hand was splayed across the small of her back, urging her forward.

It was funny how, though Silas's hand held far more hard strength than Nick's, she somehow wanted to relax into his touch rather than shrink back from it. That might be funny, but what was definitely not was the discovery that, instead of moving forward, she really wanted to turn sideways instead, and move closer to Silas.

Why? she derided herself, deliberately trying to whip up awareness of her own foolishness. So that she could get another look at his mouth? Another taste of his mouth? But her body's reaction, far from being an appropriate recognition of her folly, was a wilful misunderstanding of the message she was sending it. It, it seemed, would very much like another taste of Silas.

When had she become the kind of woman who actively liked courting danger?

CHAPTER THREE

'*HOLA*, SEÑOR.' The receptionist beamed up at Silas from behind the desk. 'Here is your key.'

His key? Julia stared at him.

'You aren't staying here?'

Silas was a 'five-star hotel and nothing less' man. No—correction. Silas was a 'private villa and his own personal space' man who, she was pretty sure, had never stayed at a three-star hotel in his life.

'I've booked us a suite and asked them to move your stuff to it from your room. That way Blayne won't be under any misapprehensions about us or our relationship.'

A suite? Us? Their relationship?

'Something wrong?' Silas asked her.

'Do you really need to ask?' Julia challenged him as soon as she had got enough breath back to speak. 'Silas, no way am I going to sleep with you.'

'*Sleep* with me?'

'You know what I mean,' Julia told him crossly.

'We'll discuss it in our suite, shall we?' Silas suggested in a gentle voice that felt like a very thin covering over very hard steel as it fell against her frazzled nerve-endings. 'Unless, of course, you feel that having the hotel staff witness a potential quarrel between us is going to add reality to our relationship?'

Since he was already standing next to her, bending towards her in a way that no doubt looked sensually lover-like to their audience but, Julia nastily decided, was just another example of the dictatorial side of his nature she had always disliked, she didn't have much choice other than to allow him to propel her towards the rackety lift.

'I suppose this wretched suite is on the top floor,' she complained as the lift started to lurch upwards.

'Since Señora Bonita has assured me that it is possible to see the sea from its windows, I imagine that it must be,' Silas concurred, so straight-faced that Julia had to look at him very carefully to catch the smallest of small betraying quivers lifting the corners of his mouth.

'And you believed her? The sea is miles away.'

'No doubt the *señora* assumes we will be far too busy gazing at one another to concern ourselves over her enthusiastic laundering of reality.'

'This lift takes for ever, and I'm not even sure that it's safe,' Julia complained. For some reason she wasn't prepared to explain, even to herself, it seemed a very good idea to keep her gaze concentrated on the lift door and not on Silas.

'"A long, slow ride to heaven" was how the *señora* poetically described it to me.'

Forgetting her determination not to look at him, Julia turned round and accused him, 'You're making that up.'

Silas gave a small shrug.

'Silas, why are you doing this?' Julia demanded, then her eyes widened as the lift suddenly shuddered theatrically and then dropped slightly, throwing her off balance and against Silas.

Immediately his arms went round her to steady her, and equally immediately he released her and moved back from her.

'Something wrong?'

Julia glared at him. What was he trying to imply?

'This lift isn't safe,' she told him.

Silas watched the emotions chase one another across her face. She had always had the most expressive eyes, and they were telling him quite plainly now exactly what she thought. Fortunately, he was rather more adept at guarding his own expression, otherwise she would have been able to read equally clearly in his eyes exactly what he had really wanted to do when he'd had her in his arms.

Her grandfather's gruff comment to him that he was worried about her had brought him here to Majorca, but ironically it was thanks to Nick Blayne that he was at last able to manoeuvre himself into a position of intimacy with her. Even if that intimacy was, for the moment, merely fictitious.

'Silas, you can't possibly really intend to marry Julia,' his mother had protested unhappily the night they had both attended Julia's eighteenth birthday.

'I take it you don't approve?' Silas had challenged her.

'Do you love her?' his mother had demanded, equally sharply.

'Sexual love is little more than an emotional virus, and in my opinion should not be used as the basis on which to build a relationship. I have thought for some time that Julia would be the perfect wife for me—once she has matured.'

'Silas…'

'I've made up my mind. After all, who could possibly be a better wife for me? She knows exactly what her duties would be once I inherit, both as a countess and as the mistress of Amberley. It will make the old boy happy—and tidy up a lot of loose ends. From a practical point of view, a marriage between us makes good sense.

She's too young at the moment, of course. But I don't want to leave it too long.'

'Good sense? Silas, you're talking about marriage as though it's a...a business deal.'

'No, Mother, I'm merely being practical. As well as my responsibilities to Amberley, I've got to think of the Foundation as well. I don't want a wife who is going to change her mind and demand a huge divorce settlement. Julia has been born into a tradition of arranged marriages that goes way, way back. She understands these things.'

'Does she? My money is on her refusing you, Silas. Julia is a very feisty and passionate young woman. And an arranged marriage—that is so archaic!'

'They worked very well for hundreds of years, and they kept families and property together.'

His mother had sighed faintly and told him grimly, 'Sometimes you sound more like those dry dusty trustees you inherited from your father than a young man in his twenties. Don't you care that you will be depriving Julia as well as yourself of sharing your lives with someone you love?'

'Mother, love is merely an illusion—a delusion, in fact. A marriage built on mutual understanding and shared goals is far more practical, and far more likely to survive.'

'I doubt that Julia will agree with you. Look at her!' his mother had demanded, and dutifully Silas had looked across at the short spiky brown- and pink-striped head that had been all he could see of her over her dance partner's shoulder.

'Helen said that she came back from school with her belly button pierced and talking about having a tattoo— the family coat of arms, if you please.'

That had been the year Julia had fallen passionately

in love with the leader of a local animal rights group, Silas remembered. The love affair might have been short-lived, but the results of it were still very much in evidence. The group, led by Julia, had defied her grandfather's gamekeeper and 'rescued' the young pheasants he had been rearing, with the result that one could not travel within ten miles of Amberley now without encountering wandering cock pheasants.

It was also this relationship that had been responsible for the five engaging greyhounds Julia had 'rescued' and brought home and who now lived a life of luxury, having won her grandfather's heart via their shared misery at winter rheumatism and their love of a good whisky before bed.

Julia wasn't eighteen any more, though. And Silas had decided that it was time to put his plan into action. Julia's grandfather was growing frail, and Silas was very fond of him. It would mean a great deal to him to see his granddaughter married to his heir, Silas knew. Like him, the old Earl was also a very practical man—and what could be more practical than for his heir to marry his granddaughter, tying together the two remaining strands of the family and securing the future of Amberley at the same time?

It was very fortuitous that fate had decided to weigh in on his side and assist him in bringing his plans to fruition. Not that Silas considered that he needed to have fate on his side. He was perfectly capable of constructing his own good fortune.

The lift had finally stopped its sawing motion. Julia got out with relief, not sure whether to be appalled or triumphant when she realised that the 'penthouse suite' was actually in the rafters of the house, and that the tiny window in the corridor beside the lift was so low that an adult would have to kneel down in order to be able to look out of it.

She watched whilst Silas inserted the key into the lock of the heavy-looking door, and then opened it.

The room that lay beyond it was furnished as a sitting room, its double doors open to reveal the bedroom that lay beyond it. And a *huge* bed.

'Apparently there are two bathrooms,' she heard Silas informing her. 'And the sofa in the sitting room area converts to a double bed.'

'In case we want a foursome?' Julia couldn't resist saying lightly.

There was a cold steeliness in the look Silas lanced in her direction.

'The only kind of bed-sharing foursome I find acceptable is the non-sexual variety with a couple and their two children. And if Blayne's been dragging you down into that kind of gutter—'

Julia's face burned.

'It was just a joke, that's all. I didn't mean anything… I suppose you're expecting me to sleep on the sofa bed?'

'No. You can take the bed. After all, I'm not the one who has the problem waking up in the morning, am I?'

It was true that she was more of an owl than a lark, Julia knew, and it was also typical of Silas that he wouldn't have forgotten that as a teenager she had preferred to sleep late in the mornings—especially when she was on holiday.

'Which side of the bed do you prefer to sleep on?'

Julia gave him a suspicious look. 'If I've got the bed to myself it doesn't matter, does it?'

Silas exhaled slowly and warningly.

'Julia, it would help us both if you were able to refrain from looking for a sexual connotation in everything I say. My question about which side of the bed you prefer was provoked quite simply by a desire to know which of the two bathrooms it would make sense for you to use. That is to say, if you sleep on the left-hand side of the bed then, should you need the bathroom during the night, you would probably automatically use the one on the left. On the other hand—'

'All right, Professor, I get the picture.' Julia stopped him crossly. 'Why on earth couldn't you just say that, Silas?'

'Why couldn't you simply answer my question?'

'This is never going to work,' Julia told him, raking her hand impatiently through her hair.

'It certainly won't work if you don't want it to,' Silas agreed succinctly. 'If we want it to work then it's up to us both to make sure that it does.'

She certainly didn't want another run-in with Nick like the one she had had earlier in the evening, But his behaviour towards her had set her wondering just how he treated Lucy, and if in helping to preserve her marriage she was truly doing her friend a favour.

'There's no way I want to be the cause of Lucy being hurt,' she agreed. 'But if she's unhappy in the marriage too, then—'

'Has she told you that she's unhappy, or are you relying on Blayne for that piece of information?'

'I haven't discussed her marriage with Lucy, but—'

'But you have discussed it with her husband?' Silas pointed out coolly.

Julia slanted him a sideways and slightly wary glance. He was angry with her now; she could tell that just from the way in which his voice had hardened.

'This isn't the eighteen hundreds, Silas, when a

woman couldn't speak to a friend's husband or have male friends.'

'It isn't your friendship that Blayne wants, though, is it?'

She was tired, and a small dull ache at the back of her eyes was steadily becoming an insistent stabbing pain. All she wanted to do was to have a bath and go to bed, not stand here arguing with Silas.

'Why don't you climb down off your moral high horse?' she suggested grittily. 'After all, you aren't in this just out of altruism, are you?'

'What do you mean?'

He went so still so quickly, like a hunter suddenly on the watch, that her own body tensed as well.

'I mean that aside from wanting to protect Gramps, there has to be something else in this for you.'

'Such as?'

'This woman you no longer want, for instance? The one you were happy to take to bed but don't want to get seriously involved with?'

'Like Blayne with you, you mean?'

He had relaxed again now, but he was still firing those poisoned darts, with deadly accuracy. Well, she could fire a few of her own.

Giving a small shrug, she told him, 'If you want to put yourself in the same category as Nick, then go ahead.'

She had known, of course, that he wouldn't like her comment, but she hadn't correctly calculated just how much.

When he took a step towards her she found that she was automatically stepping back, and, even more betrayingly, wrapping her arms around herself, her hands on her bruised flesh as though to protect it from further assault.

There was a look now in his eyes that she could not interpret—at least not with her brain. Her emotions were reacting to it with a sudden rush of hot miserable tears that burned the backs of her eyes.

'I can't understand what on earth you're even doing here in Majorca,' she burst out, exhausted. 'I suppose it must be something to do with the Foundation?'

There was the smallest of pauses before Silas agreed quietly, 'Yes.'

'Another acquisition, I suppose?' She was just too tired to argue now.

'In a manner of speaking. Although this one is very special…unique, in fact.'

'And worth the trouble this fake relationship with me is going to cause?' Julia asked him wryly.

'Well worth it,' Silas confirmed softly, before continuing, 'Now, which side of the bed?'

'The left. No, the right… I really don't mind. Which side do you prefer?' Julia asked him, and then went bright red. 'No, I didn't mean that. What I meant was, which *bathroom* would you prefer…?'

When he continued to look at her, she bit her lip, and then told him huskily, 'I can imagine what you're thinking, but I don't want to have sex with you, Silas.'

Just the lazy way in which he raised one eyebrow was enough to up her heart-rate.

'I wasn't aware that I had invited you to. But, if I had, why would you want to refuse me?'

'Why?' Julia took a deep breath and gave him an outraged look. 'Isn't it obvious? We don't mean anything to one another—we don't even like one another, never mind lust after each other. And even if we did… Well, it would just be too... Sex carries implications and...and responsibilities. And it's...' She was beginning to flounder and she knew it.

Before she could sink any further, Silas told her, 'You know, Jules, you are beginning to sound more and more like an anguished outdated virgin than the sexually experienced modern young woman I know you to be.'

'Well, I'm not,' she told him flatly. 'Not a virgin, I mean.'

'So why all the fuss and panic?'

Why indeed? She could hardly answer that question for herself without having to face certain previously unrecognised realities, never mind admit them to Silas.

Instead it was far easier and safer to take refuge in insouciance and say, as light-heartedly as she could manage, 'Maybe I was worried that my experience wouldn't match up to your own well-documented expertise. After all, that supermarket chain heiress you dated made it quite plain that she thought you were a real stud...and put that video of the two of you having sex on her website to prove it.'

'You watched it?'

'No! But I read about it in the papers.'

'That was three years ago, and since you never actually saw a face the man in the video could have been anyone. Still, I'm surprised by your attitude. I should have thought you'd have welcomed the opportunity to enjoy my so-called expertise and learn from it.'

Now what was she supposed to say?

Yes, please?

'Actually, we do have a client who runs, amongst other things, ''Learn to love your orgasm'' classes,' she told him truthfully.

'Learn to *what*?'

'You heard me. ''Learn to love your orgasm'' classes. I suppose it means that you…you know…learn to feel comfortable about…erm… not being in control…'

'A sort of sexual female primal scream,' Silas offered, not quite straight-faced.

'It isn't funny,' Julia protested, but the giggles were already rising in her own throat and within seconds she was helpless with laughter herself.

That was the thing about Silas, she acknowledged later, as she luxuriated in a wonderfully deep bath, full of blissfully hot water, safe in the knowledge that the door to her bathroom was firmly locked. No matter how much he infuriated her, somehow he always had the knack of being able to make her laugh. She and Silas definitely shared a similar sense of humour.

Unlike Nick. Nick had never made her laugh. Nick's sense of humour involved being cruelly unkind to and about others.

Nick.

She looked at her upper arms where the flesh was already beginning to show the bruise marks he had left there.

CHAPTER FOUR

JULIA stretched luxuriously beneath the bedclothes. She could smell coffee and she could hear voices. One of them a familiar voice. Silas's voice, she recognised, at virtually the same second as she realised *why* she was hearing it.

She opened her eyes and stared towards the now open double doors that led from the bedroom to the sitting room.

'Are you awake yet, sleepyhead?'

Silas himself appeared in the doorway, his legs bare beneath the hem of the robe he was wearing. He was holding a cup of coffee. Her mouth started to water. Coffee. She could live quite happily on a combination of caffeine and the buzz she got from her shoe habit. And this morning she was going to indulge that habit, having spent all week being tormented with longing for those impossible-to-resist little darlings she had heard about the day she had arrived.

'If you're waiting to shower and get dressed, don't let me stop you,' she informed Silas pointedly.

'I'd forgotten how grumpy you are when you wake up. Come and have a look at this view.'

And *she'd* forgotten how relentlessly and unnecessarily cheerful *he* was, Julia decided antagonistically.

'Shouldn't you put some clothes on?' she suggested.

'What for?'

What for? For her peace of mind, that was what! There was something seriously disturbing about having

50

to cope with Silas wandering around in a bathrobe that was both too short and too small, so that it exposed a large amount of tanned, hair-roughened chest, in addition to somehow making it plain that those thighs it was just about covering were hugely powerful and very male. And surely he could have tied the belt a bit more securely, and put something on his feet. There was something distinctly sexual about a man's bare feet. In fact there was something distinctly sexual about Silas this morning, full-stop.

That familiar frisson of sensation she was feeling right now, which she had always previously put down to healthy antagonism, had somehow astonishingly morphed into a staggeringly acute sexual awareness of him. Beneath the bedclothes her nipples peaked with delight, ready and willing to show him the effect he was having on them, whilst the tension gripping her lower body made her wonder hollowly if she was on the point of losing her sanity.

How could she be lusting after Silas? She knew it had been a long time since she had last had sex, and it was true that she couldn't even remember the last time she had woken up to find a semi-naked man wandering around, but this semi-naked man was *Silas*, for heaven's sake. Silas, who had laughed out loud the first time he had seen her dressed up to go out on a date. Silas, who had threatened to 'beat her butt black and blue' when she had given the pheasants their freedom. Silas, who had threatened even worse violence to her person when he had found two of the greyhounds playing tug-of-war with his favourite Brooks Brothers shirt.

'I thought you'd prefer to have breakfast up here. So I've ordered you some coffee and juice, and I remembered that you like your eggs over easy.'

Coffee. Caffeine. That was what was wrong, Julia told herself feverishly. She was in caffeine shock. She had heard it could do weird things to you, but she hadn't realised just how weird.

'Are you sure you're wearing the right bathrobe?' she demanded. 'Only it doesn't seem to be your size.'

'Well, if you end up tripping over the hem of yours we'll have to swap. But until you get out of that bed we aren't going to know, are we?'

'I can't get out of bed with you standing there.'

'You can't? Why not? Worried about the effect the Mickey Mouse PJs might have on me?'

'That was when I was ten,' Julia told him awfully.

'So was the teddy bear hot water bottle, but last time I visited the old guy there it was, hanging up along with the others.'

Muttering at him, Julia mentally cursed herself for getting into bed naked in the first place. It would serve Silas right if she just clean got out of bed starkers. Mickey Mouse PJs indeed. Huh. That would show him.

After all, it wasn't as though no man had ever seen her naked. Several had, even if right now she could not remember ever having felt this hot-shot tingle of fizzing, trepidation-coated excitement before.

'Your eggs will be cold,' Silas warned her.

That was all he knew, Julia decided feverishly. Right now her 'eggs' were feeling pretty hot, and ready for the kind of action that led to one and one becoming three. Or maybe even four, if they had twins. She had always thought twins must be fun...

She gave a small yelp of protest against her own thoughts and hurriedly got out of bed, forgetting her nudity in her eagerness to escape from the images inside her head of two adorable dark-haired babies with Silas's ice-blue eyes.

'What happened to the tattoo?'

She was very careful not to turn round, but instead to look back over her shoulder as she stood sheltering behind the half-open bathroom door.

'What tattoo?'

'The family coat of arms. Mother said you'd had it tattooed across your butt.'

'I did—for a dare. But it wasn't permanent. Anything else you want to know?'

'No, not right now. I guess it tells a guy quite a bit about a woman when he can see that she doesn't sunbathe in the nude.'

'Haven't you heard of sun damage?' Julia retorted smartly. 'If I want an all-over tan I have it sprayed on.'

'Take it from me, the cute white triangles are much more of a turn-on. Any guy would feel good knowing he was getting to see something the world at large hadn't had access to. I'd forgotten how small you are without those ridiculous shoes you insist on wearing.'

'Small?' Julia stepped angrily towards him and then shot back, her face pink. 'I'm five foot five.'

'Like I said, I'd forgotten how small you are,' Silas drawled.

'Well, I haven't forgotten what an arrogant, know-it-all you are,' Julia snapped back at him crossly, before disappearing into her bathroom and firmly closing the door.

To her own disgust she was actually trembling slightly, with a mixture of rage and emotional frustration. How could she have forgotten just how much and how easily Silas had always managed to infuriate her, with that lordly belief of his that everything he said and did was both superior and right?

What must it be like to be so impervious and invulnerable? The problem with Silas was that he had never suffered. But whilst wealth and position had protected him from financial hardship and the rigours of modern-day life, it was surely his nature that had ensured he was impervious to emotional vulnerability and self-doubt. No one had ever successfully challenged his beliefs or made him question them. No one had ever made him doubt himself or what motivated him. Even that wise gentleman her grandfather treated him with respect and deference.

But she wasn't going to do so! What she wouldn't give to be around on the day when Silas discovered what it felt like to be human and hurt, Julia decided savagely as she showered and dried.

She pulled on her own waiting bathrobe, which of course was not oversized and meant for a man, but instead exactly the same as the one Silas was wearing.

Of course it was oversized on her, but the fact that it wrapped round her with fabric to spare and reached the floor was not, in her present mood, a disadvantage.

She found Silas standing beside the open windows of the sitting room, drinking his coffee.

'There's a balcony out there, but I'm not sure how safe it is,' he warned her. 'Want some coffee?'

'I'll pour my own, thanks,' Julia told him sharply.

'I'd eat your eggs first.'

'I don't eat eggs any more.'

It wasn't the truth, but it was well worth depriving herself of them to have the joy of rejecting his authority.

But of course Silas wasn't so easily outmaneuvered.

'No wonder you look thin,' he told her disparagingly.

'I am not thin!'

'What's on the agenda for today?'

'Nothing much, really. The Famous Couple and their people are flying out this afternoon, and presumably, Dorland will be going to see them off safely. But we aren't involved in that. Lucy and Nick are due to return to England tonight, and, like I said, I'm booked on a flight for Naples.'

'So that leaves you with a free morning?'

Julia hesitated. She had no intention of handing Silas the opportunity to further deride her by informing him that she intended to spend her free morning indulging in her shoe habit. Why should she, when even her closest friends shook their heads over it so much that secretly she did sometimes feel guilty?

'Not exactly. I've got a few errands to run, some laundry to collect, and I want to go to the bank—that kind of thing.'

'Fine. I'll come with you. It will give me an opportunity to look round the old part of the town.'

'No! I mean, there's no need for you to come with me. You'd only be bored. I've got some paperwork to catch up on as well, and some phone calls to make.'

'I see.'

Did she really think that he couldn't work out that she was planning to see Blayne? Silas wondered cynically.

If it hadn't been for the fact that he knew the other man was flying back to the UK later in the day, whilst *he* was accompanying Julia to Italy, he might have been inclined to do something about it, but he could see no sense in pushing her into doing something stupid like running off with Blayne.

It was a pity that she hadn't remained at Amberley after leaving school, riding her horse, doing good works and keeping her grandfather company while she matured enough for him to marry her. He had not been too concerned about her involvement with Prêt a Party because it had freed up time he was able to put to good use in focusing on streamlining the operation of the Foundation.

Now, however, things were different. Now he was ready to put into operation his decision to make her his wife. She was, after all, in so many ways the perfect wife for him. They shared a common history, but their blood tie was not too close. She had virtually been brought up at Amberley, as had her mother, and would have no problem fitting in or running it. Julia, via her family history, understood the duties of a marriage such as theirs. Her grandfather would naturally approve of their union, and, whilst there was no obligation on him to submit his marriage for the older man's approval, life would be easier all round if he did approve of the woman who would one day run his beloved home.

Not that Silas had any intention of basing himself permanently at Amberley. He was an American, after all, with responsibilities and duties to fulfil to the Foundation established by his own grandfather. Julia, he felt sure, would make an admirable wife in that respect, especially with his formidable mother to guide her. Their children—and there would be children—would grow up in a secure emotional environment, because there would be no divorce. He had already decided that after the birth of their first child he would commission Julia's portrait, with her wearing the Maharajah's gift, just like her ancestor.

Naturally, Silas was aware that many people—Julia included—would not appreciate his unemotional and practical view on marriage, but a man who was responsible for ensuring that billions of dollars and an earldom were passed intact down through the generations could not afford the folly of being governed by his emotions.

But now, like a small flaw in the middle of an otherwise perfect diamond, there was Nick Blayne. It was Silas's belief that a person made his own luck, but he was forced to admit that it had been a bonus in his favour to be in a position to drive a wedge between Nick and Julia and at the same time take advantage of Julia's loyalty to her friend by proposing their own fake relationship.

He certainly wasn't prepared to have all his plans disrupted by the inconvenience of Julia getting involved in a messy divorce.

He wasn't going to press the issue now, though. Blayne would be going back to London with his wife, whilst he intended to make sure that when Julia returned to the UK it would be in order to prepare for their marriage. And he had from now until the end of the year to achieve his goal.

True, there was the irksome and irritating problem of a certain spoiled American heiress who was declaring to anyone who would listen to her, without any encouragement from him, that she was passionately in love with him. It was no secret in old money New York society that there was more than a suspicion of mental instability in her family tree, but Silas had grown impatient of her dramatic and over-emotional behaviour. It wasn't even as though he had actually dated her—although she seemed to think that the fact that she continually stalked him, turning up uninvited at events she knew he was attending, constituted some kind of relationship. If she had known the first thing about him she would have known that she was wasting her time, and that by sending him a video of herself having sex with two well-endowed musclemen would not tempt him to fall in love with her, as she had repeatedly insisted she knew he would. Silas had no intention of doing anything so impractical as falling in love with anyone.

Still, a beneficial side effect of the announcement of his engagement to Julia was that it would, thankfully, bring Aimee to her senses—or at least what senses she possessed, Silas decided unkindly.

She had managed to leave the hotel without anyone stopping her to ask where she was going, and Julia could feel her heart starting to beat that familiar little bit faster as she turned into the alleyway that led to the shoe shop.

She stopped guiltily to look back over her shoulder. Of course she should feel ashamed of herself, and no doubt she would later, but right now all she could think of were the shoes. And there they were, in the window, with their darling high delicate heels, and the kind of low-cut front that she knew would show just the right amount of toe cleavage.

She could stand here all day and look at them. But if she did that someone else might buy them, and she couldn't bear that. Hurriedly she pushed open the shop door.

Over an hour later she left the shop, clutching two carrier bags, her face flushed and pink with happiness and her eyes shining. It had been so impossible to choose between the two pairs of shoes she had fallen for that in the end she had decided she had to have both. They had been just too beautiful to resist.

*   *   *

'No Nick, Lucy?' Silas enquired, putting down the newspaper he had been reading as Lucy walked into the pleasantly shaded patio area at the back of the hotel.

'No, he had to go into town to attend to a few things. He must have his mobile switched off as well, because I've just tried to ring him.'

Her innocent statement confirmed his own suspicions, and it was on the tip of Silas's tongue to suggest cynically that she try Julia's instead.

'I hope he gets back soon. Dorland has just been on the telephone to say that there's a big panic on at the villa. Apparently, the Tiffany necklace has gone missing.'

'Don't tell me he's surprised?'

When Lucy looked puzzled, Silas explained, 'Martina is known for her acquisitive nature, and it won't be the first time she's held on to a piece of loaned jewellery and refused to hand it back.'

'But Dorland will have to pay Tiffany for it. Because they loaned it to *him*,' Lucy protested, looking shocked.

'I doubt the odd million or so would make much of a dent in Dorland's bank account, and in fact I wouldn't be surprised if the whole thing wasn't some kind of publicity stunt. My guess is that Dorland will have informed the media first, and not the police.'

'Silas, you are far too cynical,' Lucy told him gently.

'It isn't cynicism, it's common sense,' Silas corrected her, glancing at his watch and then putting down his paper. 'Julia went into town earlier—she should be on her way back by now. I think I'll take a walk and see if I can spot her.'

'Julia's gone in to town?' Lucy's forehead crinkled into a small frown. 'Oh, I thought she said last night that she intended to spend the morning with you?'

'She'd probably forgotten then about the laundry she had to pick up.'

It wasn't his business to protect Lucy Blayne's feelings, Silas reminded himself, but the poor girl was so obviously vulnerable—and besides, it wouldn't serve his purpose to create suspicion and mistrust between Julia and her best friend.

She really didn't know which pair of shoes were her favourite, Julia mused dreamily as she sauntered back to the hotel. True, the pair she had seen in the shop window had been her first love, and she had had to have them, but then the assistant had shown her the other pair, and a pang of such acute longing had gripped her that she had just not been able to choose between them. Thank heavens she had had the good sense to buy both pairs.

'Hello, Jules.'

She came to an abrupt and wary halt as the alleyway opened up into a small square and Nick materialised in front of her. The square was quiet and empty, apart from two old men sitting outside a small café, both of whom looked as though they were asleep.

'I'm just on my way back to the hotel,' Julia announced, trying to assure herself that if she acted as though Nick's aggressive attack on her had not actually taken place then somehow that would require him to behave decently.

'Well, well,' Nick murmured. 'Look who's here.'

Julia gave a small gasp of dismay as she looked across the square and saw Silas walking purposefully towards them.

'Let's see how he likes looking at this, shall we?'

Before she could stop him Nick had pushed her back

against the wall and was kissing her with mock passion, as she fought to break free of him.

He didn't release her until Silas's shadow was falling across her face, and kept his back to Silas before he turned to saunter triumphantly away, so that only she could see the cruel satisfaction in his eyes.

'It wasn't like it seemed—' she began shakily, as Silas stood in front of her, blotting out the warmth of the sun so that she felt so chilled she actually started to shiver.

'Do you remember what I threatened to do when you set those wretched pheasants free?' Silas asked her, almost gently.

Julia was not deceived; she had heard that dulcet note in his voice before and knew exactly what it meant.

'Yes, you said if I ever did anything like that again I'd feel the flat of your hand on my butt, good and hard. You couldn't get away with threatening me like that now. It's illegal to smack a child.'

'But you aren't a child; you are an adult—even if you don't seem to possess the ability to reason like one. And right now the best way, in fact the only way I can think of letting you know how furious you have made me, would be for me to apply the weight of my hand to that pretty little *derrière* of yours, until it blushes pink with shame for you.

'Can't you see what you're doing? You said that you didn't want to hurt Lucy, and yet you lied to me and to her so that you could sneak out and meet up with her husband. What if she had been the one to see Blayne pushing you against that wall as though he were about to take you right there and then?'

There was no gentleness left in his voice now, and Julia quailed beneath the savage lash of its anger.

She was no weak-willed pushover, though, to be

treated like a child and threatened with the kind of humiliation Silas had just described.

'I did not sneak out to meet Nick! I'd only just bumped into him. He kissed me like that deliberately, because he had seen you. He's angry because I've told him I won't sleep with him, and now he wants to hurt me and get at you as well!'

Her voice was trembling slightly with both indignation at Silas's accusation and reaction to her own mental image of his open palm, spanking teasingly and sexily down on her bare behind whilst she tried to squirm free. She couldn't help feeling a little bit turned on both by the image and her own reaction to it. There was something definitely rather naughtily delicious about the thought of such teasing love-play. Not that she was into anything as potentially painful as true S and M, but a little gentle game of forfeits with the kind of 'punishment' that would involve her partner indulging in some pretend bottom-spanking could be fun if she was in the right mood. And with the right man... A man like Silas?

Julia could feel herself starting to blush a little at the inner excitement caused by her own thoughts, but Silas soon brought her back to reality, insisting, 'You claim you met Blayne by chance, and yet it was obvious to me this morning, when you said you intended to go into town, that you were hiding something.'

'But it wasn't a secret meeting with Nick,' Julia protested.

'Then what was it?' Silas challenged her.

Julia looked down at the bags Nick had made her drop.

'Shoes,' she muttered guiltily.

'Shoes?'

Silas looked from the carrier bags to her flushed face and then back again.

'You didn't want me to know you intended to buy *shoes*?' he questioned, bemused.

Julia could only shake her head. If Silas didn't know about her shoe addiction then she certainly wasn't going to expose herself to his mockery by telling him.

'Come on, we'd better get back to the hotel,' he announced, reaching down to pick up her bags.

Immediately Julia tried to stop him, not wanting to allow her precious purchases out of her own control.

'Julia, I'll carry them for you,' Silas insisted, taking hold of her arm to hold her back so that he could pick them up, but he was gripping her arm exactly where Nick had bruised it the previous evening, and Julia couldn't stop herself from giving a small, agonised gasp of pain.

'What…?'

The sleeves of her tee shirt just about covered the bruise marks—or at least they did until Silas pushed one of them up to reveal them.

'Who did this?' he demanded quietly.

Julia didn't even think of trying to lie.

'Nick,' she told him shakily. 'Last night. He was furious when I told him about you…'

'So he did this to you?'

The surge of angry protectiveness that gripped him caught him off guard. Of course no man should hurt a woman, but he was not used to experiencing such intense or possessive emotions.

He looked across the square in the direction Nick had taken.

Julia put a restraining hand on his arm. 'I don't think he meant to hurt me, Silas.'

'But he did. Your arms are black and blue—'

Julia started to laugh.

'What's so funny?' Silas demanded.

Mischievously, Julia reminded him, 'As my bottom deserved to be, according to you.'

Silas looked at her. Her lips were parted and her face was flushed. There was a look in her eyes that told him...

He put down the carriers and said softly, 'Something tells me that you find the prospect of a little spanking rather erotic.'

Julia laughed and looked away demurely. 'You're the one who keeps threatening to punish me,' she told him breathlessly.

Heavens, she couldn't really be flirting like this with *Silas*, could she?

'Mmm, but you're the one who keeps reminding me that I haven't carried out my threat as yet,' Silas murmured. 'And the one who keeps on provoking me...'

'Provoking you?'

'You certainly provoked me this morning, with that cute, peachy little butt of yours.'

Now it wasn't just her flirting with Silas. He was flirting right back. And the heady excitement of what they were doing was irresistible.

'You said I was thin,' Julia pouted.

'I guess maybe I didn't make a close enough appraisal.'

He was actually moving closer to her and reaching behind her, and—oh, lordy—he was sliding his hand right down her back and cupping—no, caressing—one firm buttock. Helplessly Julia leaned into him, even her shoes forgotten.

This was definitely *not* part of his game plan, Silas

recognised as he looked down at her closed eyes and parted lips. He wanted his—their—kids to be conceived after they were married, not before.

He bent his head and kissed her briefly, ignoring the look of disappointment in her eyes when she opened them as he released her.

'We'd better get back. I saw Lucy at the hotel, and apparently Dorland's in a sweat because the necklace he had on loan from Tiffany has gone missing.'

'Oh, no! Poor Dorland. Maybe they'll have found it by now,' Julia suggested, as Silas picked up her bags. 'Stuff like that happens all the time. These big stars have such a huge retinue that no one ever seems to know what anyone else is doing. One of the PRs has probably put the necklace somewhere safe.'

She was growing more sexually attracted to Silas by the hour, Julia admitted to herself—or had the attraction always been there without her wanting to recognise it?

'Oh, there you are. Nick's gone over to the villa to see if he can be of any help to Dorland,' Lucy began as they walked into the hotel, only to look accusingly at Julia's carrier bags before exclaiming, 'Jules—not more shoes!'

'I had to have them.'

'How often have I heard that before? You do realise, I hope, Silas, that Jules has a very serious shoe habit?'

'Lucy, wait until you see them. They've got the perfect toe cleavage shape,' Julia burst out enthusiastically. 'And the heels—they had one pair with the cutest little kittens, and another with serious stilettos...and...'

'You had to buy them both!'

Julia hung her head.

'No wonder you snuck out this morning without telling me where you were going,' Lucy accused her.

'You're going to have to find a way of restraining her, Silas,' Lucy warned him, mock seriously.

'Yes, I think I am,' Silas agreed gravely, but when Julia looked across at him the wicked glint in his eyes told her that the kind of restraint *he* was envisaging, had nothing whatsoever to do with preventing her from buying shoes.

What in the world was happening to her? She didn't really know—but she certainly knew what she would like to happen, Julia admitted ruefully as she looked discreetly but very interestedly at the tell tale bulge that no amount of expensive tailoring could completely hide.

Sex with Silas. Mmm…

'Jules, will you please stop looking at Silas like that? You're embarrassing me.' Lucy laughed.

'So, tell me some more about this shoe fetish thing you've got.'

It was after lunch and Lucy and Nick had gone upstairs to pack, and Julia and Silas were still sitting outside, finishing the bottle of wine Silas had bought to go with the alfresco lunch they had eaten in the small hotel courtyard.

'It isn't a fetish. It's just that I can't help wanting to buy shoes.'

'Uh-huh. And toe cleavage? What exactly is that?'

Honestly—men. They didn't know anything! Julia shook her head and explained in a kind voice, 'It's when the front of your shoe shows a bit of your toes, and it's seriously sexy.'

'Show me?'

'I can't—not properly anyway—because I'm not wearing the right kind of shoes,' Julia told him. 'You'll see what I mean when I wear them.'

'I can't wait.'

'I'd better go up and pack. We need to leave for the airport for our flight to Naples at five.' Would he offer to come with her? And if he did...

'I've got a few phone calls to make.'

Julia tried not to feel disappointed.

'And, by the way, I've cancelled your booking at that guest house and booked us both into the Hotel Arcadia instead.'

'The Arcadia? But that's the most exclusive hotel in Positano. It costs the earth to stay there, and Lucy—'

'Stop panicking. Naturally I shall be paying the bill. Did Lucy say that Dorland was going to come over?'

'Yes. About three.'

Upstairs in the suite, Julia packed quickly and efficiently—leaving plenty of room for her new shoes. Her normal travelling work 'uniform' consisted of her current favourite pair of jeans, (her love affair with jeans came a close second to her shoe addiction—Julia was simply not what she called a 'suit and two veg' fan), several tee shirts and strappy tops, a swimsuit just in case she got the chance to have a lazy day, and a long, sleek, very plain jersey dress that rolled up into a ball, which she wore when she needed to be dressed up. Added to these basics were casual cut-offs and a few boho-type tops, plus a much loved floaty skirt.

Julia adored accessorising her clothes with one and sometimes more of her trademark boho 'finds'. Her personal look was very different from the designer 'footballer's wife' style adopted by so many of their clients. One of her most cherished moments was the time a stylist for *Sex and the City* had stopped her in the street to ask where she had got the top she had been wearing. Julia's current favourite accessory was a dark brown wide leather belt, ornamented with leather flower petals sewn with tiny turquoise beads to form the flower stamens. She had bought it from a stall at Camden Market, and wore it at every opportunity. She had been seriously tempted to buy a pair of Aztec-inspired turquoise earrings she had also seen on the stall, but had managed to resist.

Her packing finished, she looked at her watch—the plain but oh, so elegant Cartier that Lucy had so generously insisted on buying for all three of them out of her first profits.

Those had been happy, heady days, filled with fun and laughter. Julia frowned. The initial success of the business seemed to have been replaced by a series of financial problems, causing poor Lucy to have to dig deep into her trust fund to provide Prêt a Party with more capital. No wonder her friend was looking so stressed.

It was almost three o'clock. She might as well go back down and wait for Dorland to arrive. Most of the necessary organisation for his end-of-summer party had already been done by Dorland himself, but, as Julia knew, he liked to fuss and fret over every tiny little detail, and virtually every day she received anxious urgent e-mails from him.

She had just stepped out of the lift into the guest house's dusty, faded hallway when her mobile rang.

'Darling!' She heard her mother's voice exclaiming. 'How naughty of you not to tell us about you and Silas. I couldn't believe it at first when Mrs. Williams showed me the article about the two of you in that celebrity gossip magazine she buys. Such a lovely photograph of the two of you, darling, but I must admit I was rather shocked. Not that we aren't all thrilled. We are, of course—especially Daddy. I drove straight round to see him, and he was so pleased that he instructed Bowers to open a bottle of the wine he put down when you were born, to celebrate. It's what he's always longed for. Of course I had to ring Nancy. So silly of me to get the time difference wrong, but naturally she is as excited as we are. You'll be married at Amberley, of course—every Amberley bride always is, but have you decided on a date yet? I do so think that winter weddings have a certain *élan*.'

With every excited word her mother spoke, Julia's insides churned a little bit more tensely.

'Ma…' She tried to protest when she could eventually interrupt her excited happiness, but it was no use. Her mother, as high as a kite on maternal delight, was too busy listing all the many sections of the family who would want to supply a potential bridesmaid.

Silas was on his own in the small courtyard. Julia didn't waste any time announcing in despair, 'Ma's just been on the phone. She thinks we're getting married.'

When Silas refused to react with the shock she had expected, she added, 'She's told your mother, and Gramps was so pleased he instructed Bowers to open a bottle of the wine he put down when I was born.'

'The Château d'Yquem, eh?' Silas looked impressed. 'He's obviously pleased, then.'

'What? Of course he's pleased. According to Ma it's what he's always wanted. But that isn't the point. We *aren't* engaged—we aren't even in a *relationship*. Can you imagine what it's going to do to him when he finds out the truth?'

'You're right,' Silas agreed firmly. 'We can't let that happen.'

Julia had the unnerving feeling that she was a passenger in a car that had suddenly taken a dangerous curve at high speed and left the road completely.

'Silas…'

'For his sake we're just going to have to go along with the situation for now.'

'Go along with it? Ma's already planning the wedding—right down to the number of bridesmaids!'

'Mothers are like that,' Silas agreed gravely.

Julia glared at him.

'You aren't taking this seriously,' she accused him.

'Because it isn't serious,' Silas told her. 'Okay, it's unfortunate, but it's hardly the end of the world. People get engaged to one another every day.'

'Yes, but *they* have a reason for being engaged,' Julia told him through gritted teeth. 'We don't.'

'No, but we do have a reason to maintain the fiction that we are engaged.'

'Gramps?' she guessed helplessly.

'Exactly,' Silas agreed. 'No matter what our personal feelings—or lack of them—I am sure we are both agreed that not upsetting your grandfather is of more importance than they are.'

'Yes, of course,' Julia agreed immediately.

'So, then, we are both agreed that for his sake there is nothing we can do other than to accept that we are now "engaged".'

Julia swallowed—hard. 'But ultimately…'

'Ultimately a solution will have to be found,' Silas agreed calmly. 'Either by us or perhaps by life itself.'

Julia looked at him. 'You mean that Gramps might…that he may not… I know his heart isn't very strong, but—'

Before she could continue, the door to the courtyard opened and Dorland hurried in.

'I suppose you've heard about those wretched diamonds? How on earth can they be lost? Martina swears
she remembers taking them off and putting them back
in their case, and asking someone to give them to the
bloody security guard—who I paid a small fortune to do
nothing other than watch over them. He says he never
got them, Martina can't remember who she gave them
to, and she screams every time I try to get her to remember. And George—would you believe it?—was
shagging one of the waitresses when Martina took them
off. I've got Tiffany on the phone every five minutes,
demanding that I pay them a million dollars for their
necklace. Thank goodness I managed to persuade the
Beast to pay for an exclusive account of how George
was discovered *in flagrante*, the very night he had reaffirmed his marriage vows. You should see the photograph they've done—George and this girl, naked apart
from a diamond necklace.'

'The *Beast*?' Silas questioned.

'Dorland's pet name for a certain red-top daily,' Julia
explained.

'My little joke, Silas.' Dorland beamed. 'The editor,
the dearest boy, has a fondness for dressing up as King
Kong, as part of his mating ritual.'

'Dorland, I've got a bone to pick with you,' Julia informed him grimly.

'Oh?'

'My mother's daily showed her an article in *A-List
Life* with photographs of me and Silas and the information that—'

'I'm sorry, sweetheart, but I just couldn't resist.'
Dorland stopped her, looking more smug than repentant.
'It was such a tempting tidbit. Fortunately the photo-
graphs I told the guys to take of the two of you turned

out well, and I told Murray to make room for them. I thought up the headline myself. "Keeping it in the Family." Then it said, "My spies tell me that one of *A-List*'s favourite party girls is soon to be planning a wedding. And guess who to? Her grandfather, the Earl of Amberley, is bound to be pleased, since her husband-to-be is also his heir, the American billionaire Silas Cabot Carter." You'll be getting married at Amberley of course?' he continued, unconsciously echoing Julia's mother.

'Of course,' Silas agreed smoothly. 'But not yet. I haven't forgotten my promise to Lucy.' Really, Silas reflected inwardly, things couldn't have begun to work out better if he had planned them this way himself.

'Jules, I've been thinking—the fireworks. Do you really think it's a good idea to colour-co-ordinate them?' Dorland demanded, having obviously lost interest in their 'engagement'.

'I think it's an excellent idea,' Julia assured him, well aware how much it would cost if she were to instruct the firework suppliers to change the order she had already given them.

'Lucy, I know you're about to leave, but have you got a minute?'

'Of course. Nick's gone down with our stuff to wait for the taxi.'

She hated doing this, Julia thought. No way did she want to lie to her best friend, but with her grandfather having sent off a notice of her supposed engagement to *The Times*, Lucy was bound to wonder why on earth she hadn't said something.

'Silas and I are getting engaged.'

'Jules!' Immediately Lucy threw her arms around her

and hugged her fiercely, her face alight with happiness. 'Oh, I am so pleased for you. You're perfect for one another. Oh, Jules, how exciting—and you never said a word...'

'It's all been very sudden,' Julia told her uncomfortably. Well, that much at least was true.

Despite the fact that her friend was obviously happy with the news, Lucy looked weary.

'You're happy, aren't you, Lucy?' Julia demanded abruptly. 'I mean, with Nick?'

'Of course I am,' Lucy told her immediately. 'Why shouldn't I be?'

'A word with you, if you please, Blayne,' Silas demanded quietly.

This was the first time he had managed to catch Nick on his own following Julia's revelations.

Nick shrugged. 'Sure. How can I help?'

Silas studied him assessingly. Was it only another man who could see that the too-handsome face hinted at weakness?

'You're walking a very precarious line right now, and whilst your marriage is not my concern, Julia's well-being is.'

'You're warning me off?' Nick asked lightly, smiling. He gave another small shrug. 'Jules has a very passionate nature. She's never made any secret of the fact that she has a bit of a thing for me—'

'Really? And what do you have a thing for, Blayne? Apart from assaulting women, of course.'

An angry red tide of colour had begun to seep up under Nick's tan.

'I don't know what she told you, but she was—'

'Trying to tell you that she wasn't interested in having

sex with you. Let me give you a friendly warning. You've been lucky. You married Lucy. Don't push that luck too far, otherwise you could very easily find yourself unmarried to her. Right now she's all that's stopping me from turning your life inside out. You're scum—you know that, and I know that. So, in case you want what we both know to become public knowledge, I suggest that in future you remember what a very lucky man you are.'

'It's all very well for you, standing there all high and mighty with your billions of dollars behind you,' Nick burst out savagely. 'You don't even begin to know what the real world is all about. If you did—'

'If I did, I still wouldn't use a woman to satisfy my own needs if that wasn't what she wanted. Money has nothing to do with morals, Blayne. We've all got freedom of choice.'

'Bastard,' Silas heard Nick mutter venomously as he walked away from him. But the sudden compression of his mouth into a hard line wasn't caused by Nick's aggression.

He had claimed a moral superiority over Blayne, and it was true that he would never physically abuse or force a woman in any kind of way, but according to his mother in planning to marry Julia he was using her.

'A marriage between us will benefit her as much as it will me,' he had told her.

'Only if she shares your thinking, Silas, and I have to say that I don't think she will. You claim to be a practical man who has no desire for a marriage based on love. I doubt that Julia will share that point of view.'

Silas stopped himself. This was hardly the best time for him to start indulging in a guilt trip over Julia's feelings.

Any practical person would agree with him that a marriage between them would be extremely beneficial to both of them. In and out of bed. He considered himself to be an aware and fair lover, and Julia hadn't flirted with him earlier on because she *didn't* want to have sex with him, had she? There was no reason why they shouldn't share a mutually very satisfying sex life. If they did, then he was certainly prepared to remain a faithful husband, and he felt confident that he could keep Julia satisfied enough not to want to stray herself. Their marriage would certainly have a far stronger foundation than one based on 'romantic love'. One only had to look at the tragedy of Lucy's marriage to Blayne to know that.

CHAPTER FIVE

THERE were undeniably some advantages to her 'engagement' to Silas, Julia reflected as their chauffeur-driven limousine swept them down toward Positano, and first-class travel had to be at the top of the list.

Julia knew that many people found Silas dauntingly formidable. His unemotional practicality had certainly irked her over the years, but there were times when a practical man was a bonus and this was definitely one of them. She considered herself to be a modern, independent woman, but she had certainly enjoyed having nothing to do other than sit back and relax and admire the awe-inspiring Amalfi coastline.

Silas, predictably, had been working, his BlackBerry handheld PDA device in constant use as he phoned and e-mailed, while the chauffeur with true Italian *élan* and a breathtakingly macho disregard for the coaches lumbering the other way.

'Relax,' Silas had murmured at one point, when she had audibly drawn in her breath, sure that they would go over the cliff. 'He knows he won't get a tip if we don't survive.'

It had astonished her that he had noticed her apprehension. He certainly hadn't been looking at her. She knew that, because every time she had looked at him he had been totally focused on e-mailing.

What would it take to shake Silas out of that cool, distancing manner of his and into the heat of raw human passion…or rather who would it take? She would certainly need to be a very strong woman, and a very determined one. What would he be like as a lover? Experienced, certainly, and knowledgeable about what pleased a woman for sure. Silas set high standards for himself, and his skills. And a woman would be able to trust him to take care of everything there was to be taken care of. Silas would have a clean bill of health and an awareness of what could be safely risked and what could not. He would take due care to make sure that his lover experienced the maximum amount of pleasure without inflicting on her any kind of pain.

Physically, perhaps, but what about emotionally? Was Silas, with his cool distance from the rest of the human race and their untidy emotions, capable of understanding what it meant to be hurt emotionally?

'I've e-mailed your grandfather, apologising for not asking his formal permission for our engagement. I told him that your impetuosity overwhelmed us.'

'*My* impetuosity?' Julia challenged him.

Silas smiled at her.

'Well, he would hardly be likely to believe me if I said it was mine, would he?' I've also e-mailed my mother, and the New York society columns.'

'Have you told her that my impetuosity is to blame as well?' Julia asked wryly.

'My mother doesn't need an explanation.'

Whilst Julia was silently digesting his comment, Silas added, 'You're going to need an engagement ring, but, I've suggested to your grandfather we wait until you can return to New York with me.'

'Silas, I don't want a ring.'

She might just as well not have spoken.

'It seems appropriate to me that you should wear the Monckford diamond.'

'*What?*' Julia stared at him. 'You mean the one the Sixth Earl fought that duel over?'

'Actually, it was his wife's honour over which he fought the duel, but since it was the fact that she was foolish enough to be wearing the ring when she went to meet her lover, yes, I do mean that one. Traditionally it was the family betrothal ring, so it seems fitting that you should wear it now.'

Julia took refuge from her own chaotic thoughts by saying crossly, 'I thought you were supposed to run the Foundation, not spend your time trying to repossess every bauble the family ever owned.'

'The Monckford Diamond is hardly a bauble. In fact, it is an extremely rare and historic stone.'

'Thank heavens I don't have to wear it permanently. If it looks anything like it does in the Countess's portrait, it must be incredibly ugly,' Julia could not resist saying disparagingly.

Silas had always incited her to this kind of angry tit for tat, as though somehow they both had to try and outdo one another. But, no matter how much she goaded him, Silas never reacted with a satisfactory show of emotion.

They had reached Positano, its rows of pastel-washed buildings clinging to the steep hillside whilst the Mediterranean lay blue and calm below them.

No wonder artists and poets had fallen in love with this place, Julia reflected as she gazed out of the car widow in silent appreciation. And no wonder too that the Silverwoods had wanted to come here, to the place where they had first met, to celebrate two such special family events.

As regular visitors to Positano, the Silverwoods had a favourite hotel where they always stayed, and Julia had managed, after some incredibly difficult negotiations, to ensure that they would have the exclusive use of a private dining room there, that opened out onto a terrace overlooking the sea, for the celebratory meal. Not unnaturally, the manager of the hotel had demanded a large fee for the use of both dining room and patio, at what was virtually the height of the summer season.

Privately Julia was not sure she would have chosen such an exclusive and expensive venue for the celebration of an eighteenth birthday, and during initial discussions she had recognised that the Silverwoods' teenage son was not as excited about the prospect of the double celebration as his parents. Diplomatically she had suggested to her clients that they might think about throwing a more robust type of event exclusively for their son, so that he could celebrate his coming of age with his friends.

The car turned in to the entrance to the Arcadia hotel, past the discreet plaque that bore the legend 'Leading Hotels of the World'. She already knew that the Arcadia had been built in the eighteenth century as a private villa, and had been opened as a hotel in the early 1950s. Its rooms were apparently still furnished as though it were a private home, with carefully chosen antiques and *objets d'art*, and certainly the reception area bore out this description.

They were shown almost immediately to their suite, and Julia caught her breath as she saw the views from the windows. The hotel must surely command some of the best views in Positano, Julia decided as Silas tipped the porter.

'This is heavenly,' she murmured appreciatively, unable to take her eyes off the sparkling blue of the Mediterranean.

'What's the plan of action for tomorrow?' Silas asked, merely glancing briefly at the view as he reached for his BlackBerry.

'The family will have already arrived today, and by tonight so will most of the guests. For tomorrow, we've organised the hire of a private yacht that will take everyone to Capri, where they will have lunch. Then tomorrow evening there will be a champagne reception at the hotel. Some of the guests won't make it in time for the Capri trip, so the following day those who wish to do so can go to Amalfi. For those who don't, a buffet lunch will be provided at the hotel, with the main event—the formal dinner—taking place that evening.'

'And that's it?' Silas asked her.

'That's it,' Julia agreed, straight-faced. 'Except, of course, for the flowers, and the hairdresser, and the food, and of course the wine, plus getting the presents here, et cetera, et cetera.'

He had put down his BlackBerry and come to study the view. There wasn't very much room on the small balcony, which meant that he had to stand behind her, so close that she could feel the heat coming off his body.

'I think tonight we'll dispense with the separate sleeping arrangements.'

'What?' Julia started to turn round and then stopped as she realised that turning round would bring her body to body with him.

'This really is a wonderful view,' she blurted out in panic.

'Wonderful,' Silas agreed kindly.

He had put his arm around her—both arms, in fact, Julia discovered.

'I don't think this is a very good idea,' she warned him in a wobbly voice.

'No? Are you sure?'

His mouth was brushing hers. How could such a cool and remote man have such a warm and sensual mouth? Like fire under ice, or her favourite dessert, hot sauce on cold ice cream. Mmm, delicious… Just like the feel of Silas's mouth on her own, in fact. Mmm.

As she sighed her appreciation of his kiss, she moved closer to him and put her own arms around his neck.

His tongue probed her lips, slowly but oh, so deliberately, letting her know that he would not stop until she had given him what he wanted. Her body shivered with pleasure as she let him thrust firmly between her half-parted lips. Oh, but he was good. Or was it just that it was just so long since she had last been kissed? Her whole body had become the ice cream now, melting in the heat of the deliberately slow and sensually symbolic thrust of his tongue within the eager wetness of her mouth.

His hand claimed her breast, moulding it firmly and then caressing it rhythmically, his fingertips teasing her nipple before his hand slid back so that this palm was rubbing erotically against it, the caress repeated so firmly and insistently that her whole body began pulse to the rhythmic movement of his hand. Instinctively she wanted to return the intimacy of his touch, to hold the stiff hot flesh of his erection in her hand so that she could explore its veined hardness and see his pleasure whilst she did so.

It had been so long since she had last had sex. She had truly believed that she wasn't bothered, but now she realised that she must be, because she was already aching with frantic need for Silas.

Silas!

Abruptly she broke the kiss.

'What's wrong?'

'We shouldn't be doing this…'

'Of course we should,' Silas told her promptly. 'We're engaged.'

When she looked at him, he added softly, 'And, more importantly, you want to.'

'Do *you*?'

The way he looked at her as he took hold of her hand and placed it against his erection made her heart turn over inside her chest.

'What do you think?' he demanded.

Julia was too caught up in the discovery that his bank account wasn't the only thing about him that was larger than average to make any kind of response.

A part of her was thinking that this couldn't be her, actually thinking of having sex with Silas, but another and much more assertive part was saying it would hate her for ever if she didn't allow it to satisfy the fiercely urgent need that had taken hold of her.

Even so…she had her responsibilities…

'I ought to go over to the hotel and just check…'

'How do I know that isn't just an excuse to sneak off and indulge your shoe habit?' Silas teased her.

She had a shoe habit? She didn't remember. In fact she couldn't think of anything other than what it was going to feel like to lie naked under Silas whilst he filled her with his gorgeous thick strength until he had satisfied the ache that was pulsing from her clitoris right up to her womb.

'Okay, come on,' Silas announced, his voice suddenly crisp. 'Let's get unpacked, and then go down and get some dinner.'

Unpacked? Dinner? There was only one hunger she wanted to satisfy right now. And as for clothes...

Silas watched her with a small satisfied smile. She wanted him and she wanted him badly. That was good. Establishing a sexual bond with her prior to persuading her to marry him might not have been part of his original game plan—sexual satisfaction within their marriage hadn't been particularly high on his original list of priorities—but a plan could be adapted. Why shouldn't he make use of such an excellent opportunity, especially when doing so would be very pleasurable for them both? And not just pleasurable in the short term, but potentially very pleasurable in the long term as well, bonding Julia to him in a way that could only be beneficial to their marriage.

The truth, if he was honest with himself, was that the speed and intensity of his arousal had caught him totally off guard. He prided himself on his sexual self-control, but right now he could feel himself straining and pulsing with his need to push slowly and deeply into Julia's wet heat until she had taken all of him, and then, equally slowly, to ease himself out again before thrusting slickly back in, slowly and deeply, until she raked his back with her nails and held him in her, whilst she moaned her pleasure and urged him to move harder and faster...

Abruptly he made himself think of something else. He

might have decided to marry Julia eight years ago, but since he hadn't spent those years fantasising about having sex with her, he saw no reason why he should allow himself to do so now.

He was suddenly and uncomfortably aware that if he hadn't already been planning to marry Julia, then the intensity of his physical desire for her might have been a problem. And there was no place for problems in Silas's life—just as there was no place for situations he could not control.

His mother was a shrewd and emotionally strong woman, but as a young widow she had bowed to the pressure put on her by her late husband's financial advisers and accepted the Foundation's trustees' insistence on helping her to shape and direct the way in which Silas was groomed to take on the role which would one day be his almost from the day of his birth.

The burden of being responsible for the future of the Foundation and its billions of dollars was not one that could be taken on lightly. Her husband, Silas's father, had died before his twenty-fifth birthday, and these trustees even then had already been in their late middle age, considering the heat and excitement of youthful passion something to be deplored and strictly controlled. Through their guidance and teaching Silas had not just learned how to protect the Foundation, but had also absorbed almost from his cradle certain old-fashioned attitudes to life. Silas had, in short, been raised to put the Foundation first, to exercise self-control, and to be practical and unemotional. The trustees were all dead now, but he knew how much they would have approved of his decision to make Julia his wife. He saw what he had learned from the old men who had been his male role models as an asset, and indeed it was one he fully intended to pass on to his own sons.

Julia watched him, wondering what he was thinking and if he was as astonished and bemused by what was happening to them as she was herself.

That was the trouble with Silas: one could never tell what he was thinking.

She picked up her bag and searched for her mobile. She hadn't had time to charge it before leaving Majorca, so she had switched it off to preserve what was left of the battery.

Her fingers closed over her phone and she extracted it from the bottom of her handbag and switched it on, making a small moue as she saw how many messages she had to check through.

'You should upgrade to a BlackBerry,' Silas told her as he observed what she was doing.

'I should. But right now the business isn't making enough money for that.'

Silas frowned. 'I saw Blayne using one.'

'Oh, yes, Nick's got one. But then he does a lot more travelling than anyone else.'

She started to check though her messages, slightly alarmed to see how many there were from her client.

As she played them her alarm became anxiety, and then dismayed disbelief. Switching off her mobile, she turned to Silas.

'I've got to get over to the venue. There's been some kind of mix-up and I need to get it sorted out asap.'

'What kind of mix-up?' Silas demanded.

'When the client asked to look over the private dining room the hotel told her that the booking for the celebratory dinner party had been cancelled. Of course she immediately got in touch with Lucy, and both she and Lucy have been trying to get hold of me to find out what's going on. I've got to get over there. There's obviously been some mistake. I made the booking myself, and there's no way I would have cancelled it—not after all the trouble we had persuading the hotel to let us have exclusive use of the room and the terrace.'

'Can't you phone them?' Silas asked.

Julia shook her head.

'I could, but I'd much rather go over and sort things out in person.'

'I'll come with you,' Silas told her.

'Thank you, but no.' Julia refused his offer firmly. 'This is my problem, not yours. There's obviously been some kind of mix-up, and hopefully it won't take too long to get it sorted out.' She was still wearing the clothes in which she had travelled, and she felt grubby and tired, but her own comfort would have to wait.

Half an hour later, having decided it would be simpler and quicker to walk to the hotel venue, Julia was standing at the reception desk trying to sound calm and professional as she explained who she was and asked to see the hotel manager. Her hope was that she would be able to sort out whatever the problem was prior to announcing her presence to the clients.

However, when she saw the dubious look the immaculately groomed receptionist was giving her, she couldn't help wondering whether it might have been wiser to have taken the time to shower and change, instead of panicking and rushing over here. But of course it was too late to worry about that now.

She was kept waiting in the hotel's reception area for well over fifteen minutes before the hotel manager finally emerged from his office to beckon impassively to her to come forward.

There was no way she intended to discuss the situation in such a public arena, with the reception desk between them and her very much the supplicant on the wrong side of it. So, as diplomatically as she could, Julia curved her mouth into what she hoped was an appealing smile and asked softly if they might talk somewhere more private.

For several perilous seconds she thought that he was going to refuse, but eventually he pursed his lips and said brusquely, 'Very well, then. Come this way.'

The office to which he showed her was much the same as its counterparts all over the world. A large desk dominated the small space, and the chair he waved her into was slightly uncomfortable and too low, whilst his own gave him some extra inches of height he did not in reality possess.

Prêt a Party secured its business by word of mouth, and no matter how frankly she might express her opinions in her personal life, in her professional life Julia had taught herself to speak with a honeyed careful tongue and to use tact and diplomacy at all times. Especially these kinds of times.

As soon as she was seated she smiled and offered a calm apology for the inconvenience being caused by what was obviously a mix-up of some kind before insisting firmly, 'Obviously there has been a clerical error somewhere, because I can assure you that I have not cancelled our booking. You will remember, I know, our negotiations when the original booking was made—'

'Indeed I do. And I also remember it was agreed that

you would pay a holding deposit of one half of the estimated bill for the evening.'

'Of course. And I explained your requirement to our clients, who agreed to your terms.'

The manager's mouth thinned ominously.

'But you did not abide by those terms, did you?'

Julia frowned, but managed to stay calm.

'I'm sorry. I don't understand. What do you mean?'

'I mean that you did not forward the sum agreed to us, and, what is more, you ignored the several e-mails I sent to you requesting it—including my final e-mail warning that if payment was not immediately forthcoming the booking would be cancelled.'

'No—there must be some mistake,' Julia protested.

'I have copies of the e-mails here—and I have shown them to your clients.'

Julia couldn't understand what had happened. She could clearly remember receiving the Silverwoods' cheque and passing it over to Nick, who dealt with the accounting side of the business. After receiving the Silverwoods' cheque Nick should have paid it into their bank account and then issued a cheque to the hotel: that was the way in which they worked. Right now, though, what was more important than discovering who had been at fault was ensuring that her clients' event ran smoothly, and as they had arranged.

She would have to throw herself on the hotel manager's mercy—even if right now he looked far from showing her any.

'I can only apologise again,' she tried softly. 'Obviously there has been some mistake…'

'There has been no mistake here,' the manager told her coldly. 'We have e-mailed your accounts department on several occasions, requesting payment of this deposit, and yet we have not once received a reply.'

Small cold fingers of despair gripped Julia's stomach. 'There has obviously been a communication breakdown at our end,' she told the manager, as calmly as she could. 'And of course I apologise for that. As soon as I return to London I shall look into it to find out exactly what has happened. But in the meantime I know that both of us will want to do everything we can to ensure that Mr. and Mrs. Silverwood's celebration is everything that they want it to be.'

The hotel manager gave a dismissive shrug.

'As to that, I have already told them that it is impossible for us to allow them to have exclusive use of the dining room now. And, even if it was, we have not made the necessary arrangements in the kitchen. We cannot simply provide a meal such as they had requested at such short notice.'

Julia was beginning to feel slightly sick. The origination of this event and its smooth running was her responsibility and hers alone. The Silverwoods had come to them on the recommendation of a friend, and right from the start Mrs. Silverwood had made it plain exactly what she wanted and how important the event was. To have to tell her now, at this late stage, that not only could they not have the dining room but also that it was not possible to organise the meal she had planned in such minute detail would not just damage Prêt a Party's reputation—more importantly, it would ruin what should have been a very special event.

Julia did her utmost to put across to the manager all of this, and to appeal to him to think not so much of her error but instead of the unhappiness it would cause their mutual clients if the dinner could not go ahead.

'The hotel is full, and we have many people here who have already booked tables in our dining room. It is, after all, one of the most famous assets of our hotel. Everyone who comes here wants to dine in it and look out over Positano.'

'*Signor*, please.'

'No. I am sorry, but it is just not possible.'

The hotel manager wasn't just standing up now, he was also moving purposefully towards the door, obviously intent on getting rid of her. However, before he reached it it suddenly opened inwards, and a very upset and determined Mrs. Silverwood was pushing her way past the receptionist who had tried to stop her from entering the office.

'Julia, what on earth is going on?' she demanded immediately. 'You assured me that the dining room was booked for our exclusive use, but Signor Bartoli insists that it isn't.'

Silas looked at his watch. He had showered, redressed, dealt with his e-mails and right now he was more than ready for his dinner. Julia had been gone for over an hour—more than enough time in which to sort out a minor misunderstanding.

It took him fifteen minutes to walk to the hotel venue, and precisely fifteen seconds to persuade the harassed-looking receptionist to admit him to her manager's office.

Silas could hear the raised voices even before she opened the door—chief amongst them the hotel manager's.

Julia was standing in a corner of the room looking trapped and white-faced as he harangued her, whilst another woman, whom Silas assumed must be Julia's client, sat sobbing on a chair, demanding to know why her party had been ruined.

'Signor Bartoli?'

As all three occupants of the room turned towards him Silas looked first at Julia. She looked shocked and very worried, her eyes widening as she saw him.

The hotel manager looked as though he were about to burst a blood vessel, his face red with angry frustration, whilst Julia's client looked as any woman would having discovered that a year's worth of careful planning was in ruins.

'Who are you and what do you want?' the enraged manager demanded. 'If you are yet another person here to insist that I throw my guests out of their own dining room in order to accommodate a party that has not been paid for, then—'

'I am the Honourable Julia's fiancé,' Silas answered him calmly, shamelessly making use of Julia's title. 'Perhaps we might talk with one another man to man, *signor*? You are a businessman, but I am sure that you are also a very reasonable and compassionate man,' he added, taking advantage of the momentary silence he had created to remove his chequebook from his pocket.

'I am also sure that it is possible for us to reach a mutually acceptable solution to this present *impasse*. Mr. and Mrs. Silverwood have only the very happiest memories of your hotel, *signor*, and I am sure we would both want them to continue to feel that way. Mrs. Silverwood has set her heart on celebrating here. I am sure that it is not beyond your power to grant her this very special desire, despite the misunderstanding that has occurred. Naturally, I am prepared to make full recompense to you for the inconvenience this misunderstanding has cost you. Furthermore, I am sure that a man such as yourself has the skills to explain the situation to those guests who are not taking part in the celebrations, and I am equally sure that they will very generously agree to eat their dinner somewhere else in order to accommodate Mr. and Mrs. Silverwood. In fact, I have already spoken to the manager of my own hotel, the Arcadia, on this very subject, and he has confirmed that your guests may dine there—at my expense.'

Without turning his head to look at Julia, Silas told her, 'Perhaps Mrs. Silverwood would like to a have a restorative glass of champagne, Julia, whilst Signor Bartoli and I discuss this matter further.'

It was ten o'clock, and Silas had warned Julia that if she took longer than ten minutes to shower and change then he was going down to dinner without her.

She had managed it in eight minutes flat, and now they were seated opposite one another at a table in the restaurant, having just ordered their food.

'You can't believe I did what?'

'You know what I mean! Paying Signor Bartoli an extra twenty thousand euros on top of the bill to change his mind and let Mr. and Mrs. Silverwood have the dining room after all.' She gave a small disbelieving shake of her head.

'What went wrong?' Silas asked her.

'I don't know,' Julia admitted. 'Our system is that our clients pay all the bills we incur on their behalf themselves, via us. That way we keep our own overheads down and they get to see exactly what the costs are. All we charge them for is our professional services as organisers.'

'Surely when you received those e-mails it must have alerted you to a potential problem.'

'Well, yes, it would have done if I had seen them, but I didn't—' She broke off to smile at the waiter as he brought their first course.

Her stomach was still churning with anxiety-induced adrenalin. The scene in the hotel manager's office had left her feeling so physically and emotionally on edge that the last thing she wanted to do was eat. She didn't want to tell Silas that, though.

It was bad enough that he had witnessed her humiliation and been obliged to rescue her from it, without letting him see how stupidly upset and shaken she still felt.

Silas had scant tolerance of other people's emotional vulnerability, and that was an aspect of his personality that had always made her feel defensive and wary. He always seemed so invulnerable, which highlighted her awareness of her own weaknesses. He seemed to think that in paying the hotel manager to change his mind he had solved the whole problem, but Julia was now sick with worry about how on earth she was going to repay him. The business certainly could not do so. Lucy had confided worriedly to her that they were barely breaking even, never mind making any profit. Julia had no money of her own, and whilst her stepfather was a relatively wealthy man Julia could not imagine asking him to give her twenty thousand euros.

Silas watched her pushing her soup round and not

drinking it for several seconds before demanding, 'What's wrong?'

'Nothing. I'm just not hungry.'

'It's over twelve hours since you last ate. How can you not be hungry?'

'I'm just not. But I am tired. In fact, if you don't mind, I think I'll go up to…to bed.'

Silas gave a small shrug.

'If that's what you want to do, go ahead.'

It was his dinner he wanted, not her company, he assured himself, as Julia pushed back her chair and stood up. And that sharp little knife-twist he could feel, of something that was almost pain, wasn't a pain at all. It was just a pang of irritation caused by Julia being Julia.

Julia stared at the figures she had written down on the piece of paper in front of her. Her head was beginning to ache and she felt sick. No matter how much she juggled with the figures, there was just no way she was going to be able to find twenty thousand euros. She didn't like to go into debt and didn't even possess a credit card—but nor did she in the way of savings, either (she bought too many shoes!). Her family was wealthy but their money was all tied up in property—such as the Estate at Amberley and the London flat where she lived—assets that were supposed to be preserved for future Earls and so weren't hers to sell. Perhaps she would have to try and raise a loan—but it was not as if she had any property to borrow against.

Silas picked up his wine glass and looked sombrely at the contents. It held a robust, energetic rioja, with a good parentage, that should have tasted warm and well rounded instead of slightly sour. Or was it his mood that had turned sour and not the wine? Why should that be? Not, surely, because Julia had left him to eat alone? Silas often ate alone. In fact he preferred to. He glanced down at his plate. His steak was cooked just as he liked, but he might just as well have been eating sawdust, he realised, as he pushed his plate away from himself and signalled for the waiter.

As the hotel lift took him up to the suite, he wondered what the hell was happening to him? Why hadn't he simply stayed where he was and finished his meal? Why had both it and the evening lost their flavour and become flat and unappealing without Julia's presence?

Engrossed in the figures in front of her, Julia did not hear the outer door open, or see Silas walk in until he was virtually standing in front of her.

'What's this?' he demanded, picking up the piece of paper and studying it.

'Nothing,' Julia fibbed, but Silas wasn't listening to her. He stared at the small, worried little sums, written down over and over again, and something inside him that he hadn't known was there moved a painful little notch, like the cranking of some long-unused mechanism, its movement all the more agonising because of that.

'You don't seriously think that I expect *you* to repay me, do you?' he demanded sharply.

'Why not? Someone has to,' Julia told him. 'And I know that Lucy can't. The business is barely breaking even, and if the business can't repay you, then naturally I feel morally obliged to do so myself. Because I dealt with the Silverwoods' event.'

Her eyes widened as Silas suddenly screwed up the

piece of paper with an almost violent movement of his hand and threw it into the wastepaper bin.

He had no real idea quite why Julia's comment should affect him so strongly, nor why he should feel so enraged because she didn't realise that he didn't want to be repaid.

'You're my fiancée, remember? The money I gave to the hotel manager I gave because I did not wish to see my fiancée being harassed and distressed. Therefore it was for *my* benefit as much as anyone else's. There is no reason for Lucy to know about it and even less for her to pay me back,' he told her grimly.

'But our engagement isn't real,' Julia pointed out. 'And even if it were I'd still want to repay you.'

Silas looked at her. 'Why?'

'Because I would. Because I don't like what it does to a relationship when one person uses the other—financially or in any kind of way. How could you respect me? How could I respect myself if I let you carry me financially? I can't match you for money, Silas, but if we were really a couple I would want to match you in respect and…and…all sorts of other ways…'

Silently Silas digested what she was saying. She had surprised him he admitted. How could this young woman who had admitted openly to a constant need to buy shoes also manifest such a deeply ingrained sense of responsibility and pride? And how could he not have known that she did?

'Since your clients insist they sent you a cheque, and moreover the cheque has been cashed, it seems to me there must have been some kind of accounting mistake. The money must be in Prêt a Party's accounts somewhere. Who deals with the day-to-day finances of the business?'

Julia exhaled slowly, and then told him reluctantly, 'Nick.'

'Blayne?' Silas demanded sharply.

Julia looked away, reluctant to admit to Silas that she was beginning to remember some odd and very worried comments Carly had made before she had left Prêt a Party to marry Ricardo.

Could it be that Nick was doing something fraudulent with the company's money?

Julia was reluctant to speak openly to Silas about her burgeoning suspicions in case she was wrong. Nick might have threatened to punish her for refusing his sexual advances, but there was no way he could have carried out that threat by allowing the booking to be cancelled. The timing simply wasn't right. Unless he had somehow or other tampered with her e-mails...But that would mean that Nick was stealing from his own wife, and why on earth would he do that?

And then she remembered that Nick had wanted to come to Positano with her.

'Now what's wrong?' Silas queried, as he watched the way her expression changed and anxiety shadowed her eyes.

'I was just thinking about Nick,' Julia said.

CHAPTER SIX

JUST thinking about Nick? Hardly. No, what she really meant was that she wanted Blayne, despite having insisted previously that she didn't. And despite, too, having responded physically to *him*.

Silas wasn't used to hearing a woman express desire for another man when she was with him. And he certainly wasn't used to the feelings he was now experiencing. Anger, pain—*jealousy*? What on earth was happening to him?

Oblivious to the interpretation Silas had put on her words, Julia took a deep breath and then asked uncomfortably, 'Silas, you don't think that Nick could be—?'

'I don't think he could be what? So unhappy in his marriage that he should leave Lucy for you?' Silas demanded savagely.

'Leave Lucy for *me*? I've already told you that I don't want him!'

'But you can't stop thinking about him?'

'What? No! I'm not thinking about him like *that*,' Julia protested. 'It's Lucy I'm concerned about.'

When Silas continued to look unconvinced, she told him, 'Nick deals with the financial side of the business, and I can't help wondering...'

It was hard to come out and say what she was actually thinking, but she could see from Silas's expression that she was going to have to—unless she wanted him to continue to think she wanted Nick. Although quite why it suddenly seemed so very important to convince him that she didn't, and that there was no one else in her life, she wasn't prepared to analyse too much.

Instead she took a deep breath and said uncomfortably, 'I'm probably being stupid about this, but I can't help worrying that Nick might be...' This was so difficult! 'Silas, you don't think he could be doing anything wrong, do you?' she appealed anxiously.

'Wrong? What kind of wrong?'

When she began to chew anxiously on her bottom lip and looked uneasy, Silas suddenly realised what she was trying to say.

'You think that Blayne might be defrauding the business?'

Relief replaced Julia's earlier discomfort. 'Yes! Well, no. I don't know. I mean, why should he, when he's married to Lucy? But I *know* that I never saw those e-mails from the hotel. I know that I passed the cheque on to Nick, along with the invoices it was supposed to cover.'

'You said yourself that the business was struggling to make money—maybe the situation is worse than you know and Blayne simply couldn't pay out the deposits because there wasn't enough money?'

'In that case why didn't he say something to me? Warn me? He was very angry that he wasn't going to be coming to Positano with me. I thought it was because I'd told him I wasn't going to have sex with him, but if he knew that there was going to be a problem here... Oh, Silas, I just don't know what to think or do. Lucy is one of my two closest friends. Prêt a Party is her business. The last thing I want is to do something that might hurt her.'

It was only natural that he should be relieved to discover that Julia had not lied to him, Silas assured himself. But a taunting inner voice told him mockingly, Relieved, yes. But surely not almost euphoric?

'Would you like me to make some discreet enquiries?'

'I don't know,' Julia admitted. 'Maybe if you left it until I've been able to speak to Lucy and…and check everything.'

'You're worried that Lucy might be implicated as well?' Silas guessed.

'No! Lucy would never do anything dishonest.'

'But you think that Blayne could have involved her in something *he* has done that is dishonest?'

'I don't know, Silas…and, like I just said, I don't want to do anything that could hurt her. I feel so sorry for her, and I feel a bit guilty as well. If it hadn't been for me she would never have met Nick in the first place.'

'You can't say that. She might still have met him without you.'

She looked so distressed that Silas immediately found he wanted to comfort her. And not just verbally, he realised, and he discovered that somehow or other he had moved closer to her.

'I am grateful to you for what you did at the hotel, Silas,' Julia told him huskily. Silas was being so very kind and understanding.

'I just wish…' She stopped speaking as Silas reached out and drew her purposefully into his arms.

'Why don't we forget about Prêt a Party and focus on this instead?'

So much had happened that she had almost forgotten the thrill of anticipation and excitement she had felt earlier. Almost, but not entirely. And now immediately it was back, her pleasure even hotter and sweeter this time as Silas kissed her with deliberate thoroughness.

'Mmm.' Julia slipped her arms round his neck to hold him closer as she savoured the deepening passion of his kiss, and then shivered in voluptuous pleasure as his hands sculpted the curves of her body before taking possession of her breasts.

Her own arousal was hot and fiery and immediate. Behind her closed eyelids she could see erotic images of them together—Silas's hands and mouth on her naked body, possessing it and her. She could see herself writhing in eager urgency whilst his lips played erotically with the tight, hot jut of her nipples, his hand slipping between her legs to open her to his sensual exploration.

But who needed to imagine when what he was already doing to her was so effective? She loved the way his fingertips stroked her breast, so slowly and tantalisingly, and then drew erotically on her waiting nipple, savouring its hardness through the layers of fabric.

He lifted his mouth from hers and started to kiss her jaw, causing her to arch back her head so that he could plunder the soft, sweet flesh of her throat, and then move lower to that special secret place where her neck ran into her shoulder and where just the warmth of his breath was enough to make her shudder in wanton need.

Being held, and touched and kissed like this, with nothing to do other than let Silas build her arousal, was the most deliciously sensual and self-indulgent pleasure. She exhaled slowly on a luxuriant sigh of delight and stroked her fingertips through the thick hair at the back of his neck. His flesh felt warm and firm, and oh, so wonderfully male. A feeling of harmony and happiness, of *rightfulness*, stroked slowly through her like a delicious extra layer of physical pleasure. She traced the curve of his neck and then the rigid hardness of his collarbone with delicate fingertips, savouring his male difference.

'Mmm. Lovely strong muscles.'

The approving, almost purring pleasure in her voice caused Silas to tug urgently on her nipple and then bite gently at her earlobe before whispering thickly, 'Why don't we get rid of some of these clothes?'

Beneath his hands her body arched fiercely in eager response.

'I thought you were never going to ask,' Julia admitted huskily.

Silas had switched off the electric lights, but the doors to the balcony were open and uncurtained. The sky was so bright with stars and a full moon that more than enough silver light was shining down on them for him to see her clearly. Her eyes shone with liquid desire, her lips slightly swollen and flushed with colour from his kisses. Not even the fact that she was fully dressed could conceal her arousal: the stiff thrust of her nipples was plainly visible. He reached out and traced a slow circle with his fingertip around the one he had been caressing, watching with totally male satisfaction as her whole body tightened and she exhaled fiercely. Inside his head he could already see the naked flesh of her breast, creamy pale against the puckered darkness of her nipple; he could feel the way her body would shudder as he teased the tight peak with the tip of his tongue before taking it fully into his mouth. He could even hear her wild cry of erotic pleasure as she called out to him to satisfy her.

What was Silas waiting for? Julia looked up at him

questioningly, and then reached out to touch the hard ridge of his erection, stroking its fabric-covered heat with delicate fingertips, seeking and finding the sensitive place where its head bulged thickly from his foreskin.

Silas discovered that he could scarcely bear to so much as breathe as he stood stiff and still whilst her fingertip mapped and teased him, in case somehow he missed a fraction of the almost unbearable pleasure of her touch.

It wasn't very often that Silas felt any need to give thanks for the gifts life had given him—he was, after all, a man who dealt in practicalities, not emotions—but suddenly he recognised that unexpectedly he had received a very special life-enhancing bonus. He wanted Julia and she wanted him, and the desire between them was so hot and so fierce, so immediate and so damned right, that it almost made their marriage a necessity in its own right.

Whatever he had envisaged when he had thought about marriage to Julia, it had not been that he would feel like this. But now that he did feel like this... Silas gave a low, tormented moan of raw male pleasure as her fingertips slowly and rhythmically worked his foreskin over the pulsing head of his penis, whilst she used her free hand to unzip his trousers and then unfasten his belt.

She wanted them to get naked? Well, so did he.

Silas could be both ruthless and inventive when he wanted to be, Julia decided happily only seconds later, as her clothes were removed so speedily and determinedly that it seemed to her that one minute she was fully dressed and the next she was standing in the moonlight wearing only her very brief lace thong, with Silas kneeling on the floor in front of her. Or rather she was almost wearing it. Because Silas had slid his hands beneath the thin lace-covered elastic that had been resting on her hips and was circling her belly button with his tongue-tip.

His hands moved to her bottom, kneading the rounded flesh whilst his tongue teased a line of fire just above the triangle of lace fabric covering the firm, mound of her pubic bone.

He had loved one hand from her bottom and was sliding it between her legs, stroking the sensitive flesh on the inside of her thighs, his touch making her sigh with soft pleasure.

Somehow the warmth of his lips teasing the sensual spot just above the soft dark curls that covered her mound, the slow, explorative stroke of his fingers as they moved up her thigh and under the lacy barrier between them, and the eager swelling of the soft fleshy lips concealing her sex seemed to link the two parts of her body together via an almost electric invisible arc of sizzlingly erotic pleasure. It made her want to push deeper into his touch. It made her want to wantonly demand that he give her more, so very much more. It made her want to urge him to make those tiny flutters of sensation she could feel pulsing deep inside her wet heat become much stronger and fiercer. In short, it made her want…

'Oh, Silas…' she groaned warningly, her helpless moan of pleasure turning to a sharp gasp as his fingertip stroked through her wetness to caress her clitoris. Almost immediately her body was seized with a violent shudder of delight that left her quivering helplessly whilst Silas picked her up and carried her over to the bed, placing her on it and then stripping off his clothes whilst she lay watching him.

In all the years they had known one another she had never so much as seen him wearing a pair of swimming shorts, she realised as her eager gaze delighted in the sight of his wide shoulders tapering down to a flat stomach. His skin was lightly tanned, his body hair dark and soft-looking, lightly covering his chest but making an erotically denser line down the centre of his body before thickening out around his penis.

'Mmm…' Julia purred happily as she reached up to touch him. 'You've got a gorgeous, sexy body, Silas. Just looking at it makes me melt inside with anticipation.'

He had always known that she had a tendency to be outspoken and say whatever came into her head, but he hadn't known just how much pleasure that outspokenness was going to give him, Silas thought, as a certain part of his 'gorgeous, sexy body' showed its appreciation of her compliment by stiffening even more.

'Mmm.' Julia reached out and ran one fingertip around the engorged glossy head, her touch making Silas fight to smother a groan of pleasure and a small bead of milky fluid began to form.

Very gently Julia caught it with her fingertip and looked up at Silas, laughing softly. 'Ooh. Baby gravy.'

'You want my baby?' Silas heard himself demanding thickly.

'Silas…' Julia began to protest. But Silas was already kissing her so passionately that it was impossible for her to say or do anything other than respond to him.

'I'd forgotten just how good skin on skin feels,' Julia murmured sleepily as she snuggled into Silas, her hand spread flat against his chest, registering the post-orgasm slowing of his heartbeat.

'Has it been a long time since the last time, then?' Silas asked her casually.

'Aeons,' Julia admitted frankly. 'In fact so long that I can hardly remember it. You know what it's like, Silas. When you're in your teens and you've got all those hormones jumping about all over the place sex is all you can think about, but then somehow life takes over, doesn't it? Setting up the business and then running it has taken up so much time there just hasn't been any left for anything else. Even if I had met someone I wanted to go to bed with, I wouldn't have had time.'

'You met Blayne,' Silas reminded her.

'Well, yes, but Nick dropped me for Lucy before we'd got as far as having sex.'

'So your passionate response is more likely to be the result of frustration than any actual desire for me?' Silas probed.

'Who said I was frustrated?' Julia demanded.

'You did.'

'No, I didn't. I said I'd forgotten how good skin on skin felt. And that's different. After all, I've got Roger to make sure I don't get frustrated.'

'Roger?' Silas queried.

'Yes Roger. My Rabbit. My *vibrator*,' Julia explained, when he looked at her uncomprehendingly, a smile dimpling the corners of her mouth. 'Jessica Rabbit—a single girl's best friend. Only I call mine Roger because he…'

Silas started to laugh. 'Okay, yes—I get it, Roger as in "to roger"—the good old-fashioned English word.'

'A vibrator's okay, but no way can it compare with being with you. It was really good for me, Silas,' Julia told him softly. 'In fact...' She hesitated, her fingers curling into the soft hair on his chest, her lashes sweeping down to conceal her expression, but Silas could still see the heat warming her face.

'In fact?' he encouraged, noting in fascinated male bewilderment that *now* she was blushing.

The dark lashes lifted and she was looking at him with those huge amazing eyes of hers.

'In fact, it was the best sex I have ever had,' she admitted huskily.

A sensation that was both physical and emotional, and so strong that momentarily it almost stopped his heartbeat, gripped Silas by the throat. It had to be caused by the realisation that he was being given the perfect opportunity to achieve his goal, he told himself practically, before saying, 'Really? Good enough to make it worthwhile turning this fake engagement of ours into a real marriage?'

'What? You're joking!'

Silas shook his head. 'No. I'm completely serious,' he told her truthfully.

'But...but why on earth would you want to marry me?' Julia demanded, her forehead pleating into a small frown.

'Oh, the usual reasons,' Silas told her lightly. 'You turn me on. You give good head. And I love the way you yell, ''Siii—lasss!'' when you come.'

Julia giggled and punched him playfully on his arm.

'Those are not good reasons.'

'I can't think of any better,' Silas told her. 'Unless it's the pleasure I get from filling you with baby gravy.'

Julia laughed, and then stopped, her face anxious.

'Silas, you don't think...?'

'I don't think what?'

Julia started to chew her bottom lip.

'We didn't use a condom, and I'm not using any contraception. What are we going to do?'

'You want kids, don't you?'

'Yes, of course.' And that speaking of them as 'we' had turned her heart to melting chocolate, Julia realised.

'So, what are we waiting for?'

'Silas!' Julia protested as he turned to reach for her.

'Okay, maybe it would not be such a good idea for you to walk down the aisle wearing a tent. We'd better buy some condoms—and bring the wedding forward.'

Quite how it was possible over the course of two short days for her to go from thinking of Silas as someone she preferred to see as little of as possible to knowing that she was passionately in love with him and wanted to spend the rest of her life with him, preferably making babies, Julia was far too blissed-out and far too sexed-out to worry about.

All she needed to make her whole world perfect was Silas. Silas and a bed. Silas and a shower large enough for two people. Silas and a magical walk along the seashore, with shadows deep enough for them to hide in body to body whilst their shared passion drove them to forget everything but one another. Silas, whose taste she still had on her tongue and whose scent she could still smell on her skin and in her hair. Silas, who always gave that funny little grunt before he gave in to his own orgasm. Silas who filled her and thrilled her, who satisfied her and aroused her, as no other man ever had done or would do.

She was obsessed with him, Julia admitted cheerfully

to herself, her mouth curving into a wide, happy smile. Obsessed with him and totally, totally besotted by him. She felt like a particularly smug Bridget Jones-type singleton. The kind who would write deliriously in her diary, *2 days and 20-plus shags*. Silas had to be the world's best lover, even if he protested generously that her partisan enthusiasm was encouraging him to previously unreached heights.

Only this morning he had cupped her face and kissed her nose as the sweat of passion dried on their damp bodies, and told her softly, 'Don't ever take off those rose-coloured glasses you view me through, will you.'

Rose-coloured glasses? As if! The wonderful thing about falling in love with Silas was that she already knew everything there was to know about him, so there couldn't be any unpleasant shocks waiting to wreck their relationship.

'Julia, my dear, have I told you how wonderful all of this is?' Mrs. Silverwood enthused emotionally as she left her guests to come and stand with Julia. 'And all thanks to your wonderful fiancé. I do not know what we would have done if he hadn't managed to persuade the hotel manager to relent.'

On the other side of the restaurant Silas, whom the Silverwoods had insisted on including in their dinner party, finished his champagne and enjoyed himself watching Julia. He had laughed more in these last two days than he had laughed in the whole of the rest of his life. Laughed more and loved more too.

He sincerely hoped that their children would inherit their mother's blithe spirits and sense of humour. Their children. Desire hardened his body, causing him to move discreetly back into the shadows. Sex with Julia was like no sex he had ever had before. He simply couldn't get enough of her, and when his body did cry enough he was filled with a sense of such intense satisfaction that he had no past experience in his life he could compare it to.

This sexual hunger for one another that had overtaken them both had brought a whole new urgency to his determination to marry Julia. The end of the year was way too long to wait. He wanted to tie her to him now, as tightly and permanently as he could. Which was why he had spent hours on the telephone this afternoon, whilst she had been checking over the final arrangements for the dinner. The result was worth the time he had spent, though, even if he *had* had to twist the arms of both the American and British Ambassadors just slightly in order to get what he wanted. Now all he had to do was persuade Julia.

It was four o'clock in the morning, and the streets of Positano were empty as Silas and Julia walked arm in arm back to their own hotel.

'The Silverwoods seemed pleased with the way the event went,' Silas commented.

'Yes, thanks to you. I nearly died when the hotel chef threw that tantrum yesterday and threatened to walk out. That was really quick thinking on your part, to let him think that the chef from the Arcadia would be happy to take over.'

Silas laughed. 'Quick thinking, maybe, but not entirely true. Still, it did the trick. Am I right in thinking that now we've got ten days before we need to be in Marbella for Dorland's party?'

'The party isn't for another ten days,' Julia agreed.

'But we'll have to be there well before that in order to make sure everything is properly organised.'

'How well before?' Silas asked. 'Will three days be enough?'

'At a pinch,' Julia agreed. 'Why?'

They had almost reached the hotel and Silas stopped walking, drawing her into the shadows with him as he leaned back against a convenient wall, his hands on her hips, guiding her between his parted legs.

Just the scent of him was enough to turn her on. Julia pressed closer to him and lifted her face for his kiss.

'Let's not wait to get married.'

His voice was thick and raw, sending a shudder of pleasure jolting through her whilst her heart thudded out a stunned tattoo.

'What—what do you mean?' she demanded uncertainly.

'I mean, let's not wait to get married. Let's do it now. Here in Italy.'

His words fell honey-sweet against their ears; her heart lifted in excited pleasure. So far neither of them had spoken the 'L' word, but, knowing him as she did, that he should feel such an urgency to commit to her told her just how he felt about her. Even so...

'Silas, we can't,' she protested.

'Of course we can. I've already checked it out. We could be married within the week—less, if I put some more pressure on our Ambassador.'

'Why the rush?' she teased him. 'Don't you trust me?'

Silas laughed. 'Yes, I trust *you*. But I'm not sure that I trust the condoms to withstand the rigours we've been subjecting them to.'

Julia giggled.

'Silas, we couldn't…could we?' she breathed excitedly.

'You want to?'

She closed her eyes and then opened them again.

'Do I want to be your wife and have guaranteed wonderful sex for the rest of my life? Of course I do,' she told him extravagantly. 'But what about the family…what about Gramps?'

'We could still have a religious blessing in Amberley Church, and even a reaffirmation of our vows and a formal post-wedding breakfast afterwards, if that is what you want.'

'What I want? All I want is you,' Julia told him simply, and she raised herself up on her toes to kiss him.

CHAPTER SEVEN

'I STILL can't believe we're actually doing this,' Julia whispered nervously to Silas as they stood side by side waiting for their papers to be checked. The American Embassy had recommended that they consult an Italian official well versed in the complexities of the correct procedure to enable other nationals to marry in Italy, and, with a speed that had impressed Julia, all the necessary paperwork had been assembled and submitted. And here they were, just an hour or so short of five days after Silas had suggested they do so, actually about to be married to one another.

'It will be a civil ceremony,' Silas had told her.

'Oh, but that will make whatever we do at home all the more special,' Julia had told him in delight. 'It would be really cool if we could reaffirm our vows at Amberley, like you suggested, Silas. Almost like having a second wedding.'

Since the Monckford Diamond was still in New York, Julia had no engagement ring to wear with one of the matching plain gold bands she and Silas had chosen in a small jeweller's, down a narrow side street in Rome.

Emotional tears filled Julia's eyes as they stood together and made their vows. In some strange way being alone together actually made exchanging them all the more special.

As she slid Silas's ring onto his finger she bent her head and brushed it with her lips, promising him silently, *I shall love you for ever.*

She had discovered that Silas was not a man who found talking about his emotions easy. But she was sure he loved her, even though he had not said so. He had married her, after all. A small naughty smile curved her mouth. Before they celebrated their first wedding anniversary she would have taught him to say that he loved her, and that was a promise to herself she was not going to break.

They had agreed that they wouldn't wear their rings until they could go back to England and tell her grandfather what they had done.

'I don't want him to hear about it via Ma's cleaning lady and Dorland's wretched magazine,' Julia had told Silas when they had been discussing the matter.

'Fine—that's okay by me,' Silas had agreed.

Her husband. Julia looked up at Silas, her face glowing with happiness. They would have one night together here in Rome before they flew to Spain tomorrow, and Silas had booked them into the most wonderful hotel.

'I thought we'd go straight back to the hotel,' Silas told her now. 'Unless you'd prefer to do something else?'

'What? Rather than go to bed with you? No way,' Julia told him, shaking her head.

It was so refreshing to be with Julia, Silas acknowledged. She never tried to play controlling mind games, and he loved the way she was so open with him about her sexual desire for him. Not that their mutual sexual desire for one another was the only thing they shared. She was passionately committed to seeing Amberley preserved for future generations—but not, as she had put it, '…like some kind of museum. Amberley—the real Amberley, as it is today—is what it is because of the way each generation had lived in it, because it has been a real home. Not because it has been kept exactly as it was when it was first built. I know Gramps opens it to the public for several months a year, and I know that the state rooms are too grand really to live in...'

'So what would you do with them?' Silas had asked.

'Oh, all sorts of things. We could hold musical evenings in the green salon, so that young musicians could play Handel in the kind of setting for which he wrote his music. We could have literary readings in the library. We could do things with the house and for it that would benefit other people as well. Imagine what it would mean to children learning to play an instrument to be able to have some of their lessons in the green salon, for instance. And then there's the home farm. It know it's a bit run down now, but there's more than enough land for us to have rare varieties of free range hens and ducks...'

'My life is focused on New York,' he had reminded her. 'I have a duty and a responsibility toward the Foundation.'

'I know that. But we could travel between Amberley and New York, couldn't we?'

'Of course.'

She had wrinkled her nose at him in that delicious semi-teasing way she had, and then said hesitantly, 'Silas, I'm afraid I don't know very much about the workings of the Foundation. You're going to have to explain to me exactly how it runs and what *if anything* I can do to help you.'

Yes, he had every right to congratulate himself on his perspicacity in deciding to marry Julia, Silas decided. She was, as he had told his mother on Julia's eighteenth birthday, the perfect wife for him.

The hotel Silas had booked them into was old and elegant, hidden away down a maze of narrow streets which opened out into a quiet piazza, where an ornamental fountain splashed water down into an ornately carved marble basin and equally ornate marble statues stood on marble plinths. The austere grandeur of so much marble was broken up by huge classically shaped urns filled with a tumbling mass of flowers.

Their own suite had a balcony that overlooked the piazza, and Julia glanced up towards it now, a delicious thrill of excitement gilding her happiness as she anticipated what lay ahead.

Having sex with Silas was always wonderful, but this time would be extra special—because this time they would be doing it as husband and wife.

She looked down at her ring. She couldn't wear it permanently yet, of course. If she did someone was bound to see it.

'I thought we'd have dinner in the suite tonight,' Silas told her as they walked into the hotel foyer. 'But first there's something I want to show you.' He took hold of her arm, guiding her down a dark vaulted corridor, suddenly stopping to demand, 'Where's your hat?'

'Here,' Julia told him, showing him the hat she was holding in her other hand. She had thought that he would laugh, or even object, when she had insisted on wearing the pretty semi-formal straw hat for their marriage, but instead he had actually given a small nod of approval.

They had reached a set of highly polished heavy wooden doors, which Silas opened for her.

Beyond them lay another corridor, its walls plain, almost roughly hewn stone, and Julia shivered as she felt the cold coming off them, turning to look enquiringly at Silas.

'The hotel has its own private chapel, where the family who owned the original house used to celebrate Mass. It was a condition that the family made when they sold the house that lighted candles would always be kept burning in the chapel, and that it would always be open to those who wanted to come here to pray and to give thanks.'

They had reached another set of huge double doors. A little hesitantly, Julia looked at Silas.

Smiling at her, he reached out and took her hat from her, and set it very gently on her head.

'That is why I have brought you here, Julia. So that I can give thanks, and because I sensed when we were being married that a part of you was thinking of the church at Amberley.'

Silas was opening the doors. Beyond them Julia could see candlelight, blurred by her own emotional tears.

Taking hold of her hand, Silas led her into the chapel, their footsteps echoing on the worn stone floor.

Silently they walked past the empty pews towards the altar, beyond which an ancient stained glass window reflected the light of the candles. The air smelled of age and damp and that indefinable smell of old churches: a mixture of incense and peace and faith, all bound together with humility and acceptance.

Julia bowed her head. Silas was still holding her hand. She watched as he removed both their rings and then handed her his own.

Silently they exchanged rings. Could there be anything more profound or meaningful than this? Julia wondered. Automatically she knelt in prayer, as she had been taught to do as a small child. This might not be her family church, or her religion, but its spirituality reached out to her and touched her like angels' wings.

Even Silas was standing with his head bent, as though he too felt the same sense of awe and humility she was experiencing.

'Silas, thank you.'

They had just walked into their suite, and as he locked the door Silas cocked an enquiring eyebrow and demanded, 'What for?'

'For what you just did. The chapel. My hat. Understanding how I felt. Everything.'

'You've got just under an hour to get changed before dinner.'

It was silly of her to feel disappointed, and even more silly of her to feel hurt because Silas was changing the subject—cutting her off, almost, as though her emotional words irritated him. She had felt so close to him in the chapel, but now she was suddenly aware of how he was distancing himself from her.

His mobile started to ring, and he turned away from her to answer it, but not before Julia heard a girlish female voice exclaiming, 'Silas, darling—surprise! It's me—Aimee!'

Automatically Julia stiffened, but Silas was already walking away from her, his voice too low for her to hear what he was saying as he stepped out onto the balcony.

Aimee DeTroite was a high-maintenance New York socialite heiress, whose sexual adventures had been the subject of a great deal of celebrity gossip. Private videos of her having sex with a variety of male partners—consecutively and concurrently—had apparently been stolen from her apartment and then shown over the Internet to whoever was prepared to view them. She had the reputation of being an extremely difficult and very spoiled young woman, who claimed that her famous tantrums were not caused by an over-fondness for the white powder, as some articles had claimed, but instead by the fact that she was 'bi-polar'.

Of course Silas knew other women, and had women friends—had had other lovers, Julia told herself stoutly. The fact that one of them had chosen to telephone him now might be bad timing, but she was hardly to be blamed for that, and neither was Silas. And calling a man 'darling' hardly meant anything at all any more! Everyone did it. Even Silas when he was talking to her— in public.

Outside on the balcony Silas's fingers tightened on his mobile. He had no idea how Aimee had managed to get hold of his new mobile number, but he wasn't going to waste any time asking her.

'Silas, how could you do this to me? How could you get engaged to someone else when you know how much I love you? I won't let her have you—you know that, don't you? You're mine, Silas. Mine!'

Her voice had started to rise in familiar hysteria. As Silas switched off his mobile, cutting her off, he could hear her starting to scream at him. Grimly he looked into the bedroom, wondering if Julia had heard. If she was upset… He started to frown, his earlier unfamiliar mood of lighthearted tenderness flattened by Aimee's unwanted telephone call. Of course it made sense for practical reasons that he didn't want Julia to hear another woman telephoning him on *their* wedding night. But that didn't totally explain the anger he was feeling because Aimee had intruded on his privacy with Julia.

'Is everything all right?' Julia asked as lightly as she could when Silas stepped back inside the room.

'Everything's fine.' Silas's voice was curt, and she could see that he was frowning. 'Why do you ask?'

'No reason.' Julia fibbed.

Her earlier happiness had vanished, and she was miserably aware both of Silas's withdrawal from her and the fact that another woman was responsible for it.

He was handling things very badly, Silas acknowledged as he registered Julia's small intake of breath and the look in her eyes.

'I'd forgotten I'd promised Aimee I'd buy some tickets for a charity benefit she's organising.'

Julia forced herself to smile. 'I know you dated her at one time.' Thanks to Nick, who had made a point of telling her.

'I have *never* dated Aimee,' Silas denied forcefully. 'I simply know her, that's all.'

'But what about that video when you and she—' Julia blurted out.

'That was—' Silas broke off, and tried to control the angry thumping of his heart. Was he going to be forever pursued by Aimee's malice and the lies she had told about him and their supposed relationship? A relationship that was nothing more than a figment of her own fantasies.

'I just don't want to talk about this, Julia. I am married to you, and that should tell you all you need to know about my relationship with you.' Silas's voice was clipped and sharp.

Julia didn't say anything, but it perturbed her that Silas should be so angrily vehement—almost excessively so, in fact. It was so out of character for him. The action of a man with something to hide?

She didn't want to pursue such thoughts, Julia told herself firmly, and she wasn't going to do so.

*   *   *

They had eaten—a delicious meal—and talked, and Julia
rather suspected that she had drunk just a little too much
champagne. And now every bit of her was fizzing with
anticipatory excitement as Silas reached for her hand and
drew her towards him.

The phone call he had received earlier and the woman
who had made it had been firmly and determinedly banished from her thoughts. This was, after all, her wedding
night, *their* wedding night, and no way was she going
to let another woman spoil it.

'I still can't believe that we're married,' she whispered. 'You and me, of all people!'

Silas was cupping her face in his hands and it was
impossible for her to say any more, because he was
slowly and deliberately kissing her mouth with individ-
ual kisses that tasted every curve and angle of her lips.
His tongue-tip began to probe deeper, making her moan
and cling tightly to him. All she was wearing was a
pretty silk chiffon wrap, which she had tied around herself, half uncertain about whether or not she had gone
too far in deciding to leave off her underwear.

Now, though, the knowledge that there was so little
to come between her flesh and Silas's touch was a potent
aphrodisiac that added to her excitement and arousal.

'You are a complete and total sensualist. You know
that, don't you?' Silas demanded thickly as he rubbed
his palm slowly over her chiffon-covered nipple, enjoying watching the pleasure darken her eyes as much as
he was enjoying the feel of her hard nipple, growing
tighter between his rhythmically plucking fingers.

Already beyond logical conversation, Julia could only
moan and grind her hips eagerly against him. The silk
wrap was so sheer that it barely veiled her body, the
light shining through it to pick out the dark, sensual

ripeness of the aureoles of flesh surrounding her nipples as well as her nipples themselves. It was tied at the front, and when she moved Silas kept getting brief, tormenting glimpses of bare flesh.

He parted the fabric, his hand gripping her naked hip as he bent his head and drew one chiffon-covered nipple into his mouth, caressing it with his tongue-tip whilst Julia writhed helplessly in erotic delight.

But that pleasure was nothing compared to what she felt when Silas caressed the eager wetness of her waiting sex, stroking the full length of her from back to front in a caress that made her cry out and arch into his touch, then cry out again as he played delicately with her clit, nurturing its tight bud into ripe fullness before he finally gave in to her incoherent pleas and slid his fingers into her hot waiting wetness, making her climax so violently that Julia was half afraid she might actually pass out.

'Oh, Silas, that was heavenly.' She wept emotionally as he held her shuddering body. 'Purr-fect. Who would ever have thought that being married to you could be like this?'

'I'm going to take that as a compliment,' Silas told her dryly, as he picked her up and carried her over to the waiting bed.

Laughter gurgled in Julia's throat as she leaned over and kissed him.

'And I'm going to take you as well—unless you've got some objection?'

'No objection. Just a warning that I probably won't come again. Not after an orgasm like that,' Julia cautioned him.

'Want to bet?' Silas asked her.

He was just leaning over her when the telephone

started to ring. Immediately Julia stiffened. Was it Aimee ringing him again?

Silas released her and reached for the room telephone at the same moment as she recognised that it was not his mobile ringing.

'That was the reception desk, wanting to know if we'd booked a car. I told them they'd got the wrong room. Now, where were we?' Silas asked softly.

No way was she going to let Aimee spoil what she was enjoying with Silas, Julia assured herself as he took her back in his arms. She closed her eyes tightly, willing herself not to think of anything or anyone other than the two of them and what they were sharing, and gave herself over completely to the physical delight of his hands on her body.

An hour later, after the final ripples of their shared climax had died away and Silas had gathered her into his arms to draw her close to him, Julia decided blissfully that there could be no greater happiness than this, and that she had been silly to worry about that earlier phone call.

She was almost on the verge of falling asleep when she remembered something very important.

'Silas!' she gasped urgently.

'What?'

'We didn't use a condom.'

'No, we didn't, did we?'

If Silas wasn't concerned that they might be risking her conceiving his child, then he couldn't possibly be involved with another woman could he? She had been silly to worry, Julia reassured herself.

CHAPTER EIGHT

MARBELLA in September: the month of summer when the tiresome tourist crowds had gone, along with their noisy children, and the only visitors were those who were rich enough or A-list enough to know that this was the time to be here. Or at least that was what most of the guests invited to Dorland's party were likely to believe, Julia thought cynically, as the chauffeur-driven limo swept them up to the main entrance of Marbella's *luxe de luxe* home from home for the celebrity set—the world famous Alfonso Club, Golf Resort and Spa—or the Alfonso, as most of those in the know referred to the hotel a European prince had created from what had originally been merely a family *finca*, or rural property.

Supposedly, sooner or later everyone who was anyone stayed at the Alfonso. Her smile deepened as she reflected on how very different this fashionable celebrity watering hole was from the hotel they had stayed at in Rome.

Marbella, like St Tropez, St Moritz and a handful of other places worldwide, had held on to its exalted status through many decades. Julia suspected that nowhere else in the world, apart from possibly Palm Springs, was home to quite so many nipped and tucked seventy-something women pretending to be thirty-something. They came here in the summer to bask in the sunshine, like so many stick-thin locusts, bronzing their leathery bodies before retreating to some discreet Swiss clinic to be pampered and prepared for another summer.

Marbella was like nowhere else, being a place where it was almost *de rigueur* to sport a tan, a proper hairdo, diamanté-studded sunglasses and gold leather Gucci-style loafers.

Not that Marbella didn't attract the younger celebrity crowd—it did, and in droves, a fact which Dorland had recognised when he elected to throw his end-of-summer bash here.

Silas had booked them into one of the club's private villas, and as they were shown to it Julia decided she would have to do something about extending her wardrobe. She had seen how sad her small case looked in contrast to the mounds of Louis Vuitton being removed from limousine boots. Already she had spotted at least three famous film stars, plus an all girl-group and their entourage, all of whom she knew had been invited to Dorland's party.

To Julia's delight their villa not only had its own private garden, it also had its own private swimming pool.

'Oh, Silas, this is just too blissful,' she exclaimed happily as she stood looking out of the villa's patio doors towards the pool.

'I thought you'd like it,' Silas agreed, making her both laugh and blush at the same time.

'Just because I happened to say that I'd love to swim naked with you and then have sex outside, in the open air, that doesn't mean you had to find a way to make it possible,' she told him.

'Meaning that now that I have, you've changed your mind?'

'No way,' Julia assured him vehemently. 'Though I'll have to go and find Dorland later.' She gave a small shudder. 'I don't want any more traumas or mistakes of the kind we had in Positano. I still can't believe that actually happened. What is it?' she demanded, when she saw the way Silas was looking at her.

'I've had an e-mail from the person I asked to make some discreet enquiries into both Blayne and Prêt a Party.'

'And?'

'Let's get settled in first. You must be hungry. I'll order something from Room Service, shall I?'

'Silas, it's bad, isn't it?' Julia guessed.

'Let's get sorted out first.'

Julia reached out and touched his arm, sensing that he was trying to distract her.

'No, please tell me now.' She could see from his face that Silas was beginning to wish he hadn't said anything. 'I know you only want to protect me, but I'm not a little girl any more,' she told him gently. 'And Lucy is my friend.'

'All right. But at least let's sit down.'

Her mouth had gone dry, Julia realised as Silas sat in one of the comfortable easy chairs and she perched on the arm of it next to him.

'From what my source has discovered—and I've no reason to doubt him; I've used him in the past to investigate sensitive issues for me—it looks very much as though Prêt a Party has some very serious financial problems.'

'Oh, Silas.' Julia placed her fingertips to her mouth, her eyes shadowing with distress.

'There's worse, I'm afraid. It seems that there is every likelihood that Blayne has been defrauding the business—and Lucy herself as well.'

'Oh, no! Poor Lucy—but how can that have happened? Lucy is always complaining that her trustee won't let her touch her trust fund without his say-so.'

'Maybe not, but he has allowed her to guarantee Prêt a Party's overdraft facilities. And that means that the bank has been able to call upon her to clear it via her trust fund. From what my source has discovered, it seems that large amounts of money have been withdrawn from the business by Blayne, which have caused an overdraft that Lucy has had to make good. It seems that there is no real business reason why he should have withdrawn such large amounts, and my source suspects they have gone straight into his own pocket—if Lucy isn't aware of what he's doing.'

'She can't be.' Julia defended her friend immediately. 'Lucy is scrupulously honest, Silas.'

'Maybe she was. But she loves Blayne, and if he has been pressuring her…'

'No.' Julia shook her head vigorously. 'No matter how much Lucy loves Nick, she would never agree to anything underhand. She just isn't like that. Oh, Silas. Poor, poor Lucy.'

Tears shimmered in Julia's eyes. 'This is just so awful. Imagine loving someone who would do that to you. And Nick…how could he do such a thing?' She bit her bottom lip and then looked unhappily at Silas.

'It's going to be so dreadful for Lucy when she finds out what Nick's been doing.'

'Yes, but you can't interfere,' Silas warned her.

'Silas, she's one of my two closest friends,' Julia protested. 'Lucy, Carly and I have been like sisters. I can't just stand by and let Nick destroy her.'

'What I've told you is merely, at this stage, the informed opinion of my source. What do you think will happen if you do tell Lucy and she refuses to believe you? Blayne is her husband. She's besotted with him.'

'But we must be able to do something.'

'Maybe I could sound out her trustee discreetly.'

'Marcus, you mean? Lucy hates him.'

'Maybe, but he's still the best person to deal with the situation on her behalf. I've told my source to double-check and then come back to me. Until he does we can't really do anything. Was Blayne supposed to pay any bills for this party of Dorland's?' Silas asked.

Julia frowned. 'No, we worked together with Dorland, and he paid for everything himself. I'm going to be more a hostess for him than anything else. But why are you asking me that?'

'If Dorland had given Prêt a Party money then it's pretty likely it would have found its way into Blayne's pocket—and then we would have a repetition of what happened in Positano.'

'No, Dorland has definitely paid for everything himself,' Julia told him, adding with relief, 'Thank goodness.'

Julia was still thinking about Lucy several hours later, when she knocked on the door of Dorland's suite.

'Julia! What—no fabbie jewels?' Dorland exclaimed as he opened the door to her himself and immediately examined her left hand. 'Don't tell me the engagement is off?'

Julia laughed.

'Not yet,' she answered mischievously. She had no intention of giving Dorland any kind of hint that she and Silas were actually married, and she certainly wasn't going to let him guess why.

Dorland pouted, and then batted what Julia saw were fake turquoise eyelashes at her.

'I thought he was going to load you down with heir-looms.'

'The insurers wouldn't let him,' Julia answered, straight-faced.

'You must watch that, Julia. There is nothing worse than a mean billionaire,' Dorland warned her, ignoring her comment.

'Silas isn't mean.'

'Oooh, so it is a love thang, then, is it? I thought so! Sex is all very well, but take it from me, diamonds are better.'

'Speaking of which, did the Tiffany necklace turn up?' Julia asked him.

'No, and Tiffany are being absolutely *howwid* to me about it. You wouldn't credit it. Still, we won't talk about that now. Not when all I want to talk about is my fabby party. Everyone is coming…a certain celebrity European princess, plus an even more celebrity Hollywood couple—you'll know who I mean. They are all so famous I'm not allowed to so much as breathe their names,' he added coyly. 'Just the whole of the A list are going to be here—even a certain international footballer and his wife are coming, and guess who they are bringing with them?'

'Er…who?' Julia asked dutifully.

'Only Jon Belton!'

Julia looked suitably impressed at the mention of the ultra-famous pop singer.

'Oh, Jules, I am just *sooo* excited,' Dorland exclaimed excitedly. 'It is going to be the party of the year—and of course *A-List Life* will have an exclusive on it. Now, sweet, down to business. I've already spoken to the hotel people and arranged for a piano, but you know, I was thinking—wouldn't it be fun to have the balloons printed with a piano motif—black balloons with a white piano,

perhaps encrusted with just the teeny-weeniest bit of dia-
manté? So retro and so Liberace. I can see it now!'

So, unfortunately, could Julia.

'Do you think that's a good idea?' she asked cautiously.

'Of course I do. Why? Don't you?'

'Well, it could be just a tad over the top, don't you
think?'

'Julia, I am Dorland Chesterfield—*nothing* I do could
ever be too over the top,' Dorland told her theatrically.

'How's it going?'

Julia shook her head as Silas reached for her hand and
held it firmly in his own. He had been waiting for her
when she finally left Dorland's suite, and now they were
walking back to their villa through the hotel gardens.

'Dorland is wearing false eyelashes—turquoise false
eyelashes. Apparently he's going to be wearing tur-
quoise-coloured contact lenses for the party. And he's
going to be sprayed with fake tan.'

'I'm beginning to fear the worst,' Silas murmured
wryly.

'He's had a shirt specially made for him by Roberto
Cavalli, and he's going to wear a white suit.'

She could feel Silas starting to shake with laughter.

'Silas, it isn't funny. He's bought a white poodle—
and a diamond- and turquoise-studded collar.'

'For whom?'

'The poodle, of course. At least, I assume it's for the
poodle. I haven't told you the worst yet, though.'

'Could it be any worse?'

'Yes. He keeps on talking about Liberace—Silas, stop
laughing. *Silas!*' Julia protested breathlessly as he suddenly stopped walking and pulled her towards him.

'We're almost back at the villa,' she told him huskily, as his hands moulded her against his body.

'I can't wait that long.'

His skin smelled of warm night air and that sexy indefinable smell that was just him, and his lips were cool and slightly salty as they teased and cajoled hers.

Julia looped her arms around his neck and traced the shape of his mouth with the tip of her tongue, glorying in the now familiar starburst of erotic delight fizzing eagerly inside her. It wouldn't always be like this between them, of course; one day this fierce, intoxicating passion would become a warm and familiar comforting glow rather than something that still filled her with half-shocked delight. One day. A long, long time from now, when they were old...

Growing old with Silas. The rest of their lives together. How very lucky she was—and how very, very happy. She held him tighter, kissing him passionately, making a small soft sound of pleasure deep in her throat as she felt him start to unfasten her cut-offs and then slide his hand inside the opening.

'You're so wet...'

'Mmm, I know... Uhh. Ohh. Mmm, Silas...' Her body was already moving rhythmically against his caressing fingers, her own hand closing round him whilst she shuddered in pleasurable anticipation. He fitted her so well. Filled her so well, making her feel each time that she almost might not be able to take the pleasure of the depth and intensity of his thrusts, and yet at the same time miraculously somehow making her feel that she wanted to stretch, to have more and more of him.

'Silas, I'm going to come,' she warned him.

'No. Not yet. I want to watch you when you do…'

He removed his fingers, slowly and gently, and then kissed her tenderly, keeping her close to his side as they walked the last few yards to their villa.

CHAPTER NINE

JULIA lay in bed next to Silas, dreamily watching the early-morning sunshine stroking golden warmth onto his bare skin. Silas had the most perfect male body she had ever seen, and just looking at it—at him—filled her with such a deep well of wonder and happiness. She had never imagined that she would know this level of joy and fulfilment, or feel that her future stretched out in front of her in a rose-coloured pathway sparkling with gold dust. She was just so happy—and all because of Silas.

'I thought you said you wanted to be up early today, with it being Dorland's big day.'

'Mmm, I did,' she agreed reluctantly.

She was going to be tied up for most of the day, and they had agreed that Silas would leave her to do what she had to do whilst he got on with some work of his own. But not yet. Definitely not yet. She snuggled closer to Silas, drawing sexy shapes on his bare shoulder with the tip of her tongue and then, nibbling his earlobe and whispering in his ear.

'You've got to guess what I'm drawing, and if you're wrong you have to pay a forfeit.'

'Which is?'

'Either massage my feet or shag me.'

'And if I get it right and win?'

'You get to massage my feet *and* shag me,' Julia told him generously, before adding dreamily, 'I'm keeping a count of how many orgasms I've had with you.'

'What for? Comparison or posterity?'

Julia giggled. 'Well, it isn't for comparison—no one could compare with you, Silas. Do you think I should count all those little mini multiple "o"s I had last night as one or individually?'

As Silas moved, the bedclothes slipped down past his waist, revealing the thick hard jut of his morning erection for her adoring and admiring approval.

'How close are you to double figures?' he asked lazily.

'Mmm…with the multiples I'm over it, and without I'm just over halfway to triple. Oh…that is so nice…' She exhaled heavily as his tongue caressed the nipple of the bare breast closest to his mouth whilst his fingers worked sensually on the other.

Drawing her with him, Silas lay flat against the bed, so that she was arched over him on her hands and knees.

Watching her excitement as she responded to the sure guidance of his hands, Silas was sharply aware of how unique she was. He had had sex, and he had had good sex, but he had never had sex with a woman who responded to him with the openness and enjoyment, the complete naturalness and the sheer happiness manifested by Julia. She showed him in so many different ways that having sex with him gave her pleasure and delight and made her feel good, and as a consequence of that she made him feel good. In fact she made him feel one hell of a lot more than merely *good*.

Her breathless 'Oh, Silas, look!' had him pushing aside his thoughts to obediently look down his own body to where she was straddling him, and slowly and joyously taking him into her inch by inch.

'Mmm, doesn't that look good? It feels good too… You are just so big!' she cooed delightedly.

Foolish, flattering words. But the insane thing was that Julia quite plainly actually meant them.

She eased down on him a little more, using her muscles to gently squeeze and then stroke his erection in a movement that made him close his eyes and fight for self-control.

But Julia obviously had other ideas, and he could hear her laughing softly as she took him deeper and held him harder, and his control exploded in the red heat of his need to drive into her over and over again, his hands gripping her hips as she moaned and writhed above him.

Outwardly she might look businesslike and in control but inside she was just a delicious boneless mass of sexually satisfied woman. Very sexually satisfied woman, Julia congratulated herself, as she listened to a very Notting Hill type who obviously fancied himself describing to her the birthday party he had attended in Venice earlier in the year.

'And we were all taken to the party on these fantastic gondolas along the canals. Everyone was in costume. It was terribly Thirties and decadent. I've heard that an American TV network is filming Dorland's party for one of those fly-on-the-wall docudrama things. Is it true?'

'I really don't know, Charles. You'll have to ask Dorland,' Julia answered truthfully.

'And which famous people are going to be here?'

'I haven't seen the guest list,' Julia replied. Which wasn't true.

'Julia—darling!'

Charles was shouldered aside by a trio of frighteningly stiff-faced women whom Julia vaguely recognised from school—not fellow pupils but their mothers. One of them, or so it was whispered behind closed doors, had not—as she liked to claim—been in her youth a high-priced model, but rather a high-priced whore.

'So clever of you to bag Silas.' Cold sharp gazes swept her from head to toe.

These women were part of the new social order—fifty-something divorcees, prepared to fight dirty in order to look more like thirty. While their ex-husbands used their money to replace them with younger models, these women used their divorce settlements to try and turn back time. And the better-informed ones sometimes actually managed it, Julia knew, thinking of at least half a dozen high-profile society hostesses who genuinely looked as though they had been able to turn the figure five into a three.

Unfortunately for them, though, these three were not among that half-dozen.

'Yes, isn't it?' Julia agreed, flashing them a very happy smile.

'All that money, and a title—and best of all, he's wonderful in bed.'

Scarlet and green was never a good colour combination on aging faces, Julia decided smugly, and she left them with their red faces and jealous eyes to go and see how things were progressing with the decorating of the large marquee which had been put up for the occasion.

All the invitations had specified that Dorland's guests were to wear either their own most 'papped' (papparazzied) outfit, or a copy of one worn by someone else. And Julia had privately predicted that at least half the female guests under thirty-five (and that meant all the female guests, since none of them was likely to admit to being older) would be wearing a copy of the designer Julien Macdonald's itsy-bitsy sparkly dress, as worn by a certain top international star when she upstaged the bride at a celebrity wedding. With this in mind, Julia had suggested to Dorland that they keep the interior of the marquee quietly elegant and in colours that would act as a foil to the celebrated dress.

Dorland had resisted her advice at first, having fallen in love with the idea of mimicking a certain branded and banded couple's wedding, with gold throne-like chairs studded with fake jewels instead of the simple, plain cream-covered dining chairs Julia had suggested, decorated with glittery grey and black and white ribbon tied into bows.

When Julia reached the tented anteroom of the main marquee, the construction people were just finishing setting up the champagne fountain Dorland had fallen in love with, and Dorland himself was busy giggling with a bevy of ultra-thin leggy blondes, who all seemed to be clutching small hairy dogs.

The combination of shrill yaps—from both pets and owners—was positively eardrum assaulting, Julia decided as she hurried out again—only to come to an abrupt halt as she saw Nick standing blocking her path.

'I hear you really ballsed up in Positano,' he told her unkindly.

Julia didn't like being bullied, and she lifted her chin and told him sharply, 'Someone certainly did.'

She thought for a minute that Nick was going to challenge her to explain what she meant, but instead he looked at her left hand and said mockingly, 'He's still not given you a ring, then?'

'Actually, he has,' Julia semi-fibbed. After all, Silas had told her that he wanted her to wear the Monckford Diamond.

'I must say you've surprised me, Jules,' Nick drawled nastily. 'I wouldn't have thought you've got what it

takes to hook a man like Silas. Has he told you about
Aimee DeTroite?'

'Whatever Aimee may have been to Silas, that is now
in the past,' she told him lightly.

'You mean Silas has *told* you she's in the past. So far
as she's concerned she is still very much in his present
and his future—but of course he won't have told you
that.'

What had she ever seen in Nick? He was a loathsome,
vile, repellent toad, and she hated him for what he was
doing to Lucy.

'No, he hasn't,' she agreed coolly. 'But he has told
me about you.'

'What does that mean?' Nick demanded.

'You know what it means. It means that Silas has
checked up on you and the business. How could you do
this to Lucy, Nick?'

'What have you said to her?'

'Nothing—yet. But I—'

'Jules—there you are. Have you got a moment?'

'Of course, Dorland.' Julia smiled, walking away from
Nick to go and see what Dorland wanted.

Had Nick just been trying to upset her when he had told
her about Aimee? Or did the other woman genuinely
have grounds for claiming that she was involved in an
on-going relationship with Silas? An *affair* with Silas
now, in fact, since Silas was married to her.

Julia could feel her heart thumping painfully. She felt
sick and dizzy from the mixture of anxiety and confusion
and adrenalin hurtling through her veins. She was determined to hang on to her belief that whatever had happened before her in Silas's private life was his alone to
know about, if that was what he wished. Aimee was

certainly not the type Julia would have thought would appeal to Silas. But Silas had dated her. And Silas had appeared in one of those stolen videos. She had not seen the video, but she had read the gossip when the story had first broken earlier in the year.

Nick was a troublemaker, she warned herself, and Silas was entitled to have a past. A past, yes. But right now she needed to know that not only was she his present and his future, but also that she was going to be his *only* present and future! And she needed to know it because she was wildly, passionately and totally in love with him.

Because he was the best shag she had ever had?

How shallow was that? Loving someone was about more than a ten-second orgasm, surely? About more than even double figures of them. Loving someone involved things like respect, and wanting to share the rest of your life with them, in sickness and in health. It meant that being with them added an extra dimension to your life. It meant that they were the light that filled your life, the extra special someone without whom your life felt empty and for whom your heart ached.

And that was exactly how she felt about Silas.

When she eventually got back to their villa, Silas was waiting for her.

'Sorry I've been so long. Dorland was waffling on for ever about Jon Belton. I think he might have a crush on him. Oh, and Silas, guess what? Nick's here.'

'Blayne? Why?'

'I don't know. Dorland interrupted us before I could ask him. I can't understand now why I didn't realise how loathsome he is when I first met him. I told him we know what's going on, and how much I hate him for what he's doing to Lucy.'

'I thought we'd agreed that nothing was going to be said about that until it could be proved?'

'Well, yes. I know you did say that. But he made me so very angry, and it just sort of slipped out.'

'What do you mean, he made you angry?'

'Oh, he said that he couldn't understand why you wanted me, and he asked me if I'd asked you about your relationship with Aimee DeTroite.' Julia looked at him, but Silas had turned away from her.

His body language positively bristled with 'keep off the past' signs that sent a shiver of female anxiety icing down her spine. As a woman she could think of only one reason why he was making it plain he didn't want to talk about Aimee, and that was because he still had feelings for her. No woman ever minded about talking about a burned-out love affair, especially not when doing so might help to underline her besotted adoration for her current love interest, Julia reasoned, so it must be the same for men.

Therefore, by one of those lightening and complicated equations so familiar to the female mind, she was very quickly able to work out that Aimee plus silence equalled unrequited love—which, when added to physical frustration plus male pride, added up to marriage to her. And that equation, when totalled with her own sum of total love for Silas, plus insecurity, plus jealousy, plus uncertainty, equated to the chemical effect of a lighted match being dropped straight into a keg of gunpowder.

The result was immediate and explosive.

'You just married me because you can't have her, didn't you? She rejected you, and so to make her jealous you pretended to be engaged to me! Well, I don't care how many sexy videos you made with her, she's—

Silas!' Julia protested as he started to stride away from her.

'What the hell is this?' Silas demanded angrily as he turned to look at her. 'You're my wife, not a federal judge, and besides…'

'Besides what? You've only had sex with her?'

Silas couldn't believe his ears. Did Julia really think that he…? Aimee DeTroite was a head case—totally off the wall and dangerous with it.

'Look, Julia, just ease off on the histrionics, will you? I married you—'

'And you shagged Aimee—the whole world knows that, and most of it has seen the video,' Julia told him nastily.

The vicious slamming of the door as Silas brought their argument to an end shuddered through the whole villa.

Dorland's party would be starting in half an hour, and it was time for her to go over to the marquee—even though she hadn't made things up with Silas, Julia realised miserably.

All the time she had been getting ready she had been hoping he would walk into the bedroom. But he hadn't, and her own pride would not let her go in search of him. After all, she had done nothing wrong.

She looked at her watch. She couldn't delay any longer. Even so she still dawdled in the villa's entrance hall, and dropped her bag on the tiled floor to alert Silas to her presence just in case he did want to make amends, but her husband maintained an obstinate absence and silence.

She must not start howling now, Julia warned herself

as she opened the villa door, and she blinked fiercely, firmly straightening her shoulders.

Silas removed his frowning concentration from the e-mail he had just received on his BlackBerry for long enough to watch as Julia hurried away from the villa. She was wearing a long black dress that clung sensually to her body. Round her hips she had wrapped what looked to Silas very much like the Hermès scarf his mother had given her for her birthday, and over that she had fastened a heavy belt set with turquoise stones. The whole effect was *very* Julia, Silas decided.

His frown disappeared and his mouth started to turn up at the corners. She would look stunning in the Maharajah's jewels, and she would probably devise some innovative way of wearing them that would shock the purists rigid. The sound of his own laughter startled him, and then made him frown slightly as he put down his BlackBerry.

There was no getting away from the fact that Julia had the most extraordinary effect on him. By rights he ought still to be angry with her, but instead he was laughing—and he was tempted to drop the BlackBerry and race after her. She was the most ridiculous, infuriating woman there could possibly be, aggravatingly sunny-natured and welded to those rose-tinted glasses through which she seemed to view humanity. She was illogical and stubborn and sometimes just plain crazy. And she made him feel…

Feel? He did not 'feel' things. He analysed and dissected them; he applied practical reasoning to them—just as he had applied practical reasoning to their marriage. But how could you apply practical reasoning to a woman who wanted to know if a multiple orgasm counted as one or not; a woman who referred to your penis as a 'gorgeous, sexy hunny-bunny of a shag shaft,' cooing the words in between stroking and kissing it; a woman who asked you in all seriousness if you thought that, if she whispered a few words to them, 'all the sperm in your baby gravy' would paddle like mad to make her pregnant.

Practical reasoning and Julia were poles apart—at opposite ends of any scale—which was why she needed him to keep an eye on her. And that, of course, was the only reason why he was going to get showered and changed and go and join Dorland's ridiculous ego fest of a party.

It was nearly midnight, the party had been going on for hours, and she still hadn't seen any sign of Silas—even though she had spent what felt like the whole night looking for him.

'Julia.' She stiffened as she saw Nick approaching with a group of louche-looking young men—the sons of some of Dorland's older guests, Julia recognized, most of whom looked rather the worse for drink.

'I've brought a few of your admirers over to say hello to you.'

The boys—for they were little more, Julia decided—blushed and brayed and generally behaved as male teenagers do under the influence of drink and raging hormones.

'Are you enjoying the party?' Julia asked them in a kind voice, at the same time looking round discreetly to see if she could spot Silas anywhere.

'Any one for more champagne?' Nick demanded, revealing the unopened bottle he was carrying.

'Not for me, thanks,' Julia refused, showing him her already half-full glass.

'Rubbish—of course you want some,' Nick insisted, taking it from her and turning away to put it on a table while he opened the bottle, then filling it and topping up everyone else's glasses. 'Here you go.'

Julia took a polite mouthful of the drink and tried to keep up her smile as the men gathered around her, making drunken attempts at wit and charm.

'Has anyone ever told you that you've got great tits?' one of the boys asked her.

Pretending she hadn't heard him, she moved slightly away from him. She finished the champagne and put her glass down on a nearby table, wanting to get away.

'Is that Silas over there?' Nick asked Julia, and watched in satisfaction as she turned her head to look where he was indicating, towards the marquee.

In the darkness on the other side of the large people-packed stretch of gardens that separated him from Julia, Silas frowned as he saw her with Nick and a group of young men. As he watched, she put down her glass and seemed to be trying to edge away from the group.

She had her back to him, and something about her stance made Silas think of a young fox surrounded by out-of-control baying hounds. Blayne was obviously saying something to her, because she suddenly turned her head to look in the opposite direction from the table. Behind her back, one of the group of young men refilled her glass while another dropped something into her drink.

Anxiously, and oblivious to what was happening, Julia continued to look in the direction Nick had indicated, even though she could see no sign of Silas.

'Julia!' Even though he knew she wouldn't be able to hear him, Silas still called out her name in sharp warning as he started to thrust his way through the crowd towards her.

'Come on, Jules—drink up,' Julia heard Nick urging her affably, as he proffered a second glass of champagne. Reluctantly she turned to face him, taking a polite sip. 'I really have to go now,' she told him. 'Dorland will be wondering where I am.'

'Oh, but we aren't going to let you go yet—are we, boys? Come on, drink up. That's right.'

There was a look in Nick's eyes that was quite frightening, Julia saw uncomfortably. A mixture of excitement and cruelty that made her desperately want to get away from him. And the boys with him, although no doubt charming as individuals, in their present overheated and drunken state reminded her far too much of hungry, mob-minded pack animals.

Nick was already holding on to her arm now, and the boys were pressing much closer to her than she liked.

Anxious to get away from them without any unpleasantness, Julia took a gulp of her champagne.

'Come on—you've got to drink it all. Hasn't she, lads?' She could hear Nick speaking, but oddly the words seemed to be reaching her from a distance. Even more oddly, her mouth seemed to be going numb, whilst her body felt heavy and all she could see were blurred images.

She was being sucked down into a vortex of darkness. Darkness and harsh mocking laughter, whilst hands reached for her and tugged at her clothes.

'What have you given her?'

Silas was standing cradling Julia's inert body in one arm, Nick's blood crimsoning the knuckles of his free hand, whilst Nick himself lay where he had fallen, in a tangle of wrought-iron chairs and pot plants, nursing his bruised jaw. The least drunk of the young men were rapidly sobering up, and looking white-faced with fear.

'Liquid X—you know, GHB,' one of them volunteered, shamefaced. 'Couple of doses, I reckon, 'cos Nick put some in too.'

Nick glowered at Silas silently.

'Blayne told us she was up for it,' another of them insisted. 'Said he'd see us all right if we helped him.'

Whilst Silas's attention was on them Nick managed to struggle to his feet. Damn that bloody bitch Julia. He had been determined to have his revenge on her, and to make sure that no one would ever take any accusations she might make seriously. If Silas hadn't intervened right now the Honourable Julia would have been on her way to becoming the Dishonoured Julia, in the cheap apartment Nick was renting. He had already set up everything he would need to film Julia enjoying the intimate attentions of the drunken youths he had planned to incite to take full advantage of her and the situation she was in.

By tomorrow morning he would have had a video of the whole thing that would have earned him a small fortune and humiliated and humbled Julia. No way would his sanctimonious wife have believed a word her precious friend had to say once his video became public property.

Silas could see Nick scuttling away, but he wasn't prepared to leave Julia to go after him.

He had reached her just as she collapsed, and had heard her terrified whimper of protest as she felt his hands on her body, her own trying desperately to push him away.

The images inside his head of what her fate would

have been if he hadn't witnessed what was happening and got to her in time, filled him with fury and anguish. His arms tightened protectively around her as she lolled helplessly against him.

'You—go and find a doctor and bring him here,' he instructed the most sober of the youths grimly. 'There should be one at the first aid station. And as for the rest of you…I won't forget what nearly happened here to-night.'

CHAPTER TEN

SILAS stood sombrely beside the bed watching Julia as she slept. He had spent most of the night catnapping in an armchair so that he could both watch over her and be there should she wake and need him, and now the golden bars of morning sunshine striping the bed in honey-eyed warmth contrasted sharply with the darkness of his thoughts. Yes, Julia was here, and safe, but she might so easily not have been. And that would have been his fault. He could have made up their small quarrel before she had left the villa, but he had chosen not to do so, deeming it practical that she should be punished just a little for raising issues he did not want to discuss.

His fault. A surge of aching emotional anguish battered savagely against his once impervious belief in his own rightness.

Julia made a small sound and immediately he leaned towards her. The doctor who had seen her the previous night had assured him that there would not be any lasting long-term effects from the drug she had been given.

'But,' he had warned Silas gravely, 'in the short term it may well be that she will suffer from physical symptoms such as nausea and dizziness—and, more unpleasantly, emotional and mental panic, flashbacks, even paranoia. She will feel vulnerable and sometimes threatened. Fortunately, because you were able to rescue her, you will be able to reassure her that she has nothing to fear from what she can't remember.

'One of the most harrowing aspects of the way certain

depraved and vicious men are using this drug against
women is the fact that their victims cannot remember
what happened. They have flashbacks, dream sequences
of events, but these are shadowy and insubstantial, and
it is my experience that a woman who has suffered rape
via this kind of drug tortures herself over what she
cannot remember as much as what she can. In fact, in
one particularly traumatic and tragic case I had to deal
with some months back, the young woman concerned
actually took her own life. Your partner has been very
fortunate.'

Silas made a small abrupt movement, unable to continue with his own train of thought, and then sat down
on the side of the bed.

Immediately Julia opened her eyes and looked at him,
starting to smile, her eyes alight with warmth and love.
And then, as though a protective seal had been torn from
her, her expression changed, all the joy leaching from it,
as swiftly as dry fine sand running through a man's hand,
leaving behind it an empty hollow that quickly became
filled with darkness and pain.

Silas could see the fear and confusion filling her—
sense it almost like a cold, thick, impenetrable fog.
Automatically he touched her arm, wanting to comfort
her, his heart thudding with the violence of his emotions
as she recoiled from him.

'No, Silas, please,' she whispered. 'You mustn't touch
me. Something horrible has happened.'

Her eyes were filling with tears and the look of agonised shame she gave him ripped at his heart.

'Julia, it's all right…'

'No. No, it isn't. You don't know what's happened.'

As she wept Julia lifted her hands to her face, pressing
her fingers against her temples.

She felt so weak and confused, somehow aware that something unbearably dreadful had happened to her but unable to remember what it was. Images flashed through her head like lasers. Nick looking at her with a vicious cruel smile. Sounds: the braying laughter of men. Sensations. Hard male hands touching her. And, woven through them all, binding her with icy fear, the most terrifying and intense surges of panic.

'Jules, it is all right, I promise you.' Silas could hardly speak himself, his voice thick with a mingling of anger, guilt and an emotion he didn't recognise but that ran as pure as liquid gold, carrying only his desire to protect and comfort her.

'No!' Julia shook her head and wept. 'Nothing can ever be right again, Silas. You don't know what happened. Nick…'

As she shuddered and closed her eyes Silas took hold of her, binding her to him. 'Nothing happened,' he told her thickly.

'Yes, it did. But I can't remember what. All I can remember is that Nick made me drink some champagne. I didn't want to, but he insisted. And then…I can't remember what happened, but I know it was something horrible. And I'm afraid… You'll have to divorce me, Silas.'

'What?'

'I've heard about things like this happening…women being drugged and then… You don't know what's happened, because you can't remember, but you just get sort of flashbacks, and the men always claim that you were willing… Nick hates me, and if he…if they…'

The look in her eyes shocked and tormented him into speechlessness.

'If there were to be a child…' she whispered rawly, hanging her head. 'I don't know if I could—'

'Julia, you mustn't torment yourself like this. There's no need. Nothing happened!'

'You keep saying that, but you don't know—'

'I do know! I saw Blayne slip the drug into your drink. By the time I got to you it was too late to stop you from drinking it, and you were on the point of collapsing, but that was all that did happen.'

'But I will never know that, will I?' Julia told him quietly. 'I'll never know if that's true or if you're just saying it to protect me. And I'll have to live the rest of my life wondering if you're married to me because you want to be or because you feel honour-bound to be. I can't do that, Silas. I can't live like that. And I can't bear thinking about what might have happened. They *were* touching me!' Julia wept. 'I felt their hands…'

'Those were my hands.'

Julia pulled away from him and looked up at him, her eyes dark with despair.

'Julia, I give you my word that what I am telling you is the truth. I understand how you must feel, and why you feel it, but I have to say that I don't like thinking that you neither believe me nor trust me.'

'I feel afraid, Silas, and…and dirty. And… How can I ever have sex with you again when I don't know what might be happening inside my own body? When I don't know what might have happened—what things could—'

'Your body is no different this morning than it was yesterday afternoon when you left the villa. I am not in any way unwilling to have sex with you, Julia, because I know there is no reason for me not to do so other than my concern for you. And if you want me to prove that to you…'

'Where is Nick now?' Julia asked, without responding to his challenge.

'I have no idea. Dr. Salves has already advised me that if you want to press charges against Blayne, then—'

'No!' Julia stopped him violently. 'How can I do that when he is married to Lucy?' she demanded, adding weakly, 'My head hurts, and I feel sick...'

She was trembling almost violently, and Silas didn't waste time, simply scooping her up out of the bed and carrying her to the bathroom.

Julia looked out of the bedroom window towards the patio area of the villa, where Silas was sitting beside the pool, wearing only a pair of shorts despite the fact that it was already almost dusk. She could hear his voice, although not what he was saying, as he spoke into his BlackBerry. It was nearly a week since she had been drugged. Dr. Salves had told her two days ago that physically she was fully recovered, and she had told him truthfully that her feelings of acute panic and terror had begun to lessen. But, despite that, she was still haunted by the fear that Silas, out of kindness, had lied to her when he had told her that nothing had happened to her.

A little shakily she turned round and headed for the open patio doors.

When he saw her walking towards him Silas switched off his BlackBerry and stood up without moving, letting her walk to him instead.

'Silas, tell me again what happened with...when... I can't bear it that I can't remember!' She choked out in a tortured voice, stepping back as Silas reached out for her.

'Nothing happened.'

'You keep telling me that, but how can I believe it when I can't remember? How can I know that it's the truth and that you aren't just saying it to protect me?' Julia demanded emotionally. 'Dr. Salves says I may never have total recall, so how can I know if I can't remember?'

She flinched as Silas took hold of her left hand, clasping it between his own, but he refused to let her go.

'When I married you I took on certain responsibilities,' Silas began sombrely.

'Yes, I know, and it's because of that that I'm afraid you are just protecting me,' Julia burst out.

'One of those responsibilities,' Silas continued, as though she hadn't spoken, 'at least for me, is to ensure that our relationship, our *marriage*, has the strongest foundations it can possibly have. And for me the strongest foundations any relationship can have are those of trust and honesty. Trust is a two-way thing, Julia. A person may give it freely, or it may have to be earned. But both the person who gives it and the one who takes it have an irrevocable duty to honour it. I trust you to honour our marriage because I know the person you are, and I know without it having to be said that having married me, you will give your responsibilities to our marriage and to me priority above everything else. I give you that trust because I know that I can—because, if you like, I *know* you.

'And I promise you that you can have the same trust in me. Yes, I do believe it is my responsibility to protect you, and I blame myself for not being there to prevent what happened right at the start. But I would not be protecting you now if I lied to you about what happened and left your fears and doubts to fester. A clean, sharp, open wound always heals better than one that is hidden away. Had you been physically abused in any kind of way I would have told you. But you were not. I reached you as you collapsed and the only hands to touch you were mine. You were not abused, and you were not raped, and that is the truth. I promise you that on my word as your grandfather's heir. I cannot give you back the memory you have lost, but I can and do give you my promise that you can and will always be able to trust me to tell you the truth—just as I already know that I can and do trust you to be equally honest with me and for me.'

Julia's eyes stung with bittersweet emotional tears. How could she reject the precious gift Silas was offering her? She remembered how only this morning she had twisted away from him, refusing to let him kiss her, explaining reluctantly that she still felt contaminated and afraid, even though Dr. Salves had assured her that she was perfectly healthy.

'Julia?'

Unable to speak, she shook her head and then turned and ran back to the villa.

From their bedroom Julia watched as Silas walked to the far end of the pool. The subtle nightscape lighting illuminated the privacy of their enclosed patio and pool area and showed her the clean hard lines of his body, the strongly toned width of his shoulders that she had loved so much because they were so male and made her feel so safe, the nicely muscular firmness of his torso, arrowing downwards in a perfect V shape. Silas was muscular enough to look healthy and fit without looking mirth-provokingly like a contestant in a Mr. Muscle contest.

The shorts he was wearing, hip-hugging and long-legged, in black and white patterned cotton, were the kind favoured by surfers, and secretly she thought them far more sexy than the tight, skimpy posing pouches favoured by some men.

She wanted him so much, but at the same time she was filled with an unfamiliar sick fear at the thought of having sex with him. Silas might assure her that neither Nick nor anyone else had raped her, but Nick had certainly raped her of her delight in her physical relationship with Silas. And that physical bonding was such an important part of what had made things good between them.

But was she really going to let Nick do that to her? Was she really so weak and doubting that she was going to let him destroy their marriage? Or was she strong enough to trust in Silas, to truly trust in him from the depths of her being? The choice was hers.

Outside, Silas was swimming lengths with a powerful driving crawl that barely rippled the surface of the water.

Julia stepped back from the window.

Marriage obviously changed a man's thinking at some deep and profound level, Silas decided. There was certainly no other practical explanation for the way he was feeling and behaving right now. Logically, until Julia had overcome her present problems, it made sense for him to return to New York, where he had any amount of work waiting for him, rather than remain here. Practical explanations and solutions must always be any right-thinking man's preferred choice. And yet here he was, ploughing up and down a swimming pool, trying to work off the physical ache of his desire for her, and totally unable to find any kind of exercise that would do the same for the mental turmoil he was experiencing.

To say that he felt guilty and helpless and filled with

savage anger came nowhere near to describing just what he did feel. He wanted to take Julia in his arms and hold her protectively safe. And at the same time he wanted to take her with his body and somehow bring back to life the happy, sexy, joy-filled lover who, he was only now beginning to realise, had completed and satisfied him as no other woman ever had. He wanted to tell her that nothing could ever happen to make him want to end their marriage. It couldn't; he simply couldn't envisage his life without her. But he also wanted to tell her that he ached and needed to have back the Julia she had been—the Julia who had laughed and joked and filled the hours they shared with her own special unique sunshine. And he missed that sunshine just as he missed waking up in the morning with her cuddled up against him, just as he missed that special feeling of male satisfaction and triumph that came with holding her tight whilst their heartbeats slowed to post-orgasm normality.

It seemed incredible to him that he could think of nothing and no one else other than Julia, that she filled his thoughts to such an extent that there simply wasn't room for anything or anyone else. It was because she represented a problem that needed a solution, he told himself. Because the way things were now was interrupting the smooth flow of the life and the future he had planned for them. Because this morning, when she had backed away when he had tried to kiss her, her eyes filling with tears, he had damn near wanted to cry himself.

And practical men did not cry. They found solutions instead.

'Silas…'

He stopped swimming in mid-stroke and rolled over to float and look up to where Julia was standing at the

edge of the pool, wearing a sleekly fitting swimsuit that
dipped to a deep V at the front.

'I thought I'd come and join you.' She held out her
arms and told him, 'Catch me.'

The feel of her body in his arms as she slid into the
water brought his aching tension into full-on hard urgency. She had pulled free of him and started to swim
away from him, but she was nowhere near as powerful
or skilled a swimmer as he was himself.

Taking a deep breath, Silas kicked down with a powerful enough stroke to carry him underwater towards her.
His fingers closing round her ankles, he pulled her down
to him.

The scent of the night air combined with the silky
warmth of the water and the touch of Silas's hands on
her body would once have been enough to have her virtually orgasming at the very thought of the pleasure in
store for her, Julia thought bleakly as she closed her
eyes, but she was helplessly aware of the empty noth-
ingness that numbed her.

Wrapped tightly against Silas, she felt the powerful
upward surge of their bodies as he kicked down and sent
them up to the surface whilst her breath escaped in a
stream of small bubbles.

Silas was kissing her, and mechanically she responded, her lips parting obediently, her eyes closing,
her body as still as the soft air as his free hand gently
caressed her and then closed over her breast.

Immediately she broke away from him, and swam towards the shallower end of the pool where she could
stand up.

Silas followed her, taking her back in his arms. His
body felt warm and heavy against her own, and a small
shiver of something that wasn't either despair or pain

flickered to life inside her. Hope or uncertainty? Did she really want to know which?

Determinedly she pressed closer to him, refusing to allow herself to draw back from the hard pulse of his erection. Instead she made herself draw a mental picture of his hardness, drawing it with the love and happiness she could remember but not feel. Warm, amorous mental brushstrokes of delight and excitement created a mental image of firmly muscled maleness, fleshed in skin that shaded from creamy olive to arousal-flushed deep rosy red, ridged and veined to bring it to three-dimensional power and life instead of flatness.

Inside her head she imagined herself touching it, stroking and kissing it, licking its shiny tight head. And all the time she was giving herself a mantra. This is Silas. This is Silas. This is Silas…

And this was Silas who was pulling her so close to him, slipping the straps of her swimsuit from her shoulders and baring her breasts and the protruding stiffness of her nipples to the soft glowing light, Silas bending his head to kiss her.

She flung her own arms round him and returned his kiss with passionate desperation. He broke the kiss, his hands cupping her breasts and his mouth caressing first one and then the other, bathing her cooling skin in delicious wet heat whilst Julia waited, checking and monitoring herself, tensing herself against the flash of memory she was dreading and the surge of fear and loathing it would bring with it.

Silas was guiding her out of the pool towards the comfortably cushioned loungers. Picking her up, he placed her gently on one of them, then reached for a towel and began to dry her with it, removing her swimsuit as he did so. Each touch of his hands was a caress that he made deliberately increasingly intimate, until her body was moving helplessly against his touch. He was taking her to a place she was afraid of going because of what she might find there, but she couldn't stop him because her own body didn't want her to stop him.

He had removed his own swimming shorts and her gaze fastened eagerly on his erection as it strained impatiently from the thickness of his body hair.

He knelt over her and she reached out to touch him, but he evaded her, parting her legs with his hand and bending his head over her. His lips brushed the sensitive flesh on the inside of her thighs and delight rippled through her. His tongue stroked upwards, and of her own accord she stretched wider to meet it, sighing happily in aroused anticipation as he folded back the fleshy outer lips of her sex and stroked the full length of her with his tongue-tip. Beneath its urgent stroke she could feel her clitoris swelling and pulsing. She cried out to him, joyfully giving herself over to sensation, the fear that had stolen away her sexual sense of self swept away by the sheer intensity of what she was feeling.

There were no hidden demons, no dark places, waiting to destroy her. There was only this, and Silas, and an overwhelming need to share with him her joy in the pleasure he was giving her.

'That was wonderful.' Her voice trembled and her eyes were wet with tears of completion and relief.

They were lying side by side on the sun lounger, and Silas leaned over her, gently kissing the tears from her face before brushing her mouth with his own.

It had been wonderful, he acknowledged, wonderful, wondrous, and perfect. He just wanted to lie like this, holding her and giving thanks for what she was and what she had given him, for the rest of his life.

Earlier, when he had entered her, complying with her achingly sweet urgent demands for him to thrust deeper and faster, he had been flooded with the most profound sense of awe and humbleness. And when, seconds later, he had spilled himself hotly into her, that feeling had become ever more intense and meaningful.

She was his soul mate, the only woman who could ever move him to such heights; without her his life would be meaningless and empty. Was this what people meant when they said they loved someone? Was this awesome, intense experience what love was? Was this…*love*. Was he *in love*?

CHAPTER ELEVEN

JULIA smiled contentedly as she slipped her feet into the funky shoes Silas had pointed out to her earlier in the week when they had been in Marbella.

Then she had laughed and refused to be tempted, but this morning she had weakened, and decided to slip into Marbella whilst Silas was catching up with some work— a necessity, he had claimed, now that they had been in Spain for over six weeks.

Technically there would have been time for them both to return to their respective homes and spend some time there before the beginning of November, when Julia had to leave for Dubai and the post-Ramadan party, but Silas had felt that it made sense for them to stay in Marbella, where neither of them was likely to be put in the uncomfortable position of having to lie to anyone about the fact that they were already married. Plus they would have the added advantage of being together.

How could she have argued with that when she loved being with Silas so very much? When, in fact, being together with him just went on getting better and better? Not even the pleasure of trying on such beautiful shoes could come anywhere near matching the dazzling, breathtaking happiness being married to Silas gave her. Just thinking about it filled her with a fizzing, bubbling joy that had to be the emotional equivalent of the world's very best champagne. She had never known anything like it. She woke up each morning with her heart dancing in eager delight, and she fell asleep in bed every night knowing that all she wanted in the world was contained in the man lying there with her.

Emotionally she felt as though she were living on a different plane, and every bit of her radiated with the happiness she felt. It awed her that after all the men she had met and dated who had not been right, Silas—who was—had been there in her life all the time. Wisely she acknowledged that what she had suffered because of Nick had actually helped her to see just how fortunate she was to have what she had found with Silas. She felt so incredibly blessed and fortunate. She knew that Silas felt Nick should be pursued and punished via the courts for what he had attempted to do to her, but she knew too that he understood and accepted that she would not do so for Lucy's sake.

Silas. She had already been away from him for far too long and she was missing him. She looked down at her feet. The shoes were lovely. And then out of the corner of her eye she saw a small display on the other side of the shop. Tiny, perfect replicas of the shoes she was trying on, made for little baby feet.

Her heart skipped a beat and then gave a rapid flurry of small, excited and eager thuds. Her eyes were misty with emotion. Silas's baby; their baby. If she felt deliriously happy now, how on earth was she going to feel when ultimately she conceived Silas's child?

She went up to the tiny shoes and touched them with a tender fingertip. How very sweet they were.

'You want?' the salesgirl asked, but Julia shook her head.

'Not yet,' she told her, as she handed her the shoes she did want to buy.

Not yet—but maybe soon? Silas would want an heir

and her grandfather would be delighted if she were to make him a great-grandfather, especially now.

Julia smiled at her taxi driver when he pulled up outside the main entrance to the Alfonso, tipping him generously and considering whether or not to go into the club and order a cool drink or to hurry back to the villa to see Silas.

Did she even need to think about it? Of course not.

She didn't bother trying the front door of the villa, going instead to the small half-hidden gate that opened into the garden, just in case Silas had finished working and was sitting by the pool.

When she saw that he wasn't, she crossed the patio and opened the patio door, then stopped in shock as she heard a female voice she recognised saying, with cool sharpness, 'Silas, I can't believe that you've done this.'

'And I can't believe that you've flown all the way from New York to tell me that, Mother,' Julia heard Silas respond, equally coolly.

What was Silas's mother doing here? And what did she mean?

'Of course I haven't. Julia's mother wanted to talk to me face to face about the wedding plans, so I flew to London to meet her. She wanted to know if I thought she had missed anyone off the guest list and who else I might want to invite. She's trying to keep the list down to five hundred names because Amberley Church is so small.'

When Silas did not respond to her dryly given information she continued briskly, 'She also told me that you and Julia were here in Marbella—Julia, it seems, keeps in better contact with her mother than you do with yours. And, since I was already in England, I decided that I might as well fly home via Spain so that I could find out what exactly is going on.'

'You know what's going on,' Julia heard Silas retort dismissively. 'Julia and I are getting married.'

'Where is Julia?'

'In town. Buying shoes.'

Julia winced a little as she heard his mother sigh. She had always secretly suspected that Silas's mother thought of her as foolish and lightweight, and her sigh seemed to confirm that.

'Silas, I had hoped for better than this.'

Julia felt her heart take a high dive and plunge downwards with sickening speed. It was worse than she had feared. Silas's mother did not think she was good enough to marry him.

'There is no better wife for me than Julia,' Silas answered curtly, his defence of her making Julia's heart soar up again.

'I meant better *from* you, not better for you,' his mother responded immediately, causing Julia to go into semi-shock. 'And you know that. When you informed me on Julia's eighteenth birthday that you planned to marry her not because you loved her but because from a practical point of view she was the perfect wife for you, I told you what I thought.'

'You said that you didn't believe Julia would accept me,' Silas agreed.

His mother's visit had come as a total surprise, adding more complications to what was already a very delicately balanced situation. He and Julia were married, but as yet no one knew. Julia naturally wanted to tell her mother and grandfather before they went public, and equally naturally she wanted to do it in person. Silas had given consideration to flying back to England before they went to Dubai, but at the moment he was reluctant to share Julia with anyone else at all. Plus, he had wanted to see her restored to her pre-Blayne sunny happiness before plunging them both into the emotional storm the news that they had married in secret was bound to cause—especially with Julia's mother.

And then there had been that final consideration to make him hold back—that sharp, thorny, and very steep belief journey he had had to make from his denial that love was a concept even worth including in his calculations to admitting that it was a force that had rewritten his emotional and mental rule book.

Admitting to himself that he loved Julia had been the hardest thing he had ever had to do, and doing so had left him feeling acutely exposed and vulnerable. He needed more time to get accustomed to this new aspect to his personality, to feel comfortable with it and himself before he could go public and start telling the world that he was passionately in love with his wife. And he was damn certain that the first person he was going to tell was not going to be his mother. Especially not when those three small words he had been mentally sweating over for the last four weeks, whilst he imagined himself whispering them to Julia, had not actually been said yet.

Nope; so far as his mother was going to know, the status quo was exactly as he had told her it was going to be all those years ago.

But there was one thing he could safely say.

'Julia *is* the perfect wife for me.' Perfect in every way, but most of all in the joy she had brought into his life and the love he had for her.

Outside in the hallway, hidden from their view, Julia battled fiercely with her own feelings. Silas's mother's revelations had shocked and hurt her. But perhaps there was more of Silas's practicality in her than either of them had realised. Either that or his attitude had begun to change the way she thought herself, she decided bleakly. Because honesty compelled her to admit that Silas had never said that he loved her. She had simply assumed that he must because of her own feelings for him—and because it had never occurred to her that he would marry her for any other reason.

Now she could see that she had been hopelessly naïve. So what was she going to do now? Throw an emotional tantrum and blurt out that she loved him? Demand a divorce because he didn't love her?

But what was love? Did it always and only have to be the hearts and flowers outward trappings of romance familiar to everyone? Couldn't it sometimes be something else? Perhaps…something like a practical man protecting the woman who was his wife. Like that same man scrupulously ensuring that he secured her future and that of their children. Like that same man giving a high priority to their shared sexual pleasure. Were these things not in their own way a form of love? Or was she deluding herself? Trust and honesty were to be the foundations of their marriage, Silas had told her. She had accepted that she could trust him. Could she accept the sharp bite of his honesty as well?

'Well, right now, Silas, my concern is not how perfect a wife Julia will make you, but how happy a woman you will make her. I intend to wait for her to return, and when she does I intend to make sure that you have not pressured the poor girl in some way into agreeing to marry you…'

Julia took a deep breath, and then, before she could change her mind, she stepped out of the shadows and into the room, saying lightly, 'I'm afraid I've been eavesdropping. I got back a few minutes ago, and didn't want to break up your mother-and-son chat, but…' Was her smile everything he wanted it to be? Calm and serene and very much that of a woman who admired the man who wanted to marry her because it was practical to do so?

'I have to say, mother-in-law-to-be, that everything Silas has said makes perfectly good sense to me. In fact I totally share his feelings. I think we have more than enough in common to make our marriage work very well.'

'But you are not in love with him?'

'Being in love is not necessarily a prerequisite for a good marriage,' Julia answered Silas's mother firmly.

So far Silas hadn't said a single word, and when she looked at him she was surprised to see that he was looking back at her almost blankly, as though somehow what she had said was unwelcome to him.

Automatically she moved closer to him and reached for his hand, before saying huskily, 'Silas, I think we should tell your mother the truth.'

She *knew* that he loved her?

'The truth?'

'Yes,' Julia agreed, facing her mother-in-law determinedly as she said quietly, 'We haven't told anyone else yet, but actually Silas and I are already married.'

Julia watched as Silas's mother's gaze dropped suspiciously to her stomach and then lifted to Silas's face before switching back to her, and her own face grew pink as she read all the unspoken messages those three looks contained.

'No, he did not *have* to marry me,' Julia burst out indignantly, speaking the unspeakable as only she could, Silas decided ruefully.

His mother might have wrongly assumed that they had married in such haste because they had discovered that Julia was pregnant, but he doubted that she was likely to guess the real truth—which was, as Silas himself had only just come to recognise, that he had rushed Julia into marriage because quite simply he loved her and wanted to tie her to him in every single way that he could.

'You might have backed me up when I told your mother that you didn't marry me because I was pregnant, instead of laughing,' Julia complained crossly to Silas as he poured her a cup of tea.

It was just over an hour since they had returned from seeing Silas's mother off on her homeward flight, and Julia had begun to feel very tired.

'I was in shock,' Silas told her dryly.

'*You* were in shock?'

'I hadn't realised that you had such a practical turn of mind.'

Julia knew immediately what he meant.

'Well, I could hardly tell your mother that I wanted to marry you because you are quite simply the world's best shag, could I?' she asked lightly.

No way was she going to spoil what they had by bursting into tears and begging Silas to say that he loved her.

'Maybe not in those exact words,' Silas conceded. 'Although I dare say she would not have been averse to hearing that you feel passionately about me.' He knew that he certainly wouldn't.

'I do. Like I just said, I feel passionate about you being the most wonderfully orgasmic shag.'

Why did that make him ache inside with pain instead

of with delight? Why was he suddenly feeling that sex on its own wasn't enough, and that he craved a connection with her that went deeper and was more profound?

'You don't think she'll say anything to Ma or Gramps, do you?'

'About shagging?'

'No. Silas, you know what I mean. Your mother won't tell them that we're married?'

'No. Although I must admit I don't really understand why you actually told *her*.'

'I thought from the way she was acting that she might actually drag me back to New York with her to save me from you,' Julia told him lightly.

'And you didn't want that?'

No! I want to spend the rest of my life with you and I can't bear the thought of living any other way, Julia thought. But of course she couldn't say that to him.

'Not really. Did you?'

'What? And miss being woken up every morning by you holding a one-to-one conversation with my penis? What do you think?'

'I think that the best place to drink a cup of tea is in bed.' Her world might have come crashing down around her, but, Julia reminded herself sturdily, no one else was going to know that.

'Mmm, nice thought—but maybe later,' Silas told her lightly, immediately standing up. 'I've got some e-mails to send…'

'To Aimee?' she challenged jealously.

Immediately Silas frowned. 'Why on earth should I want to e-mail her?'

When Julia made no response, Silas exhaled and told her grittily, 'I have no desire to either e-mail Aimee DeTroite or to bed her, if that's what you're worrying about. I do not want her, I have never wanted her, and I would not want her if she was the last woman left on earth. So far as I am concerned she is a neurotic whose behaviour borders on being dangerously destructive—to herself and to others. Now, if you don't mind, I need a break from all this emotional self-indulgence.'

Julia put down her cup so that Silas wouldn't see how much her hands were trembling. He might have denied wanting Aimee, but he had also rejected her hint to him that they have sex as well.

As he walked away from her Silas told himself that, feeling the way he was right now, there was no way it made sense to take Julia to bed. If he did he couldn't guarantee that he wouldn't be able to stop himself from showing her that sex simply wasn't enough for him any longer. And no way did he want to do that after she had made it plain that it was all she wanted from him.

The irony of what had happened made him smile bitterly. He had been so wrapped up in his own desire to marry Julia for practical reasons that it had never occurred to him to question her motives for marrying him.

CHAPTER TWELVE

'I'VE sorted everything out with the travel agent. Apparently Sheikh Al Faisir is going to provide us with a private villa in the grounds of the Jumeirah Beach Club.'

Silas had been dealing with the arrangements for their trip to Dubai, and Julia nodded wanly as she listened to him, trying to concentrate on what he was saying. She had felt so nauseous this morning when she woke up, and yesterday as well, and now she just felt so incredibly tired.

'The Sheikh is connected to the ruling family of Dubai, and this post-Ramadan party we are doing for him will be attended by members of that family as well as his corporate guests,' she explained briefly.

'It's going to be a pretty grand affair, then?'

'Very much so,' she agreed, abandoning her mental attempts to backtrack over the last few weeks and work out some all-important dates. 'We suggested to the Sheikh that we keep to a glamorous Arabian Nights-based theme for the décor, with a sophisticated exotic fantasy element. For instance, the party is being held on a private beach with access to some of Dubai's most exclusive hotels. The guests will be able to sit and eat inside specially designed pavilions. They'll be covered in richly coloured silks and velvets—the whole effect will be rather theatrically over the top and very lush. Sort of Cecil B DeMille meets Bollywood, only much richer.

There'll be the usual fireworks, and those things that produce strawberry-flavoured smoke—they're really big over there. We've got a floorshow as well—magicians, sword-swallowers, a snake charmer, all that kind of stuff—and a belly dancer—the real thing. She's a superstar over there in her own right. They take belly dancing very seriously. It's a complete art form, of course. And we've got live music, and a guest list that includes loads of famous names from the horse racing scene and the pro golf world, plus quite a few Formula One stars. Then there are the celebs who have bought property out there on the Palm Islands. Over a thousand guests have been invited in total. It's a hugely important contract for us.'

'And a very profitable one too, I should imagine.'

'I hope so, for Lucy's sake. She sort of hinted that it was Marcus who got us the business.'

'Blayne is not likely to turn up, I hope?'

'That wasn't the plan. We only got the contract after we'd drawn up the schedule for the year. Both Lucy and Nick were already involved with other projects, which is why I got it.'

'So where's Blayne now?'

'I don't know.' Julia started to frown. 'It's rather odd, really, because although I've spoken to Lucy pretty regularly she hasn't mentioned him at all.'

'According to my source, he isn't in London—or at least, if he is, he isn't living at home.'

Julia didn't want to talk about Nick. She had far more important and personal things on her mind. Was it nearly five weeks since she had last had a period or was it closer to six? And if it was closer to six did that just mean that she was late, or did it mean something else? Her heart bumped against her ribs.

'Silas, I… There's something…' she began huskily, but he was looking at his watch and exclaiming urgently.

'Hell—is that the time? I'm going to be late teeing off if I don't leave now.'

And then he was leaning over to give her a brief kiss before heading for the villa door.

Julia sighed ruefully. Was she pregnant? She certainly hoped so. Perhaps she should go into Marbella and buy a home pregnancy testing kit before she started getting too excited and making announcements to Silas. But first she had some work to do.

Silas had been gone just over an hour, when Julia heard someone knocking on the front door of the villa. Thinking it might be their maid, coming to see if they wanted the fridge restocked, she padded barefoot to the door and pulled it open.

An impossibly thin white-blonde young woman, with equally impossibly large unmoving breasts, was standing outside, a heavy fur coat draped over one arm and a tiny snakeskin handbag clutched in the diamond-encrusted fingers of her other hand.

Julia recognised her immediately.

'Aimee DeTroite.'

'I have to see Silas,' she burst out, pushing past Julia and marching into the villa. 'Where is he?'

'He—he isn't here,' Julia told her. It was the truth, after all.

'You aren't that aristocratic distant relative he's engaged to, are you? No, you can't be. Silas hates brunettes. He adores elegant blondes. Where is he anyway? I can't wait to see him and tell him our news.'

Their news—what on earth did she mean? Anxiety was beginning to tighten its grip on Julia's body.

'You *are* related, aren't you? He can't possibly marry

you. He's going to have to marry me instead. You see…'
Aimee paused for effect before announcing, 'I'm having
his baby.'

Julia felt as though a trap door had opened under her
feet, sending her hurtling downwards into sickening
darkness. Don't you dare faint, she warned herself
grimly.

Trust. Trust and truth were the foundations on which
their marriage was going to be based—Silas had told
her. And she had believed him because she knew that
she could. Somehow she was going to find a way to hold
on to that belief now.

'Really?' she heard herself saying. 'How very interesting. Are you sure it's Silas's?'

The puppy-brown eyes hardened into cold little peb-
bles.

'Of course I'm sure. Otherwise I wouldn't be here. I
love Silas and he loves me, even if he refuses to admit
it. He's all I've ever wanted. He knows that. We are
destined to be together. Our souls have sped together
through time and space to bring us here now. My astrologer has done our charts. He says he has never seen
a couple so harmoniously linked to one another. I told
him that our son will be a Lord…'

'An earl, actually,' Julia corrected her flatly.

Could it be true? Could Aimee be having Silas's
child? Her belly was so flat and her body so thin that it
didn't seem possible for her to have so much as a pinhead inside her, never mind a baby, but appearances
could be deceptive. Her own stomach was still concave
at the moment.

'If I were you I'd start packing right now,' Julia heard
Aimee telling her smugly. 'After all, there's no point in
making things harder for yourself, is there? I mean, Silas

is not going to want you around, is he? He'll have to marry me now that I'm having his baby. Naturally a man in Silas's position needs a son, and I know that my baby is going to be a boy.'

It wasn't in Julia's nature to be manipulative or deceitful, but rather shockingly she heard herself announce calmly, 'Well, I'm afraid if you want to see Silas you'll have to go to London.'

'London? I was told he was here.'

'He was, but his mother stopped over a short time ago and asked him to go to London to attend to some business for her.'

'So when will he be back?'

'I don't know. He said not to expect him until the end of next week.'

'Next week? I've got a manicure booked the day after tomorrow. Whereabouts in London is he?'

'He normally stays at the Carlton Towers,' Julia told her truthfully.

'You won't be able to keep him, you know,' Aimee warned her. 'Silas is mine, and I'm going to have him— no matter what it takes. Where do I get a cab?'

'From the hotel.'

'You mean I've got to walk back there in these?' she demanded, displaying thin high-heeled lizard-skin shoes for Julia's inspection.

'Manolos?' Julia guessed appreciatively.

'Sure. I get the same design as the Hilton woman, only mine are higher. But then I guess my bank account is bigger than hers as well.'

Your ego certainly is, Julia reflected acidly. 'I'll walk back with you if you like.'

Anything to get rid of her before Silas got back.

'Sure. You can carry my coat for me. I had it specially

made. There's this guy who breeds these special cats with long fur…'

Julia's stomach heaved.

Silas couldn't love this woman, she decided. It was totally impossible. Apart from anything else, there was something unwholesome and skin-pricklingly not quite normal about her.

Because she was anxious to get rid of her, Julia took a short cut to the hotel. It took them past one of the swimming pools which had been emptied prior to being cleaned. Julia was careful to avoid stepping too close to the tiled edge—more because of her companion's high heels than anything else—and her attention was on the weight of the heavy coat she had been forced to carry, so the sudden sensation of someone pushing her caught her off guard, causing her to cry out as she felt herself losing her balance. As she cried out she felt herself being pushed towards the empty pool, and the crazed violence in the brown eyes staring into her own as she turned her head towards Aimee in shocked disbelief turned her whole body cold with horror.

Aimee was trying to hurt her.

Neither of them had seen the three workmen who had come to finish cleaning the pool and now saw what they thought was one woman trying to help another as she fell. Of course they immediately rushed to help, grabbing Julia just as she was about to slip over the edge of the pool at its deepest end.

Julia didn't risk waiting for Silas to return to the villa. She was waiting for him when he came off the golf course.

'What is it? What's wrong?' he demanded as soon as he saw the anxiety in her eyes.

'Aimee DeTroite came to see you,' Julia told him.

'What?'

She could see how shocked he was.

'Do you love her, Silas?'

She had to know before she could tell him anything else. She had to hear him say the words—even though she felt she already knew his answer. Or at least she knew the answer the man she thought he was would give.

'What?' he repeated.

'I said, do you love her?'

'No, I don't,' he told her grimly.

I will always be honest with you, Silas had told her. She had believed him then and she believed him now. Very slowly she let her pent-up breath leak out of her lungs. Silas would not lie to her. Whatever she did not know, whatever she could not trust, she knew that and she trusted him.

'Aimee says she loves you, though, Silas. And she says—'

Silas cursed audibly—something Julia had never heard him do before.

'We can't talk properly about this here. Let's go back to the villa. She isn't there, is she?'

'No. I told her you had gone to London.'

'Thank heaven for that. Julia, I don't know what she's said to you, but I promise you she means nothing to me—'

'And I believe you. But she seems to think the two of you are fated to be together.'

'She's an obsessive. A while back, in New York, I began to feel like she was stalking me.'

'Well, according to her she's done a lot more than

that,' Julia told him lightly as she unlocked the door to the villa.

'Like what?' Silas demanded.

Julia turned to look at him. 'She told me that I would have to give you up to her because she's having your child.'

Julia waited to hear him tell her that it was impossible. When he didn't, something inside her felt as though it was breaking in two.

She wasn't a child. She knew that men had sex with women for a wide variety of reasons that had nothing to do with having an emotional connection with them. But somehow she had thought that Silas was above all of that.

'She's crazy.'

'But it is possible that she *could* be having your baby?'

They were inside now, and Silas had closed the door.

'Yes,' he said carefully. 'It is possible.'

There were any number of dignified responses she could have made, but for some reason she chose instead to say, overbrightly, 'Oh, what fun! Because it just so happens that I think I might be pregnant as well. I wonder which of us will produce first? Her, I suppose.'

And then she burst into tears.

'Are you feeling any better now?'

Julia nodded her head. She was tucked up in bed, and Silas was sitting on the bed beside her.

'But explain it all to me again, please, Silas.'

He sighed. 'Very well. Aimee is an obsessive, and some time ago she decided that she was in love with me. She started turning up wherever I went; she called my friends, she invited herself to events she knew I was attending. She even tried to bribe my doorman to let her into my apartment, but thankfully he refused. She got into the boardroom at the Foundation and was found lying naked on the table—she claimed I'd told her to wait for me there. Luckily I was out of the country at the time. She sent me letters and photographs—'

'And videos,' Julia put in.

'Yes. It got to the stage where I was thinking about getting an injunction against her. I found out she had a history of mental problems, a compulsion/obsession complex that her family had kept hidden, so I told them that if they didn't get her some kind of medical help then I would.'

'Would you have done?'

'Probably not. But I didn't know what else to do to get rid of her. And then one evening when I was at a fundraiser she turned up. I was talking to one of my old frat buddies when she came over to join us. He started talking about when we were at Yale and how a few of us had been persuaded to donate sperm to this doctor guy who was setting up a sperm bank—supposedly to provide women who couldn't have children with sperm from intelligent, healthy men from good families. I can't believe now that I was ever credulous enough to believe that. I guess we were all going through some kind of idealistic phase. Anyway, Hal was saying how this doctor had expanded his donor bank and become something of a media personality, and that far from providing sperm free, as we had been told, he was charging thousands of dollars for it. Aimee joined in the conversation and started asking Hal questions about the doctor—who he was and where he was, that kind of thing. I suppose I should have guessed what was going through her head, but I didn't.'

'And now you think she could have bought your sperm from this doctor?'

'What I think is that she could have bought *someone's* sperm from him and convinced herself that it is mine—we were guaranteed anonymity, but, yes, there could be a small chance that she may be carrying my child. Julia, don't cry, please…'

'I can't help thinking about the poor baby. Silas, we must do everything we can to make sure it's going to be safe. Once she knows you aren't going to leave me and marry her, she might not want it any more.'

'Julia, it might not be my child.'

'But it might, and if it is it's only right that we should do everything we can for it. Do you think she'd let us adopt him, Silas? We could bring them both up together? I can't bear to think about the poor little thing growing up thinking you don't care and feeling unwanted. Even if she won't let us adopt him you can make sure that he knows you, and that he comes to stay with us…'

Silas started to shake his head.

'There'd have to be DNA tests first.'

'I don't think that would be a good idea,' Julia protested.

'Why not?'

'Silas, Aimee is having this baby because she thinks it's yours. If it turns out that he isn't, she might just reject him. Then he'll have no one. You can't do that to him. It's too cruel.'

He had thought he knew her, Silas acknowledged, but now he realised that he had not known her at all. He had thought in his arrogance that he was her superior—intellectually, emotionally, and morally. Now he knew that the opposite was true. She had just shown him such a

breadth of wisdom, such a depth of compassion and such
a wealth of love that he felt humbled and shamed.

'You must think me the worst kind of fool for giving
that damned sperm in the first place,' he told her bleakly.

Julia shook her head.

'No, I don't. Actually, Silas I admire you tremen-
dously for it. It makes you human and caring. I think it
is emotional and meaningful and a very special thing to
have cared enough to want to give another person the
gift of a child they cannot have for themselves.'

'Oh, Julia, don't. I love you too damn much as it is,
without you making me love you even more.'

Julia stared at him, her lips parting.

'Would you mind saying that again?' she gulped.

A thin red tide was creeping up under his skin.
'Why?'

She started to pleat a piece of the bedspread with nervous fingers.

'Well, for one thing I want to make sure you actually
did say that you love me before I tell you that I love
you too. And...'

She was smiling at him, that lovely, light-filled Julia
smile that felt like sunshine touching his heart.

'Did you really tell your mother you were going to
marry me all those years ago?'

'Yes. But I didn't realise the real reason why I wanted
to until a whole lot later.'

'How much later?'

'When all that mattered to me was seeing you smile
again after Blayne had drugged you. When I knew that
your happiness was more important to me than anything
else in my life. I knew then that it wasn't practicality, it
was love.'

'But you told your mother...'

'I told my mother that you would make me the perfect wife. And so you do. Hell, Julia, I couldn't tell my mom that I loved you when I hadn't even told you yet.'

'You were so stiff and scratchy with me after your mother left that I thought you didn't want me any more.'

'I was scared stiff of touching you in case I lost control and told you how I felt. And how could I do that when you'd told me that you agreed with my reasons for marrying you?'

Julia reached up and touched his face tenderly.

'I love you so much.'

'Is there any chance of me having a practical demonstration of that?' Silas asked softly.

Julia gave an ecstatic sigh of happiness and held out her arms invitingly to him.

'No chance—just total certainty,' she managed to whisper in between the passionate kisses and hot words of love, with which he was claiming her as his own.

EPILOGUE

'OH, SILAS, look—it's snowing!'

Julia was snuggled up on the faded velvet-covered sofa, in Amberley's winter parlour, her six-month-old son, and eventual heir to Amberley and its history, lying fast asleep in his travel cradle next to her.

It had been Silas's idea that Henry Peregrine Gervaise Carter, to give him his proper name—or baby Harry, as his family called him—should be christened at Amberley Church on the anniversary of the day his parents had reaffirmed their marriage vows there. And of course Julia had been only too delighted to agree.

The birth of his great-grandson seemed to have given the Earl a new lease of life, and he was insistent that he intended to live long enough to sample the special wine he'd had laid down when Harry was born at his great-grandson's coming of age.

'It's early for snow. Oh, you don't really call this snow, do you?' Silas teased as he went to the window to look outside and then came back to sit down next to her. 'How's Lucy getting here? If she's coming by train, I could pick her up from the station.'

'I spoke to her earlier. She says she's going to drive down. I'm so glad she's agreed to be one of baby Harry's godmothers. She's had such a terrible time of it this last year. First finding out that Nick was having an affair and him demanding a divorce, and then all the problems she's had to face with the business.'

'Personally I think she's far better off without Blayne,

although I agree that it can't have been easy for her dealing with the financial mess he left behind.'

'I wish she'd let you help her with that, Silas. I hate thinking of the struggle she must be having when we've got so much money.'

'She's got her pride, Julia, and we've got to respect that. I did have a word with Marcus, though, to tell him that he can always call on us to help her out. Where did that come from?' Silas demanded suddenly, as he saw the copy of *A-List Life* magazine lying on the floor next to Julia.

'I bought it when I went into town this morning,' Julia confessed. 'I haven't read it yet, though. I fell asleep after I'd finished feeding Harry. I have to tell you that your son has a very healthy appetite.' She reached down to pick up the magazine, flicked through it and then tensed, her eyes widening as she stared at one of the pages.

'Silas, look at this!'

'What?'

'This!' she told him, showing him the page that had caught her attention and reading aloud from it. '"One of New York's wealthiest heiresses announces her engagement. Millionairess Aimee DeTroite has just announced that she is to marry her personal astrologer, Ethain LazLo, the society stargazer who claims to be descended from Rasputin and who sports a similar hairstyle. Aimee and Ethain plan to marry on Twelfth Night, a date that Ethain has deemed to be predestined to unite them."'

'Well, I wish them luck with one another. They're certainly going to need it. Still, if he's as good at telling the future as he likes to claim, no doubt he'll already know what's in store for them.'

'Silas, that's not very kind,' Julia protested, but she didn't press the matter. She knew that Silas still felt angry about the way Aimee had behaved.

After claiming that she was having Silas's child she had refused to attend any of the medical appointments Silas's legal team had made for her, claiming publicly that she was afraid that the well-known and highly respected gynaecologist Silas had nominated to confirm her pregnancy was being paid by Silas to force a termination on her.

However, Silas's legal team had then spoken with the doctor who ran the sperm bank to which Silas had contributed his own sperm, and he had insisted that his donors' anonymity had never been compromised or their confidentiality breached, and that, whilst Aimee *had* contacted him and begged him to supply her with Silas's sperm, he had made it clear to her that this was not going to happen. In fact in the end, because he had been so concerned about Aimee's mental state, he had advised her that he felt she should undergo a course of extra counselling in addition to the pre-conception counselling all those to whom he supplied sperm had to undergo.

In a private letter to Silas he had further announced that in the fifteen-plus years since Silas had donated his sperm, technology had made such huge advances that he had decided to dispose of any sperm over three years old and start afresh. Therefore, even if he had been willing to help Aimee, he would have been unable to do so.

Four months after telling Julia that she was carrying Silas's child Aimee had announced via her lawyers that she had made a mistake and that she was not pregnant after all.

'You don't think that she was, and that once she knew that trying to force you to marry her wouldn't work she had her pregnancy terminated, do you?' Julia had asked Silas unhappily at the time.

'Trust you to think that—and to break your heart over it.' Silas had sighed. 'No, Julia, I don't think that—and neither do my lawyers. I must admit I was surprised that Aimee didn't try to claim she had miscarried, rather than admitting she had lied, but the attorneys say that the reason she didn't do that was because her own lawyer would have advised her that if she did we could ask to see medical records as confirmation of her claim. Miscarrying at six or even seven months isn't like miscarrying at three, after all—we'd have been talking about the death of a fully formed child. Even her own lawyers admit that this isn't the first time she's tried to pull this particular trick. There was a similar situation when she was seventeen, but then she claimed the guy raped her as well.'

Baby Harry had woken up and was gurgling happily to himself. Immediately Silas reached down and lifted his son out of the cradle, holding him expertly in his arms. The look of doting male pride and love in his eyes made Julia smile as she watched father and son communicating with one another.

The anxiety they had suffered because of Aimee's lies had brought them even closer together, and to Julia's delight Silas had not only been totally open with her, telling her everything that was happening, he had also asked for her opinion and taken it on board, so that all the decisions they had made had been made jointly.

They were a team now, a unit, bonded firmly together by their love for one another.

'I'll have the final arrangements to make for the fundraiser when we get back to New York,' she reminded him. 'I hope it's going to be a success.'

New York's society hostesses had an enviable reputation for the excellence of their charity fundraising events, both in terms of money raised and exclusivity, and Julia knew that whilst on the surface she had been welcomed and accepted by the wives of Silas's peers, the success or lack of it at her first personally organised fundraiser was the real test she needed to pass.

She had spent the last six weeks sitting for the portraitist Silas had commissioned to paint her wearing the Maharajah's jewels, with baby Harry lying on her lap, holding one of the priceless bracelets.

The portrait was to be unveiled for its first public viewing on the night of her fundraiser, along with the jewels themselves, and Julia felt that the jewels alone should guarantee her event was in a class of its own.

Her charity of choice was one for orphaned and homeless children, and she had deliberately chosen to have displayed, alongside her own portrait and some beautifully done photographs of the jewels, a set of hauntingly painful photographs of children living in the most desolate of circumstances—obscene riches portrayed alongside equally obscene poverty. Her aim was to raise for the charity a sum that equalled the ten million dollar value of the Maharajah's jewels—for surely no material possession should ever be held to be of more value than the life of a child?

'Thank you,' Silas murmured as he leaned forward to kiss her.

'What for?'

'For everything. I was right all those years ago. You *are* the perfect wife for me—perfect in every single way there is. And I love you more than I can ever find the words to say.'

Blackmailing the Society Bride

PENNY JORDAN

CHAPTER ONE

'So what you're saying is that my ex-husband has damaged my business so badly that it and I are both virtually bankrupt?'

Lucy stared at her solicitor. A deepening sense of sickening shock and fear was gripping her, a feeling that the situation she was involved in was so frightening and unbearable that it could not possibly be real.

But it was real. She was here, seated in front of Mr McVicar, while he told her that her ex-husband had so badly damaged the reputation and financial status of the event organisation company she had set up with such enthusiasm and delight prior to their marriage that it was no longer viable.

Nick had cheated her sexually and financially all through their brief marriage...but then, hadn't she done some cheating herself? A guilty conscience wasn't going to help her now, Lucy warned herself, as she struggled with the massive weight of the problems she now faced.

'I've got some commissions for events for the rest of this year,' she told the solicitor, crossing her fingers behind her back and hoping that he wouldn't ask her how many, since in reality there were so few. 'Perhaps, in view of that, the bank...?'

Her solicitor shook his head. He liked his pretty young client, and felt very sorry for her, but in his opinion her nature was too gentle for the unforgiving world of business.

'I'm sorry, my dear,' he told her. 'As you've already

said yourself, several potential clients have cancelled their events and asked for their deposits back already, and I'm afraid... Well, let's just say we live in a harsh world, where confidence is something no one can put a price on.'

'And because of what Nick has done no one will have any confidence in Prêt a Party any more—is that what you mean?' Lucy asked him bitterly. 'Even though Nick is no longer a part of the business, or my life, and I was the one who started it up in the first place?'

The solicitor's sympathetic look was all the answer she needed.

'I dare say I shouldn't blame clients for backing out. After all, I suppose in their eyes if I was stupid enough to marry Nick then I can't have much credibility,' Lucy said with bitter humour. That was certainly what Marcus believed. She knew that well enough.

Marcus. If there was one person she would like to somehow magically remove from her life and her memories for ever, that person wasn't Nick, but Marcus.

'Is there nothing I can do to save the business?' She appealed to her solicitor.

'If you could find a new partner—someone of probity and known financial stature, whom people respect and trust, and who is willing to inject enough capital to settle all Prêt a Party's outstanding obligations...'

'But I intend to pay those off *myself*. I still have money in my trust fund,' Lucy interrupted fiercely.

'Yes, of course. I realise that. But I'm afraid that clearing Prêt a Party's debts, whilst a very honourable thing to do, will not revive client confidence in you, Lucy. Regrettably, the actions of your ex-husband have damaged the reputation of the business virtually beyond repair, and the fact that both your partners have left Prêt a Party—'

'But that's because they both got married and have other

responsibilities now, that's all. Not because of anything else! Carly's pregnant and has her son to look after, as well as working alongside Ricardo with the orphanages he has set up, and Julia has a new baby to look after—plus she's involved in the Foundation—'

'Of course.' Her solicitor soothed her sympathetically. 'I know all this, Lucy, but unfortunately the eyes of the outer and greater world—the world from which you hope to attract new business—do not see it. I really am sorry, my dear.' He paused. 'Have you thought of approaching Marcus? He—'

'No! Never! And I absolutely and totally forbid you to say anything about any of this to him, Mr McVicar.' Lucy spoke fiercely, standing up so abruptly that she almost knocked over her chair. Panic and misery gripped her by the throat as powerfully as though it were Marcus himself closing his fingers around it. How he would love this. How he would love telling her that he had warned her all along that this would happen. How he would look down that aristocratic nose of his with those ice-cold eyes while he ticked off a list of all that she had done wrong, all the ways in which she had failed.

Sometimes, in the eyes of her family and Marcus, Lucy felt as though she had spent the whole of her life failing. For a start she had been a girl and not a boy, a daughter and not a son—a daughter to be married off and not a son to be an heir. And, even though her parents had gone on to have a son, Lucy had somehow always felt she had let them down by being born first, and the wrong sex. Not that her parents had ever said that she was a disappointment to them, but Lucy had been born with a sensitive kind of nature and did not need to be told what people felt. She had sensed her parents' disappointment—just as in later years she had recognised Marcus's impatient irritation with her.

Not that anyone ever needed to *guess* what Marcus thought or felt. She had never known anyone more capable of or uncompromising about saying exactly what he thought and felt. And he had made it plain from the first moment he had confronted Lucy across the large desk in his London office that he did not approve of the fact that her late great-uncle had left her such a large sum of money.

'I suppose that's why you agreed to be my trustee, is it?' Lucy had accused him. 'Because you don't approve of me having the money and you want to make life as difficult for me as possible!'

'That kind of remark merely confirms my concern about your late great-uncle's mental state when he made his will,' had been Marcus's caustic response.

'I suppose you were hoping he would leave his money to you?' Lucy had shot back.

In response, Marcus had given her a look that had made her face burn, and made her feel as though she wanted to crawl into a corner.

'Don't be so bloody infantile,' he had told her coldly.

Of course she hadn't realised then that Marcus had millions, if not billions of his own, tucked away in the vaults of his family's merchant bank, of which he was the CEO.

Mr McVicar watched her sympathetically. He knew perfectly well of the tension and ill feeling that existed between his client and the formidably wealthy banker her late great-uncle had appointed as trustee for the money he had left her.

That money had nearly all gone now—swallowed up by the greed and fraudulent actions of Lucy's ex-husband and the failure of her once-successful small business.

But in his view there was still no one better placed to

help her in her present difficult situation than Marcus, whose business savvy was both awesome and legendary. Mr McVicar himself had urged her not to agree to her bank's request that she secure Prêt a Party's finances by pledging her inheritance, but she had refused to listen to him. Morally Lucy was beyond reproach, but unfortunately she had been too gullible for her own good, and she was paying the price for that now.

He returned to the problem at hand. 'If you could attract a wealthy business partner who would be prepared to put money into the business, then—'

'Actually, that's exactly what I've been doing.'

As soon as the words had left her mouth Lucy wondered what on earth she was doing. Was it Mr McVicar's reference to Marcus that had prompted her into lying to him and creating a fictional potential backer? Lucy closed her eyes in helpless acknowledgement of her own vulnerability. Somehow just hearing Marcus's name was enough to goad her into a fury of defensiveness.

Mr McVicar looked both relieved and surprised.

'Well, that is really excellent news, Lucy. It puts a different complexion on matters entirely,' he told her enthusiastically, looking so pleased that her guilt increased uncomfortably. 'The very best outcome one could have hoped for, in fact. But obviously it is something we shall need to discuss. I think we should set up a meeting with your proposed partner and his or her legal advisers just as soon as we can. Oh, and of course we must let your bank know what is in the wind. I am sure that they will be inclined to be far more flexible once they know that fresh capital will be injected into Prêt a Party. I also think it would be a good idea to go public, even perhaps take a half-page announcement in those papers most frequently read by your clients stating once again that your ex-husband now has no access to or involvement with any aspect of Prêt a Party's business, and that moreover you now have a new partner. That should do a tremendous amount to offset the upsetting effect Nick's fraudulent behaviour has had on the business.'

Lucy felt as though she were trapped in ever-deepening mud of a particularly sticky and clinging consistency. Why on earth had she let the thought of Marcus's disapproval propel her into such stupidity? What on earth had she done? How could she admit now to Mr McVicar that she had lied—and why?

'Er, I can't tell you who he is at the moment, Mr McVicar,' Lucy began uncomfortably. 'It's all very much a secret. Negotiations are...um...well, you know how it is...'

'Of course. But I must urge you to remember, Lucy, that time is very much of the essence here.'

Nodding her head, Lucy made her escape as quickly as she could. How could she have lied like that? It went against everything she believed in. Now she felt sickeningly guilty and ashamed of herself, and she had to blink away her self-pitying tears as she stood outside her solicitor's Mayfair office in the bright autumn sunshine.

What on earth was she going to do? It would take a miracle to save her now. Automatically, she turned the corner and hurried into Bond Street, not bothering to glance into the windows of the expensive shops lining the street. Designer label clothes were not really her thing. She liked vintage clothes, salvaged from street markets and family attics. Their fabrics were so lush, the feel of them against her skin something she treasured and loved: real silk and satin cashmere; sturdy wool; cool cotton and linen. Man-made fibres might be more practical for modern-day city living, but in many ways she was an old-fashioned girl who craved a return to a quieter, more gentle way of life.

The truth was that secretly she would have loved nothing more than to marry and produce a large brood of much-loved children whom she and her husband would raise in an equally large and loved country house. She envied her two best friends their happy marriages and new young families more than they or anyone else knew—after all, she had her pride, just like anyone else. It was that pride that had led her into setting up Prêt a Party in the first place. The very same pride that had just led her into telling that stupid, stupid lie, she reminded herself miserably.

The magazines on a nearby newsstand caught her eye, and she stopped to study them. To the forefront, as always, was *A-List Life*. Lucy started to smile.

Its eccentric owner and editor Dorland Chesterfield had been such a good friend to her, using Prêt a Party to organise several of the events he had hosted—events attended by the world's top celebrities. She might even have considered turning to *him* for help to get her out of the mess Nick had left her in were it not for the fact that she knew if there was anything guaranteed to overwhelm his genuine kind-heartedness it was his love of passing on gossip. The last thing she needed right now was to have the story of her downfall spread over the pages of *A-List Life*.

Of course both her friends—now ex-partners in Prêt a Party—had extremely wealthy husbands, and both of them had in turn come to see her and gently offered financial help, but Lucy could not accept it. For one thing there was that wretched pride of hers, and for another it was not just money she needed, but someone to work in the business with her. Being given money to clear Prêt a Party's debts was a kind gesture, but she wanted—*needed*, in fact—to prove that she was not the silly fool everyone obviously thought her, and that she could make a success of her business.

Yes, marrying Nick had been a mistake, and, yes, she had—as Marcus had unmercifully pointed out to her—rushed into the marriage, but she'd had her own reasons for doing that. Reasons she could never, ever allow Marcus to discover.

She picked up a copy of *A-List Life* and handed over some coins, giving a reciprocal smile to the newsstand vendor before turning to cross the road. The sunlight glinting on her shoulder-length naturally blonde hair caused the driver of a large, highly polished, diplomat-plated Mercedes to slow down and study her appreciatively.

As she regained the pavement Lucy flipped open the magazine and quickly checked the contents—more out of habit than anything else. It was over three months now since Prêt a Party had managed a large event of any kind, never mind one glitzy enough to merit page-space in Dorland's magazine, but to her astonishment she suddenly saw Prêt a Party's name beneath the words: *A-List Life*'s Favourite Party of All Time.'

Bemused, she turned the pages, her eyes widening as she recognised the photographs covering the entire mid-section of the magazine. They were from the huge summer party Prêt a Party had organised for *A-List Life* the previous year.

Tears stung her eyes. It was so typical of Dorland to do something so generous—and it *was* generous of him to republish those photographs, even if at the same time it was also a way of blowing his own trumpet.

Although at the time she had refused to admit it to anyone, she had known then that her marriage had been a mistake, and she had known, too, that Nick was being unfaithful. She had known that Nick was cheating on her, yes, but she had not known that he was also defrauding her business and her customers—even if her two best friends Carly and Julia *had* suspected what was happening.

Out of concern for her they had kept their suspicions to themselves. Not so Marcus. Lucy knew that she would never be able to forget the searing humiliation of having to stand in front of Marcus whilst he listed with cold fury the fraudulent activities Nick had been engaged in whilst in charge of finances in Prêt a Party.

'Why the hell did you marry him in the first place?' he had demanded savagely, before adding, 'No, don't bother to tell me. I already know the answer. Did it never occur to you that you could have sex with him *without* marrying him?'

Lucy's face burned hotly now, just remembering how Marcus had looked at her.

'Perhaps I wanted more than sex,' she had countered. She *had* wanted more, certainly, but she had not received it. But then, neither had she given Nick more. And as for the sex... Her face burned again, but for a different reason.

The Nick who had spoken so urgently and flatteringly of his desire for her before their marriage had very quickly turned into a Nick who derided and taunted her for her lack of sexual expertise and desirability after it. And who could blame him? The effort of maintaining the fantasy of hot, urgent longing for him with which she had thrown herself into their relationship had proved too much for her to sustain once they were married. Nick had taunted her for her sexual inexperience, claiming that she was frigid and she turned him off, and she had been in too much torment, compounded by her guilt and self-loathing, to protest.

'More than sex? Really? And you actually thought you

would get more from someone like him?' he had demanded sarcastically.

'It's all very well for you to stand there and—and criticise me,' Lucy had told him wildly. 'But I don't see that *you* are exactly having any success with a long-term relationship!'

'Maybe that's because I haven't chosen to commit to one. I can certainly assure you that when I do my commitment to it and my conviction about it will be properly thought out and permanent. My decision won't be made off the back of imagining myself in love following an alfresco holiday shag.'

Lucy's hands tightened into impotent fists now, just remembering those contemptuous words, and the manner in which they had been delivered, with Marcus looking at her with that arrogant, obnoxious, *Marcus* look of his.

She had tried to defend herself, of course. 'That was not—I was not—'she had begun, but typically Marcus had refused to allow her to continue. 'Oh, come off it, Lucy,' he'd said harshly, 'we all know what happened. After all, the photographs were plastered all over the celebrity gossip rags. You, minus bikini top, draped all over Blayne, saying that you were up for a good time and looking for everything that went with that.'

'Goodness,' she had retaliated, in a brittle voice, 'you've actually remembered the caption word for word. Did you have to practise repeating it for very long to do that, Marcus?'

Of course she had regretted the idiotic quote recorded in the magazine. But when you were jet lagged, and you'd packed in such a rush that you'd omitted to pack matching bikini tops and bottoms, and you got caught out and papped by some prowling paparazzi with nothing better to do and no one better to photograph, you naturally did your best to make a joke of your plight—especially when those same paparazzi could sometimes be so important to the success of your business.

Not all celebrities, no matter what they might choose to say in public, genuinely wanted to avoid those camera lenses. Many actively sought out the events and parties where they would be spotted and photographed. Thus, Lucy had felt she could not afford to offend the guy who had snapped her, no matter what her own personal feelings.

If he'd seen her twenty-four hours later, then the photograph he would have taken would have been a very different one. Then, after a decent night's sleep and with the loan of a bikini from Jules, she would probably have been in control enough to tell him truthfully that she was simply taking a much-needed holiday from the mounting stress of running a successful business.

Unfortunately the photographer had taken it into his head that her life was far more interesting than it actually was, and from then on neither he nor his camera had been very far from her side.

Nick had revelled in the attention. At the time she had taken that as a sign that, unlike the other men she had dated, he would be able to cope with her work and its effect on their personal life. She hadn't realised that for Nick everything had its price—including photographs of them together, if not actually having sex in a variety of exotic locations then as close to it as was possible, given that she was wearing bikini bottoms and he was wearing swimming shorts.

She had had no idea that she was being set up with a view to them being taken until it was too late and they had been published. And by then she and Nick were married—

Naturally in public she'd had to shrug off her real feelings and pretend that she welcomed her new image as a randy, anything-goes, up-for-it and eager for sex party girl, only too delighted to let the whole world see how much she wanted her new husband. Even if by then that same new husband had been privately calling her frigid and useless in bed, and spending more nights out of their marriage bed than he was spending in it with her.

She looked at her watch a little bit anxiously. She had spent rather longer with her solicitor than she had expected, and she was due to put in an appearance at her great-aunt Alice's ninetieth birthday party this afternoon.

Great-Aunt Alice lived in Knightsbridge, in a huge old-fashioned apartment that was always freezing cold because, despite her wealth, she refused to have the central heating on.

No one in the family ever wanted to visit her in winter, and even in summer the wise visited equipped with extra layers in the form of cardigans, pashminas and the like, to ward off the icy blasts which Great-Aunt Alice insisted were necessary for good health and were the reason she was still hale and hearty at ninety.

'Balls,' Lucy's younger cousin Johnny had always claimed. 'The reason she's still alive is because she's too bloody mean to die. God knows, I could do with my share of her millions.'

'What makes you think you'll get a share?' Lucy's brother Piers had asked wryly.

'I'm bound to,' Johnny had replied smugly. 'I'm her favourite.'

'Yah? Well, you certainly work hard enough at it,' Piers had mocked him.

Nineteen-year-old Johnny, with his slightly louche lifestyle, permanent lack of money and winning ways, had a reputation within the family of being someone who was constantly wheeling and dealing. Lucy suspected that

Marcus probably disapproved of Johnny almost as much as he did her.

Marcus! But *she* didn't disapprove of *him*, did she? And that was the cause of, if not all, then surely most of the problems in her life. It had, after all, been to escape from loving Marcus and the knowledge that that love would never be returned that she had thrown herself into Nick's arms. And it was because she still loved Marcus now, despite all her attempts to stop doing so, that she treated him with hostility and resentment. That was her shield, her only protection against the potential humiliation of Marcus—or anyone else—ever discovering how she felt about him.

CHAPTER TWO

'GOODNESS. It's actually *warm* in here!' Lucy removed the cashmere wrap she had pulled on over her delicate silk chiffon dress the moment she walked into Great-Aunt Alice's hallway.

'Yes, I bribed Johnson to put the heat on.' Her brother Piers grinned.

'You might have told me that before,' Lucy grumbled affectionately, as she fanned herself with her hand to cool down her flushed face. 'How warm did you tell him to make it? It's like a sauna in here. The flowers I've bought Great-Aunt Alice will have wilted before she gets them.'

'Never mind your flowers—what about my chocolates?' Piers told her ruefully.

'Piers thought Johnson was probably still working in Fahrenheit,' Lucy's father chipped in. 'So he told him to set the temperature gauge at sixty-eight. None of us realised what had happened until Johnson came back and said that the gauge only went to forty.'

Lucy joined in the good-natured laughter at her brother's expense, and then suddenly froze as the door opened and Marcus walked in.

Was it her imagination or was there really a small, sharp silence—as though not just she but everyone else was aware of just how formidable and commanding Marcus was?

It wasn't only that he was tall—just nicely over six foot—or even that he was sexily broad-shouldered and taut-muscled. It wasn't even that combination of thick dark

18

hair and striking ice-grey eyes which could sometimes burn almost green.

So what was it about him that made not just her own sex but men as well turn and look towards him? Turn and look up to him, Lucy amended.

Could it have something to do with the fact that he ran the merchant bank which had been in his family for so many generations? Because of that he was in a position of great trust, responsible not just for the present and future of his clients, but in many cases for the secrets of their ancestors as well.

But even if one took away all of that—even if he had walked in as a stranger off the street—women would still have turned their heads to look at him and would have gone on looking, Lucy acknowledged. Because Marcus was sexy. In fact, Marcus was *very* sexy. Her heart attempted to do a high dive inside her chest, then realised it was attempting the impossible and ended up crashing sickeningly to its floor. She gulped at the glass of champagne Piers had handed to her as much for something to do— some reason not to have to look at Marcus—as for Dutch courage.

He was wearing one of his customary hand-made plain dark suits, a typical banker's white shirt with a blue stripe, and a red tie.

She took another gulp of her champagne.

'Want another?' Piers asked her.

Lucy shook her head. She wasn't much of a drinker anyway, and her work meant that it was essential she kept a clear head in social situations, so she had quickly learned to simply take a small sip from her glass and then abandon it discreetly somewhere. The up side of this was that she always had a clear head, but the down side was that her body was simply not up to dealing with anything more than one small glass of anything alcoholic. But right now the numbing effect of a couple of glasses of champagne was probably just what she needed to help her cope with Marcus's presence, intimidatingly up close, if not exactly as personal as her foolish heart craved.

'Oh, good. Marcus has made it after all,' Lucy heard her mother exclaiming to Lucy's great-uncle in a pleased voice. 'Charles, do go over and ask him to join us.'

'Goodness, it *is* hot,' Lucy said wildly. 'I think I'd better go and get these poor flowers into some water.'

Her heart was thumping its familiar message to her as she made her escape, champagne glass in hand, heading for the rambling patchwork of corridors and small rooms to the rear of the huge apartment which her great-aunt still referred to as the servants' quarters.

How on earth did Johnson and Mrs Johnson, aided only by a daily, manage to cope with looking after somewhere this size? Lucy wondered sympathetically as she hurried down one of the corridors and into the 'flower room'. A row of vases had already been assembled on the worktop, ready filled with water, and Lucy unwrapped her own offering and busied herself placing the flowers stem by stem into water.

Was she really so afraid of seeing Marcus? Her hands trembled. Did she really need to ask herself that question? How old was she? Twenty-nine. And how long had it been since she had come down from university and looked at Marcus across the width of his desk and known...?

Tears suddenly blurred her vision.

Oh, yes, she had known then, immediately, that she had fallen in love with him, but she had known with equal immediacy that he did not return her feelings—that in fact, so far as he was concerned, her presence in his life was an inconvenience and an irritation he would far rather have been without.

She had been young enough then to dream her foolish dreams regardless, to fantasise about things changing, about walking into Marcus's office one day and having Marcus look at her as though he wanted to drag her clothes off and possess her right there and then. She had whiled away many an irascible lecture from Marcus by allowing herself the pleasure of imagining him standing up and coming towards her, taking hold of her and putting his desk, or sometimes his chair, more often than not both of them, to the kind of erotic use for which they had definitely not been designed.

But the reality was, of course, that she was the one who wanted to tear *his* clothes off. And then one day she had looked at him and seen the way he was looking at her. And she had known that her foolish erotic fantasies and her even more foolish romantic daydreams were just that. Marcus did not either want or love her, and he was never going to do so. That was when she had decided that she needed to find someone else—because if she didn't one day her feelings were going to get too much for her and she was going to totally humiliate herself by declaring them to Marcus.

A husband and then hopefully a family of her own would stop her from doing that, surely? she'd thought. But she hadn't even managed to get *that* right, had she? Her marriage had been a disaster—privately and publicly. Very publicly.

She wasn't the kind of person who wanted to be alone. She loved children, and had known from a young age that she wanted her own. Although she loved them both dearly, sometimes she felt wretchedly envious of the love and happiness her two best friends had found with their husbands.

And one day she knew Marcus would marry—and when he did... A shudder of vicious pain savaged her emotions.

When he did, she made herself continue, she hoped to be protected from what she knew she would feel by the contentment and love she had found with another man and her family. How foolishly and dangerously she had deluded herself.

She couldn't stay here in the flower room for ever, Lucy realised, and with any luck Marcus might actually have already left by now. Giving her flowers a final tweak, she turned to leave.

As soon as she opened the door into the drawing room the first person she saw was her cousin Johnny, who grabbed her arm and announced eagerly, 'Great—I've been looking for you. More champagne?' Without waiting for her to respond, he took a glass from a passing waiter and handed it to her.

'Must say the old girl isn't stinting with the champers. It must be costing her a pretty penny to put this do on. Champers...waiters. Did you organise it?'

'Yes,' Lucy said ruefully, remembering the hard bargain her great-aunt had driven over costs, and how in the end she had given in and suggested she give Great-Aunt Alice the business cost as her birthday present, provided her great-aunt supplied the champagne, the *hors d'oeuvres* and the waiters' wages. Which probably explained the lack of any food, Lucy decided.

She tried not to look at Marcus, who was standing the full width of the room away from her but facing towards her, and watching her, she could see, with a very grim look tightening his mouth. She took a quick, nervous, sustaining sip of her champagne, and then another. She couldn't bear to think about what would happen if Marcus ever got to hear about that idiotic lie she had told Mr

McVicar. In the absence of a miracle, she was going have to dispose of her supposed investor as speedily as she had invented him.

'Actually, Luce, there's something I need to discuss with you.'

'What?' Somehow or other Lucy managed to drag her attention away from Marcus.

'I need to talk to you,' Johnny repeated patiently.

'You do?' Immediately Lucy was alert to her own prospective danger. 'Johnny, if it's a loan you're after,' she began warningly, 'I haven't forgotten that you still owe me fifty pounds from last time. Even if you have.'

'It isn't anything like that,' Johnny assured her earnestly. 'Fact is, sweet cos, it just so happens that a business acquaintance of mine has asked me if I would introduce you to him.'

'He has?' Lucy said cautiously.

'Mmm. Have another glass of champagne,' he added encouragingly, removing Lucy's half-empty glass before she could refuse or protest and summoning the still-circulating waiter so that he could hand her a fresh glass.

On the other side of the room Marcus's unwavering focus on her had hardened into a grim-mouthed coldness that caused Lucy's hand to tremble so much she almost spilt her champagne.

'If he's thinking of commissioning Prêt a Party to do an event for him...' she began, trying to move round so that she couldn't see Marcus, and failing as he moved too.

'No, what he's got in mind is making an investment in Prêt a Party.'

'What?' Now she did spill a few drops of her champagne, before managing to take a steadying gulp of it.

'Oh, yes. He's a bit of an entrepreneur. He's made absolutely stacks of money from this turnkey business he owns. You know the kind of thing...' Johnny enlarged. 'He employs cleaners, cooks, someone to wait in for the gas man, someone to collect your cleaning—all that kind of stuff—for these rich City types who can't afford the time to do it themselves. He saw the spread in *A-List Life*, and heard that you're my cousin, and he said that Prêt a Party is exactly the kind of investment he's looking for. So I said I was seeing you today and that I'd sound you out.'

'Johnny...' Her head was spinning, and it didn't occur to her to connect that with her unfamiliar consumption of champagne.

'Why don't you let him talk to you and tell you what he's got in mind himself? I could give him your office phone number...'

When she had reflected that she needed a miracle she'd never imagined she would get one—and certainly not one of this potential magnitude. She felt positively light-headed with relief, almost dizzy.

'Well, yes—okay, Johnny,' she agreed gratefully.

'Great.' Johnny looked at his watch, announcing, 'Lord, is that the time? I've got to go. His name's Andrew Walker, by the way.'

She hadn't finished her champagne, but she put her glass on the tray as the waiter went past, absent-mindedly picking up a fresh glass and wincing slightly as she did so. She knew she shouldn't have worn these high heels. Shoes were Julia's thing, not hers, and she had only been persuaded into buying the strappy sandals with their far too high thin heels because they were the perfect shade of cornflower-blue to wear with one of her favourite dresses.

Unfortunately, though, they were not parquet-floor-friendly—especially when that floor had been polished in the old-fashioned way and was as slippery as an ice rink.

She looked round the room, but she couldn't see either

her parents or her brother, and she was just wondering if she could make her own escape when suddenly Marcus was standing in front of her, announcing grimly, 'Don't you think you've had enough?'

Enough of what? Lucy wanted to ask him. *Enough of loving you? Enough of wanting you and aching for you? Enough of dreaming of you whilst the man I married because I couldn't have you slept in bed beside me? Enough of knowing that you are never ever going to love me?* Oh, yes, she'd had enough of that.

'Actually, Marcus, no—I don't.' The familiar pain was back, and it was intensifying with every second she had to spend in his company. It seared her and drove her, maddening her with its agonising ache so that she barely knew what she was saying.

Marcus was looking at her with familiar contempt and irritation. Lucy gasped in dismay as someone standing behind her accidentally bumped into her. The combined vertiginous effects of stilettos and Marcus-induced heartache was definitely not good for one's balance, Lucy thought miserably, as Marcus gripped her arm firmly to steady her.

'Just how much champagne have you had?' Marcus demanded grimly.

'Not enough,' Lucy answered, with a flippancy she didn't feel.

Marcus was looking at her with a blend of irritation and impatience. 'You can hardly stand,' he told her critically.

'So what?' Lucy tossed her head. She was defying Marcus—baiting him, in fact! What on earth was happening to her? She was winding him up, and pushing her luck as she did so. She knew that, but somehow she couldn't help herself. Somehow she needed to see that look of angry irritation mixed with contempt in his eyes just to remind herself of the futility of dreaming impossible dreams.

'Actually, I rather think I'd like some more champagne. I'm celebrating, you see,' she heard herself telling him, uncharacteristically and recklessly emptying her glass before he could remove it and then looking round for the waiter with what she didn't realise was champagne-induced vagueness. Her lips did feel slightly numb, it was true, but then so did her toes, and they hadn't had any contact whatsoever with the champagne, had they?

'Celebrating what?' Marcus demanded tersely, his hold on her arm tightening.

'My miracle,' Lucy responded, forming the words very carefully.

She might have imagined it, but she thought Marcus actually swore softly. 'The only miracle here is that you're still standing,' he muttered.

The waiter was almost level with her. She reached out to pick up a full glass of champagne from the tray he was carrying, but Marcus got there before she could lift the glass, the fingers of his free hand closing hard on her own.

'Leave it where it is, Lucy,' he commanded her calmly.

'I'm thirsty,' Lucy protested. Thirsty for the nectar of his kiss, thirsty for the feel of his mouth on her own, on her skin, *everywhere*, whilst she drank in the taste of him. She looked at his hand, at his long, strong fingers curled around her own. She wanted to put her other hand on top of it, so that she could touch him. She wanted to lift his hand to her mouth so that she could breathe in the scent of his skin as she explored it with her lips and with her tongue. Longing burned through her, leaping from nerve-ending to nerve-ending until she was filled with it, possessed by it...

'I think it's time we left.' The cool hardness of Marcus's voice chilled her overheated thoughts.

'We?' she queried warily.

'Yes. *We.* I was just about to leave—and, unless you want the remainder of your great-aunt's guests to witness the unedifying sight of you sprawled on her parquet floor, I rather think you would be wise to leave with me. In fact, I am going to insist on it.'

'You're my trustee, Marcus, not my guardian or my keeper.'

'Right now, I'm a man very close to the edge of his patience. And besides, I need to talk you about Prêt a Party.'

Lucy stiffened defensively.

'If you're going to lecture me about Nick again—' she began, but Marcus simply ignored her and continued as though she hadn't interrupted him.

'You may remember me mentioning some time ago that my sister Beatrice wants to plan a surprise party for her husband's fiftieth birthday?'

'Yes,' Lucy agreed. Beatrice was Marcus's elder sister, and her husband George was something very important in the mysterious highest echelons of the civil service.

'I have to go and see Beatrice later this week, and she suggested that I should take you along with me so that she can discuss her party with you. I thought you might want to check your diary before we fix on a date.'

Lucy exhaled weakly. She was grateful to be given any business right now—even if it meant having to spend time with Marcus in order to obtain it.

'I've got a fairly free week,' she responded, as nonchalantly as she could. The truth was that she had a wholly free week; in fact the only event she had coming up in the whole of the next month was a launch bash for a sportswear manufacturer.

Somehow or other they had actually reached the door to the hallway, where her great-aunt was already saying goodbye to some of her other guests, and it was obvious that Marcus had every intention of hauling her through it. If she dug in her heels, would he literally drag her across the parquet?

'You're walking too fast,' she told him breathlessly, and then gave a small startled 'oof' of exhaled breath as he stopped so suddenly that she cannoned straight into him.

She was standing body to body with Marcus, and he had one hand on her arm whilst his other was pressed into the small of her back. She could smell the faint lemony scent of his cologne, mixed with warm man scent. Suddenly the back of her throat prickled treacherously with tears. How many hours had she wasted after she had first smelled it on him haunting the men's toiletries departments of up-market stores? Sniffing and testing and searching, hoping that she might recognise it and find out just what it was he wore, so that she could buy some and put a little on her pillows, so that she could wear it herself if necessary— anything just to be able to feel closer to him. But she had never discovered what it was.

Body to body with Marcus. If only by some miracle he would draw her closer now, and bend his head and cover her mouth with his—if only, if only...

'Marcus, dear boy—so good of you to come. And Lucy...'

Lucy could feel her face burning as Marcus stepped back from her but still continued to hold on to her arm.

The almost flirtatious warmth of her voice as her great-aunt had greeted Marcus chilled quite distinctly over her own name, Lucy noticed cynically. Was there any woman on the surface of the earth who was immune to Marcus's personal brand of male charm?

'A truly delightful occasion, Alice. Thank you for inviting me.'

'My dear boy, how could I not? After all, your family have been taking care of our family's financial affairs since before the Peninsular War. Of course there should have been food, but I'm afraid Lucy rather let me down there.'

Lucy gasped in outrage.

'That— Ouch!' she protested as Marcus trod on her toes, then hustled her out into the street—just as though she were a prisoner under armed guard, Lucy decided indignantly.

'You do realise that you stood on my toes, don't you?' she objected, as she breathed in the familiar scent of the sun-warmed city.

'Better my foot on your toes than your foot in your own mouth, don't you think?' Marcus suggested.

It took Lucy several seconds to recognise what he was saying, but once she had she glowered indignantly and told him, 'It was Great-Aunt Alice herself who decided not to have any food. It was nothing to do with me.'

'You amaze me sometimes, you know, Lucy,' Marcus told her grimly. 'Has no one ever told you that a little tact goes a long way towards oiling the wheels of business and reputation?'

'You're a fine one to talk! You never bother using tact when you talk to me, do you?'

'Some situations call for stronger measures,' Marcus answered grimly.

'If you mean my marriage—' Lucy began hotly, and then stopped.

Her marriage was just not something she felt safe discussing with Marcus. The last thing she wanted was to have him probing into the whys and wherefores of her relationship with Nick. There was no point in allowing herself to be drawn into an argument she already knew she was not going to win.

'You can let go of me now, Marcus,' Lucy hissed valiantly several seconds later, when he was still holding on to her. But Marcus ignored her, keeping a firm grip on her arm as he flagged down a taxi and then opened the door for her, almost pushing her inside it. Lucy resentfully moved as far away from him as she could as he sat down beside her.

'Where to, guv?' the taxi driver demanded.

'Wendover Square. Number twenty-one.'

'Arncott Street.'

They had both spoken together.

'Make yer mind up,' the cabbie complained.

'Wendover Square,' Marcus repeated, before Lucy could speak, leaving her to glower angrily at him.

'It would have been easier if he'd dropped me off first, Marcus.'

'I want to talk to you,' Marcus told her coolly.

'So talk,' she said recklessly.

'In private,' Marcus informed her in a very gritty voice.

The taxi driver was turning into Wendover Square, its elegant Georgian houses overlooking one of London's most attractive private squares.

Marcus's house—the same house his grandfather and his great-grandfather had lived in, in fact all his ancestors right back to the Carring who had first begun the bank in the days of the Peninsular War—had just about the best position in the whole square. Four storeys high and double fronted, with a proper back garden, it was a true family house, and Lucy could see how impressed the cabbie was as he pulled up outside it and unlocked the door for them.

'I do hope that whatever you want to say to me isn't going to take too long, Marcus.' Lucy was trying to sound as businesslike as possible—a difficult task when suddenly, for no discernible reason, her tongue seemed to be slipping and sliding over her words, and the motion of the taxi had made her feel very dizzy indeed.

'No Mrs Crabtree?' she managed to articulate, when Marcus opened the door and there was no sign of his housekeeper. As Lucy knew, the woman treated her employer as though he were at the very most one step down from god status.

'She's gone to stay with her daughter, to help look after her new baby.'

'Oh!' Lucy gave an exclamation of surprise as she semi-stumbled in the hallway.

'I told you you'd had too much to drink,' Marcus said grimly. 'And you're certainly in no fit state to go anywhere on your own.'

His accusation stung—and all the more so because it was just not true. She didn't drink! But before she could say so, he was continuing curtly, 'You're out of touch, Lucy. The tipsy, thirty-something, Bridget Jones-type female is over. The in thing now is the committed working mother with two children and a husband—and if you don't believe me take a look at your own friends. Carly and Julia are both married now, and both mothers.'

As though she needed reminding of that! Lucy thought miserably.

'I am not thirty-anything,' she told him crossly instead. 'And, just in case you had forgotten, I've been married.'

'*Forgotten?* How the hell could anyone forget that?'

'And I have not had too much to drink,' Lucy added forcefully.

The look Marcus gave her made her whole body burn, never mind just her face.

'No? Well, all I can say is that if this is the state you were in when Nick Blayne picked you up, it's no wonder—'

'It's no wonder what?' Lucy stopped him. 'No wonder that I went to bed with him? Well, for your information, I went to bed with him because—'

'Spare me your reminiscences about how much you loved him, Lucy,' Marcus told her flatly. 'Blayne saw you coming and took advantage of you—financially, emotionally, and for all I know sexually as well. He used you, Lucy, and you let him. Couldn't you see what he was?' he demanded in exasperation. 'I should have thought even a sixteen-year-old virgin could have recognised that the man was a user.'

'Sixteen-year-old virgins probably have better eyesight than twenty-plus unmarrieds,' Lucy retaliated flippantly. How many times had she used flippancy as her defence against the powerful blasts of Marcus's irritated broadsides? Surely more than enough to know how much they increased his ire. But what else could she do? Without her protective shield of nonchalance she might just break down into a sobbing wreck of pleading female misery, and he would like that even less!

'I loved Nick,' she lied wildly.

'Did you? Or did you just want to go to bed with him?'

'A girl doesn't have to marry a man in order to have sex with him these days, Marcus. She doesn't even have to love him. All she needs to do is simply do it.'

She could see the contempt flashing through his eyes as he looked at her.

'Have you any idea just how provocative that statement is? Or how vulnerable you are?'

Lucy stared at him. 'What do you mean?'

'I mean that right now *any* man could get you into his bed.'

'That is so not true!'

'No? Want me to prove it to you?'

'You couldn't,' Lucy objected recklessly.

'No?'

He reached for her so suddenly that she didn't even have time to think about evading him, never mind actually do so. One minute she was standing in his hallway, the next she was in Marcus's arms, held securely against him. His mouth came down on her own, hard and sure, hot with male pride and anger, and he took her half-parted lips in a victor's kiss. And she didn't care, she didn't care one little bit. A feeling far more potent than the bubbles from a thousand bottles of champagne hit her emotions. He was kissing her. Marcus was kissing her.

Marcus was *kissing* her.

Marcus was kissing her!

CHAPTER THREE

'OH. MMM. Oh...' Greedily Lucy clung, both to the sensation and to the man delivering it, reaching up to wrap her arms tightly around Marcus's neck as she caved in to her own need. She had wanted him too much and for too long to resist this...this miracle of miracles, she decided headily, and she moved even closer to him, trying to ease the ache deep inside her body by arching into him and moving her body against his.

'Oh, Marcus...' she sighed ecstatically, as she felt the unmistakable surge of his erection pressing into her.

'Lucy...no!' He pushed her sharply away.

Bereft and stunned, she stared reproachfully at him.

'You see, this is exactly the kind of situation I've brought you here to avoid,' he told her brusquely. 'If I'd let you make your own way home—'

'But what if I don't want to avoid it?' Lucy demanded provocatively. 'What if I want...' What on earth was she saying? Another minute and she'd be telling Marcus that this was what she had been dreaming from the first time she had stood opposite him in his office. Dreaming of, lusting after, longing for...

'Never mind what you want,' Marcus told her acerbically. 'What you need right now is to sleep off that champagne.'

Reddening and humiliated, Lucy started to walk towards the door. 'Well, in that case I'd better go home, then, hadn't I?' she said petulantly. The truth was that, whilst she wasn't drunk, the glass and a half of champagne she'd had was a whole glass more than she normally had to drink—on an empty stomach, too. And there was no doubt that the combined effect of Marcus's presence, the privacy of his house, plus the intensity of her feelings for him were all working together to make her want to put into practice the feverish lust-filled desires she had kept hidden for so very long. However, dizzy with lust and longing though she was, she was still in control enough to recognise that the best place for her right now was somewhere with a comfortable bed and no Marcus.

'No way.' Marcus stopped her. 'You can sleep it off here. Come on—this way.'

He had turned her round and was practically frog-marching her up the stairs, Lucy recognised wrathfully. She tried to pull away from him, and to her chagrin over-balanced on her spindly heels.

'Right—that's it,' Marcus announced, swinging her up into his arms before she could stop him as he climbed the last couple of stairs.

With her face buried against his shoulder, and her hand splayed out across his shirt, perfectly able to feel the crisp male hair beneath it, Lucy felt as though she had suddenly become a sort of sexual Lucy in Wonderland, fallen into a magical fantasy world.

Still carrying her, Marcus strode down the landing and in true Hollywood hero fashion pushed open a bedroom floor with one highly polished shoe. How typical of Marcus that he would wear such traditional-looking shoes, Lucy acknowledged, whilst her stomach muscles cramped in pleasure at the exciting discovery that said shoes looked rather bigger than those worn by her unmourned ex-husband. They must be at least a size eleven, maybe even larger...

The room they were in was obviously a guest room,

pristinely neat and decorated in a rather old-fashioned and very unadventurous mix of traditional chintz and heavy inherited family furniture.

Not that Lucy had very much inclination to study the furniture—not when Marcus was sliding her down his body in such a delicious and delirium-inducing way. Sliding her down his body and trying to step back from her, she recognised. But she wasn't going to let him.

The shock of her own thoughts was a powerful adrenaline surge, filling her with a determination that was turning her into someone she hardly recognised. Someone who was demanding to know why she should not have what she wanted; why she should not do as others did and simply take what she wanted. Why she should not for once in her life simply put herself and her own needs first.

She had never experienced anything so alluringly tempting, so wonderfully empowering, so overwhelming irresistible. Why should she try to resist it? Why shouldn't she seize this opportunity? Why shouldn't she allow herself to seduce Marcus into taking her to bed? Why shouldn't she do what other women did all the time instead of denying herself what she so desperately wanted? Why should she always be the one to go without? Why shouldn't she allow herself this one night?

And tomorrow? When she had to face Marcus's anger and rejection?

But this wasn't tomorrow. It was today. It was here and now. She was already dealing with Marcus's rejection and had been for years. Why shouldn't she sweeten it with the kind of memories that would burn within the shrine of her most secret places for ever?

'Marcus... *Marcus*...' she whispered fiercely against his lips, and she lifted her mouth to his, wriggling as close to him as she could, oblivious to the fact that her movements had caused the press-studs fastening her fragile silk dress to pop open until she felt the unwanted presence of its small cap sleeves halfway down her arms.

The unwanted intrusion of her dress and its unfamiliarly draped sleeves was easily dealt with. She simply dropped her arms and let it slide down to the floor, to pool round her feet, then stepped out of it. Thus freed, she lifted her arms and wrapped them tightly round Marcus's neck, standing in only one shoe, a thin silk camisole and matching fluted-legged brief French knickers. Ridiculously, perhaps, one of the first things she had done after Nick's betrayal and their subsequent divorce was to go inside the Agent Provocateur shop she walked past most days on her way to her office and treat herself to the kind of underwear that every sensual woman had a right to enjoy—even if her husband had labelled her as sexless.

Marcus was trying to say something to her, she realised, as she rubbed her nose against the bare flesh of his throat with open sensual pleasure, breathing in the scent of him. And she could feel his fingers biting into the soft skin of her upper arms, too. But she was too lost in the sheer wonder of the moment, and what was happening, to pay any attention to what he might be trying to say. Why speak, after all, when they could be doing this? Lucy decided giddily in adrenaline- and love-fuelled need, as she created around herself the familiar fantasy that had comforted her Marcus-deprived body for so long. The fantasy in which Marcus just could not resist her and didn't even want to. Poor Marcus. He was probably dreadfully uncomfortable in all those clothes—that tie, that buttoned-up shirt—surely it behoved her to aid him with their removal?

She tried for the tie first, her tongue-tip pressed firmly against her teeth as she worked at the knot with eager fingers.

'Lucy!'

'Mmm?' She had worn a tie at school, as part of her uniform, so surely unknotting this one...?

'Lucy...' Marcus's hands covered her own. Lucy looked up at him and gave him an approving smile. Obviously he shared her own eagerness for him to be rid of his clothes and wanted to help her. She intended to say as much to him, but suddenly she became distracted as she looked at his mouth, and then she couldn't look away again.

'Marcus.' She whispered his name in dizzy delight as she looked at it and longed for it, touching her own tongue to her lips as her eyes darkened with the heat of her own hunger for him.

Reaching up, she pressed her mouth tenderly against his. His lips felt firm and strong, his flesh sensuously distracting and hunger-inducing as she breathed tiny kisses against it, little nibbles that grew bolder as each taste fuelled her need for more. Marcus's hands left her arms and gripped her waist.

It was nice to be held so tightly, she acknowledged, but it would be even nicer if he were to touch her breast. So much easier, surely, for her to simply take his hand and place it against the warm swell of her own flesh beneath the thin silk of her cami and hold it there whilst her tongue darted excitedly against the closed line of his mouth, begging for entrance to the pleasures that lay beyond them...

'Lucy!'

What was Marcus doing? He couldn't be pushing her away. Frantically she reached out to him, then lost her balance and started to fall backwards onto the bed behind her.

Immediately Marcus made a grab for her, but it was too late, and somehow or other she was lying on the bed, with Marcus on top of her. The full weight of his body was pressing her down into the mattress and it felt so good. In fact it felt, *he* felt like heaven...like everything good she had ever experienced in the whole of her life, only ten times more than that. She exhaled in delighted bliss and wrapped her arms tightly round his neck, pressing her mouth against his, her lips parted invitingly.

She heard Marcus make a thick muffled sound. Surely not a groan? And then his hands were in her hair, his fingers hard and warm against her scalp as he held her head in sensual imprisonment and his mouth moved on hers.

Had she imagined she knew what a kiss was? She had known nothing—less than nothing, Lucy admitted, as the emotional champagne bubbles of delight and disbelief exploded inside her and raced along her veins into every part of her body. Most especially to those bits of her body that were particularly receptive to the kind of pleasure Marcus was giving her. Even her toes were curling, in a silent exclamation of thrilled awe.

So this was what it felt like to be truly aroused by and responsive to a man. No wonder in times gone by mothers of impressionable daughters had guarded them so ferociously. Already she was hooked on what Marcus was giving her; already she wanted and needed more. His tongue-tip teased the sensitivity of her lips with small, almost whip-like tormenting caresses before suddenly hardening and thrusting deep into her mouth, not just once but repeatedly, until her whole body was shuddering in rhythmic response to those thrusts.

Dizzily Lucy reflected that she'd asked for one miracle but had actually got two! Was that how it worked with this miracle thing? Once you had tuned in to miracles, so to speak, did they just keep on coming? Little miracles popping up here, there and everywhere?

'Oh, I do so hope there will be more,' she whispered ecstatically as Marcus released her mouth.

'What?' he demanded, looking down at her, all blazing impatience and irritation and lethal male desire.

'More,' she repeated sweetly, giving him a beatific smile. 'I would like more, Marcus. Much more,' she emphasised.

'You want more?' he repeated.

Why was he looking at her like that? As though he couldn't believe what he was hearing? As though the hard pulse of his erection didn't exist?

Lucy wasn't going to let herself be dragged out of her fantasy.

'Oh, yes,' she agreed. Now that he had kissed her, and she had tasted him, her body was so fixated on him that it would probably mount an all-out rebellion if it was denied him now. She wanted him and she was going to have him, she decided firmly. She deserved to have him.

'It's been such a long time, you see,' she told him. And it had. Such a very, very long time since she had first looked at him and wanted him. And now here was her very own personal miracle, making it possible for her to have him. So of *course* she wanted more of them—and of him, too. But right now she didn't have time to explain all of that to him because right now...right now she had far more important and exciting things she wanted to do.

She looked up into his eyes and then gave in to the temptation to stroke her tongue-tip along the line of his throat. She heard him groan, felt him shudder, and then his hands were on her body, as she had so much longed for them to be, cupping her breasts whilst she tugged off his tie and her fingers worked busily to unfasten the buttons of his shirt. The pads of his thumbs were stroking her erect nipples, working the silk of her camisole against them until she moaned in helpless delight at the effect his deliberate stroking of the fine silk against her sensitive flesh was having on her.

But she got her own back. She had unfastened his shirt and was free to slide her hands inside it, palms flat against the hard muscle of his chest. She lifted her head and kissed his collarbone, stringing tiny kisses together in mute arousal. His fingers plucked erotically at one nipple whilst her own urgent movements brought the other free of her cami. She flicked her tongue-tip urgently against the small stone hardness of Marcus's flat male nipples, tasting first one and then the other, tormenting herself with the knowledge of the pleasure that lay ahead of her when she allowed her hands and her mouth to move down over his body.

Marcus bent his head and kissed her throat. His fingertip traced the shape of her ear whilst his teeth nibbled gently on her lobe, and then his mouth caressed the flesh just behind it. A spasm of intense pleasure and longing shot through her, and she arched her back to bring her breast fully into his hand, a small, keening moan bubbling in her throat. Her toes curled, and automatically she opened her legs in eager supplication.

Against her body she could feel the erect heat and hardness of Marcus's own arousal, whilst what he was doing to that tiny spot of flesh was practically bringing her to the point of orgasm all by itself.

His hand stroked her hip and then slid lower, finding the soft curve of her bottom beneath the wide silky leg of her fluted French knickers. Some women thought thongs were sexy, but right now Lucy felt that what she was wearing and the access to all areas they gave Marcus was far more alluring. Without any need to remove them, his hand had already moved from her bottom to the soft silky curls of hair between her legs, and his thumb was massaging slow circles against her mound before his fingers started to tease her open.

Lucy moaned and writhed and lifted her body up to his hands, then gasped as he stroked deftly into her wetness in the very same heartbeat as his lips started to caress her tight nipple.

She felt as though a magical cord was somehow stretched from her breast to her belly, and that what Marcus was doing to her was tightening it to the point where she wanted to scream with urgent longing for him to do more, to take her further, deeper.

'Marcus, I'm going to come,' she protested thickly. But instead of heeding her warning and removing his clothes, so that he could slide into her, he lifted his head and looked steadily at her whilst his fingers moved more purposefully over her. Over her and into her. Stroking her, teasing her, until she was so hot, and so wet, and so wanting...

'I'm not coming until you're inside me,' she told him, panting out the words as she struggled to hold back her orgasm, her fingers closing over him through the fabric of his clothes and her body shuddering violently in excitement as she realised how thick and strong he actually was.

He undressed with speedy efficiency, scarcely giving her time to enjoy the pleasure of looking at his naked body. Then he undressed her as well, and then positioned himself between her welcoming, eager thighs.

'Missionary position?' she huffed, pulling a small face.

'It's all we've got time for if you want me inside you when we come,' Marcus told her rawly, before bending his head to kiss her naked breasts in turn whilst he rubbed the hard hot head of his erection against her clitoris until she called out frantically to him, begging him to satisfy her.

Lucy felt her orgasm seize her in its seismic grip with his third thrust, her muscles fastening round him to hold and caress him, to draw from him the sharp, sweet juice of life itself.

She knew the moment she opened he eyes that she wasn't in her own bed. But it was several seconds before she realised just whose bed she was in—or rather whose bedroom, since the room she was in was obviously a guest room. Marcus's guest room. In Marcus's Wendover Square house.

She gave a small despairing groan as the events of the previous afternoon and evening formed images inside her head—images she was forced to view without the protection of her earlier adrenaline-induced armour.

What on earth had possessed her to behave like that? Granted, she loved Marcus, and always would love him, but last night she had... She swallowed uncomfortably whilst her whole body burned in the flames of her own shocking memories.

She looked at her watch. Ten a.m.

She shot upright in the bed. It couldn't possibly be! She'd always woken up at seven at the very latest—always. Even on her honeymoon.

But last night with Marcus she'd had the kind of sex, the quality of sex that she most definitely had not had with Nick—either on her honeymoon or at any other time.

Marcus? Where was he? She hauled up the duvet, holding it to cover her naked breasts, even though some sixth sense told her that the house was a Marcus-free zone. Her clothes, which she could blush-makingly remember abandoning all over the place, had been thoughtfully retrieved

and neatly folded—although she couldn't see her knickers—and there was an envelope propped up on the tallboy
with her name written across it in Marcus's imperious
hand. Keeping the duvet wrapped around herself, she got
out of bed and padded over to the tallboy. Inside the envelope was a piece of paper on which Marcus had written
economically.

*Your underwear is in the dryer. Don't leave without
having some breakfast—coffee, fruit, cereal, etc, in cup-
boards and fridge. Will be in touch this p.m. re visit to
Beatrice.*

Her knickers were in the dryer! How domestic, how
authoritarian—how Marcus.

And how lovely to know they would be clean. If she
had one tiny little hang-up, it was that she was almost too
neat and tidy—and everything that went with that, Lucy
admitted as she hurried into the bathroom. But then boarding school did that to a person, she reflected, as she stood
beneath the refreshing sting of the shower, lathering her
skin and her hair.

The décor in Marcus's house might be slightly old-
fashioned, but the guest bathroom was well stocked with
everything that an overnight visitor minus her sponge bag
might need. Lucy smiled approvingly when she found a
new toothbrush as well as toothpaste in the basket beside
the basin, along with a new comb, a small unopened jar
of face cream and even deodorant.

Fortunately her hair was naturally straight, so she had
no need to do anything other than wash and comb it, knowing that by the time she reached her office it would have
dried. And even more fortunately, given the time and the

fact that she had a considerable amount of paperwork to attend to, she could go straight there and change into a pair of jeans once she got there. She always kept several changes of clothes there, just in case.

Her head had begun to ache unpleasantly—a combination of anxiety about what Marcus might be likely to say to her about last night and lack of caffeine, Lucy decided as she made her way downstairs in her silk dress but minus her stiletto shoes.

Marcus's kitchen was, of course, immaculate. Having retrieved her underwear from the laundry room and quickly put it on—no matter how saucy it might be, she simply was not a 'no knickers' girl, Lucy decided firmly—she hurried into the kitchen, desperately in need of a very strong cup of coffee.

Ten minutes later, after going through every cupboard and finding only decaf, she was forced to admit that there was an unbridgeable gap between her idea of what constituted a proper breakfast drink and Marcus's.

Decaf. She screwed up her nose in distaste as she made herself a cup and munched half-heartedly on a banana.

Those butterflies in her stomach weren't there just because she needed her caffeine fix. They were there because last night she had seduced Marcus. Because she had thrown herself at him—and onto him. Her face started to burn, and not just with the guilty embarrassment she ought to be feeling. Her mental self might feel guilt and shame and be dreading having to face Marcus, but her physical self was positively crowing with delight, reliving with relish every single intimate caress and kiss. It certainly had no intention of feeling any kind of shame whatsoever.

But what about her emotional self? Lucy wondered sadly as she let herself out of the house, carefully checking that the door had locked behind her before setting off to walk the short distance to her Sloane Street office. Her emotional self was caught between the two opposing forces of her mind and her body. Her emotional self loved Marcus and yearned for him to love her back. Her mental self said that it was simply not possible, and warned her of the pain and humiliation she was courting. Her physical self, on the other hand, was still wallowing in the triumphant afterglow of sex with a lover who had elevated the experience to a plane hitherto unknown to her other than via fevered fantasies and lustful daydreams.

Add to all of that the fact that the thought of seeing Marcus again was making her feel physically sick with apprehension, and it was no wonder her head was pounding, Lucy decided as she hurried into the coffee shop she regularly used to obtain her daytime caffeine fix. To her relief she was the only customer.

'Your usual?' the girl behind the counter asked cheerfully.

'Please, Sarah—no, make that two,' Lucy told her. 'And a couple of chocolate brownies as well.'

Sarah gave her a wicked grin.

'Caffeine and carbs? It must have been a good night last night.'

'The best—at least what I can remember of it,' Lucy agreed, rolling her eyes and grinning back. But the truth was that the first bit of her light-hearted response to Sarah's teasing was exactly that—the truth. It had been the best—and was likely to remain so, she reminded herself grimly as she gathered up her double espressos and her brownies and stepped back into the late-morning sunshine.

Marcus would certainly not want a rerun, and now that she had had her fantasies come to life—now that she knew just how far short they had fallen of the reality of the heaven of Marcus's arms around her, Marcus's mouth on hers, Marcus's lovemaking—she was going to have to spend the rest of her life not just knowing she could never love anyone else but also knowing that she was never going to want to have sex with anyone else.

It was a miserable thing to have to admit to herself as she hurried into the building that housed Prêt a Party's offices, pausing to exchange smiles with Harry the doorman as she did so.

Once, Prêt a Party's offices had been filled with the busy hum of telephones ringing, clients calling, the laughter of her two best friends and partners. But now they were empty and silent. Kicking the door closed as she balanced her coffee, Lucy fought the temptation not to think about how Marcus had kicked the bedroom door open last night—and what had happened after he had.

Five minutes later, her dress exchanged for a tee shirt and a pair of jeans, and her French knickers carefully parcelled up to be rewashed and kept as a very personal souvenir, Lucy savoured the last delicious gulp of coffee whilst she scrolled down her e-mails.

No new requests for Prêt a Party's services, she saw gloomily. The only commission she had pending was the sportswear manufacturer's launch of a new football boot, which was to be held at a very trendy nightclub of the type favoured by TV celebs, models, premier league footballers and the like.

Everything was already in place for the launch, but while she drank her second coffee Lucy brought up the worksheets for it to check them over.

She had based the whole event on the manufacturer's logo and colours, playing on a 'team event' theme, since they were launching a football boot. Cheerleaders dressed in a highly-sexed version of a football strip would provide the main entertainment by chanting the client's name, a new cocktail was going to be served, and Lucy had decided that the food was going to be miniature portions of that favourite laddish treat—curry and chips in a plastic carton.

When her telephone suddenly rang she stared at it apprehensively. Marcus. It had to be! She picked up the receiver and flicked her tongue nervously over her dry lips.

'May I speak to the Honourable Lucy Blayne, please?'

How was it possible for her heart to sink with relief? Lucy wondered, as she corrected her caller discreetly by responding, 'Lucy Cardrew speaking.'

'Oh, hi. It's Andrew Walker here—your cousin Johnny...'

Andrew Walker. The miracle who might be going to save Prêt a Party and what was left of her trust fund.

'Oh, yes—of course!'

'Look, I know it's short notice, but I'm going to be out of the country from tomorrow, so I wondered if there was any chance that you might be free for lunch today so that we could talk things over and set the ball rolling, so to speak.'

Lucy looked at her watch. It was gone twelve now.

'I could make a late lunch at half one?' she suggested.

'Great. Is the Brasserie in Pont Street okay for you?'

'Perfect,' Lucy confirmed. Pont Street was virtually round the corner from her office, and the Brasserie was one of her favourite eateries.

'Excellent. I'll see you there at one-thirty, then.'

Replacing the receiver, Lucy looked down at her jeans. She would have to change them for something more suitable for a business lunch. The Armani suit, probably— referred to by her friends as 'the armour', because Lucy invariably wore it whenever she had a business meeting to attend. And always when she went to see Marcus to ask him to release more money from her trust fund.

CHAPTER FOUR

AT DEAD on one-thirty, fortified by two more cups of espresso and armoured with the Armani, Lucy fought her way past the untidy jumble of camera-toting, motorbike-riding paparazzi clustered boldly outside the Brasserie, waiting for its celeb diners to arrive and leave, and pushed open the door. She was immediately greeted with a welcoming smile from the receptionist, who recognised her.

'I'm having lunch with a Mr Walker—Andrew Walker?'

'Mr Walker is already here and waiting at the table,' the *maître d'* informed her.

'Oh, Angelo, you're back! How lovely. Did you have a wonderful time in Sydney with your son and grandchildren?' Lucy asked warmly.

'That boy—he is doing so well. He has his own restaurant now,' Angelo informed her proudly as he escorted her past the other tables to one set discreetly out of earshot of the others.

The man seated there stood up as she approached, extending his hand. 'Andrew Walker,' he introduced himself, and Lucy shook it and sat down.

'Hello Andrew—Lucy Cardrew.'

He was a middle-aged man of middle height with an unremarkable face. He was smartly if somewhat formally dressed, in a suit that—like those Marcus wore—had obviously come from a bespoke tailor. The shirt had all the hallmarks of its Jermyn Street origins, and his shoes were handmade too, but whereas Marcus always looked completely at home and at ease in the formality of his dark business suits and handmade shirts, Andrew Walker looked rather uncomfortable in his clothes, and they in turn looked new and somewhat alien to him.

As he signalled to the waiter he told Lucy, 'Your cousin will have already mentioned to you that I may be interested in investing in your business?'

'Yes,' Lucy acknowledged, thanking the waiter for the menu he was handing her and shaking her head when Andrew asked her what wine she would like.

'Just water for me,' she told the waiter firmly.

Andrew didn't resume talking about his plans until after they had been served with their food, and even then he kept his voice low and conspiratorial as he leaned across the table to tell her firmly, 'I must stress that at this stage it is imperative that you don't discuss my approach to you with anyone else.'

'But my solicitor will have to know, surely?' Lucy protested.

'Ultimately, perhaps. Although I would prefer it if my own solicitor drew up all the necessary agreements first.' He gave a small shrug. 'I have discovered that the success of my existing business has resulted in other people becoming very keen to find out what my future financial moves will be. Any market can only sustain a certain amount of business. How much business do you have in hand at the moment?'

'Very little,' Lucy told him honestly. 'I expect you know about the financial problems the business has had to face following my divorce?'

'Of course.'

'I've got a big event coming up next month—the launch of a new football boot—'

'And that kind of business is profitable?'

'Corporate business is hugely profitable compared with

private business,' Lucy explained. 'When I'm asked to organise an event where the client wants access to my address book, in order to ensure that they have enough A-list celebs at the event to assure them of maximum press coverage, I can charge more than when I am organising a private event, where the guest list is supplied by the person giving the event. Obviously any kind of launch is an event when the attendance of the right kind of high-profile celebrities is a must. For this event, for instance, the client is guaranteeing the attendance of the premier league football star who is the face of their brand, and I have sent invitations to everyone in my address book who is guaranteed to bring the press to the event.'

'"Everyone" being...?'

Lucy gave a small shrug. 'Certain top-rank models and soap stars—the top names, not the B-and C-list—a smattering of It Girl-types and rock star offspring, plus some of the more sociable dot-com millionaires. People who are glamorous and newsworthy, and who will add lustre to the event.'

'I see... So I take it that much of Prêt a Party's market value lies in its address book?'

'In some ways,' Lucy agreed.

'When it comes to organising food and drink, venues, flowers, that kind of thing, who is responsible for choosing who will supply those?'

'Prêt a Party,' Lucy told him promptly. 'I'm very strict about who I do and don't use. Prêt a Party's reputation has been built on the quality of everything we provide—and that includes the ancillary services we use, whether they are marquees or food.'

'Mmm. Have you ever thought about selling the Prêt a Party concept as a franchise?'

'No.'

'Well, that is one of the areas I am very interested in us looking into as business partners. It will be expensive to start with, of course, until the franchisee revenue starts to come in. But what I have in mind is to use the contacts I have already made via my turnkey business to build up our own ancillary service agencies—so that we can supply our franchisees with everything they need and the Prêt a Party guarantee of quality. We buy our own marquees and we provide the men to erect them. We supply the waiters, the glasses and the drinks. We provide the florists and the musicians and the cleaning staff—in fact, we supply everything and anything else our franchisees and their clients may need.'

Lucy stared at him, her food forgotten. 'That's *brilliant*,' she told him, her eyes shining. 'But it will cost a fortune...'

'Indeed it will. But I think the eventual return will make it a worthwhile investment.'

Lucy didn't know what to say. The most she had been hoping for had been an injection of capital to refloat the business so that she could build it up again, but what Andrew Walker was talking about so matter-of-factly was the creation of a whole business empire.

'As I've already said, I would like your assurance that what we are discussing is kept strictly between the two of us at this stage.'

Lucy nodded her head.

'I'd like to get things moving as quickly as possible, but obviously you're going to need time to think over my proposal. How would you feel about us meeting up again when I get back from this trip?'

'That...That sounds fine,' Lucy managed to tell him, as she fought to sound businesslike and professional rather than giddy with the delight and relief she was actually feeling.

'Here's my card,' Andrew Walker told her. 'I have just bought a new property in Holland Park. It's in the course of being renovated at the moment, but once the renovations are finished I intend to throw a large party there for my friends and my business contacts. If all goes as I hope it will, that event will be organised by Prêt a Party, and will be a means of introducing our new joint venture to everyone.'

'Brilliant,' Lucy repeated, and meant it.

It was three o'clock before Lucy got back to her office, her head buzzing with excited thoughts and plans. She could scarcely believe her good luck, and all because Andrew had happened to see that spread about Prêt a Party in *A-List Life*.

The only down side to this wonderful piece of good luck was that she wasn't going to be able to say anything about it to Marcus. Or at least not just yet. It would be such a relief to know that she didn't have to plead with him to change his mind and allow her to use what was left of her trust fund to clear Prêt a Party's overdraft and give her some much-needed working capital. She looked at the telephone. There was no message from Marcus, despite the fact that he had said he would be in touch with her. Had he changed his mind? Had he been thinking about last night and decided that he simply never wanted to see her again, just in case she tried to repeat her behaviour?

And if he did ring what was he likely to say?

She needed an espresso, Lucy decided.

Marcus frowned as he studied the view from his office window. His father, grandfather, great-grandfather and all those who had gone before them had occupied this office in their turn, and Marcus had known from the moment he had been old enough to know such things that one day he would have to take over responsibility for the bank and its clients. His father's death when Marcus had been only six years old had meant that Marcus had been brought up by his mother and grandfather, who'd made sure that Marcus was aware of how important the bank was, and the fact that he was expected to dedicate his life to it. At twenty-one, fresh from university, Marcus had resented that responsibility, and the way that life had forced it on him, even while he had felt honour-bound to accept it. His grandfather at nearly eighty had needed to be allowed to retire, and he had a duty to take over from him.

And so he had put aside his dreams of travelling the world and focused instead on doing what he had to do.

He was nearly six years older than Lucy, and the first time she had walked into his office his feelings towards her had been a mixture of irritation and impatience. Irritation because he'd had enough on his plate without having to act as her trustee, and impatience because he had seen in her eyes the dazed look of a young woman about to develop a huge and unwanted crush on him.

Marcus did not consider himself to be vain. But he had had enough relationships to know what the look Lucy had given him meant. He might have had no choice other than to do what was expected of him and take over the bank, but he had grimly and determinedly held on to what independence he did have. Marriage, so far as he was concerned, was a necessary evil he wanted to put off for as long as he could. One day, yes, he would marry, and provide the bank with its future administrator, but not yet. And he certainly had no intention of ever allowing himself to fall in love.

His mouth hardened. Marcus had seen at first hand the destruction 'falling in love' could cause. His own father had fallen in love when Marcus was six, and he had left his wife—Marcus's mother—abandoning her and his two children because of that 'love'. He had destroyed their family and left Marcus feeling betrayed and bereft. And, since he had not been able to hate the father he had loved so much, his six-year-old mind had turned its hatred on the emotion that had caused him to leave instead.

Three weeks after he had left them Marcus's father had been killed in an accident—along with his lover. Marcus had mourned him and promised himself that he would never make the same mistake as his father. He would never, ever allow himself to fall in love. Because of that he had made sure that the women he dated, the women he slept with, were sophisticated, slightly older than he was himself, often post-divorce and pre-second marriage. Women who enjoyed sex and were socially aware, women who understood the rules of the game as he chose to play it—women, in short, who were the complete opposite of Lucy.

Over the years the initial irritation and impatience he had felt towards Lucy had fused together to become a gut reaction which was activated every time he saw her, and it had been intensified to the point where it had been laced with incredulous disbelief and anger when she had married Nick Blayne.

She was supposed to be an intelligent young woman. She must have been able to see what Nick Blayne was. But she had obviously been too blinded by 'love' to care. Love and lust, if the newspaper photographs he had seen of her cavorting half naked with Blayne on the Caribbean island where she had first met him were anything to go by.

Irritation, impatience, anger—and, if he was honest with himself, perhaps a touch of guilt?

Guilt? What the hell did he have to feel guilty about? He hadn't been responsible for her marrying Blayne, or the catastrophic events that had followed. He had done everything within his power to stop Lucy destroying her own financial security and allowing her now ex-husband to plunder the trust fund, but she had refused to listen to him.

But, ridiculously, he did feel guilty. And for some reason that made him feel even more intensely irritated and angry with Lucy.

He was, he reminded himself grimly, her trustee, and he was now ruthlessly determined to protect what was left of her inheritance—from Lucy herself, if that should prove necessary.

He was well aware that her original blushing, bashful self-consciousness and virginal sexual curiosity about him had turned to resentment edged with apprehension. He had made it clear to her that he was not going to be persuaded into allowing her to remove what was left of her trust fund to put into her ailing business, no matter how much pressure she put on him to do so.

Prêt a Party was suffering the natural death throes of a business ruined by greed and mismanagement. The only thing that could save it now was a massive injection of capital and a very firm hand grasping its control. That had translated in Marcus's mind into *his* massive capital injection and *his* firm hand, but whilst he could quite easily spare the money, he could not spare the time to salvage the wreckage of Lucy's once profitable business.

He had stood by and watched—first assessingly, then reluctantly and then grudgingly admiringly—as she built up Prêt a Party into a very nice little business, even if she had continued to irritate him with her almost aggressive post-crush antagonism towards him and her refusal to listen to his advice.

But all that had been before last night! Taking Lucy to bed had been the last thing on his mind when he had removed her from the party.

But he had done so. And now...

Marcus frowned heavily. He was almost thirty-five years old—an age by which all his male ancestors had already been married and had fathered the male heir who would ultimately take over the family bank. Since he had never been in love, it was hard for Marcus to envisage what being 'in love' might feel like. His observations of love in others inclined him to the view that he was better off not knowing. He had deliberately chosen relationships which allowed him to avoid marriage, but at the same time he had known that ultimately he must marry. And over this last year he had become increasingly aware of his duty to the bank and to the past. He needed a wife and he needed an heir.

Finding a wife would not be a problem, but finding the right kind of wife—who would adapt to his way of life and understand the duties and responsibilities it carried—could be one. Especially when the kind of marriage he wanted was one based on practicality rather than emotion. Especially when one considered his wish to father an heir.

It was time for him to find himself a woman. A woman with whom he was both socially and sexually compatible. A woman, perhaps, like Lucy.

Lucy? Had he gone mad? She exasperated him as no other woman could, and her marriage to Nick Blayne had only increased his impatient anger towards her.

But last night she had enticed and aroused him as no other woman had.

The truth was that Lucy needed protecting from herself.

He would certainly be a far safer and more suitable husband for her than another Nick Blayne. A marriage between them would benefit them both. He needed a wife, and Lucy certainly needed a husband—if only to prevent her from repeating the mistake she had made in marrying Blayne.

And Lucy loved children.

Actually, for them to marry one another was in many ways entirely logical. She understood the world he lived in because it was also her world. They both wanted children, and sexually he had sown all the wild oats he wanted to sow—even if a part of him still mourned the loss of his youthful dreams of travel and adventure.

His mind was made up, Marcus decided abruptly. He intended to marry Lucy. And the sooner the better.

All he had to do now was find a way to convince her that she needed to marry him. And Marcus though he knew exactly how to do that.

The sensuality Lucy had displayed last night had surprised him, as had the pleasurable intensity of her sexual response to him. Lucy was a woman with a warm sex drive, a woman currently without a sexual partner in her life and quite clearly a woman who wanted one.

All he had to do was make her need work in his favour, Marcus decided coolly. He walked over to his desk and picked up the telephone receiver.

The message light was flashing on her telephone when Lucy walked back into the office. She had been longer at the coffee shop than she had expected. Her heart slalomed the length of her chest cavity before skidding dangerously to a halt as she played the message and heard Marcus's voice, telling her that he had arranged for them to visit his

sister and that he would pick her up from her office at four
o'clock.

Four o'clock? It was ten to now, Lucy saw, panic-
stricken.

Thirteen and a half minutes later she was on her way
downstairs, her hair combed, her lips glossed, and her heart
thudding like a drum beat.

'There you are—come on. There's a traffic warden on
the prowl and I don't want to get a ticket.'

There was no time to object as Marcus took hold of her
arm and hurried over to the Bentley parked illegally outside the office block, opening the passenger door for her
so that she could scramble in whilst he strode round to the
driver's door.

The interior of the car smelled of leather and Marcus,
and Lucy leaned back in her seat and closed her eyes,
breathing as slowly and carefully as she could.

'Our flight leaves at six—which means you've just
about got time to pack if I drive you back to your flat
now.'

'What? What flight? Where are we going?' Her eyes
snapped open and she lurched forward in her seat.

'To see Beatrice, of course,' Marcus told her patiently.
'Remember? You're going to advise her about organising
a party for George's fiftieth.'

'Your sister lives in Chelsea!' Lucy protested dizzily.

'Most of the time, yes. But she and George also have a
villa in Majorca, and that's where she is right now. She
thought it would be a good idea if you flew out to see her
while she's there, so that she can discuss George's party
with you while he isn't around. She doesn't want him to
guess what's going on.'

Silently Lucy digested what he was saying to her. It was
not particularly unusual for clients to fly her out to all

manner of places, in order to consult her or to get her opinion of their chosen venue for their event, but Marcus had said very clearly '*our* flight', which meant...

'You're going to Majorca as well?' she demanded.

'I have some family business I need to discuss with Beatrice, so she suggested we might as well travel out together,' Marcus told her calmly. 'We'll be staying for a couple of days, so you'll need to pack a few things.'

'And I'll have to get changed. I can't travel to Palma wearing armour,' Lucy protested.

'Armour?'

Lucy could feel herself going red at she recognised her slip-up.

'It's what I call my business suit,' she mumbled.

She could feel Marcus looking at her, but his only comment was a very dry, 'Mmm.'

Marcus turned into Sloane Square and then cut through a couple of narrow back streets before finally bringing the Bentley to a halt in a conveniently empty parking space right outside the block of flats where she lived.

'I'll come up with you.'

It was a statement, not a question or an offer.

Wasn't Marcus going to say *anything* about last night? She had been dreading seeing him all day, worrying about what he would say and how she could respond.

She had told herself that the worst-case scenario would be if he had simply guessed the truth and challenged her with it. She had even rehearsed the scene mentally inside her head to prepare herself.

Marcus would say: You're in love with me, aren't you?
Lucy: What? Certainly not. What on earth makes you think that I could be?

Marcus—in that horrid dry voice he could use to such dramatic effect: Last night?

Lucy—breezily, looking amused and nonchalant: Oh, that! Good heavens, no. I just fancied a shag, that's all.

But evidently that wasn't going to be how it happened.

Leaving Marcus to follow her, Lucy hurried past the concierge with a quick 'hello' and then up the stairs. Her flat was on the first floor, and tiny, but at least she owned it outright and it wasn't a drain on her finances—unlike the much grander flat Nick had insisted on them renting during their marriage.

She unlocked the door and walked into the small hall-way. The enclosed and windowless space had been made larger and brighter by the addition of two non-matching mirrors she had 'borrowed' from the attics at home. A small table, also rescued from attic oblivion, which she had painted cream just like the walls, stood under one of the mirrors. On it Lucy had arranged not flowers, since she believed that every living thing needed natural light and proper fresh air, but instead her precious Jo Malone scented candles and a collection of glass candlesticks. Would Marcus notice the tasteful effect of the arrangement as he followed her into the hallway?

Beyond the hallway lay a tiny sitting room, furnished and decorated in various shades of cream, and pin-neat.

'Before I do anything else I'm going to make myself a cup of coffee,' Lucy told Marcus. 'Would you like a cup?'

'No, thanks. We don't have very much time, you know,' he reminded her.

'You're the one who's organised this, not me, and I'm not going anywhere until I've had my caffeine fix,' Lucy informed him stubbornly, heading for the kitchen.

'Fine! Where do you keep your passport, Lucy?'

'In the bureau behind the sofa,' Lucy told him from the kitchen.

Marcus opened the bureau and saw passports immediately. Two of them were bundled together inside a rubber band. He snapped off the band and opened the top one, and then wished that he hadn't. It was the passport Lucy had had when she had been married, and the photograph inside it showed a bright-eyed, happy-looking young woman. Her current passport, though—the one she had obtained after her divorce, when she had reverted to her maiden name—showed a thinner-faced young woman whose eyes held stark pain and despair. What on earth had she seen in Nick Blayne? How could she have loved him? Was it really 'loved'?

'Did you find the passport?' Lucy asked as she walked past him with her coffee and pushed open her bedroom door. Lifting a small case from beneath the bed onto it, she began methodically opening drawers and placing what she thought she would need on her bed.

'Look—while you're doing that, why don't I pack your toiletries for you?'

Having Marcus safely out of the way and out of her line of vision, instead of standing there watching her and making her think about last night, was a very good idea, Lucy acknowledged. So she nodded her head and handed him the bag she used for such necessities, exhaling slowly when he had disappeared into her small bathroom.

Determinedly Lucy started to fold the things she had put on the bed, and place them into the flat packs she always used for travelling.

'Lucy, what about your pills?' Marcus called out from the bathroom.

Her pills! Thank heavens he had reminded her. She had learned the hard way never to go anywhere without her sun allergy pills.

'In the cabinet,' she called back. 'Second shelf down, right-hand side.'

She heard him opening the cabinet door as she placed the flat packs in her case, and then he called out again, 'I can't find them.'

Putting down the pack she was holding, Lucy walked into the bathroom, holding her breath when she was forced to squeeze past him to reach the cabinet.

'They're right here,' she told him, taking the allergy tablets from the shelf.

'Those aren't contraceptive pills,' Marcus objected.

Contraceptive pills?

'No. I don't take contraceptive pills. I don't need to. I've never needed to. Nick always used a condom. It was something he was obsessive about. He told me that he never had and never would have sex without wearing one.'

This wasn't a subject she wanted to discuss with Marcus in any way, shape or form, Lucy recognised. But she couldn't help wondering if the fact that Marcus had felt so good inside her last night had been because he had been inside her skin to skin, and she had loved the intimacy of knowing that.

As Lucy hurried back into the bedroom Marcus frowned. Last night, with unprecedented recklessness, the last thing on his mind had been the need for any kind of contraceptive or health precaution. He had to admit that hearing Lucy's ex-husband had insisted on wearing a condom was very good news.

He watched her whilst she finished her packing. He could feel his body tightening, and a very specific ache gripping it. He wanted her.

He was supposed to be focusing on getting her to want him, not allowing himself to want her.

'Ready?' he demanded tersely.

Lucy gave an unsmiling nod of assent.

CHAPTER FIVE

PALMA airport was always busy, and today was no exception. Lucy struggled to dodge the mounds of luggage and keep up with Marcus who, despite having their luggage to deal with, still somehow or other managed to have a positively 'parting of the Red Sea' effect on the crowds. They opened to allow him through, and then closed again, forcing her to fight her way through.

Marcus had now reached the exit, where he was being approached by two pretty girls wearing the uniforms of a certain car rental firm. Was it a car they were hoping to persuade him to hire, or a date they were hoping to be offered? Lucy wondered jealously as she finally caught up with him.

'I was just explaining to these ladies that the hotel will have sent a car to collect us,' he told Lucy.

'The hotel? What hotel?' Lucy demanded as he started to walk towards the waiting chauffeurs with their boards displaying clients' names. 'I thought we were staying with Beatrice.'

'Did you? The villa's quite small and remote, and since Beatrice is there to oversee some remedial work on the bathrooms I didn't think it was a good idea for us to expect her to put us up. I've booked us into a hotel instead. It's in Deia, very close to the Residencia, and supposed to be even better. And don't worry about the bill. I shall be paying it. Ah, there's our driver.'

If she stood on her tiptoes, she could just about see the

smartly uniformed chauffeur holding up a placard that read 'Hotel Boutique, Deia'.

Lucy knew Majorca quite well, since it had recently become very much one of the 'in' places to stay, following on from various celebs buying property in an exclusive enclave of villas and boutique hotels that had sprung up on a previously undeveloped part of the island's coastline. The Residencia had been *the* place to stay in this upmarket resort, and from what she had heard the new Hotel Boutique was even more special. Lucy had heard rave reviews from clients who had stayed there.

Outside the airport, the warmth of the night air wrapped round her like soft cashmere as the chauffeur opened the doors of a large Mercedes limousine for them.

Marcus slid into the sea next to her and the chauffeur closed the doors.

'Where exactly is Beatrice's villa?' she asked Marcus uncertainly as the Mercedes joined the queue of traffic waiting to leave the airport.

'Up in the hills outside Palma.'

'But that's a long way from Deia,' Lucy objected. 'Wouldn't it have been better for us to have stayed somewhere closer?'

'The Boutique has an excellent reputation, and I thought you'd prefer to stay there.'

'How long will it take us to get there?' Lucy asked.

'Not that long. Why?'

'I need another caffeine fix. I'm desperate for cup of coffee.'

And *he* was desperate for *her*, Marcus found himself thinking. 'Do you want me to ask the driver to stop somewhere?'

Lucy shook her head. 'No, I'll wait.'

She was beginning to feel tired, and more than a little

bit headachy, but despite the comfort of the Mercedes she couldn't relax properly—not with Marcus right there next to her.

The road climbed and turned, winding through the hills, and then started to drop down again. Below them Lucy could see the lights of villas, dotted either side of the river ravine, and below them the small harbour itself. Pure, perfect picture-postcard stuff.

The Mercedes turned in to a narrow stone tunnel beyond which lay a paved forecourt. Within seconds, or so it seemed, they were standing in the jasmine-scented coolness of the foyer, a huge fan whirring above their heads, traditional terracotta tiles underfoot, and the décor echoing the very best of traditional Majorcan interiors. The white walls were warmed by striking paintings and woven rugs in rich earthy colours.

'If you will follow José, he will show you to your suites.' The receptionist smiled as she handed Marcus two key cards, and a very young and very handsome young Majorcan appeared from out of nowhere to assist them.

The lift was tucked away discreetly in a corner, and as it bore them upwards José told them proudly, 'You have the best suites in the whole hotel. The King of Spain himself, he has stayed there with his family.'

The lift stopped and José held the doors open, giving Lucy a small bow as he encouraged her to step through ahead of him.

A short, wide corridor lay in front of her, its walls painted white and hung with more paintings. Lucy was tempted to linger and inspect them more closely, drawn by the richness of the oil paint, but her head was pounding and she was desperate for coffee.

Only two doors opened off the corridor. José stopped at

the first of them and opened the door, inviting Lucy to step inside.

As she did so, her eyes widened in appreciation. In front of her was a large room with a high ceiling, furnished with traditional dark, heavy wooden furniture which included a huge four-poster bed. Floor-to-ceiling wooden shutters filled one wall, and when José went to open them for her Lucy gasped in delight. The shutters concealed glass patio doors beyond which was a well-lit private terrace, complete with its own plunge pool, and beyond that an uninterrupted view of the sea and sky.

'Thank you, José. I'll find my own way around everything.' Lucy smiled and tipped him so that he could leave and show Marcus to his suite.

As soon as she had closed the door behind José, Lucy picked up the telephone and hurriedly dialled Room Service. Only when she had ordered her much-needed coffee did she start to study the suite properly.

A wooden screen that could be folded back separated the bedroom from an integral, sensually luxurious huge round bath, set into the floor right in front of the patio windows so that one might lie in the bath and look out across the terrace and beyond it.

The wall opposite the patio doors was completely mirrored, as was the wall at right angles to it, and set against the right angle was an all-glass shower cubicle, so that in effect one could bathe or shower and see one's reflection in the mirrors at the same time.

She heard a knock on her bedroom door. Her coffee! Wonderful! But when she went to open the door it was Marcus who was standing outside it.

'I've brought you this,' he told her, handing her a card key. 'I'm going to ring Beatrice in a minute, and fix up a meeting with her for tomorrow, but so far as dinner tonight is concerned, there's supposed to be an excellent restaurant down by the harbour. It's eight now, so if I book a table for ten...?'

'Yes. Fine,' Lucy agreed, exhaling in relief as she saw the waiter coming down the corridor.

Ten minutes later, with her caffeine levels replenished, Lucy explored the rest of her suite.

In addition to her open plan bedroom-cum-bathroom, she also had a self-contained dressing room and a second bathroom, with another shower plus bidet and lavatory.

She would have to change before she went out for dinner. A shower would be speedier, but she just couldn't resist the temptation to wallow self-indulgently in the bath.

Lucy lay soaking in the bubble-topped silky warm water of her bath, luxuriating in the sensuality of the experience. She had left her shutters open, so that she could enjoy the view out to sea should she feel energetic enough to lift her head off the bath pillow. Instead, though, she opened her eyes and looked towards the mirrored wall. There was something irresistibly sensual about the combination of a huge bath and a mirror in which one could see oneself using it. This was definitely a suite for lovers.

Lovers. There was only one man she wanted as her lover. Only one man she had ever wanted, full stop. And that man was Marcus.

Marcus.

Was his suite the same as her own? Was he right now lazing in a tub of hot water, his body naked beneath the suds? A shiver of sensual pleasure iced through her own inner heat, as pleasurable as ice-cream melted by hot chocolate sauce—only a thousand times more so.

But she suspected that Marcus was more likely to prefer

a fierce shower to a lazy linger in a bath. And he still hadn't said a word about last night.

Lucy closed her eyes and stroked the soapy water over her skin, imagining that it was still last night and that Marcus was here with her, touching her, stroking her. A wet heat that had nothing at all to do with the water flooded her sex. This was getting dangerous. But she couldn't resist the temptation to lie there and fantasise, to imagine and remember. She closed her eyes...

She had almost fallen asleep in the bath! And look at the time! It was gone nine o'clock. Reaching for the plug, Lucy stepped up out of the bath and reached for one of the deliciously thick, fluffy towels. The mirror threw back her reflection—white soap bubbles slithering silkily down her body, covering her sex and then revealing it. She could feel the hot beat of her own desire as it pulsed out its hungry message. Her fingers touched her own body, stroking the foam from the swell of her mound and then moving lower. She watched her own movements in the mirrors, unable to look away. Her heart had started to race, a fierce wanton urgency filling her. Slowly and delicately, her tongue-tip pressed to her teeth, Lucy ran an experimental finger along her mound and pressed lightly against her clitoris.

Marcus... Immediately her flesh swelled and glistened richly, her heart pumping...

Somewhere outside the intensity of her concentration she heard a noise that sounded like a door opening...

A door opening! Immediately she removed her hand and reached for a towel, her face burning with self-conscious heat as she realised that Marcus was standing in her bedroom.

How long had he been there? How much had he seen? Behind him she could see what must be a connecting door between the two suites. He must have knocked, but she had obviously been too preoccupied to hear him. Her face burned with the knowledge of what she had so nearly been preoccupied with!

'How much longer is it going to take you to get ready?' he asked her. 'Only it's nearly nine-thirty now.'

He, Lucy recognised dizzily, was already changed, wearing a pair of light-coloured chinos with a darker-coloured top.

'I'm virtually there,' she replied, and then blushed vividly as she realised just what connotation could be placed on her comment, and how appropriate it had almost been. She did not dare look at Marcus as she almost scurried past him and into her dressing room.

'It's a long, steep walk down to the harbour, so I've asked the hotel to provide us with a car and a driver,' Marcus announced as they walked into the foyer together, and Lucy glanced down at her strappy-sandal-shod feet. The same sandals she had been wearing yesterday. The same sandals one of which she had left on his stairs, and then found placed neatly with its twin this morning, alongside her clothes...

She wasn't normally a fan of high-heeled shoes, but the dress she was wearing had a pretty handkerchief hem and demanded equally pretty footwear.

From the hotel, the road to the harbour wound down alongside the river, the wooded slopes broken up by the lights of a scattering of expensive luxury villas,

The harbour itself was tiny, and predictably filled with sleek expensive-looking yachts—just as the restaurants fronting onto the harbour were filled with equally sleek and expensive-looking diners.

This was very much Notting-Hill-on-Sea territory, Lucy thought ruefully. Within seconds of leaving their car and taking less than half a dozen steps, she had seen at least half a dozen famous faces amongst the groups of people already seated at the tables set up outside the restaurants and bars.

'The place I've booked us into has a reputation for serving top-quality fish dishes,' Marcus told her. 'And, knowing how much you like fish, I thought you might prefer that to a more traditional tapas bar.'

'Yes, I would,' Lucy agreed, as she stifled a small yawn. 'Sleepy?'

'No, not really. I think my bath must have made me feel tired,' Lucy responded without thinking, and then felt her whole body start to burn as she tensed, dreading hearing Marcus say that he knew exactly why she might be feeling tired.

There was really no reason for her to feel embarrassed about something so natural. Heavens, she didn't know any women of her own age who were not prepared to trade opinions on the latest vibrator. But somehow the fact that Marcus might have seen her almost engaged in such a very intimate and personal act of self-pleasure made her feel acutely embarrassed. Especially after last night. Oh, yes, especially after last night. Now he might think that it was her desire for him that had prompted her to such a course of action.

He might think it, but she actually *knew* it, Lucy admitted to herself, as Marcus guided her between the packed tables and into the restaurant itself.

Typically, Marcus had managed to secure them a table with just about the best view of the harbour possible, and he had been right about the food as well, Lucy saw, when her own meal was placed in front her. Her mouth started to water. Pan-fried scallops with an Asian fusion-style warm salad. Marcus, she noted, had chosen a thick tuna steak.

'More wine?'

Lucy shook her head firmly. She was already on her second glass, and beginning to feel pleasantly relaxed. She didn't need or want any more.

Marcus had only had two glasses himself, although she noticed that, unlike her, he did not nod his head when the waiter asked if they wanted coffee.

'Espresso?' he commented after she had given her order. 'You'll never sleep.'

'Watch me,' Lucy answered flippantly, and then went bright red. Heavens, Marcus was going to think she was propositioning him if she kept on saying idiotic things like that.

Watch her? Oh, he would love to... And not only watch, either.

'What time did you say we were seeing Beatrice tomorrow?' Lucy asked Marcus hastily, trying to sound businesslike and efficient.

'She's going to ring me in the morning to confirm,' Marcus told her as he glanced at his watch. 'I don't want to rush you, but the car should be back for us any minute now.'

Her coffee had arrived and Lucy drank it greedily, relishing both its smell and its taste, while Marcus summoned their waiter and asked for the bill.

She certainly wasn't going to risk having another bath after what had happened earlier, Lucy decided as she locked her suite door and stepped out of her sandals. Instead she would make do with a shower. She yawned sleepily.

After last night, and then Marcus walking in on her and

almost finding her touching herself, she should have been on edge all evening, but instead she had actually felt very relaxed—so relaxed, in fact, that on a couple of occasions she had even laughed. Marcus had proved to be an unexpectedly entertaining and interesting dinner companion, and she had been sorry when the evening had come to an end—and not just because, given the choice, she would have so much preferred to end it in Marcus's arms, in Marcus's bed.

She undressed quickly and pulled on the complimentary bathrobe before tidying away her clothes and heading for the shower.

She had just stepped out of it and towelled herself her dry when she heard a knock on her patio window. She realised that Marcus was standing outside, beckoning to her. Like her, he too was wearing a bathrobe, but whereas on her it fell to the floor and trailed behind her, on Marcus it only just covered his knees. The sight of the bare tanned flesh of his legs made the muscles in her lower body clench in unmistakable need.

Fighting down her reaction, she went to open the door, pulling her own robe protectively around her as she did so. Marcus had obviously walked across from his own suite, she recognised, and she realised that they actually shared the terrace, which ran the full length of both suites.

'Marcus, I was just about to go to bed,' she protested.

He ignored her, taking hold of her arm and commanding, 'Come and look at this,' as he drew her towards the stone parapet that edged the terrace.

'Look at what?' she demanded, and then stood still, a soft 'Oh!' of pleasure escaping from her lips as down below their hotel, at one of the villas, fireworks exploded in a burst of scarlet stars.

'Fireworks,' she whispered, entranced.

'I remembered how much you like them.' Marcus smiled.

'They're magical—like champagne in the sky,' Lucy responded softly. 'Someone must be celebrating something.'

As he wanted to celebrate her, Marcus thought. But in a far more private and intimate way. He would gladly create sexual fireworks for her if she would just allow him.

Another burst of stars followed the first one, this time a shower of sparkling silver and white against the night dark sky.

She looked as excited and enthralled as a small child, Marcus reflected, as she hung onto the stone balustrade and watched. But she wasn't a child.

Lucy could feel Marcus standing behind her, the warmth of his body taking the chill of the evening breeze from hers and making her want to lean back against him...skin to skin...whilst the fireworks lit the sky and her own desire exploded inside her. She looked down. Marcus was leaning forward to get a better view of the fireworks, his hands either side of her own, so that she was enclosed between his body and the parapet.

A burst of gold and crimson exploded into the darkness before falling back to earth...

'Oh, Marcus...' Without thinking, she turned round. He was so close to her. So very close.

'Marcus...' She looked up at his mouth and swallowed. Oh, God, but she wanted him.

'They've finished now. I'd better go in,' she told him jerkily, almost pushing him out of her way in her desperate need to get away from him before she did something even more stupid than she had done already.

She was in so much of a rush that she didn't realise he had followed her inside her suite and was closing the patio door until it was too late.

She couldn't even move when he began to walk towards her, her mouth suddenly too dry for her to speak and her legs too weak for her to move.

In complete silence he took hold of her hand and drew her with him toward the bath and then past it, until they were standing in front of the mirror. Just where she had been standing earlier, when he had...

The colour came and went in her face as he took her in his arms and started to kiss her, holding her face in his hands whilst he brushed her trembling lips over and over again with his own, until she had forgotten everything but her own need to have his mouth on her now, longer and harder. Her own hands rose to cover his shoulders, her fingers digging deep into the muscles as she shuddered fiercely beneath the sudden thrusting possession of his tongue. She felt his hands on her body, pushing the robe off her shoulders, and immediately she dropped her arms so that she could step out of it.

Very slowly Marcus turned her round and drew her back against himself, so that she was facing the mirror and he was standing behind her. His hands skimmed her body, stroking her skin, cupping her breasts, whilst her nipples pushed eagerly against his touch and his mouth teased the sensitive pleasure spot just behind her ear.

Her whole body arched as the breath left her lungs in a sob of erotic longing. Helplessly Lucy closed her eyes— half shocked by the sight of her own naked arousal and the erotic movement of Marcus's hands over her body, and half so aroused by it that she wanted him to take her there and then. To bend her forward until she could rest her hands against the mirror, whilst her hair tumbled round her face and Marcus spread open her thighs, sliding his hands up to her hips whilst he plunged into the female heart of her in a position that was so sensually, shockingly, eternally primitive and immediate.

She was wet, so very wet, and hot and aching, her muscles quivering in anticipation of the pleasure and satisfaction her body craved.

'Open your eyes, Lucy, and look in the mirror.'

Very slowly, she did so.

Marcus caressed her naked shoulders, his hands sliding down to cup her breasts whilst he kissed her throat. The sensation of the slightly rough pads of his fingertips against the exquisite sensitivity of her tight nipples made her cry out and arch her back, to bring her breasts closer to his caress while she pressed her buttocks back against him in eager, urgent movement.

'Is that good?'

His voice sounded thicker, deeper, sending a message to her own senses like a note running along a wire. He was plucking erotically at her nipples, his tanned skin a contrast to her own pale softness and the dark hot flush of her engorged flesh.

His hands moved lower down, over her ribcage, lower... Lucy sighed and squirmed, closing her eyes in anticipation of the pleasure to come.

'No...open your eyes and watch me,' Marcus insisted thickly.

He was stroking her sex. Lucy couldn't remove her aroused gaze from the movement of his hands. Her heart started to hammer against the wall of her chest as slowly and deliberately he folded back the soft flesh—just as she herself had done earlier. She looked into the mirror and saw in his eyes that he had seen her, had known what she was thinking. What she had been wanting. What she had been on the verge of doing....

'Isn't this better?' he demanded softly. 'Why pleasure yourself, Lucy, when I can do it for you?'

His mouth caressed the magic spot just below her ear and her whole body convulsed.

'Did you know that the nerve-endings in this spot here are directly connected to your nerve-endings right here?' she heard him whisper in her ear, as he kissed her skin again and stroked his fingers over the eager, dark pink wetness of her sex, rubbed his thumb-tip slowly over her clitoris.

Once. Twice. And then faster. Until she was breathing frantically fast and her whole body was shuddering in the grip of orgasm.

She couldn't move. She couldn't even stand. She felt boneless, weightless...and pleasured. Pleasured, but not satisfied, she knew, as Marcus swung her up into his arms and carried her over to the bed.

Only when he had placed her on it and removed his own robe, only when her reckless longing had directed her fingers to reach out and stroke the length of his erection and back again, and she had allowed herself to enjoy the delicious pleasure touching him had relayed via her fingertips to each and every one of her senses, did she think to say uncertainly, 'Marcus, I don't think we should be doing this...'

'Why ever not? You enjoyed it last night, didn't you?'

Enjoyed it? Of course she'd enjoyed it. But that wasn't the issue, or the point she was trying to make.

And yet she was murmuring dizzily, 'Oh, yes, I did.'

'And so did I. So there's no problem, is there?'

'No, I don't suppose there is,' Lucy agreed weakly.

How could there be any kind of problem when Marcus was touching her like this? Kissing her like this? 'Mmm,' she sighed happily against his mouth, and she reached up and wrapped her arms tightly around him.

CHAPTER SIX

LUCY looked at the pillow next to her own. It was still squashed from having Marcus's sleeping head lying on it. She reached out and tenderly traced the indentation, a smile of soft happiness curving her mouth. Last night had been so wonderful—and what had made it even more wonderful had been falling asleep cuddled up next to Marcus, free to snuggle in against him and breathe in the scent of him. She had woken up several times during the night, just for the pleasure of reassuring herself that he was still there.

But he wasn't always going to be 'still there', was he? She had no idea what had prompted Marcus to indulge in this brief and unexpected sexual adventure with her, but she knew already how much it was going to hurt when he grew tired of it—and of her. She didn't want Marcus for a brief fling. She wanted him for life. Despair swamped her earlier euphoria.

'Come on, sleepyhead, wake up. I've ordered breakfast, and it will be here any minute.'

Marcus! Lucy shot upright in the bed, and then blushed and reached for the protection of the duvet to cover her bare beasts, all too aware of the amused and quizzical look in Marcus's eyes. He sat down beside her, firmly removed her 'protection', and bent his head to kiss first one nipple and then the other. Then he murmured appreciatively, 'Maybe I should phone Room Service and tell them to delay breakfast.'

'Mmm,' Lucy agreed weakly, and then grabbed for the duvet again when there was a knock on the door.

'I'll get them to take our breakfast through my suite onto the terrace,' Marcus offered, leaving the bed to go and close the shutters for her. 'But don't you dare go back to sleep.'

Sleep! That was the last thing she felt like doing, Lucy thought as she headed for the shower.

'I was just about to come and make sure you hadn't gone back to sleep,' Marcus told her ten minutes later, when she opened the shutters and walked through the patio doors onto the terrace.

'I've ordered coffee for you,' he continued. 'And fruit juice, and poached eggs with tomatoes and mushrooms. There's some toast as well.'

'A cooked breakfast? Yuck.' Lucy shuddered as she sat down and immediately looked longingly at the coffee pot.

Marcus was already pouring coffee for her, and she breathed in its rich aroma whilst her tastebuds prepared themselves for their morning surge of caffeine. Marcus, she noticed, was drinking green tea.

'The body needs protein in the morning,' Marcus told her firmly, as he removed the cover from his own breakfast. 'It can't function properly without it.'

'Oh, thank you, Dr Atkins,' Lucy retorted sourly as she reached for her coffee. But the eggs did look appetising. She reached out and pinched a mushroom from Marcus's plate.

'Eat,' Marcus commanded, handing her her own breakfast. 'As soon as we've finished breakfast I'll go and ring Beatrice and check what time she's expecting to meet up with us,' he added, as she tucked into her eggs and realised just how hungry she actually was. 'But first there is something I want to discuss with you.'

Lucy had to put down her coffee cup because her hand

had started to tremble. Here it was—the demand for an explanation she had been dreading so much.

'If it's about last night...and...and the day before...' she began defensively.

'It is,' Marcus agreed. 'It seems to me, Lucy, that it would be a very good idea if you and I were to get married.'

Had she head him correctly? Was he trying to make some kind of joke? 'Married? You mean, as in to one another?' she asked him cautiously.

'Of course I mean as in to one another.'

'But—but, Marcus...why? I mean, why would you—we—want to do that? I mean, you don't even like me very much!' Lucy blurted out, too shocked not to be honest.

'I think that you and I would be very well suited to one another.'

Lucy reached for her coffee cup and took a deep gulp. He hadn't said that he did like her, she noticed. And he certainly hadn't said that he loved her.

'We share a similar background, and I suspect a very similar outlook on life. We both, I think, want children, and, despite the ending of your marriage to Nick, I believe that, like me, you think of commitment made to another person via marriage as one that is made for life—for better or for worse, in a relationship to which one is totally committed. Because make no mistake—if we do marry, I shall be committed completely and totally to our marriage, and to you and to our children, and I shall expect the same commitment from you.'

Total and complete commitment from Marcus to her? Was she dreaming?

'But—but...'

'But what?' Marcus demanded coolly. 'As the last two

days have proved, we are exceptionally sexually compatible.'

'But people don't get married just because they are having good sex together!' Lucy protested. 'You can't want to marry me because of that, Marcus.'

'There are other reasons,' he agreed.

'What other reasons?'

'I'll be thirty-five in December,' Marcus told her calmly. 'All the men in my family—my father, my grandfather, my great-grandfather and back beyond that—married before they were thirty-five. It's a family tradition, and one I have no intention of breaking.'

Did he mean that if she refused him he would find someone else who wouldn't?

She thought about how it would feel, being married to Marcus without being loved by him when she loved him so much. It would hurt—and very badly. Then she thought about how she would feel seeing Marcus married to someone else because he wanted to be married before his thirty-fifth birthday.

There just wasn't any comparison. She could not bear the thought of seeing Marcus married to someone else when she could have been married to him herself.

'And we have to be aware of the fact that, since you don't take the pill and I haven't been using any form of contraception, you might already have conceived my child,' Marcus reminded her. 'I know how much you love children, Lucy, but I don't think you'd want to be a single mother—and I certainly wouldn't allow you to bring up my child without me being a part of its life. It would be far more practical for us to get married.'

Practical! She didn't want practical. She wanted undying love, and promises that she would be showered with kisses day and night.

But Marcus didn't love her, Lucy reminded herself sternly. Just as Nick hadn't loved her—and look what had happened there.

She couldn't marry him. And she couldn't *not* marry him.

She hadn't loved Nick, had she? But she did love Marcus—and besides, Marcus was a completely different man from Nick. Marcus had stated unequivocally that their marriage would be a permanent commitment, and that meant it would be exactly that. And she wanted that. She wanted it so very badly. She wanted to wake up every morning in a bed she shared with him, she wanted to conceive his children, and she wanted to grow old with him.

Love could grow, couldn't it? And Marcus did want her. Unlike Nick, Marcus wanted to have sex with her. Unlike Nick, Marcus enjoyed having sex with her—he had said so.

'Marcus, *if* we were to...to become a couple, don't you think that people might think it rather odd and ask questions?'

'Why should they? And if they do I shall simply tell them that I had always planned to marry you, and that since Blayne beat me to it first time round I'm making sure I don't lose you to anyone else.'

Tears stung the backs of her eyes. If only that was the truth.

'So, are you willing to accept my proposal? I promise you that I think a marriage between us will work very well, Lucy, and I shall certainly do everything within my power to ensure that it does.'

'I don't know. I'm so confused...'

Marcus sounded more as though he were chairing a business meeting than proposing to her. But then to him no doubt their marriage *was* a kind of business arrangement, she thought sadly.

'Perhaps I should take you back to bed,' Marcus murmured softly. 'That might help make up your mind.'

Her insides melted, then somehow she was nodding her head, and Marcus was saying coolly, 'Good, so it's agreed, then. We won't say anything official until I've had a chance to speak to your father—and besides, I'd prefer us to wait until we return to London to choose your ring. There is a family betrothal ring—so astoundingly ugly, according to my mother, that she threatened not to marry my father unless he allowed her to choose something for herself—but personally, I think that for an engaged couple to opt for a ring of their own choosing invests it with something more personal and shared than the passing-down of a family ring—'

'I agree with you.' Lucy stopped him dizzily. Was this really happening? Was she really sitting here over breakfast with Marcus, talking about their marriage and her engagement ring, having just spent a wonderful night in bed with him?

'We're virtually in October now,' Marcus continued. 'My birthday is in early December, so I'd like to be married before the end of November if possible. Just a small affair—if that's all right with you?'

'Oh, yes. Of course. A simple register office ceremony...'

'No.' Marcus shook his head, silencing her. 'No, I'd prefer a church service, Lucy. After all, I think we're both agreed that we are making a lifetime commitment to one another—I certainly view our marriage as a permanent commitment. Since you and Blayne didn't marry in church, there is, in my opinion, no moral or legal reason why we should not do so. And even if the actual wedding

has to be in a register office I'd like a church blessing, if
possible. I imagine the Brompton Oratory would be the
best choice. You'll want to be married from your parents'
London home, and since that is in Knightsbridge...'

Lucy stared at him. The Oratory was *the* church of
choice for lots of society brides and their mothers, and very
grand.

Marcus was looking at his watch.

'It's nearly eleven now, and we're meeting Beatrice at
twelve-thirty in Palma to have lunch with her. So that only
leaves us half an hour to get ready—besides which, I'd
better give her a ring and remind her. She's got possibly
the worst memory of anyone I know.'

They both stood up, and then on some impulse she
didn't want to investigate too closely Lucy put her hand
on Marcus's arm and tugged at the sleeve of his robe, so
that he bent his head towards her. Raising herself up on
her tiptoes, she pressed her mouth to his and kissed him
softly.

She could feel the rigidity of his muscles, and her face
burned as she released him and stepped back from him.

Marcus watched her through narrowed eyes. It was one
thing for her to want him, but he wasn't sure how he felt
about the intensity with which he wanted her back. It
would suit his purposes very nicely for her to lose control
in his arms, but he certainly did not want his own self-
control to be breached—and he didn't like having to admit
that it could be—especially not by Lucy.

Even so, he couldn't afford to risk alienating her at this
stage by appearing to reject her.

Lucy exhaled in shock as Marcus reached for her and
drew her back into his arms.

How and when had Marcus's hands slipped inside her
robe to her naked skin? she wondered blissfully, when she

suddenly realised that the sensation of his mouth on hers wasn't the only sensual pleasure she was experiencing.

Instinctively she moved closer to him, and discovered to her delight that he was aroused and hard. She made a small sound of female pleasure and approval as she pressed even closer—and then reluctantly she remembered Beatrice.

'You said we should get ready to meet your sister,' she reminded him, the words semi-mumbled beneath the increasing passion of his kiss.

'To hell with Beatrice,' she heard him respond thickly, but he started to release her, giving her one last hard kiss as he did so, acknowledging, 'Yes, you're right. We'd better make a move.'

She was going to marry Marcus. She still couldn't take it in.

They had arrived in Palma five minutes earlier, having been driven there by the hotel's chauffeur service.

'I thought we'd be going to Beatrice's villa to discuss the party,' Lucy commented.

'Beatrice suggested we meet up for lunch instead,' Marcus answered. 'The restaurant's just down here.'

Lucy knew Palma quite well, and the restaurant in front of them was one that was patronised by wealthy locals and visitors alike. Knowing how elegantly and expensively Marcus's elder sister dressed, Lucy had decided to wear something a little bit more formal than she would normally have chosen—and now that she had seen where they were to have lunch she was glad of that fact. Her linen skirt with its row of pretty eyelet details just above the hem, teamed with a white strappy top worn under a crunchy cotton-linen asymmetrically styled cardigan-type jacket, had been a good choice; virtually every other woman in the restaurant seemed to be wearing a combination of very stylish linens and cottons, in that smart way that continental women seemed to be able to adopt so easily.

'Beatrice obviously hasn't arrived yet, but we may as well go straight to our table and wait for her there—unless you want a drink in the bar first?' Marcus suggested.

'No, let's go straight to the table,' Lucy told him. She didn't want him thinking that she couldn't get through half a day without an alcoholic drink, especially when it wasn't true. Coffee, now—well, that was different.

They had been waiting for about five minutes when the restaurant door opened and Marcus's sister came hurrying in. Tall and dark-haired, like Marcus, she was wearing black linen pants and an oatmeal-coloured cotton top, her hair drawn back off her face, her large Oliver's People sunglasses perched on top of her head.

'Marcus!' she exclaimed as she hurried over and kissed him. 'I am so sorry I'm late. And Lucy—how very kind of you to give up your time like this.'

'We haven't ordered anything yet, Bea. Would you like something to drink?' Marcus asked, as the waiter drew out her chair for her.

'Oh, yes—a spritzer, please. I'm driving. That's why I was late. I couldn't find anywhere to park. What's the weather like at home? When I spoke to Mother the other day she said it was raining. I'm going to have to stay out here until half term, and the wretched plumber says now that he can't get the tiles we ordered, which means that when Boffy and Izzy come out for their half term break we'll only have one bathroom.'

Lucy already knew that—contrary to her rather formidable appearance—Beatrice was something of a 'dizzy brunette', but it still bemused her to hear Beatrice expressing such sentiments when the only reason Lucy was here was so that they could talk about George's surprise birthday party without him knowing.

'I can definitely recommend the food here, Lucy,' Beatrice told her. 'Especially the fish. Although perhaps not the bouillabaisse—it is rather an acquired taste.'

The menus arrived, and while Marcus and Beatrice talked, or rather Beatrice talked and Marcus listened, Lucy studied hers.

'Have you had any thoughts about George's party, Beatrice?' Lucy asked, once the waiter had taken their orders.

'What? Oh, not really. George wants something small—just a few family and friends. He has this thing about castles, and he did wonder if we might hire one somewhere. What do you think?'

'Well, that's certainly possible,' Lucy agreed, mentally rolling her eyes.

Their food had arrived, and Lucy eyed her plate hungrily. It must be all the sex she was having that was giving her such a good appetite, she decided, and then went bright red as the thought of sex and appetite somehow led to thoughts of those two elements combined together, and all the ways that Marcus might satisfy her hunger for him.

'Goodness, Lucy, you look quite flushed. Are you all right? It is warm in here. I think we can talk more about George's party once I'm back in London. After all, I've got until next year, and right now these wretched workmen have got me in such a state I can't think about anything else.'

They had all finished eating, and Marcus turned to Lucy and asked calmly, 'What about pudding?'

'Not for me. But I would love an espresso.'

'An espresso? Lucy, my dear, is that wise? All that caffeine in your system will have you chattering non-stop for the rest of the day.'

Lucy had to bite the inside of her cheek to stop herself from giggling, and then she made the mistake of looking at Marcus. He looked every bit as amused as she felt, and when he gave her a small, rueful and very private smile Lucy felt as though she had been handed the keys to heaven. She and Marcus were sharing an intimate moment of understanding and humour, just as though they were really in a *proper* relationship.

Suddenly Lucy felt as though she could touch the sky and reach for anything—even one day, perhaps, Marcus's love.

'I can't wait to ring Mother and tell her that I've seen you both,' Beatrice announced twenty minutes later, after they had walked her back to her car. She then not only hugged Lucy but also kissed her affectionately as well, before saying meaningfully, 'Mother is going to be so pleased. She's always had a soft spot for Lucy...'

'Marcus, I think Beatrice has guessed about us,' Lucy warned him after they had waved goodbye to her.

'I should hope so, after all the hints I dropped,' Marcus agreed dryly.

'What? You said we weren't going to tell anyone yet!'

'I haven't told her. I've just dropped a few hints. Knowing Beatrice the way I do, it won't be very long before she's convinced herself that she guessed about us ages ago—and that should help to ease away any uncomfortable questions about the speed with which things have happened.'

It would also place another barrier in the way of Lucy changing her mind and backing out of marrying him, Marcus reflected cynically.

'We've got another hour before the hotel chauffeur is due to pick us up. How about a walk?'

'Lovely,' Lucy told him, and meant it.

What she hadn't been prepared for was that Marcus would choose to walk in the direction of a very expensive-looking jewellers and then draw her towards its windows. 'See anything you like?' he asked.

'I thought you said we wouldn't get a ring until we get home?'

'Yes, of course—for one thing I thought you might want to choose a stone and then a setting—but I wasn't thinking of a ring right now, Lucy. You've just agreed to be my wife, and, whilst your engagement ring will be a public acknowledgement of that fact, I would like to celebrate it with something rather more personal—a pair of earrings, perhaps? Something like those?' he added, indicating the very pair of diamond studs Lucy hadn't been able to stop gazing at.

'Marcus, you don't have to buy me anything,' she protested.

'That's right. I don't have to,' he agreed blandly as he rang the bell for admittance to the shop. 'But I do want to.'

They were inside the shop—all thick carpets, glass display cases, the quiet and very serious hum of air-conditioning and wealth, and immaculately groomed young male and female sales assistants.

As soon as Marcus told one of them what he wanted, they were taken to a small private room and offered comfortable seats.

'Perhaps you would care for a drink—water, coffee?' the sales assistant offered.

'Oh, coffee please.' Lucy thanked him, ignoring the way Marcus lifted his eyebrow. 'Okay, so you don't do caffeine,' she hissed, as soon as they were alone. 'But I do.'

'Caffeine and champagne,' Marcus agreed dryly.

The salesman was returning, carrying Lucy's coffee and accompanied by an older, obviously more senior member of the shop's staff. It was too late for Lucy to defend herself on the champagne charge.

'You have an excellent eye if I may say so, *señora*,' the senior salesman told Lucy approvingly as he spread the roll of fabric he was carrying on top of the immaculate glass and then placed the earrings on it.

'These stones are excellent quality, and without any blemish. They are D quality, which means they have exceptional clarity and purity. They are one and a half carats each, and set in platinum.'

And they would cost a fortune, Lucy recognised, as she mentally said goodbye to them.

'They are lovely,' she began 'But—'

'Why don't you try them on?' Marcus overrode her.

Reluctantly, Lucy did so, and then looked at her reflection in the mirror the salesman gave her. The stones burned with blue-white fire and were, as he had said, of exceptional purity.

'Please excuse me a moment,' the salesman murmured, getting up and leaving the room.

'Marcus, you mustn't buy me these,' Lucy told him as soon as they were alone.

'Why not? Don't you like them? Personally, I think they suit you very well.'

Not like them? Was he kidding? No woman could possibly not like diamonds such as these.

'Of course I like them. But that isn't the point.'

'No? Then what is?' he challenged her.

'The cost, of course. Marcus, these are going to be dreadfully expensive.' She looked so worried, with her forehead creased in that small frown and her eyes shadowed with anxiety, that it actually made him frown himself. She was the first woman he had ever bought jewellery for who had begged him not to do so because of its cost.

The salesman had returned, carrying a small square box.

'We'll take the earrings. My fiancée loves them,' Marcus announced coolly.

The salesman beamed. 'Ah, *señor*, you will not regret their purchase, I do assure you. They will more than keep their value. And it occurs to me that you might like to see this bangle, which has the same quality of stones, but of only one carat each. The bangle itself is made of platinum and white gold. The design is modern but delicate,' he enthused, removing the bangle from its box so that they could see it.

Once again Lucy found that she was holding her breath. The bangle was beautiful, simple and elegant, its simple curving lines set with three diamonds all offset from one another.

'Try it on,' Marcus urged her.

Lucy shook her head. 'No,' she told him firmly, standing up with a determination that rather astonished her. 'It is beautiful,' she agreed, turning to the salesman. 'But I don't wear very much jewellery, other than my watch. The earrings are more than enough.'

Lucy waited discreetly in the main part of the shop whilst Marcus paid for her earrings, then automatically fell into step beside him as they walked back outside into the late-afternoon sunshine. She longed to move closer to him, to slip her arm through his, or even better for him to take her hand in his. But of course he did no such thing. A small, unexpectedly sharp pang of pain seized her.

'Thank you for my earrings, Marcus,' she told him quietly, fighting back her longing to turn towards him and kiss him. 'They are beautiful, but really you shouldn't have.'

She watched as he gave a dismissive, almost uncaring shrug. 'Of course I should. Is there anything else you'd like to look at? Only our car should be here in another few minutes.'

Lucy shook her head. If she was honest, what she wanted to do right now, more than anything else, was to go back to their hotel so that she could be on her own with Marcus.

The ache that had begun earlier in her bedroom, when he had kissed her, had gradually but very determinedly been increasing in intensity all the time she had been with him, and it was now an urgent pulsing female need that was overriding any other desire she might have had. She wanted Marcus and she wanted him desperately, eagerly, completely and utterly. And, what was more, that wanting had nothing whatsoever to do with the diamonds or anything else he might buy her.

'How do you feel about having dinner here on the terrace this evening? We can go out, if you like, or dine in the hotel restaurant. But I thought in view of the fact that we shall be returning to London tomorrow morning, in our new role as an engaged couple, this evening might be a good opportunity to discuss any concerns you might have about the future.'

'Dinner on the terrace sounds wonderful,' Lucy told Marcus truthfully. They were in her suite, having just returned from Palma.

'We're going to have to talk about Prêt a Party, and how you visualise its future at some stage,' Marcus continued.

Prêt a Party! Lucy realised with shock that she had barely given her business a thought since she had Marcus had stepped onto their flight to Palma.

'Oh, you don't—' She began immediately to reassure Marcus that he did not need to worry that she would be expecting him to rescue her ailing business from debt, and then stopped. Andrew Walker had said that he didn't want her to mention their discussion to anyone at this stage, and until he actually came back to her with a firm offer there wasn't really anything to discuss, was there? If she told Marcus now that her problems with her business were over, that Prêt a Party had a potential investor, and then had to tell him that she had been let down, she was going to look very silly and gullible. Just as she had done when Nick had cheated her. She could still remember how angry and contemptuous Marcus had been then. She didn't want that to happen a second time.

'Must we talk about Prêt a Party tonight?' Lucy asked him. 'Only...'

'Only what?' Marcus probed.

'Only I thought that tonight could be for...us,' Lucy whispered, pink-cheeked. She could feel her blush deepening as she saw the way he was looking at her.

'For us? Well, it certainly might be a good idea if we discuss some of the practical issues we need to sort out.'

Disappointment filled her. That was not what she had meant at all.

'Practical issues?' Did he mean things like contraception? Lucy wondered uncertainly. If so, she would have to find the words to tell him that she relished the experience of feeling him inside her without anything between them so much that she would prefer it if she made herself responsible for that side of things and took the contraceptive pill.

'Yes. Practical issues,' Marcus repeated. 'Such as where we are going to live. I'd prefer to keep my Wendover

Square house as our London home. After all, it's been in my family for nearly two hundred years.'

'It is a lovely house,' Lucy agreed, 'especially with the garden. But I'll want to redecorate it. And I'll definitely want an espresso-maker in the kitchen,' she added teasingly.

'The decorating I do not have a problem with,' Marcus returned dryly. 'The espresso machine might require some in-depth discussion and a compromise. Perhaps even some compensation. But I like the idea of us looking for a house in the country,' he continued.

'Mmm, I'd like that too. Though I'll want to continue to work, Marcus.'

'Of course. So shall I,' he agreed drolly, before looking at his watch and telling her, 'But remember, since we have been having sex without contraception, you could already be pregnant. Running a business and caring for a new baby wouldn't be easy. Look, it's six o'clock now and I need a shower. Why don't I go to my own suite, order dinner for eight, have a shower, get changed, make a couple of phone calls and then meet you outside on the terrace at, say, seven-thirty?'

'Perfect,' Lucy told him, although she was disappointed when he walked over to the communicating door, opened it and walked through it without kissing her before he left.

She would have a shower herself, she decided. Then a small smile curled her mouth as she glanced towards the bath. The thought of enjoying a long lazy soak was very tempting, especially with her memories of the erotic pleasure it had led to later.

She hadn't brought any 'occasion'-type clothes with her, which was another reason to prefer having dinner on their own terrace.

She reached for the telephone and pressed the numbers

for Room Service, so that she could order some coffee, then closed the shutters and pulled out the folding door that enabled her to close off the shower and bathroom area from the rest of the bedroom. Being surprised in the bath by Marcus was one thing; having one of the waiters walk in whilst she was in the shower was something else again—and something that she most definitely did not want to happen.

It didn't take her long to shower. She loved the luxury of thick, fluffy and constantly replenished hotel towels and bathrobes, she reflected, as she dried herself and then smoothed her body with delicious-smelling lotion before pulling on her robe and folding back the sliding doors.

Her coffee had arrived, and she went over to the occasional table to pour it, pausing with a small frown when she saw the dark green, gold-embossed gift-wrapped box lying on the table next to the coffee tray, beside the complimentary hand-made chocolates provided by the hotel. She recognised the name embossed on the ribbon immediately. It was the name of the jewellers they had been in that afternoon.

This hadn't been provided by the hotel, Lucy reflected, as she picked up the box and started to unwrap it. And it was too large to contain her earrings. Her suspicions turned to certainty when she removed the wrapping paper and opened it to find inside the bangle they had been shown in the shop.

Marcus had bought it for her? As well as the earrings? He really was spoiling her. Materially, yes, he was spoiling her. But she would much rather have been spoiled by his love.

In the end they decided that they might as well stay in their robes for dinner. There was no one to see them, after all, and besides, it added a special intimacy to their eve-

ning. Lucy looked down at the bangle she was now wearing. The full moon was bathing the terrace in its cool sharp
light. Lucy picked up one of her prawns and dipped it in
mayonnaise, licking her fingers after she had finished eating it, and then smiling.

'What's the smile for?' Marcus asked.

'I was just thinking about that scene in Henry Fielding's
Tom Jones—you know, the sex and food one...'

'Oh, yes? Is that a hint?'

Lucy shook her head. 'Certainly not,' she retorted self-
consciously, but when he stood up and started to walk very
purposefully towards her, her heart did a backflip in giddy
excitement and anticipation.

But when he stopped in front of her it wasn't to take
her in his arms, as she had been hoping. Instead he produced the small box that contained her earrings.

'I should have given you these.'

He sounded so abrupt and cold that Lucy frowned. He
might have said that he wanted to marry her, but he certainly wasn't behaving as though he did.

'You shouldn't have got me this as well,' she told him,
touching her bangle. 'The earrings are more than enough.'
As she spoke she reached for the box, but to her surprise
Marcus shook his head and reached for her hand, pulling
her firmly to her feet.

She had to hold her breath as he carefully inserted the
earrings into her earlobes. Not because she was afraid he
might be too rough, but because she was afraid that she
might betray to him just how she felt about him. The sensation of his warm breath on her bare skin was so sensuously erotic that it made her whole body melt with longing
for him. She knew that she was trembling inside with the
intensity of her feelings, and that very soon she would be
trembling outwardly as well.

The earrings were in place, and, had he loved her, this surely should have been the moment when Marcus bent his head and kissed her—a truly special and intimate moment they would both remember for ever—but instead he was moving away from her.

And then, so suddenly, so shockingly that her whole body thrilled erotically, he came back to her, pushing the robe off her shoulders with hard knowing hands that kept her arms straight so that it could fall away completely, while he kissed her so fiercely that she could feel the heavy, erratic thud of his heartbeat as though it were throbbing inside her own chest.

The only sound to break the silence was the acceleration of their combined breathing, and then, as abruptly as he had taken hold of her, Marcus released her mouth and began to caress her eagerly responsive flesh.

Moonlight celebrated the beauty of her naked body. The terrace was private enough for Lucy to know that they could not be overlooked, and there was something gloriously erotic and exciting about standing naked in the moonlight as Marcus caressed her skin with delicate fingertips, brushing his lips against her throat.

'You're wet,' Marcus murmured thickly as his fingers dipped into her sex.

'You made me like that,' Lucy answered him shakily. After all, it was true.

Marcus looked at the night-dark peaks of her nipples and then bent his head to suckle erotically on one of them, whilst his fingers stroked deeper and more firmly. Still caressing her, he arched Lucy back against his arm so that her whole body was offered up to him.

He could feel her moving urgently against him as her desire quickened.

'Marcus,' Lucy moaned, 'I think I'm going to come...'

'Good,' he told her thickly, as he lifted his mouth from
her breast to her lips. 'I want you to.'

'I want you inside me,' Lucy begged.

'Later. Don't talk now,' he told her. 'Just enjoy.'

Don't talk. Lucy closed her eyes and gasped as her body
tightened and pleasure began to shudder through her.

CHAPTER SEVEN

'MARCUS, are you sure we're doing the right thing?'

They had just returned from visiting her parents, who were overjoyed about the fact that they were to marry, and yet despite the delight with which everyone had greeted the news of their engagement, since they had returned to London Lucy had begun to be gripped by an increasingly intense feeling of sadness and foreboding.

Her vision was clouded with emotional tears as the October sunshine shone in through the windows of the pretty breakfast room overlooking Marcus's garden and bounced off the facets of her engagement ring. She had fallen in love with the simple rectangular diamond with its emerald cut facets the moment she had seen it, and when Marcus had picked it up and said quietly, 'I rather like this one, but of course it must be your choice,' she had been so thrilled she had almost cried with happiness. She had been happy—then!

In Majorca, swept away on a tide of sex and fantasy, she had felt as though anything was possible—even Marcus coming to love her—but now, back in London, certain realities were refusing to go away.

'What exactly do you mean?' Marcus demanded. He was frowning at her with that familiar blend of impatience and irritation that always cramped her stomach and squeezed her heart with pain. 'I should have thought from the response we've had from our families to the news of our impending marriage that it is obvious that we are very much doing the right thing.' He stood up and strode to the window, and Lucy gripped her mug of coffee with tense fingers. It was clear that he didn't want to continue the discussion, but she needed to. She needed... She needed his love, she admitted helplessly. And in the absence of that she needed some kind of acknowledgement of her own fears, and his reassurance that there was nothing for her to fear. She needed hope, and the belief that he could grow to love her. But she couldn't tell him any of those things, she admitted painfully, because she knew that he wouldn't understand her needs and that he would be irritated by them.

'Our families assume that...that we care about one another,' she told him carefully instead. 'They don't know the truth. And I don't know if a...a relationship—a marriage—without love can survive.'

'Love?' Marcus shook his head, his expression darkening. 'Why is everyone so obsessed by this delusion that what they call love is something of any value? It isn't,' he told her harshly. 'You should know that. After all, you married Blayne because you *loved* him, and look where that got you.

'You and I have the kind of practical reasons for marrying one another that are far more important than love. I need and want a wife who understands my way of life and who shares my desire for children—I certainly do not want to be the first Carring not to produce an heir or heiress. Sexually, as we have both already shown, we are compatible. You want children, and you are not the kind of woman who would want them outside a committed relationship. You married once for so-called love, Lucy. I should have thought you were intelligent enough to recognise that that was a mistake, and not want to repeat it.'

'But what if one day you fall in love with someone else, Marcus?'

'Fall in love?' He looked at her as though she had suggested he murder his own mother. 'Haven't you listened to anything I've been saying? So far as I am concerned sexual love is merely a cloak to cover juvenile and self-ish—self-obsessed!—emotional folly, allied to lust. My father fell in love, or so he claimed, when he left my mother. He abandoned her and us because of that *love*, and if it hadn't been for the accident that killed him he would have destroyed the bank as well as my mother's happiness. I saw then what *love* was, and I swore that I would never ever allow myself to indulge in such a thing.'

But you were six years old! Lucy wanted to protest. But wisely she refrained from doing so. She had had no idea that Marcus held such strong and bitter views about love, or that he was so antagonistic toward it.

Her coffee had gone cold, but she still kept her hands wrapped around her mug, as though she was trying to seek warmth and comfort from it.

'What is it?' he demanded when he looked at her and saw the despair in her eyes.

She shook her head. 'I...I'm not sure we should get married, Marcus.'

'It's too late for second thoughts now,' he told her sharply. 'For one thing your mother is busily planning the wedding, and for another...' He paused and then reminded her, 'Let's not forget that you could already be carrying my child. We are getting married, Lucy,' he reinforced calmly. 'And nothing is going to change that.'

Just as nothing was going to change the way he felt about love, or his antagonism towards it, Lucy recognised with despair. How could she have deceived herself into believing that he would grow to love her? Marcus would never love her. Marcus didn't want to love her. He didn't want to love anyone.

'I want to talk to you about Prêt a Party,' he continued briskly.

Lucy tensed. She didn't want to talk to Marcus about her business. She had had a letter from Andrew Walker, reiterating that he didn't want her to discuss their meeting with anyone and explaining that he was still out of the country on business and would be in touch with her on his return. Of course there should be no secrets between husband and wife, but she had given her word and she had no intention of breaking it—and besides...Nick's betrayal of her trust had left a painful scar. She knew that Marcus would never cheat her financially, but her growing insecurity about the future of their marriage made her want to hold on tightly to the security of Prêt a Party. If at some future date Marcus chose to decide that their marriage wasn't working with the clockwork efficiency that he had decided that it should, she might need her business—not just to support herself financially, but to validate her as a person.

'I've decided that the simplest way to deal with the current situation would be for me to inject enough capital into the business to clear its debts,' he said.

'No! No—I don't want you to do that.'

Lucy could see that her outburst had surprised him.

'Why not? Less than two months ago you begged me to let you utilise what was left of your trust fund to put into the company.'

'That was different,' she told him stubbornly. 'That was my money, not yours. And besides...' She bit her lip. She couldn't tell him about Andrew Walker—not yet—and even if she did she suspected that he would not understand why she felt able to accept both financial assistance and financial involvement from someone else, but not from him. Having one husband involved in her business and virtually destroying it, and her, had taught her a harsh lesson. It wasn't one she wanted to repeat.

Marcus frowned as he looked at her. It was obvious to him that Lucy was having second thoughts about their marriage. Was it because, despite all that he had done to her, she still loved Nick Blayne? And why was she rejecting his offer to pay off Prêt a Party's debts?

'Lucy...'

She stopped him fiercely. 'Prêt a Party is my responsibility, Marcus, and I want to keep it that way.'

Her responsibility and her salvation, perhaps, should he ever decide to end their marriage.

A feeling of intense inner aloneness filled her. Sometimes it seemed as though her whole emotional life involved keeping painful secrets she could not share with anyone else. She badly wanted to cry, but of course she must not do so. Her two best friends had been so lucky, finding men who were their soul mates and true partners— men with whom they could share every part of their lives and themselves, from their most mundane thoughts to those that were most sacred and private to them. But not her. She never had and now would never be able to share her innermost longings and feelings with anyone.

She gave a small shiver. Marriage to Marcus would mean closing the door on the deepest of her feelings and shutting them away for ever. But she knew she simply wasn't strong enough to let him walk away from her and find someone else. The pain would simply be too much for her to bear. And, as Marcus himself kept reminding her, it could already be too late for her to back out of their coming marriage. She might already have conceived.

Lucy looked at her watch. Marcus would be in Edinburgh by now. He had said that he would only be away for a couple of days, but already she was missing him.

Tonight was the launch of the new football boot—the last of Prêt a Party's major events. She was pleased with the response she had received to the invitations she had sent out, and even Dorland was going to be there. Although corporate events, no matter how lavish, were not really his style.

Her mobile rang, jerking her out of her thoughts, and her heart leapt when she saw that it was Marcus who was calling.

Although she wasn't officially living with him yet, she was spending more nights in Marcus's bed than she was her own.

'Has your mother sent out the wedding invitations yet?' he asked.

'They went out yesterday,' Lucy told him. Her mother had spent several afternoons cloistered in the Holy Grail of stationery requisites that was the basement of Smythson's Sloane Street premises, poring over samples of wedding stationery. 'Although she's telephoned people as well, in view of the lack of time. You do realise just how many guests are going to be at our wedding, don't you, Marcus?' she cautioned him.

'Two hundred and rising at the last count—and that isn't including my second cousins four times removed from Nova Scotia—at least according to my mother and Beatrice,' he relied promptly.

'What? No, Marcus.' Lucy panicked. 'It's more like—'

'Two hundred *each*. That is to say, *my* mother is planning on inviting two hundred guests, whilst I understand *your* mother can't get her list down under two hundred and fifty.'

'Oh, Marcus,' Lucy wailed. 'We said we wanted a quiet wedding.'

'Talk to your mother—apparently that *is* a quiet wedding,' Marcus told her dryly.

Lucy sighed. 'Thank goodness it isn't summer. Ma said the other night that if it had been she thought it would have been a good idea to tent over the gardens in your square.'

'Yes, I've seen it done.'

'So have I, and I know exactly what hard work it is. Anyway, I thought we both agreed that we just want a simple wedding breakfast, somewhere like the Lanesborough—not five hundred people and a ballroom at the Ritz.'

'Well, maybe *we* do, but we aren't our mothers. Stop worrying about it,' Marcus advised her, 'and let them get on with it and enjoy themselves. I don't want you too worn out to enjoy our honeymoon.'

Lucy could feel her face stating to burn.

'If I am, that won't be because of the wedding preparations,' she told him valiantly.

'Shagged out already?' Marcus asked her directly.

'Totally,' Lucy agreed lightly. There was no point in wishing he had spoken more lovingly. 'When will you be back?'

'Oh, not so shagged out that you don't want more?'

'I was asking because of the christening,' Lucy told him in a dignified voice.

'Uh-huh? Well, don't worry, I haven't forgotten that we're driving down to the christening on Thursday.'

Julia and Silas were having their three-month-old son christened at the weekend, and Lucy had been asked to be one of his godmothers along with Carly, the third member of their trio.

Although Silas was based in New York, he and Julia

spent as much time as they could in England, mainly because of Julia's elderly grandfather, and the christening was being held in a small village close to his stately home.

'I'd better go; take care of yourself,' Marcus told her calmly, before ending the call.

No *I love you*; no *do you love me*... But then, how could there be? Marcus didn't love her.

'I'm going now, Mrs Crabtree,' Lucy called out to the housekeeper, forcing back the threatening tears clogging her throat.

Marcus's housekeeper had made it plain that she welcomed the idea of Marcus being married, and she and Lucy had spent several very happy afternoons discussing how best to renovate the slightly old-fashioned kitchen.

'There's a parcel just arrived for you, Lucy,' she called back.

'Oh?' Lucy hurried into the kitchen and stared at the large box sitting on the table.

There was a note attached to it, in Marcus's handwriting.

Hope that this will make our mornings together worth waking up to.

Slightly pink-cheeked, Lucy started to open it. Marcus had already ensured that she thought he was worth waking up to, and it was difficult to imagine how he could make their mornings any more of a sexual pleasure than they already were.

But she realised that had been wrong as she opened the box to reveal not some *outré* sexual toy, but an espresso coffee machine.

'Oh, Marcus!' she whispered, suddenly overwhelmed by the emotions she had been trying to suppress.

'He said as how you were missing your espresso in the morning,' Mrs Crabtree told Lucy with a wide smile.

She desperately wanted to ring him and thank him, but she contented herself instead with simply texting him—in case he was already with his client.

Lucy exhaled slowly in relief. It looked very much as though the evening was going to be the success her corporate clients had hoped for. Having half a dozen Premier League football stars here had certainly been a good draw, and the models and It Girls clustered around them were making heavy inroads into the orange and red striped cocktail invented to match the orange and red flash on the new football boots being promoted.

If so far as the female guests were concerned the footballers were the main attraction, then her clients were equally delighted by the number of media people attending, and had told her so.

The cheerleaders had done their bit and been wildly applauded, and even her tongue-in-cheek curry and chips mini-suppers had been greeted with enthusiasm—especially by the footballers.

'Lucy!'

'Dorland.' Lucy smiled affectionately as the magazine owner and editor took hold of her arm and guided her to one of the tables.

'You're a very naughty girl not telling me about you and Marcus,' he told her, wagging his finger in front of her. 'I had to read about your engagement in *The Times*.'

Lucy gave what she hoped was a convincing laugh. 'Blame Marcus for that, Dorland, not me. But you are coming to the wedding, aren't you?'

His expression softened. 'Of course.'

Lucy had insisted that Dorland was to be invited as a guest, even though her mother had not totally approved.

'Lovely stiffie by the way, sweetie. Very grand. It has pride of place on my mantelpiece.'

Lucy giggled. These days, 'stiffie' didn't mean 'upmarket invitation' to her.

'Lucy, there's something I want to talk to you about,' Dorland added, suddenly looking unfamiliarly serious. 'Come here and sit down for a minute.'

'What's wrong?' Lucy asked him, as soon as they were tucked away in a corner.

'One of my snappers mentioned that he'd seen you having lunch at the Pont Street Brasserie the other week with Andrew Walker.'

Lucy could feel herself starting to colour up guiltily. What bad luck. She had seen the paparazzi outside the Brasserie, and she should have guessed she would be spotted. Dorland had eyes and ears everywhere.

'He knows my cousin,' she answered as casually as she could, but Dorland was shaking his head.

'He's a really bad guy, Lucy. Don't get involved with him.'

The shock of Dorland looking so serious and saying something so appalling made her stare at him uneasily. 'What do you mean?'

'How much do you know about him?' Dorland asked her.

'He's a very successful entrepreneur who has built up a turnkey business based in London supplying concierge services for wealthy people who don't have time to sort out their own domestic support services.'

'That's the legitimate tip of the iceberg of his business,' Dorland told her flatly. 'The truth is that he works for a group of Eastern European mafia-type thugs, fronting a

money-laundering exercise. The workers he uses in his
turnkey business are mostly illegals, brought into this
country to work in fear for their lives. The poor sods have
to pay thousands to get into this country in the first place,
and then when they get here they're told that they can be
sent back at any minute if the authorities find out about
them. So they're forced to work for next to nothing and
housed like battery chickens.

'And that isn't the worst of it. Young women—*girls*—
sometimes sold by their families, sometimes just stolen,
are sold into prostitution and passed from owner to owner.
What he's involved in is the cruellest business in the
world. He traffics in human misery and degradation. And,
by the way, Andrew Walker isn't even his real name.'

'How can you know all this?' Lucy protested.

'I know because last year he approached me with an
offer to buy his way into *A-List Life*. He said that he was
looking for somewhere to invest the profits from his turnkey business. He talked about taking *A-List Life* into
Europe and even Russia. I admit for while I was tempted,
and not just because of the money he was talking about—
which was phenomenal. But once I started looking a little
deeper and asking questions all sorts of stuff started crawl-
ing out of the woodwork.

'The reason he wanted to buy into *A-List Life* was because he's looking for ways and means to launder the
money he's making from trading in refugees and prostitutes. He told me about an idea he'd had for us to employ
our own *A-List Life* girls as "hostesses" at celeb events.
The way he described it, it sounded perfectly above board
and respectable.' Dorland shook his head. 'It wasn't. What
he meant, of course, was that he wanted to use *A-List Life*
to supply upmarket prostitutes.'

With every word Dorland spoke, Lucy's heart was hammering harder.

'I'm not going to pry into your personal business affairs, Lucy, but I know how these people work—they offer of a terrific business deal made in secret and kept that way. If that's why you were having lunch with him, then take my advice and don't get involved.'

'But if he's as bad as you say, why haven't the authorities done anything about it?' Lucy asked Dorland unhappily.

'Probably because he's too clever for them to prove anything. The only reason *I* know is because I asked around—and I asked the right people. London has its share of Russian oligarchs, some of whom I happen to know, and they know people who know other people, et cetera. They aren't involved in any way with him, or what he does, but they have contacts who have contacts, and they know the people he does business with. And I was told—don't get involved. He and those he works for play very dirty. Have you told Marcus about lunching with him?'

Lucy shook her head.

'No. And I...I couldn't. Not now.'

'No. He definitely wouldn't like it,' Dorland agreed.

'We only had a meeting, that was all,' Lucy stressed. 'Nothing more.'

'Well, if I were you, Lucy, I'd make sure that there aren't any more meetings. And I'd also make sure that Walker knows you aren't interested in any proposals he may put to you, either now or at any time in the future. It's none of my business, I know that, but I've always had a bit of soft spot for Prêt a Party and for you. You've got class, Lucy, and I like that. I admire what you did with Prêt a Party, even if things haven't worked out. But it's just the kind of outfit he's looking for, and once he drags you down into the dirt with him I'm afraid you'll have the devil's own job getting out of it again. These people know how to keep their victims trapped and dependent on them, and like as not they'll drag Marcus down with you.'

Lucy looked at the letter she had just finished checking. It was to Andrew Walker, telling him that since she was shortly to get married she had decided against going ahead with the business venture they had discussed. Her husband was going to become her new business partner, she had added, untruthfully.

She signed it, then folded it carefully and put it in the envelope she had already addressed.

Just to make sure that Andrew Walker did receive it she was going to the post office with it right now, so that she could send it for guaranteed delivery.

She gave a small shudder as she sealed the envelope. Thank heavens Dorland had alerted her to the real nature of Andrew Walker's business. She just wished that the authorities could do something to prevent him from continuing with his evil trade. But when she had said as much to Dorland, Dorland had shaken his head and told her grimly, 'Removing him wouldn't solve the problem. There will be a hundred or more other men all too willing to take his place. Illegal workers are big business, and men like Walker get a double pay-off—firstly when the poor devils pay for what they believe is going to be their freedom in another country, and secondly when they have to pay over most of their wages to buy the silence of the very people responsible for them being there. They can't win, and men like Walker can't lose. And that's why it's so hard for the authorities to do anything. Their victims are too afraid to say anything.'

And Prêt a Party would have been an ideal money-laundering vehicle for them, Lucy recognised. All the more so because it was so labour-intensive, and in a way that used casual labour.

Thank goodness she hadn't told Marcus about it. He would probably have been too worldly aware to fall into the trap she had, and she could just imagine what he would have had to say about the situation if he'd known how easily she had fallen for Andrew Walker's smooth words. No doubt he would have also immediately reminded her that she had already proved her naïveté once, by marrying Nick and letting him defraud her, and that there was no need for her to compound her folly.

Marcus. He would be back later this afternoon, and then tomorrow they were driving down to the country for the christening.

Marcus. Didn't she already have enough to worry about without this added problem of Andrew Walker and the trap he had set for her?

'You're very quiet.'

'Am I?' Lucy gave Marcus a too-bright smile, glad of the glaring sunlight that meant she could hide behind her sunglasses as Marcus drove them towards the motorway, *en route* to the christening. They were going down a couple of days early so that Lucy, Carly and Julia could have some time together before the other guests arrived, and Lucy was really looking forward to seeing her two oldest friends.

Marcus had booked them into a small manorhouse hotel, teasing her that they could 'practise for their honeymoon,' which they were actually taking in the Caribbean.

She had missed him desperately while he had been away, but last night when he had returned she had felt so on edge about the Andrew Walker business, and so guilty, that she had just not been able to relax with him.

Not even in bed.

'How did the football boot do go?'

'Oh, fine.' Lucy could feel her face burning, simply because of the association between that event, Dorland's revelations and her own guilt.

Marcus frowned as he listened to her. Something had changed while he had been away. Lucy had changed, he thought grimly. Why? Because she was still having second thoughts about their marriage? His mouth hardened. He had no intentions of giving her up. Not to anyone. And if her doubts were being caused by a longing for Nick Blayne, he was most certainly not giving her up. Couldn't she see how much better off she would be with him?

'I've spoken to McVicar and told him that I intend to make a cash injection into Prêt a Party's bank account sufficient to clear any outstanding debts, and the bank overdraft, plus allow for a small amount of working capital.'

'No!'

Lucy realised that her instinctive objection had been louder than she had anticipated, but she pressed on doggedly. 'I've already told you that I don't want you to do that. I have enough left in my own trust fund to do almost all of it, Marcus.'

Marcus's mouth thinned, whilst Lucy's face burned from her anguished dread of Marcus reminding her of what a fool she had been over Nick. But how could she tell anyone, and most especially Marcus, that she had felt so guilty about marrying Nick when she didn't love him that she had felt unable to question anything he did?

'I realise that you are so rich it doesn't matter if you have to pay off my debts for me, Marcus, but I don't want

you to do that. I'd rather pay them off myself. I don't want
to feel financially indebted to you over my business.'

'Very well, then. If you feel like that, why don't I join
you in Prêt a Party as a partner? We could be—'

Sleeping partners, he had been about to say. But before
he could do so Lucy burst out sharply, 'No! No. I don't
want that.'

Why? Marcus wanted to ask her. But he could see how
upset and angry she was getting, and he was afraid... He
was afraid, Marcus acknowledged, on a sudden unfamiliar
surge of shock that gripped his belly in sharp talons and
caused a pain he had never previously experienced.

He was afraid of losing her, he recognised. Did she still
love Blayne, despite the appalling way in which her ex-
husband had treated her? Blayne had left her for another
woman, but was Lucy hoping that one day he might come
back? Did she think that by hanging on to Prêt a Party she
might one day entice him to return?

What was happening? She had seemed happy to be with
him, happy about their future—and certainly happy with
him in bed. *Had seemed*... But last night she had stood
stiffly in his arms until he had let her go, and now, today,
she was behaving though he was the last person she
wanted to be with.

On a coruscating surge of pain, he recognised that
Lucy's refusal to allow him to help was actually *hurting*
him. How could that be? Why could it be?

Lucy pressed her fingers to her aching temples. She
wished desperately that their relationship were different,
that she could confide in Marcus and tell him all about
Andrew Walker and his approach to her. But she couldn't.

'We're leaving the motorway at the next junction,' she
heard Marcus telling her after a while, adding, 'The hotel
is only a few miles further on. I thought we'd go there

first, and leave our things. What time did you say Julia
and Silas are expecting us?'

'Any time after two, Jules said. So there's no immediate
rush.' Would he recognise that she was trying to hint to
him that she would welcome some time alone with him
before they went to see Jules and Silas and the new baby?
It could be an opportunity for her to make some small
amends for last night, to show both him and herself that
her inability to respond to him then wasn't some kind of
ominous portent. Lucy hoped so. For his sake or for her
own?

'It looks as though they're going to be lucky with the
weather too,' she added inanely. 'The forecast is good for
the whole weekend.'

'This is our exit junction,' Marcus told her.

He didn't speak much until they had travelled for several
miles down pretty country lanes and through several small
villages, other than to say casually, 'This is a very pretty
part of the country—and convenient for London. It might
be worthwhile considering it as a possibility for house-
hunting. What do you think?'

'I do love it down here,' Lucy admitted. 'I used to come
and stay with Jules during our school holidays, and I've
always thought it was somewhere I'd like to live.'

'Here's our hotel.'

Crunchy gravel and autumn leaves, smoke from chim-
neys drifting like pale grey silk across a sharp blue sky,
the scent of woodsmoke and fresh air: what could be more
evocative of an English country house? Lucy reflected, as
she stood beside the car and watched the deer in the park
beyond the house as they stared back with huge soft Bambi
eyes.

In the reception hall the smell of beeswax mingled with
lavender and rose pot pourri. The smiling receptionist,

dressed in a tweed skirt, cashmere and pearls, might have been the house's gracious owner and hostess as she explained that they had been given a suite in the barn conversion, separate from the main hotel.

'I think you'll like it. But do come over and have a look.'

As they crossed the courtyard Lucy could see where part of the original moat to the house had been turned into a pond, complete with two swans and a bevy of eager ducks.

'They've adopted us,' the receptionist explained with a smile. 'We have peacocks too, by the way, do please don't be alarmed when you hear them—some people don't care for the noise, but personally I think their beauty more than compensates for it.'

The stable block was a long two-storey building, with its own sunny entrance hall and a set of wide stairs.

'We have two suites downstairs and two upstairs. We've put you upstairs.'

Dutifully Lucy and Marcus followed her to the galleried landing and waited whilst she unlocked one of two doors with a heavy old-fashioned key.

Beyond the door lay a narrow short corridor, and beyond that an enormous bedroom with a huge bed and a proper fireplace.

'The suite has two bathrooms—one either side of the bed,' she explained, indicating the two doors. 'The sofas here in the bedroom convert into extra beds for families, and through here...' She led them to a door next to the fireplace and opened it, to show a pretty sitting-cum-breakfast room with a balcony and views over the countryside.

'Well?' Marcus asked Lucy.

'It's lovely,' she told the receptionist warmly.

'Good, I'm glad you like it. I'll get someone to help you with your luggage.'

'Marcus, this is gorgeous,' Lucy told him as soon as they were alone. 'Very romantic. Especially with the fire.' She moved towards him. She had been so on edge and filled with guilt last night, following Dorland's revelations, that she had not dared let him hold her in case she broke down and sobbed the whole thing out on his shoulder. But right now she was aching for him so much. Why didn't she just put the whole sorry episode of Andrew Walker behind her and enjoy being with Marcus instead?

'Mmm. Look, we'd better get a move on. It took us slightly longer to get here than I expected.'

Marcus was turning way from her, ignoring her subtle hint that she would like him to take her to bed. She recognised the signs easily. After all, she had experienced them often enough at Nick's hands.

CHAPTER EIGHT

'LUCY!'

Lucy forced herself to smile as Julia hugged her tightly, and grinned.

'You're here! Oh, I am so excited. And Marcus too. Let me see the ring. Oh, *Lucy*! Of course Silas insists that he always felt there were some pretty strong undercurrents going on between you and Marcus—don't you, darling?' Julia appealed to her husband.

'Well, let's just say that your sex doesn't always have an exclusive hold on intuition, does it, son?' Silas addressed the blue-wrapped bundle he was holding mock-solemnly. 'Actually it was Lucy who gave the game away, to be honest. It's so rare to see you getting wound up about anything or anyone, Lucy, that I couldn't help but wonder if there was something else going on when you kept on insisting that you hated Marcus. And, as we all know...'

'Hatred is akin to love,' Julia chimed in with Silas, and they exchanged amused looks.

Lucy could feel her face starting to burn. Hastily she reached out her arms and begged, 'Silas, please let me hold my new godson-to-be.'

'He's heavy, Lucy,' Julia warned her, suddenly all proud mother, wanting them to recognise her still tiny son's promise of adult male strength to come.

'Carly rang just before you arrived, by the way. She and Ricardo should be here soon. You know that they've rented a house in the village for the weekend?'

'Yes, she e-mailed to tell me.'

'I'd have liked to offer you all room here, but we've already got my family, and Silas's descending on Gramps tomorrow. Are you sure my son isn't getting too heavy for you?' she demanded. They were all standing in the large, slightly draughty drawing room Julia had taken them to, and, sensing that her friend was already eager for the return of her baby, Lucy smiled down at him, stroking his cheek gently with her finger as she walked over to Julia and handed him back.

Marcus was standing with Silas, supposedly listening to what Silas was saying about the current situation with the dollar, but he couldn't stop himself from watching her. Julia might be baby Nat's mother, but it was Lucy, with her doting, blissed-out expression, whose face was that of a traditional radiant Madonna—all soft, beatific love. There was a feeling in his heart as though it were being wrenched apart by two giant fists. Angrily he struggled to suppress it.

As she handed Nat back to Julia, Lucy couldn't help reflecting desolately that if Marcus continued to behave as coldly towards her as he had done earlier, in their hotel suite, then if she wasn't already pregnant she would probably never hold a child of her own. What was it about her that made her so undesirable and so undesired by the very men who were supposed to want her? First Nick and now Marcus. She looked over to where Marcus was standing with Silas, the two men deep in conversation.

'Lucy, come and sit down,' Julia invited, patting the empty space on the sofa next to her.

'I'm so glad about you and Marcus.' She beamed as Lucy obeyed her instruction. 'I know how unhappy Nick made you, and I've felt so guilty about that because you met him through me. Marcus will—' She broke off as a large Mercedes swept past the window, then exclaimed happily, 'Oh, good, that will be Carly and Ricardo.'

Five minutes later the large room was full of the sound of warmly excited female voices as the three women exchanged news and gossip.

'Just look at how much he's grown,' Lucy exclaimed in awe as she admired Carly and Ricardo's son before adding, 'And look at you, too, Carly—six months pregnant and yet you look as stunning and elegant as ever.'

With so much to say to one another, and two adorable babies to admire, Lucy started to relax, her earlier forced smile giving way to one that was far more natural. So much so, in fact, that when Marcus came over to where she was seated with Carly and Julia and the children, and placed a hand on her shoulder, she had to tense her whole body to stop herself from leaning into him and letting him see how much he meant to her.

'I am *so* looking forward to the wedding, Lucy,' Carly announced excitedly. 'After all, you're the only one of the three of us to have a proper regulation do.'

'Oh, yes, I'm looking forward to it, too,' Julia chimed in. 'When did you first realise you loved Lucy, Marcus?' she asked him.

Lucy immediately dipped her head, so her hair swung forward to conceal her expression.

'Not soon enough,' Marcus responded calmly. 'If I had, she would never have been allowed to marry Blayne.'

Everyone laughed, and Lucy let her pent-up breath leak away in shaky relief. What had she been afraid he might say? That he didn't love her at all? Marcus was far too cerebral to make a slip like that.

'That was a very pleasant evening.'

'I'm glad you enjoyed it,' Lucy replied as the lights of

Julia's grandfather's house were left behind them and Marcus's Bentley purred softly onto the main road.

'I'm even more convinced now, if we *are* going to think of buying a house outside London, that this would be a good area to consider. What do you think?'

'Like I said before, it is a very pretty part of the country,' Lucy agreed. 'And Julia did say that she and Silas are hoping that ultimately they will be spending more time here. Of course when Julia's grandfather dies Silas will inherit the title and the house, but they both want their children to grow up knowing their English heritage as well as their American heritage.'

She leaned back in her seat and closed her eyes. It *had* been a good evening, with the three men getting on as well as the women did themselves. There had even been whole moments when she had almost managed to persuade herself that she and Marcus were a normal soon-to-be married couple.

She certainly wished that they were. Just as she wished that right now they were going back to their hotel suite as genuine lovers who just couldn't wait to be alone together.

Lucy had fallen asleep within minutes of them leaving her friends, and as he brought the car to a halt in the hotel car park Marcus turned in his seat to look at her. He would be glad when she was safely married to him and he could once again focus his attention on the bank, instead of constantly having to be on his guard in case Lucy tried to change her mind and refuse to go through with their marriage.

He reached out and touched her arm, saying calmly, 'Lucy—wake up. We're here.'

'Marcus?' Emotion illuminated her whole face as she looked back at him. Suddenly Marcus felt as though he had been kicked in the chest and deprived of the ability to breathe. Something—a feeling—a need—roared through him, threatening to blast apart the fixed standing stones of his beliefs.

Oblivious to what was happening to him, Lucy continued sleepily, 'I was just dreaming about you and...'

'And?' Marcus probed, his voice rusty as he fought back an unfamiliar urge to take hold of her and go on holding her, so that he could satisfy his need to physically experience the reality of her.

'Nothing.' Lucy shook her head, but she could feel her face going a betraying shade of pink. It was obvious that Marcus had guessed just what she had been dreaming, too, because all of sudden there was a very definite gleam in his eyes.

'Do I take it from that pretty pink flush that it was the kind of dream I would enjoy turning into reality?' he asked, as his own body responded to the desire he could see in her eyes.

It took Lucy several speeded-up heartbeats to recognise that Marcus was actually flirting with her, and several more to take a deep breath, jettison her pride and answer him boldly. 'Well, *I* would certainly enjoy you doing so, Marcus. *Marcus*!' she protested breathlessly, as suddenly he kissed her so fiercely that she could hardly breathe.

'Come on,' he commanded, releasing her and then getting out of the car and going round to open the passenger door for her.

Their journey from the car to their suite was accomplished in between so many kisses that Lucy felt half delirious with desire by the time they reached their room. Holding her within one arm, Marcus continued to kiss her while he inserted the key in the lock and turned the handle.

A fire was burning in the hearth, the maid had been up

and closed the curtains, and the room itself smelled of pine logs and warmth and intimacy.

'Marcus...' she whispered eagerly.

'Mmm?'

'Hurry.'

'Like this, do you mean?'

He was touching her, despite the fact that they were both still fully dressed, so that her whole body convulsed.

'My clothes...' she protested, wanting to be rid of them. But her body was telling Marcus that it didn't want to wait—and, he realised fiercely, neither did his own.

He took her quickly and hotly, there and then, in the shadowy bedroom, compelled and driven by his need to possess her and make her his in a way that was totally outside anything he had ever previously experienced.

She loved what he was doing—and the way he was doing it, Lucy thought dizzily as she wrapped her legs around him and felt the swift surges of pleasure grip her. Later there would be time to undress, to pleasure one another more slowly and thoroughly, but right now this was exactly what she wanted and how she wanted it. How she wanted him.

She still couldn't fully take it in that that a few weeks from now she would actually be Marcus's wife. Lucy took a gulp of her espresso and reminded herself sternly that the reason she was here in her office was to *work*, and not to think about the many and varied pleasures of becoming Mrs Marcus Carring. Pleasures which, right now, were suppressing the doubts that had been tormenting her. It was, after all, an undeniable truth that those pleasures were *so* many and *so* varied that it was almost impossible for her not to fantasise about them. And so...

Hastily she forced herself to concentrate on what she

was supposed to be doing—namely, updating her client files and dealing with her other paperwork. The slow trickle of new business had now become a sporadic drip— little more than sympathy and family-generated events. Which was a problem, of course, so far as securing enough future income to finance her Prêt a Party debts was concerned, but not so much of a problem when she thought of the amount of time it would free up for her to get used to being married. In fact, if it wasn't for the wretched debts Nick had left her, she could have been very happy, slowly rebuilding her business on a much smaller and more containable scale.

Lucy had another gulp of her favourite caffeine fix and idly scanned the huge double-page spread of photographs from Nat's christening which, true to form, Dorland had used as his centrepiece for that week's *A-List Life*. There was one especially good photograph of her holding her new godson, with Marcus standing at her side.

Marcus. She was doing the right thing in marrying him, she told herself firmly.

There was a loud knock on her half-open office door and she swung round eagerly, hoping to see Marcus, although he had told her that he was driving to Manchester today to see a client.

'Lucy. Good, I hoped you would be here.'

Andrew Walker.

Lucy stared at her unexpected and definitely unwanted visitor in apprehensive dismay, unable to say anything more than an uncomfortable, 'Oh! Andrew. You did get my letter, didn't you?'

'Yes, Lucy. I got your letter,' he confirmed, walking past her to stand in front of the window, so that her expression was plainly revealed to him whilst he was just a fuzzy dark blur against the sunlit windows.

'I was very sorry to learn that you no longer wanted to proceed with our plans. In fact I was so disappointed that I thought I'd come and see you to see if I could find a way to persuade you to change your mind.'

Was she imagining it, or was there a subtle threat in those calmly spoken words? Lucy could feel the sharp hammer-blows of her heartbeat as it mirrored her fear.

'I explained in my letter, Andrew. I'm getting married and—'

'Yes, indeed. To Marcus Carring, I believe.'

'Yes,' Lucy acknowledged. 'Yes. And once we are married Marcus wants to become my partner in Prêt a Party.' That should convince Andrew Walker that it wasn't just her he had to contend with now, even if she was in reality fibbing to him.

'Really?'

There was something in the way Andrew Walker was looking at her that made Lucy feel afraid.

'You know, my dear, you are turning down a wonderful business opportunity here. And as for allowing your husband to be to become your partner... One never knows these days what the future of a marriage will be. Modern marriages are such very flimsy constructions at the best of times, don't you think? A sensible woman might think it a good idea to maintain her own financial independence from her husband.'

Lucy only just managed to stop herself from gasping out loud. Had Andrew Walker somehow read her mind? What he had just said echoed everything she had been saying to herself.

'My partners and I are prepared to make you a very generous offer to buy into Prêt a Party, Lucy, and I can give you my assurance that everything will be dealt with very discreetly. The cash could be paid into an overseas bank of your choice, should you want that, and no one apart from ourselves need ever know anything about the whole transaction.'

If she hadn't known the truth about him she would have been very tempted to accept what he was offering her, Lucy recognised. Because, despite the fact that Marcus physically desired her, her fear that without love their marriage could not survive would not go away. It was that fear that had prevented her from accepting Marcus's offer of finance and his suggestion that he came into the business, and that fear, too, that made her want to keep Prêt a Party under her own control and not share it with a husband.

But Andrew Walker's statement had reminded her of everything Dorland had said to her.

'No, I suppose they needn't—including those poor wretches whose lives you've ruined to get the money in the first place,' she burst out impetuously. 'I know all about why you want Prêt a Party, you know—and what you're doing.'

There was a small, tight silence and then Andrew Walker said sharply, 'Do you indeed?'

She had made another mistake, Lucy realised. And a very bad one.

How had she ever thought of Andrew Walker's face as nondescript and pleasant? Now, as he came towards her, she could see the real Andrew Walker instead of the kindly mask he had hidden behind.

Dorland had been right. This was a very bad man. Fear pooled in her stomach and her muscles tightened round it.

Exactly the same feelings of sick disbelief and fear she had experienced when she had first learned of Nick's treachery were coiling through her stomach now. And, exactly as it had been then, her first thought was that she wished desperately that Marcus were her to help her. Her second was that she was equally desperately glad that he wasn't here to witness her stupidity.

And yet she was still unable to stop herself from repeating shakily, 'I do know all about how you and your partners make your money, and why you want Prêt a Party.'

'You know, Lucy, you really shouldn't listen to gossip from jealous and unreliable sources,' Andrew Walker told her evenly. 'Why don't you take my advice and think a little bit harder about our offer, and about letting Marcus Carring become your partner? That wouldn't be a very good move, and my colleagues would certainly not be pleased were you to do that. After all, as I just said, nothing is certain in this life—especially not marriage. You've been married once already, and—'

'I won't listen to any more.' Lucy stopped him passionately. 'There isn't any point in you trying to pressure me by offering me money. I don't want it and I won't change my mind.'

'Are you sure you're doing the right thing marrying Carring, Lucy?'

His question caught her off guard.

'Yes, of course I'm sure,' she lied. 'I love him.' That much at least was the truth. 'In fact I've always loved him,' she added defiantly.

She could see that her declaration had not pleased him. He doubtless knew that he would not be able to deceive and bully Marcus the way he had tried to do her.

'I'd advise you to think very carefully about what I've just said,' he told her sharply. 'Oh, and I wouldn't tell Marcus Carring about our conversation if I were you—for your own sake and for his.' Andrew Walker ignored her attempted reply to that, and stepped past her to open the office door. 'I shall be in touch.'

He'd gone. He'd actually gone. Lucy felt sick with relief. When she attempted to stand to go and lock her office
door, to make sure he couldn't come back, her legs simply
would not support her.

She would have to close down Prêt a Party completely
now, she decided shakily. She couldn't think of any other
way to protect both herself and her business.

When Marcus questioned why she was giving up the
business she had fought so hard to keep going, she would
simply have to tell him that she had been giving the matter
a great deal of thought and that she wanted to concentrate
on them—their marriage and their future together.

Lie to him, in other words.

The sick feeling in the pit of her stomach increased.

But what other choice did she have? How could she tell
him the truth now? If she told him he would stand there
and look at her the way he had when she'd had to tell him
that Nick had not just been unfaithful to her but that he
had also defrauded the business. With angry disbelief, with
irritation and with contempt. She just did not think she
could bear that.

'It's supposed to be bad luck for you to see me in my
outfit before we get married, you know,' Lucy reproached
Marcus.

Marcus had just let them both into his house, having
picked up Lucy from her parents' home earlier.

'You aren't in your wedding outfit,' he pointed out. 'At
least, not unless you've changed your mind and you intend
to marry me wearing jeans.'

'Don't be silly. I'm not wearing the dress now, but I
was when you came round.'

'I didn't see you in it, though,' Marcus assured her, but
Lucy could see that he had his fingers crossed behind his

back, and she couldn't help but smile, albeit a little bit wanly. These last few weeks had been so stressful.

'Cheer up—it will soon be over now,' Marcus told her, as though he had somehow guessed how she felt. 'And then once we're on honeymoon you'll be able to relax.'

Lucy exhaled heavily and told him emphatically, 'I can't wait.'

There was a small potent silence during which her colour rose. She saw the way Marcus was looking at her, and then he said obliquely, 'No, I don't think I can either.'

Silently they both looked at one another.

'It's been a very long few weeks,' Lucy told him breathlessly. The look she had seen in his eyes was causing her heart to jerk about inside her chest as though he was holding it on a string.

As he stood watching her Marcus was suddenly aware of a most peculiar emotion filling him and driving him. A need—a compulsion, almost—to take Lucy in his arms and keep her there, whilst he...

He shook his head, trying to dispel the unfamiliar emotions that were gripping him. 'Why don't we...?' he began slowly, and then frowned as they were interrupted by the sound of the doorbell being rung. He went to open the door and, while Lucy watched, took a package from the waiting courier and signed for it.

'Do you want to make us both a drink while I check to see what this is?' he asked her.

She just couldn't resist the temptation to look at him, Lucy admitted to herself as she lingered to watch him as he began to open the package. When he did so, removing the contents and studying them, a couple of photographs slid free and fell onto the floor.

Automatically Lucy went to pick them up.

'No—don't touch them. Leave them.'

The harshness of his grim command instantly reminded her of the old Marcus. 'What—?' she began, and then stopped as she stared down at the floor and the photograph that was lying there face upwards.

She had heard of the expression 'her blood ran cold', but she had never until that moment imagined she might experience it as a physical sensation—as though the warmth of her blood was draining away to be replaced with something that felt like ice.

'Marcus...' Her voice a shocked, disbelieving whisper of anguish, she looked from the photograph to his unreadable face and then back to the photograph again.

On it her own face stared back at her: her mouth smiling, her eyes open, alight with excitement and delight. And the reason for that delight was...

She looked at the photograph again and her stomach heaved. Her body was naked, her arms and legs spread, held down by four sets of male hands, whilst a fifth man was positioned between her spread legs, obviously having sex with her.

Like someone in a trance, she bent down and picked up the other photograph.

'Lucy! No!'

Marcus made a lunge to stop her, but he was still holding the contents of the package. Ignoring him as though she hadn't even heard him, Lucy turned over the second photograph. This one was even worse. A woman had joined the men—a woman wearing a dildo—and she—they—she and the men—were all doing the most vile things to and with one another. And *she* was eagerly and willingly participating in it all.

She looked at what Marcus was holding. More photographs and a video. There was a picture of her on the front of the video—naked, her legs spread. The caption on it read: *Lucy Loves Lickin' Lust. Watch her in action!*

Lucy felt her stomach heave.

She ran to the bathroom and was immediately and violently sick. Shivering with disgust, she clung to the basin and turned on the taps, washing her face and then cleaning her teeth. She wanted to tear off her clothes and stand under the hottest, hardest shower she could find. She wanted to scrub at her skin and somehow remove the filth she could almost feel clinging to her.

'Lucy.'

Marcus was standing in the open doorway to the bathroom, an expression in his eyes that she distantly thought looked like pain, but which she knew must be disgust.

'It isn't me,' she told him, slowly and carefully, fixing her gaze on the far wall so that she didn't have to look at him and see in his eyes what she knew would be there. If he had looked at her before with irritation and contempt, that was nothing to how he would be looking at her now. 'I know it looks like me, but it isn't.'

Silence.

What had she expected? That he would sweep her up into his arms and tell her that he loved her? After seeing that?

'You won't want to marry me now, of course. How could you?' She was amazed at how calm and accepting she sounded. How reasoning and distanced from the wild, shrieking agony of pain and disbelief inside her.

'I'd better go home and tell everyone.' How was she managing to sound so polite? So much as though she were attending a formal tea party at her great-aunt's rather than experiencing, *enduring* what she was going through?

She certainly felt as cold as though she were at her

great-aunt's, she admitted, as her teeth started to chatter and rigours of icy cold gripped her body.

'Lucy.'

Marcus's hands felt so warm as they cupped her face, and his body was so reassuringly close, even though she hadn't even seen him cross the space between them.

'Please don't,' she begged him piteously, as her body caved in to her shock and tears welled in her eyes to roll down her face. 'Please don't make it harder for me, Marcus. I know what you must be thinking, and how you must feel.'

'Do you?' he demanded, so savagely that she flinched. 'No, I don't think you do,' he told her harshly. 'I don't think you can know how I feel knowing that *you* have been exposed to this kind of...of *filth*. That you have been dragged into it and degraded by it.'

'Marcus, I haven't. It isn't me. Please believe me. It isn't.' She couldn't hold back the words any longer, even though she knew he would not and could not possibly believe her. Not with the evidence of those horrible photographs.

She could see how darkly he was frowning at her, probably thinking she was compounding her guilt by lying about it.

'I *know* it isn't you,' he said, with an almost dismissive shrug. 'It's obvious that it couldn't possibly be you. How could it be?'

He *believed* her?

'You...you know that it isn't me?' Lucy repeated cautiously, afraid to trust in her own hearing.

'Yes, of course I know it isn't you,' Marcus replied, with familiar sharp impatience.

'But how? How can you know?' Lucy asked him shakily.

'Apart from anything else, you have a small but very identifying mole, high up on the outside of your left thigh,' Marcus told her calmly. 'And whoever posed for the body shots for this—this *abomination* doesn't.'

'Oh!'

How very weird that the most important thing in her whole life should hang on the existence of one tiny brown mole; that something not much larger than a pinhead could make the difference between happiness for the rest of her life or misery until she died—between trust and doubt, between truth and lies, between being married to Marcus and being rejected by him.

'It's obvious that someone has superimposed your face on the body of someone else.'

'But someone else without my mole,' Lucy said, as lightly as she could.

Marcus was frowning at her now.

'The mole is simply a confirmation of what I already know, Lucy,' he told her coolly. 'My own judgement is all I need to know that you could never be the woman depicted in those photographs.'

To Marcus's own disbelief he realised that he wanted to reach for her and hold her; that he wanted to tell her he would kill, breath by breath, painfully and slowly, whoever was responsible for what had happened; that he wanted to tell her that he knew not just with his intellect but also with his *heart*, with the deepest part of himself, that she would never ever indulge in the kind of scenario the photographs depicted. He wanted to tell her that he knew that she was a sensualist, a woman who loved the intimacy of one-to-one lovemaking, a woman who celebrated her womanhood in the act of sharing pleasure with just one man.

But how could he be feeling like this? He did not *feel*

things. He thought through his decisions logically and calmly. He did not 'sense' them. He did not allow his emotions to sway his judgement. And, most of all, he did not allow himself to feel his heart turning over inside his chest in a roll of raw agony because Lucy's pain was his pain. Because if he did, then that meant—

Angrily he slammed the door against the knowledge he did not want to accept.

'But why would anyone want to do such a thing?' Lucy was asking, giving him something logical to focus on and deal with. 'Never mind send those...those things to you?'

'It's probably just someone's idea of a joke,' Marcus told her, intent on refusing to analyse what was happening to him inside his head. No, not his head but his *heart*— that part of him that he had told himself, when he had finally accepted that his father had deserted them, would in future only be allowed to operate physically, never emotionally.

'A *joke*?'

'Yes, it happens all the time.' He shrugged his shoulders. 'Young idiots like your cousin Johnny, for instance, who have nothing better to do and—'

'But, Marcus, something like this isn't a joke,' Lucy protested.

'Look, let's just forget about it, shall we?' Marcus told her briskly. 'After all, we've both recognised it for what it is—at best a stupid, senseless and very tasteless joke, and at worst a malicious attempt to damage our relationship.'

'But who would do a thing like that?' Lucy asked, worry crinkling her forehead.

'Who knows? The best thing we can do now is to ignore it and to forget it,' Marcus repeated. But he knew he wasn't being entirely open with her.

He was grimly aware that only this morning he had heard that the woman Nick Blayne had left Lucy for had ended their relationship and thrown him out, and that he was now virtually penniless.

There was no note with the package, but Marcus suspected that the video and the accompanying photographs were the beginnings of a clumsy attempt to blackmail him into paying for the 'master' copies. It was the kind of thing that had Nick Blayne's grubby mark all over it, but Marcus didn't want to upset Lucy by telling her so.

Or because he was concerned that if she knew that Blayne was free again she might be tempted to go back to him?

'Marcus?'

Tears of reaction were rolling down Lucy's face. Her thoughts were a jumbled mass of fear and confusion, plus intense relief that Marcus had reacted in the way that he had. A wave of gratitude and love for him surged through her, filling her eyes with fresh tears

'It's all right, Lucy. It's all right,' Marcus told her gruffly.

'I'm not crying because I'm upset,' Lucy managed to tell him. 'I'm just crying because I'm so happy that you didn't think it was me.'

Marcus wasn't aware of moving, only of holding her in his arms whilst her whole body shuddered with reaction.

'Oh—but, Marcus, if you hadn't known about my mole...'

'Lucy, look at me.'

'My mascara's run and my nose is red,' she objected, sniffing.

'True,' Marcus agreed wryly, but his expression was warmer than she could even remember seeing it. 'But I can still recognise you, Lucy. And even if you had not had your mole I would still have known that the body in those photographs and in those situations could never have belonged to you.'

'How could you know that?'

'Because I know you,' Marcus answered her, simply and truthfully.

And it was true. He did know, at the most primitive and deepest level of his being, that Lucy could never and would never be the girl in those photographs.

And now he was beginning to know now something else as well; its message was being thumped out to him via the heavy thud of his own heartbeat.

But he still wasn't ready to give in. His desire to marry Lucy came from logic and not love. Came now? Or had originally come?

Lucy give him a small, tremulous half-smile, which wobbled slightly despite her best efforts to prevent it from doing so. 'So you still want to marry me, then?'

Marcus arched one eyebrow and told her dryly, 'Of course. It would take a far braver man than I to disappoint a mother who has planned a wedding breakfast for five hundred people.'

'I did tell her that we only wanted a quiet wedding,' Lucy assured him.

'Five hundred, five thousand, or five—frankly, my dear, I don't give a tuppenny ha'penny damn how many guests there are. All I care about is that you're there, Lucy.'

'Because you're nearly thirty-five and you want an heir?' She held her breath, hoping against hope that by some miracle he would deny her comment and declare that he loved her.

'Of course,' he agreed immediately.

Her foolish hope leaked away, leaving her starved of its comfort and filled with pain.

'I'm going to take you back to your parents' place now,' he told her.

'Marcus!' Lucy protested.

'I mean it, Lucy. You can't stay here, tonight of all nights. We both know that.'

And he knew that if he touched her he might just not be able to let her go, Marcus was forced to acknowledge.

CHAPTER NINE

LUCY had refused point blank to wear a white wedding dress, and had been on the point of giving up finding anything suitable in the short time she'd had available when she had seen a Vera Wang dress in Harrods, in ecru silk. Wonder of wonders, it had fitted her.

The long sheath-like gown had a tight-fitting corset-style bodice, a detachable skirt, and a fishtail demi-train. In order to satisfy family tradition a copy had been made of its matching close-fitting bolero-style jacket from a piece of antique family lace.

She hadn't wanted to wear a veil either, but in the end had agreed to wear a small pillbox-style hat with a very small 'almost' veil.

The promise of heavy-duty wedding-style cream lilies with appropriate greenery, a positive phalanx of pages and bridesmaids of assorted junior ranks from both their families, and the pomp and circumstance of the Oratory and Handel's music had been enough to soothe her mother's maternal angst about her not looking like a 'real' bride.

Marcus knew that she had entered the church from the excited rustle of movement that seethed along the pews behind him, and to his own astonishment felt compelled to turn and watch her as she walked down the aisle towards him.

He felt his body tighten and his heart lurch in a reaction he had been determined no woman would ever arouse in him—least of all Lucy.

* * *

It had really happened. She and Marcus really were married, Lucy realised dizzily as the Bishop intoned mellifluously, 'You may kiss the bride.'

And Marcus leaned towards her and then did just that. A cool and very distant brushing of his lips against hers that filled her eyes with painful despair and made her hand tremble within his.

Handel's musical paean of triumphal joy rang out as they walked together back down the aisle and then out into the crisp sunshine of the November afternoon, to be bombarded with rose petals by their well-wishers and guests before being swept off in a cavalcade of shiny black limousines to the imposing building built originally by a grateful nation for its hero, the Duke of Wellington, for the wedding breakfast.

'Are you sure you aren't disappointed that we didn't book into a hotel for tonight?' Marcus asked.

They were standing in his bedroom at the Wendover Square house—now *their* bedroom. It still smelled just faintly of its refurbishments—a sort of new paint, new fabric and new carpet smell, all mingled together.

'No, I'm not disappointed at all,' Lucy reassured him. 'After all, we're flying off to the Caribbean on honeymoon tomorrow, and besides...'

'Besides what?' he demanded.

Lucy shook her head. They might be married, and she might be his wife, but that didn't mean she felt she could tell him that she didn't care where they were just so long as they were together, and that anyway his house had now become inextricably linked in her emotions with the wonder of the first night she had spent there and the joy of what it had led her to.

'Nothing,' she fibbed, before admitting ruefully, 'I did

feel a bit of an idiot coming back here in the taxi still wearing my wedding dress, though. Why did you want me to keep it on?'

The look he was giving her made her whole face colour up.

'Because I want to have the pleasure of taking it off, of course. All those tiny buttons down the back have been tantalising me for hours,' Marcus told her truthfully, 'and the sooner the better, I think. Certainly before we make use of our very sensuous new *en suite* bathroom.'

'You were the one who suggested it,' she reminded him a little defensively. Her parents—very much of the old school—had shaken their heads over the waste of so much expensive London floor space on a mere bathroom.

'Mmm. I've got very fond memories of the bathroom in our suite at the hotel in Deia.'

As part of the refurbishment of Marcus's house they had expanded Marcus's already large bedroom to include a new dressing room made from one of the smaller bedrooms, plus a huge and very luxurious *en suite* bathroom which combined the best of modern, clean bathroom lines—all chrome and limestone and marble—with the sensual luxury of a large semi-sunken bath along with a separate wet room area and, of course, plenty of mirrors.

'Mrs Crabtree said that she would leave us a cold supper, and there is some champagne on ice downstairs. Don't run away while I go and get it.'

'Run away? Marcus, have you seen how narrow this skirt is? I can't *run* anywhere in it. In fact, I can barely walk.'

He wasn't gone very long—just long enough for her to glance round their bedroom and admire the clean fresh lines of its new décor.

'Here you are,' he told her, handing her a glass of the champagne he had just poured.

'I'm not sure that I should,' Lucy demurred, remembering Great-Aunt Alice's birthday party.

'I am—you most definitely should. To us,' Marcus toasted her firmly.

'To us,' Lucy whispered back, shivering with delight as Marcus leaned forward and kissed her. She could taste the champagne on his mouth, and somehow that gave an added intimacy to their kiss.

As he released her she took another sip of her champagne, and then put the glass down. She was far too excited to need any champagne-induced euphoria.

Marcus had removed his jacket and pulled off his cravat.

'When I watched you coming down the aisle to me today, Lucy, I thought I had never seen you looking more beautiful.'

'Oh, Marcus!' Lucy bit her lip, determined not to let him know that she would far rather have heard him say that he loved her.

He kissed her again, more passionately this time, and then said thickly, 'Now, exactly where do I start with this dress?'

'I'll take the jacket off first, shall I?' Lucy suggested. 'Ma wants to keep the lace and have some of it sewn on a christening robe for us, so I daren't damage it.' She blushed again as she saw the look in Marcus's eyes.

'The skirt is Velcroed to the bodice, so it might be an idea to unfasten the buttons on it first and then I can just step out of it. The bodice is a sort of corset thing as well, you see.'

She was babbling, Lucy recognised, and all because of how she felt at the thought of conceiving Marcus's child—

and she did not know yet whether or not she had already done so this month!

Marcus had moved behind her and was slowly unfastening the two dozen tiny buttons closing her skirt and train.

When he had eventually completed his task, and unhooked the skirt and train from the low-waisted corset-like bodice of her gown, she was left standing there in high heels, cream silk stockings fastened to a suspender belt that matched her gown, and a tiny pair of knickers.

'I know it all looks a bit obvious,' she told him, gesturing towards her body. 'But it wasn't my idea...'

His face, she noticed, was slightly flushed—from bending down to gather up some of the rose petals that had fallen inside her gown?

But he didn't make any response to her slightly nervous comment.

Instead he dropped down on one knee in front of her and started to kiss his way around the bare flesh at top of her stocking, pausing to slowly unclip her suspenders and then roll the fine silk down her leg, following it with the caress of his lips.

When he lifted her foot free of her shoe and then slid off her stocking, holding her foot firmly and then kissing her instep, Lucy exhaled tremulously in delirious lust.

The other stocking and her suspender belt were removed equally sensually. But Marcus hadn't finished. He slid his hands inside her knickers, pulling them down to reveal her new wax—not a summer-holiday-style Brazilian, but instead a small heart shape of silky blonde hair, something the beautician had told her was a favourite with a lot of brides.

'Mmm...pretty. Very nice,' he commented. 'But not as nice as this.' And then, while his hands held the top of her legs, his tongue probed delicately between the rose-petal-scented lips of her sex and stroked lingeringly along the whole length of her opening, right up to the now swollen and eagerly pulsing jut of flesh that was her clitoris.

Lucy moaned out aloud and buried her fingers in his hair as shuddering waves of pleasure gripped her.

'Who needs champagne when they can have nectar?' Marcus told her thickly, after his tongue had stroked her to a sweetly urgent climax.

It had still been light when they had arrived at the house, but by the time they finally made it onto the big bed it was quite definitely dark—and she was quite definitely eagerly willing to consummate their marriage. He thrust slowly and deeply into her and her muscles closed lovingly round him, her body making him its prisoner—just as he had made her love his.

'Tired?'

'Just a bit,' Lucy admitted, as they stepped out of their taxi and into the cool haven of Mustique's Sugar House Hotel.

The long flight from England in November to the warmth of the Caribbean, on top of yesterday's wedding and the long night of passion they had shared, had left her feeling slightly weary, Lucy acknowledged. Weary and disappointed—because nothing had changed—because Marcus, although a wonderfully sensual lover, did not love her.

Mustique was somewhere she had never previously visited, and she had been delighted, if somewhat surprised, that Marcus had chosen such a romantic venue for their honeymoon. A tropical darkness had already descended on the island in the short time since their plane had landed, and a handful of guests drifted through the foyer in a very

relaxed manner as Marcus signed them in and waited for
their room keys.

'Mrs Carring?'

'She means you,' Marcus told Lucy wryly as a smiling
girl approached Lucy.

Blushing slightly, Lucy returned her smile.

'We have a complimentary gift pack of vouchers for
you, for treatments at our spa facility.' As Lucy thanked
her and took the envelope, the girl added, her smile deepening, 'I can recommend our couples massage, which is a
massage that is given to you both at the same time in the
privacy of your own room.'

'If all the girls are as pretty as she was, then no way
are you going to be having a complimentary massage,'
Lucy informed Marcus pithily ten minutes later, when they
were alone in their suite.

'Aha—now you sound like a wife,' Marcus told her.
'Are you hungry? Would you like to eat now, or later?
The hotel provides an unpacking and pressing service...'

'I'd like a shower. But more than anything else I'd
love—'

'Some coffee,' Marcus finished for her. 'I'll order it for
you, shall I? And perhaps we can have an exploratory walk
whilst they unpack for us?'

'Mmm. Oh, Marcus, come and look at this,' Lucy exclaimed. 'It's a pillow menu. You can choose your own
pillow.'

Ten minutes later they were walking hand in hand
through the Great Room of the hotel. Built around an old
coral warehouse and a sugar mill, the hotel had been re-
furbished recently to a wonderful standard of luxury.

Their own master suite in the main hotel was furnished
in the style of the eighteenth century, the bed hung with
voile, the furniture elegantly styled and painted a soft,

rubbed off-white. A large freestanding double-ended hip-shaped bath and a private plunge pool added to the romantic luxury, and as they explored the gardens and stopped to admire the beach that lay beyond Lucy could well understand why this luxurious hotel was so very prestigious, and so loved by its guests. By the time they returned to their suite, via the privacy of the night-cloaked gardens and several impromptu stops to exchange kisses, their cases had been unpacked for them.

'Perhaps just a Room Service meal tonight?' Lucy suggested, stifling a small yawn.

'Good idea,' Marcus agreed.

'Oh, Marcus, this is brilliant...' Lucy sighed happily as she leaned back against him in their plunge pool, her body between his spread legs, her head pressed against his chest, with his arms wrapped around her and his hands cupping her naked breasts.

'Mmm, absolutely,' he agreed, nuzzling the sensitive spot just below her ear and making her shudder so hard that the water shuddered with her.

'You don't think anyone can see us, do you?' she whispered to him several seconds later, as they lay naked together in the water and Marcus teased her eagerly expectant body with all the touches he knew it loved.

'No...but we can go inside, if you want.'

'No, I like it here,' Lucy told him. 'There's something so nice about lying naked in the water and the sun.'

'Mmm, something very nice,' Marcus agreed, as he took advantage of her nudity to enjoy unlimited access to her body whilst encouraging her to do the same with his.

She had woken up this morning to Marcus stroking teasing fingers against her breast whilst feathering kisses on her closed eyelids, and they had gone from there on a slow journey of foreplay that had ended up with her abandoning herself willingly and completely to his thrusting possession. Now, scarcely a couple of hours later, her desire for him was already an urgent clamouring force.

Sliding away from him, Lucy slowly stroked her hand down over his body to embrace his erection.

Marcus watched whilst she focused on his pleasure, wondering if she knew just how much of it was attributable not to what she was doing but to the look of erotic delight in her eyes as she did so. Even her own body was registering its pleasure in what she was doing, her nipples tightening and her breasts lifting slightly. Beneath the water he could see how the lips of her sex were swelling and flushing.

'Marcus, we can't—not here,' Lucy protested as he reached for her, but it was too late, and as Marcus positioned her over the erection she had just been caressing she straddled him and sank slowly onto it, luxuriating in the erotic intensity of taking him into her, centimetre by centimetre, her slick muscles and flesh gripping and caressing him. He groaned fiercely and reached for her hips, pulling her down hard against him whilst he thrust into her, over and over again, then lifted his hand to place it over her mouth when she screamed out in wild ecstasy before sinking down on top of him in quivering release.

'I can't believe we're on our way home,' Lucy sighed, as they left the small plane which had brought them from Mustique.

'We've got a few hours yet before we pick up our connecting flight for London. Is there anything you want to do?'

Lucy shook her head. 'I'll go and get myself some magazines and a book.'

'I've got couple of calls to make, so I'll go and order you some coffee, shall I?' Marcus offered.

'Mmm—please.' Lucy thanked him.

Lucy was standing in the queue waiting to pay for her purchases when she saw him. The blood drained out of her face and she whispered, horrified, 'Nick!'

And, even though she knew he could not possibly have heard her, he turned his head and looked straight at her, abandoning the woman he was with to come over to her.

Immediately she shrank back from him, not wanting him anywhere near her.

'Well, well—if it isn't my ex-wife. Here on your own, are you?' he taunted her.

'No, actually, I'm with Marcus,' Lucy told him coldly. She badly wanted to ignore him, but he was standing right next to her now, and unless she abandoned the books she was holding and walked away she would have to stay where she was in the queue.

'Carring?'

She could see that Nick wasn't at all pleased—that in fact he looked distinctly put out.

'Yes, Marcus,' Lucy repeated. 'He and I are married now.' She couldn't resist the small happy boast.

'He *married* you?' Nick demanded sharply. 'How on earth did you persuade him to do that? Pregnant, are you? I thought he'd dump you the moment he saw the little wedding present Andrew and I sent him. Perhaps he has his own reasons for going ahead, does he? But if he thinks he'll force Andrew into paying more for Prêt a Party, then—'

'*You* sent those photographs?' Lucy cut him off, white-faced.

'Mmm...good, weren't they?' he mocked her. 'Especially that one of you smiling like you were really having a good time.'

She mustn't let him see how shocked and upset she was, Lucy decided frantically. Nor must she let him guess how frightened it made her feel to know that he was working with Andrew Walker, and that the two of them had tried to destroy her marriage before it had even begun.

She felt as though she was being subjected to a sensation not unlike the centre of gravity beneath her feet physically shifting, as though there had been a minor earth tremor. It scared her sick to recognise how far Andrew Walker was prepared to go to get Prêt a Party.

'You really should have accepted Andrew's offer, Lucy,' Nick was telling her. 'He isn't at all pleased with you, you know. He wants Prêt a Party, and believe me he will get it—one way or another.'

Several equally horrible suspicions were thrusting into her awareness like ice picks.

'How do you know Andrew Walker?' she demanded.

'What's that got to do with you? Let's just say that I do know him, and that I recommended to him that he look into investing in Prêt a Party,' Nick boasted. 'It's perfect for his needs.'

'Those needs being laundering money stolen from refugees who live in fear of him, you mean?' Lucy challenged Nick furiously.

'My, my—we have been nosey, haven't we? Be careful that nose of yours doesn't get chopped off for being stuck into places it has no right to be, Lucy. And think about this: you had already agreed verbally to a partnership with Andrew, so you are just as involved in what goes on as the rest of us.'

'No. We only discussed a partnership—and then I didn't know the truth.'

'But can you prove that?' Nick taunted her. 'I'm sure Andrew would be able to prove that you did if he felt he needed to. He means to have Prêt a Party, Lucy, and he wants it without Carring being involved in it. Andrew will get what he wants. He always does.'

She was beginning to feel sick again, and she knew she couldn't bear another minute of Nick's company. He made her feel so vulnerable and afraid. But she must not let him, she told herself.

Where was Lucy? Marcus left the coffee shop and went to look for her.

It was easy for him to pick her out from amongst the other travellers—and easy, too, for him to recognise the man standing so close to her, obviously engaged in a very intimate conversation with her.

Nick Blayne. What the hell...?

He could feel the anger sheeting though him. Lucy was his now. Marcus started to move towards them, but at that moment Lucy put down the books she was holding and started to walk away from Nick, heading for the coffee shop. When Marcus looked away from her, to where Nick Blayne had been, the other man had disappeared.

He caught up with Lucy just as she reached the coffee shop. She looked shocked and very distressed.

'What's happened?' he demanded tersely. So tersely that Lucy almost shrank from him. 'You look as though you've seen a ghost.'

Or an ex-husband.

'I'm just hot and tired, that's all.' Lucy could barely think straight, never mind speak, because of her own panic and fear. Nick knew Andrew Walker. Nick had told Andrew Walker about her and Prêt a Party. Nick and Andrew Walker were responsible for those photographs, that video. Andrew Walker had wanted to stop Marcus marrying her because he wanted Prêt a Party.

She hadn't said a word about seeing Blayne. Had he told her that he was free again? Was she wishing that she were too? Had they made arrangements to meet up some-where—in London, for instance? They had certainly had time.

'That's our flight they've just called,' Marcus announced.

'Marcus...' Lucy desperately wanted to tell him what had happened, to appeal to him for help.

'Yes.'

She bit her lip. 'Nothing.' How could she involve him? How could she tell him what a fool she had been? How could she tell him about the seedy and immoral nature of what she had so nearly become involved in? And what if, because of her foolishness, those dark forces and every-thing that went with them should seep into their own lives? Into Marcus's business life? Marcus was a man of honour and probity—Marcus was the total opposite of the Andrew Walkers of this world.

She felt sick and shaky, and so very, very afraid.

'Lucy. What a naughty girl you've been, not returning my calls.'

Lucy tried to stand up, but Andrew Walker had placed a hard hand on her shoulder, pushing her back into her chair. How had he got into the office? She had locked the door. She always locked the door when she had to be here now.

He waved a key under her nose, as though he had guessed what she was thinking.

'How fortunate that Nick remembered he had a spare

key to the office here. He's back in London, by the way. Has he been in touch with you yet?'

Lucy didn't speak. She didn't trust herself to do so.

'Nick very much wants to see you,' he continued. 'In fact he has told me in confidence how much he regrets the break-up of your marriage. I must say that it is a pity he is no longer involved in Prêt a Party.'

He released her shoulder and pulled up a chair, straddling it to sit in front of her, blocking her pathway to the door—which she suspected he had probably locked anyway.

'Now, about Prêt a Party, Lucy.'

'I'm closing Prêt a Party down,' Lucy told him immediately. All she had been able to think about since their return from honeymoon had been how to solve the problem she had unwittingly brought on herself. In the end she had decided that the best way was simply to make sure that Prêt a Party no longer existed. 'You'll have to look for something else.'

'Oh, no. I'm afraid we can't allow you to do that. You see, Prêt a Party is just so perfect for our needs. It really was very foolish of Nick to give up his involvement in it, and of course he knows that himself now. Indeed, it strikes me that he may very well have a claim on re-establishing his role in Prêt a Party—after all, there was never any formal cessation of the contract between you, was there?'

'Nick left me.'

'A mistake he now regrets,' Andrew Walker told her smoothly.

'I won't be dragged into what you're doing, and I shall—'

He was shaking his head.

'Lucy, I don't think you properly understand. We want Prêt a Party, and we want you as well. After all, without

you it isn't very much use to us, you know. It's your name
that makes it what it is.'

'No. I won't agree—and you can't make me.'

'Oh, dear. I'm afraid I am going to have to disillusion
you there. We very much *can* make you. How do you feel
about your husband, Lucy? Do you love him? You
wouldn't want to see him hurt, would you? And he could
be hurt—very badly hurt, too—if you don't do what we
want.'

'You're just saying that,' Lucy protested. 'You're just
trying to frighten me and threaten me—'

'Where is Marcus at the moment, Lucy? Do you know?'

Stubbornly she refused to answer him. Andrew Walker
sighed gently.

'He's in Leeds, isn't he? Why don't you telephone him?
You know his mobile number, don't you?'

'He's gone to see a client,' Lucy told him stiffly. 'I don't
want to disturb him.'

'He may have gone to Leeds to see a client, but unfortunately he didn't make the appointment. He's had a
small...accident, you see.'

He saw her expression and laughed.

'I'm going to be very generous to you, Lucy. I'm going
now, and I'm going to give you twenty-four hours to think
things over. You're a sensible woman, and I'm sure you're
going to realise very quickly that it's in your own interests
to accept what we're offering you. See you tomorrow—
same place, same time.'

Andrew Walker had gone, leaving only the smell of his
aftershave behind to mingle with the scent of her own fear.

CHAPTER TEN

LUCY felt sick. She was struggling to breathe properly. Her fingers trembled so much as she reached for the telephone to ring Marcus that it took her several attempts to do so.

When the call rang out unanswered she panicked, and then tried to reassure herself that he had simply put his calls on divert. But then, shockingly, she heard a strange male voice demanding, 'Who is it?'

Automatically she checked the number she had dialled, just in case it was wrong. It wasn't.

'I want to speak to Marcus—my husband.'

'Ai want to speak to Marcus—mai 'usband.' The man mimicked her cruelly. 'Well, there ain't no Marcus 'ere.'

'But you've got his mobile! How—? Where—?'

To her dismay the line went dead—and remained dead even though she tried over and over again to get her call answered.

Marcus's mobile had obviously been stolen—but that didn't mean anything had happened to Marcus himself, she tried to reassure herself. Mobile phones went missing all the time.

Even so... Frantically she rang the bank and asked to be put through to Marcus's PA, demanding to know who exactly Marcus had been going to see and how she could get in touch with her husband.

'Have you tried his mobile?' Jerome asked her.

'Yes, but...but a stranger answered. Jerome, I think it may have been stolen, and I'm worried about Marcus.'

'Calm down.' He immediately soothed her. 'I'm sure

there's a perfectly reasonable explanation. I'll get in touch with the client and then I'll ring you back.'

Five minutes crawled by, agonisingly slowly, and then another five. And then Lucy couldn't bear to wait any more.

This time she dialled Jerome's number direct, only to find that his line was busy. Because he was trying to get in touch with her? Immediately Lucy hung up, and curled herself into a small tight ball of anguished fear. If anything had happened to Marcus then it was her fault. Because of her and Prêt a Party...because of her marriage to Nick...

Her telephone started to ring. She stared at it for several seconds, almost too afraid to answer it, then frantically reached for the receiver, clutching it when she heard Jerome's voice saying sharply, 'Lucy?'

'Yes, it's me. Have you spoken to Marcus?'

'Yes...'

There was a note in his voice that immediately set alarm bells ringing in her head.

'What is it? Where is he?' she demanded fiercely.

'There's been a bit of an incident, but he's all right, Lucy—'

'What do you mean? What kind of incident? Jerome, where is he?'

'Leeds General Hospital.'

'*What*? Why? What's happened to him? I'm going to see him. I—'

'Lucy, calm down. Marcus is fine. He told me to tell you that he'll be home tomorrow, as planned.'

'I want to speak to him! I want to see him...'

She could hear Jerome exhaling.

'I'm afraid that you can't, Lucy. Not right now. Marcus is in Casualty—no, it's all right, there's nothing seriously wrong with him—just a few bruises and scratches.

Although from the sound of it, it could have been much worse if the crew of a cruising police car hadn't spotted what was happening and scared off the young thugs who had set about him. However, the medics want to check him over—just to be on the safe side.'

'Jerome, please... I want to know *now* exactly what happened,' Lucy demanded, as she fought back the fear his words had caused her and tried to think and speak coherently.

'Marcus was mugged by a group of youths—Eastern Europeans, he thinks. According to the police they might be illegal immigrants, but since they weren't able to apprehend any of them they can't confirm that. They were obviously after his wallet and his mobile—both of which they took, along with his watch. And of course Marcus, being Marcus, didn't make it easy for them. Fortunately the police arrived before things got too out of hand. Marcus said explicitly that I was to tell you not to worry and that he will ring you as soon as he can. Like I said, he's in Casualty at the moment, being patched up.'

'I'm going to Leeds right now to see him,' Lucy told the PA.

'No, Lucy,' Jerome said firmly. 'Marcus anticipated that you would say that, and he told me to tell you there's no need. He'll be back tomorrow evening, as planned.'

Please let this not be happening, Lucy prayed after she had replaced the telephone receiver. Please let it all be only a horrible nightmare that isn't really happening at all.

But it was happening—and it was happening because of her. Marcus had been attacked and robbed simply because he was married to her.

She was too distraught to cry, too filled with fear for Marcus to do anything other than stay where she was, unable to so much as move, as she focused on waiting to hear his voice.

Not even the familiar dull ache that told her she had again not conceived his child could break through that anxiety.

The seconds and then the minutes ticked by—half an hour—an hour—an hour and a quarter—and then the phone rang.

Lucy snatched up the receiver. 'Marcus?'

'Yes, it's me.'

The relief of hearing his voice totally overwhelmed her. She was shaking so much with reaction she could hardly speak.

'What happened? Are you all right? I want to come to Leeds.'

'I was mugged, I'm fine, and there's no point in you coming to Leeds. I'll be back tomorrow evening.'

'Where are you? The hospital?'

'I'm in a taxi on the way to see my client. The hospital have given me a clean bill of health, and apart from a bit of bruising I'm okay. Stop worrying, Lucy. Things like this happen all the time, so let's not make an unnecessary drama out of it, shall we?'

She could hear the impatience in his voice. She tried to breathe deeply, and gulped in air on a shuddering intake of breath that almost choked her.

'Look, I've got to go,' she could hear Marcus saying. 'I'm using a temporary pay-as-you-go mobile—all I've had time to get. I'll ring you tonight.'

'Promise me that you really are all right,' Lucy demanded emotionally.

'I really am all right,' Marcus assured her calmly.

* * *

This time it wasn't shock with which she reacted to Andrew Walker's appearance in her office, but instead a blend of sick despair and exhaustion.

She had been awake all night, worrying and thinking, and it showed in Lucy's face as she turned to face her tormentor.

'I do hope you've given some serious thought to what I said to you yesterday, Lucy,' he told her smoothly. 'But just in case you didn't take me seriously, I've brought along a few photographs for you to look at.'

Lucy flinched as he leaned over her and laid them out neatly on her desk. They were slightly out of focus, as though they had been taken in a hurry and not by an expert, but they were still plain enough to send a shock of sick recoil hammering through her body.

Marcus being punched and then kicked as he lay on the ground surrounded by his four assailants.

Lucy only just managed not to cry out as she saw from one photograph a boot being aimed at his face, and then in another the murderous gleam of sunlight on a sharp knife.

'This time Marcus was lucky. The police arrived in time to stop him from suffering anything more than a few cuts and bruises. Next time he won't be so lucky, Lucy. And there will be a next time.'

Very deliberately he reached into his pocket and withdrew a mobile phone—Marcus's phone, Lucy realised, as a sick, sweating trembling took hold of her.

'This time all I asked for was his telephone as proof that my orders had been carried out, but next time—'

'Stop it,' Lucy implored him. 'You can't get away with this. The police will catch the men responsible...'

Andrew Walker laughed.

'No way. Those gutter vermin know exactly how to

slink away into their sewers, and they know what will happen to them if they dare to betray me. One word to the authorities and they'll be deported—if they live that long.'

Lucy shuddered. She couldn't doubt any more that his threats were real—and enforceable. She had to do something to protect Marcus, and she knew there was only one thing she could do. Tears filled her eyes. The only thing she could do was the one thing she most wanted not to have to. But she had no choice. Marcus's safety was more important to her than her own happiness.

'It's up to you, Lucy,' Andrew Walker was telling her, with horrible fake affability. 'A partnership with you and Prêt a Party and Carring remains perfectly safe...'

Lucy managed a small uncaring shrug. She had gone over and over this so many times last night. She knew exactly what she had to do to save Marcus. She could save Marcus—but she couldn't save her marriage as well. Hot tears burned her throat raw, but she refused to think about her own despair.

'You can't blackmail me through Marcus,' she told him dismissively. 'I don't want him hurt, naturally, but frankly I wish I'd never married him. I knew it was a mistake the moment I saw Nick again.'

Well, that much was true. But not in the way she was implying to Andrew Walker.

The reason she had known her marriage to Marcus was a mistake was because Nick had revealed to her the danger she had put Marcus in—and Andrew Walker was underlining that right now.

She could see Andrew Walker was frowning, and sensed that he did not believe her. Panic twisted her insides. Very well, then, she would just have to make sure that she convinced him.

'I realised when I saw Nick at the airport that it was

him I loved,' she lied. 'I've told Marcus that, and I've told
him I want a separation.'

Andrew Walker still wore a frown.

'Well, this is a surprise. And one that I am sure will
delight Nick...if it is true.'

'It is true. But I doubt that it will delight Nick. Why
should it? He doesn't love me,' Lucy told him.

That much was true. Nick wasn't capable of loving anyone other than himself.

'Nonsense. He adores you.'

'I don't want to talk about Nick,' Lucy told him. 'Ultimately, of course, I shall divorce Marcus, but in the
meantime I shall probably leave the country and go and
live somewhere else.'

'Isn't that all very hasty and unnecessary?' Andrew
Walker cautioned her. 'I must admit that you have surprised me—if you're telling me the truth.'

'Why should I lie?' Lucy challenged him, hoping it
wasn't as obvious to him as it was to her. 'I don't love
Marcus. I don't want him hurt, particularly, but I don't
want to be involved in what you're planning for Prêt a
Party—and nothing you do to Marcus will change that,'
she told Andrew Walker shakily. 'Because I won't be.'

'Why don't you wait until you've spoken to Nick before
you come to a decision about that, Lucy?'

Andrew Walker was smiling almost paternally at her
now.

Speak to Nick? She'd rather die! Maybe she would even
die... But Andrew Walker had already told her that they
needed her name for Prêt a Party, which meant they needed
her alive. But not Marcus. They didn't need Marcus to be
alive. Marcus...

*   *   *

'McVicar rang me this afternoon, whilst I was on my way back from Leeds. He told me that you've been in touch with him to ask if Blayne could still be considered an employee in Prêt a Party since he did not sign a termination agreement,' Marcus announced coolly.

Were you hoping that he was still involved, Lucy? When I saw you with him at the airport, was that a chance meeting or a planned one? Do you want him as a partner in your bed? Instead of me?

No, that was nonsense. Okay, so after the fuss she had made over the telephone he was surprised that Lucy was behaving so distantly to him now that he was home, but he wasn't really going to let himself think he was actually disappointed by her lack of reaction to his return, was he? And he certainly wasn't going to allow himself to think that her coolness towards him hurt.

Coffee spilled from the mug Lucy was holding onto the new limestone kitchen floor. Her heart was jerking in uncomfortable, uncoordinated, irregular beats that were making her feel nauseous.

'I simply wanted to know what the situation was,' she defended herself.

'Why didn't you ask me?'

'You're my husband, not my solicitor.' She couldn't bear the sight of the bruises on Marcus's face, and was terrified of breaking down in front of him and telling him what was going on.

Mr McVicar had assured her that there was no way Nick could claim to have any ongoing involvement in Prêt a Party, but she still felt desperately afraid and worried. For herself, but most of all for Marcus.

'Has it been decided what we're doing for Christmas yet?' he asked, deliberately changing the subject.

'I spoke to my mother yesterday morning. She's spoken

to your mother, and to Beatrice, and Beatrice has suggested that we all get together.'

'Where—not in this wretched castle she wants to hire for George's birthday, I trust?'

When once she would have laughed, now Lucy could only manage the paltriest of wan smiles, Marcus noticed bitterly.

Why? Because secretly she was thinking she wanted to spend her Christmas with Blayne? The pain that thought caused him was almost beyond bearing. Where had it come from and what did it mean?

She still hadn't said a word to him about seeing Blayne, and Marcus wondered how much contact there had been between them since then.

'No.' Lucy gave him a rueful look. 'Mother is talking about us all going to Framlingdene and staying there.'

Framlingdene was the National Trust Property that had originally been the country seat of Lucy's father's family. The family had retained the right to use a suite of rooms there.

'Will there be enough room for all of us?'

'No, not really. I think it would be better if we simply stayed here in London. We normally have a big family party at Great-Aunt Alice's on Boxing Day, since she's got the space, and I imagine we could all have dinner there quite easily.'

'Well, it certainly makes more sense than driving up to Yorkshire. Lucy—is something wrong?'

His question shocked and surprised Marcus almost as much as it obviously did Lucy. Since when had he wanted to talk about emotions?

Lucy's colour came and went whilst she struggled between truth and fear—and love.

In the end, love won out.

'No, of course not. Why should there be?'

'No particular reason—other than that you don't exactly look like a glowing newly married,' Marcus heard himself saying curtly.

'Glowing newly marrieds are normally glowing because they are in love with one another,' Lucy told him lightly. 'And we aren't.'

She would have to tell him soon that she wanted to end their marriage. Soon, but not yet. Please, just let her have a little more time with him. One birthday, one Christmas...she would tell him before the New Year, she promised herself.

Lucy hesitated outside the jeweller's. It was Marcus's birthday today, and tonight they were going out for dinner with his family. She had already bought him a new silk tie, and she certainly couldn't afford to buy him one of the expensive watches displayed in the window in front her.

Besides, he would replace his stolen Rolex himself in due course. It had been insured.

Even so... There was a discreet sign in the window saying that they also sold good quality 'previous owner' watches.

She could always go in and enquire.

Half an hour later she was back on the pavement outside the shop, huddling into her coat to protect herself from the icy blast of the wind, the Rolex watch on which she had just spent virtually every penny she had in her bank account safely tucked in her handbag.

It was exactly the same model as the watch Marcus had had stolen, and she was thrilled to be able to give it to him for his birthday. Would he keep it for ever? Even after they were divorced? The pain caught her breath and held her immobile in its grip.

*   *   *

They were going for dinner at the Carlton Towers—mainly because in Marcus's opinion they served the best steak in London.

Marcus arrived home just as Lucy stepped out of the shower. By the time he had reached the bedroom she had wrapped herself in a towel and was seated on their bed, his watch carefully gift wrapped beside her.

'What's this?' he demanded as she handed it to him.

'Your birthday present.'

'I thought I had that this morning.'

'Your tie? Yes, I know. But this is something extra,' Lucy told him huskily.

She was beginning to have an effect on him that wasn't what he had planned, Marcus acknowledged as he sat down beside her and unwrapped his present.

He wasn't sure what he had been expecting. But when he removed the paper and saw the familiar Rolex box he was surprised.

'It isn't new, I'm afraid. I couldn't... But it's just like the one you lost.'

It wasn't—not quite—because the one he had lost had originally belonged to his father. But he didn't tell her that. Instead he put the watch on without a word, and then took hold of her and kissed her fiercely.

It seemed to have been such a long time since he had kissed her like this—even though in reality they had only been back from their honeymoon a fortnight. And if he had not made love to her as passionately since their return then that was very probably down to the fact that she had not encouraged him to do so. Lucy had that brief thought, and then she stopped thinking about anything as he rolled her down onto the bed beneath him and kept on kissing her.

Yearningly Lucy kissed him back. She loved him so very much...

*   *   *

'You two are late. What kept you?' Lucy's mother asked, when Lucy and Marcus hurried into the restaurant of the Carlton Towers hotel.

Automatically Lucy looked at Marcus. Thank goodness it was too dark in here for anyone else to notice the look Marcus was giving her.

'Marcus, you've got your watch back,' Beatrice announced halfway through dinner.

'Actually, no. Lucy gave me this for my birthday.'

Again he looked at her, and this time Lucy suspected that Beatrice *had* seen the gleam in his eyes, and had guessed exactly what the giving of the gift had led to, because she suddenly grinned and said quietly to Lucy, 'Aha—*now* I think I know why we weren't the last to arrive for once. I thought it was unlike my normally prompt brother to be late.'

It was gone midnight when they finally got home.

'Only another three weeks to Christmas,' Lucy said sleepily.

'Mmm. Early in the New Year would be a good time for us to start looking for that country house we've been thinking about, I suspect.'

Lucy's heart missed a beat. Early in the New Year their marriage would be as good as over, thanks to Nick and Andrew Walker.

'What's wrong?' Marcus asked her sharply.

'Nothing. What makes you think there is?'

'Oh, I don't know. Maybe the fact that the emotional temperature has just dropped by ten degrees might have something to do with it,' Marcus responded, his voice every bit as cool. 'Something's on your mind, Lucy.'

'Nothing is on my mind. I'm just tired, that's all,' she lied.

'I want to get this business of Prêt a Party's debts sorted out before the New Year,' Marcus announced. 'I think we should go and see McVicar together and—'

'No!'

'Why not?'

'I've already told you. Prêt a Party is my business and I want to keep it that way. And—and I don't want to be bullied into doing something I don't want to do!'

Marcus didn't say a word. He didn't need to. The look he gave her said it all.

Lucy wanted to plead with him to understand, but how could she do that? Dorland had not been joking when he had said to her that Andrew Walker was a bad man. People's happiness, people's lives meant nothing to him, or to those he worked for; she knew that. Ending her marriage to Marcus was the only way she had of protecting him. It was like...it was like performing an amputation to save a person's life, she told herself. But whilst Marcus would survive that amputation, and probably go on to make a perfectly happy life for himself without her in it, she knew that losing him would leave her bereft for the rest of her life.

Only a week now and it would be Christmas. All the Knightsbridge shops and of course the big stores—Harrods and Harvey Nicks—had been flaunting their Christmas finery for weeks. Lucy had done all her shopping—her cards were posted, and her presents wrapped. Mrs Crabtree had taken some extra holiday so that she could spend more time with her daughter and her grandchildren, and Lucy had been enjoying showing off her domesticity to Marcus via her cooking—even if he had turned the tables on her by cooking for her last night.

He hadn't mentioned Prêt a Party again, but there was a tension between them that hurt her—though at the same time she was clinging to every second of the time she had with him.

At least he was still making love to her—every night, in fact—with skill and passion and determination. But not, of course, with love.

The doorbell rang as she was on her way through the hall. Automatically she went to answer it, and then froze as she saw Nick standing on the steps.

She tried to close the door, but Nick pushed it open and stepped into the hall, telling her sullenly, 'What are you doing? I thought you'd be pleased to see me. Andrew said you would be when he told me to come round.'

Andrew Walker had sent him here? Why was she not surprised?

'Nick, you shouldn't have come here,' she protested. 'If Marcus saw you...'

'He isn't here, is he?'

'No, he's at work. But if he were here—'

'But he isn't,' Nick cut her off. His earlier sullenness had been replaced by the slick, facile falsity of what Nick considered to be charm and what she knew to be a shallow pretence of it.

'You know, Lucy, Andrew's right—we did rush into divorcing without giving our marriage a proper chance. I admit that I was a bit thoughtless, and selfish...'

Had Andrew Walker made him repeat those words until he had them off pat? Lucy wondered cynically. They certainly didn't ring true, and neither did they accord with the look of patronising conceit she could see in Nick's eyes as he looked at her.

'I'm not surprised you regret marrying Carring. I suppose when you compare him to me, you're bound to find him wanting—especially in bed.' He smirked. 'Bed is my speciality, after all—remember?'

Lucy longed to tell him that all she remembered of his so-called speciality was how barren and empty it had been, in every single way, but of course she could not do so.

'You were my first lover,' she told him quietly instead.

'Yeah, and I guess you took it for granted that all men would be as good as me—right? Silly little Lucy.' He shook his head mock-playfully. 'But never mind. Pretty soon you and I can start making up for lost time. In fact...' He looked towards the stairs. 'Why don't we start right now, eh? Why don't I take you upstairs and give you a very special Christmas present?'

Lucy wanted to scream at him to leave before she was physically sick. But if she caused him to think that she loved Marcus then she would be putting Marcus in very great danger—and giving Andrew Walker something to blackmail her with.

'Not here,' she demurred, trying to look regretful. 'Perhaps if I came to you...' *Never in a thousand years.*

'Came to me? How about I make you come *for* me, Lucy? And it wouldn't take long, would it? I can see in your eyes how much you want me. Come on...'

Nick was reaching for her hand and pulling her towards him. She could smell the too-strong scent of his cologne, overpoweringly unpleasant after the familiarly of Marcus's cool freshness.

'Nick—no! I was just on my way out...to meet my mother,' she fibbed.

'Andrew told me to give you a message from him,' he told her, abruptly releasing her. 'You told him that you planned to leave Carring, but you're still living here with him.'

'I can't just walk out,' Lucy protested.

'No...' Nick gave a speculative look around the hallway. 'I dare say you want to make sure you get a nice fat slice of his millions before you leave, and I don't blame you for that.'

'Yes. That's...that's exactly what I'm planning to do,' Lucy agreed untruthfully. 'And I can't meet up with Andrew at the moment, Nick. Marcus might get suspicious. In fact he's already suspicious because I won't let him become a partner in Prêt a Party.'

'Well, Andrew's getting very impatient—and so are the men he represents. Andrew said to tell you that if you don't get rid of Marcus voluntarily, then he's going to have to make arrangements to do it for you. Oh, and he said to tell you not to even think about telling Carring what's happening, because that will be as good as signing his death warrant.'

Lucy had no idea how long it was since Nick had left. And she didn't know either that her body was cramped and stiff from sitting on the stairs, her arms locked tightly around her knees as though she were trying to stanch a wound that would not stop bleeding. She did know—vaguely— that it must have gone dark outside, because the hallway was in darkness.

Dissociated thoughts and images jumbled together inside her head. The first night she and Marcus had been to bed together; the fact that this weekend they had planned to go and look for a Christmas tree—Lucy wanted a real one and, although he had grimaced, Marcus had given in and promised to take her out to get one. The espresso machine he had bought her—the thrill it had given her the first time she had woken up beside him here in this house, as his wife; the pleasure it gave her just to look at him and watch him and the pain it gave her too, as she stored every second of time she had with him with the greed that only the deprived and starving knew.

Soon now all that would be over. It had to be. Otherwise...

CHAPTER ELEVEN

'WHAT!'

'You heard me, Marcus,' Lucy repeated shakily. 'I want a divorce.'

She could see how shocked he was, how unbelieving and how white-faced with anger, even in the soft lighting of their bedroom.

'We've only been married a month.'

He couldn't believe the intensity of the pain ripping him apart.

'I know. I've counted every day of it. Every hour,' Lucy told him truthfully. 'It isn't working, Marcus. And I won't—I can't—stay in a marriage that doesn't make me happy. I'll find somewhere to live, and then we can start divorce proceedings...'

'No!'

Lucy looked up at him.

'I warned you when we married that I was making a lifetime commitment to you, Lucy, and that I expected the same commitment back from you. There won't be any divorce,' Marcus told her furiously.

He wasn't going to let her go. Not ever. She was his and he loved her.

He *loved* her? He loved Lucy?

But that wasn't possible. He had sworn years ago that he was not going to allow himself to fall in love. It was as though there was a vulnerable fault inside him, similar to those responsible for causing earthquakes, and his emotions—those emotions he had buried and denied and stubbornly refused to acknowledge could exist—were causing so much pressure within him that they simply could not be controlled.

Pain, grief, jealousy, and a determination never to let her go exploded inside him with a subterranean force that sent a mighty surge of love and need roaring through him, crashing through every barrier he had erected against them.

He loved Lucy!

His passionate refusal caused Lucy to waver between wild hope and joy—and the stark, horrifying reality of what his refusal meant. She hadn't expected this kind of reaction from him. She had expected him to tell her to pack her things and leave straight away.

'All right, don't divorce me, then,' she told him, making herself scowl and shrug, and keeping her voice cold and sharp. 'But you can't stop me leaving you, Marcus, and that is exactly what I intend to do. So far as I am concerned, our marriage is over.'

Marcus struggled to suppress an unfamiliar desire to break something—because something inside him was breaking. His heart?

He had known ever since they had come back from honeymoon that Lucy wasn't happy, and he had believed he knew why. But he had not known then what his own feelings were. He did now! Why should he let Blayne take her from him and ruin her life a second time? She was so much better off with him—even if she was too besotted with her ex-husband to see that herself. One day she would thank him for what he was doing; one day she would come to realise, as he saw with such blinding clarity himself now, that they were meant for one another. He wanted to reason with her, to plead with her, but the unfamiliarity of dealing with such intense emotions was too much for him. He could feel jealousy, burning too high and too hot. It burst out of him in a slew of bitter, angry words as he warned her savagely:

'Don't think I don't know what all this is about, Lucy. Because I do. I know exactly what's been going on behind my back.'

Marcus knew? Her heart was hammering. He couldn't, could he?

'It's Blayne, isn't it?'

He heard her give a small, betraying gasp of shocked admission.

'I saw you with him at the airport.'

Marcus had seen that? And he thought...

'That was a coincidence!'

What else could she say? Lucy wondered, as she struggled to grasp what Marcus was saying to her. Initially she had thought he meant he knew about Prêt a Party and Andrew Walker, but now she realised that Marcus thought she wanted to end their marriage because she was still in love with Nick. And wasn't it better that he should continue to think that, rather than have him become suspicious and start to ask questions she could not answer?

'A very unhappy coincidence—as I believe your common sense would tell you if only you would let it,' Marcus was continuing bitterly. 'Surely you can't have forgotten what he did to you?'

'It's different now,' Lucy told him. How true that was. 'He's changed.' And how untrue that.

'He's changed? But have you, Lucy? Are you sure you really know what you want? After all, in my bed you wanted me...'

'No!'

Yes. Yes...

'I thought I did, but I didn't. Not really.'

Yes, really—now and for ever. Only you and always you,

Marcus. This is killing me, and I can't bear it. I love you so much.

'You're lying, and what's more I intend to prove it to you.'

Marcus could hardly believe what he was saying and doing. He was a man out of control, driven mad by love.

He had reached for Lucy before she could stop him, dragging her against his body whilst his mouth took and then savaged hers in a kiss of furious male anger.

Downstairs, the Christmas tree they had bought at the weekend, and which Lucy had spent all day yesterday dressing, shimmered in the window, its lights twinkling softly with promise and hope. Upstairs, in the bedroom above it, there was no promise and no hope. Only a man and a woman locked together in an embrace devoid of both, and the savagery of Marcus's anger.

Lucy felt Marcus's hands tugging at her clothes whilst she stood motionless and numb with despair.

She heard the sound of fabric tearing as he wrenched a button from its fastening, saw the dark burn of colour staining his skin as his hands gripped the soft flesh of her bare arms.

'Have you been to bed with him since we've been married, Lucy? *Have you?*'

Please, God, let her say no.

'No.' *At least there she could be honest.*

'Not yet? But you intend to? Is that it?' Why was he torturing himself like this?

Not ever. Never. Ever again. Not with anyone if it can't be with you, my dearest, only love. 'Nick...'

'Stop it. I don't want to hear his name,' Marcus told her thickly, crushing his mouth over hers to silence the words he did not want to hear in the only way he could.

Lucy trembled—not with cold, and not with fear either,

she recognised. Even though it would have been very easy to be afraid of Marcus in this mood.

But how could she fear what she longed for so much? How could she fear what she craved so desperately? One last time. One last memory. One last sip from the chalice of bittersweet desire.

She could feel the edge of the bed behind her, she could feel, too, Marcus pushing her down against it, his removal of her remaining clothes and his own almost brutally efficient.

'I can make you want me, Lucy,' he warned her. 'And I shall do so.'

'No.'

Yes. Yes, Marcus, do it...do it now. Take me now. I want you.

He had never taken her like this before, in an angry passion that burned and seared, but she was still responding to him. Her flesh, her emotions. Her whole self was still welcoming and wanting him, ignoring his dark rage, discarding it like the shell of something sweetly craved, focusing instead on what lay within it, on what she wanted within it, taking her, transforming her, holding her in thrall to it as her body held him in thrall to her, if only for those few precious seconds out of time.

'No!' The raw denial was dragged from his lungs to burst between the sounds of their breathing, the bed moving.

What the hell was he doing? Sweat beaded Marcus's forehead as he fought against the hot tide of his own rage, pushing it back heartbeat by heartbeat, as he superimposed over his savage image of Lucy with Nick Blayne a softer, gentler image of just Lucy herself.

He must not—would not give way to his furious bitter pain.

'Yes!'

She was not going to let him go now. Not when he had brought her so close. Not when, within a heartbeat, she could take the base metal of his anger and, like some fabled alchemist, turn it into the pure gold of shared need and equally shared fulfilment. Lucy clung to him and refused to let him go, holding him with her will and her muscles, mentally and physically, as he tried to withdraw from her, moving with him, against him, on to him, slowly and rhythmically, creating a physical tune that soothed her aching need and stoked the sweet hot fires of his desire as well as her own. In this she would have her way—and she would have him. For now if not for ever, Lucy knew, as she tightened her muscles around him and drew from him the response she needed him to give.

Marcus watched Lucy, broodingly aware of how thin and fragile she looked, her face too fine-drawn and her neck so slender it looked almost too delicate to support the drooping weight of her head.

He had reiterated to her that he would not divorce her, and he had demanded from her too a commitment not to say anything about her desire to end their marriage to any members of their families over Christmas.

'Have you forgotten that there could be a child?' he had demanded harshly

'There won't be,' Lucy had told him. But she wasn't sure if that was true. They had had sex since her last period after all.

Marcus had seen the tears bleeding from her eyes then, and he had seen them there again on Christmas Eve, when they had gone to Midnight Mass with her parents and his mother.

On Christmas Day they had joined Lucy's family for

lunch, and so had his mother, Lucy's great-aunt, and his sister Beatrice and her family. Lucy had barely spoken or eaten, and Marcus had seen the surreptitious looks all the other women had given her, obviously sharing his own knowledge that she was too thin and too sad to be a happily married new bride.

The Christmas presents they had bought one another still lay beneath the tree unopened. He had declared that it was pointless for them to open them, causing Lucy to run out of the room in tears.

He wanted so desperately to keep her with him; to take her by the hand and make her look into the future; to see how happy they could be if only she would accept his love and reject Blayne.

He loved her so damn much.

Did he? Surely if he loved her, really loved her, then happiness, her desires, her tears, should matter more to him than his own?

They did, he insisted stubbornly. That was why...

That was why he was trying to force her to stay with him, was it? That was the measure of his love for her, was it?

Blayne would destroy her. He would hurt her again and again; he was just using her...

And he hadn't hurt her? He hadn't used her? He hadn't almost taken her by force physically and he wasn't now trying to do so emotionally?

Lucy looked at Marcus.

'We ought to leave. You know what Great-Aunt Alice is like.'

They were due to attend her great-aunt's traditional Boxing Day family get-together.

Lucy was wearing a soft velvet dress in a mossy green. It had lace cuffs and she was wearing a little lacy cardigan thing embroidered with pink rosebuds over it, Marcus noticed.

She looked wonderful—and heartbreakingly fragile.

'Lucy?'

He saw the apprehension in her eyes as she looked at him and he hated himself. 'I've been thinking...'

He was going to say that he wanted them to try again, that he wanted their marriage to continue, that she meant so much to him he could not give her up. Bittersweet tears filled Lucy's eyes. If only she could go to him and tell him how much those words meant...

Marcus took a deep breath. He had made up his mind and he wasn't going to falter now. He had to prove his love to himself and to Lucy by putting her needs first, by accepting that she must have free choice.

'You're right. It's pointless allowing our marriage to continue. As soon as we get into the New Year I'll instruct my solicitor to start divorce proceedings...'

Because I love you enough to let you go. Because that's what love is. It's more than a person's own feelings—it's putting the one they love first. And I do love you, my Lucy. So very, very much.

He was going to divorce her!

Lucy's stomach churned and she felt acutely sick.

But this was what she wanted.

No, not what she wanted. This was what she had to have in order to protect him.

'Lucy, you're shivering.'

'I'm cold,' she answered her mother truthfully.

'Cold? But it's lovely and warm in here. Are you all right?'

'I'm fine.'

I'm dying inside and I will never, ever be all right again. Marcus is leaving me—for ever.

'Lucy!' Lucy managed to force a smile as Johnny came swaggering over, bringing a pretty, shy-looking girl with him.

'Meet Tia. Tia—this is my cousin, Lucy. Want some champagne, Lucy?' he offered, showing her the bottle he was holding.

Lucy shuddered sickly. She couldn't even drink coffee any more, she felt so unwell, never mind champagne. And besides, champagne reminded her of that first night she had spent with Marcus.

'Have you heard about Andrew Walker being the mastermind behind some gang trafficking in immigrant workers?' Johnny asked, continuing blithely without waiting for her to reply, 'Apparently the police have been watching him for months, and now they've got the whole gang. They were involved in all sorts of dodgy scams—money laundering, prostitution, extortion. I'd no idea he was involved in that kind of thing. Dessie Arlington told me. His father's a barrister, and he was saying that the likelihood is that he'll probably end up spending the rest of his life in prison, along with the rest of the gang—I say, Lucy? *Lucy!*'

It was Marcus who caught her just before she hit the floor. Marcus too who insisted tersely that nothing was wrong, she just hadn't been feeling very well lately. But Lucy wasn't aware of that because she was still in a dead faint.

When she came round, several seconds later, she was lying on her great-aunt's parquet floor with Marcus crouched down beside her.

'It's all right, Lucy. You fainted, that's all.'

'Marcus, I feel sick,' she managed to whisper to him. 'Please don't leave me.'

An hour later she was tucked up in one of her great-aunt's spare beds, in a large chilly bedroom, while her own mother, Marcus's mother and Beatrice all vied with one another to say excitedly that they had had their suspicions but of course hadn't wanted to say so.

Lucy lay motionless in the cold bed, trying to come to terms with what her great-aunt's doctor, summoned from his house around the corner, had just told her.

A baby. She was having Marcus's baby. Why hadn't she guessed?

'Of course I was just the same,' Lucy heard her mother pronouncing. 'Just the same with both Lucy and Piers. So I had already guessed.'

'Well, I felt sure the moment I saw Lucy at Midnight Mass,' Marcus's mother insisted, not to be outdone. 'She had that unmistakable look about her.'

Lucy closed her eyes and let the tears seep out from under her eyelids. She felt so tired, so shocked...and Johnny's comment about Andrew Walker had—

Andrew Walker!

She struggled to sit up.

'Lucy, dear, do lie down.'

'Where's Marcus?' she demanded.

'Dr Holland said that you were to have a rest and that you must eat a little more.

'A good nourishing soup is what she needs.'

'Chicken broth.'

'Oh, yes. Nanny always used to say that chicken broth cured anything.'

Miserably, Lucy closed her eyes and let sleep claim her. The next time she woke up Marcus was seated beside the bed.

'Oh, Marcus...'

More tears. It must be her hormones. Marcus was holding one of her hands with both of his own.

'Marcus, we're going to have a baby.'

'Yes, I know.'

Still more tears.

'How do you feel about it?' he asked her.

Lucy looked at him.

'I...I'm glad that I'm having your baby. How do *you* feel about it?'

'I feel that I want to take you in my arms and hold you there for ever,' he told her simply. 'I love you.'

'Marcus!' Lucy stared at him in disbelief. Surely she must be imagining she had just heard him say those words?

'You love me?' she said shakily. 'But...'

'Yes, I love you, Lucy. Even if I've been too much of a fool to recognise what was happening to me, never mind admit it. I love you so much. I want to beg you to let me show you how much. I know you'd rather be with Blayne—'

'No! Never!' Lucy interrupted emphatically. 'I still can't believe that you love me, Marcus. I knew you wanted me in bed...' Her face suddenly turned pink. 'Nick might have said that I was sexless and boring because I was a virgin, but you made me feel like a woman, Marcus.'

She looked longingly at him, and then said huskily, 'Oh, Marcus, I don't want to divorce you—and I certainly don't want to be with Nick.' She gave a small shudder. 'It gave me such a shock when I saw him at the airport. I hoped that he hadn't seen me, but then he came over and he said—' She broke off and bit her lip.

'I'm glad it's just you here with me,' she told him. 'I felt so tired when our mothers and Beatrice were here. They all said that they had guessed—but I hadn't. I thought I felt so sick all the time because...'

'Because of Andrew Walker?' Marcus prompted her.

'Oh, Marcus! I haven't told you... I haven't explained...'

'It's all right, Lucy. I know what's been going on. At least, I think I do,' he told her gently. 'I've just been having a long talk with your cousin Johnny, and he told me about how Walker asked him to introduce you to him, and how he wanted to invest in Prêt a Party.'

'Is he really going to go to prison for a long time?'

'A very long time, according to George. It seems that the authorities have known what he's been up to for a while, but they've had to wait to get enough information together to convict him and the other members of the gang.'

'George? What does he know about it? I thought he was a civil servant.'

'He is—he's a mandarin in the Home Office. That's the department responsible for granting work visas and immigration documents,' he added dryly.

Lucy gave him an old-fashioned look.

'I do know that. I'm not dumb. Marcus, I've been so scared. Andrew Walker wanted Prêt a Party so that he could use it to launder money and give work to the illegal immigrants he was bringing into the country. Nick was involved as well...' Lucy shuddered.

'Why didn't you tell me? Was it because you wanted to protect Blayne?'

Lucy shook her head. 'I don't care what happens to Nick,' she told him, bluntly and truthfully. 'I should never have married him, Marcus. I only did because...'

'Because what?'

'Because I loved you so much and you didn't want me, and I was scared that I might do something silly, like burst into your office and beg you to make love to me. I thought that if I had a husband it would make me start behaving like an adult and not like a teenager with a silly crush. And besides, I'd felt such an idiot still being a virgin, because I didn't want to do it with anyone else but you... Marcus?' she whispered shakily. 'You're crying.'

'Lucy, Lucy.' He was holding her tightly, his voice muffled against her hair as he rocked her in his arms.

'Well, you wouldn't have liked me still being a virgin,' she told him practically. 'Nick didn't. And marrying Nick didn't work at all—it just made me want you even more. And when Nick didn't want to have sex with me I was glad.'

'Lucy, why didn't you tell me about Walker?'

'It didn't seem important. Not at first. And then...then it was too late. I didn't realise what he was involved in or what was going to happen until Dorland told me—and even then I just thought that once I'd told Andrew Walker I wasn't interested in a partnership with him... But he wanted Prêt a Party, and he told me that he wasn't going to let anything or anyone stand in his way. Not even you...especially not you.

'He knew about Prêt a Party before Johnny told him, too. Nick had told him. When Nick saw me at the airport when we came back off honeymoon, he told me that Andrew Walker and he had sent that video. Oh, Marcus. I was so frightened.'

'And I saw you with Blayne and I thought...'

'I would have thought the same thing.' Lucy tried to comfort him when she saw how angry with himself he looked.

'I thought you'd decided that you wanted him and not me,' Marcus told her ruefully.

'No. Like I said, I never wanted him.'

'And you married him because of me,' Marcus couldn't stop himself from saying bleakly.

'Yes, I did,' Lucy admitted. 'And that was a dreadful thing for me to do, Marcus, because I was cheating on him just as he went on to cheat on me. I knew I could never love Nick the way I do you when I married him. I met Nick and he seemed to like me and I just thought... But it never worked, and that was my fault. Because I never loved him. I just married him because I didn't want to be a nuisance to you. And then I wanted to protect you from Andrew Walker. He told me that he'd arranged for you to be mugged in Leeds. He said that he would kill you unless I left you and let him have a partnership in Prêt a Party... Oh, don't, Marcus,' Lucy protested as she saw the shine of emotion in his eyes. 'Please don't...'

'Lucy, I'm the one who is supposed to protect you. Not the other way around. Oh, Lucy, Lucy, my sweet little love.'

'Your love?' Lucy repeated wonderingly.

'My love—my one and only and for ever love,' Marcus agreed tenderly. 'And before we go any further just let me tell you one thing. Regardless of anything else—Andrew Walker, Nick Blayne, even our baby—I love you. I know that now. And I know too that I always will love you. Nothing can ever change that, and nothing will ever change that.'

'Oh, Marcus!'

EPILOGUE

One year later.

'So, LET me propose a toast, to my wife, Lucy, Business Woman of the Year, mother of my son—and holder of my heart,' Marcus added in a lower, deeper voice that only Lucy could hear as all around them everyone else raised their glasses and cheered.

'I would never have had the courage to set up a new business if it hadn't been for you, Marcus,' Lucy told him lovingly.

'Don't underestimate yourself, Lucy. You are an extremely talented woman. Junior Prêt a Party proves that.'

'I wonder what Andrew Walker would think if he knew how I'd used his idea,' Lucy said mischievously. 'It had never occurred to me before he suggested it to even think of franchising event hire, and yet really it was so obvious. And with a baby of my own, I could see that there was a real need for women to help one another organising children's parties and christenings, and for passing on not just their expertise but also practical things, like marquees, clothes, party costumes, everything. It just makes so much sense for mothers to gather together and share the cost of everything they need for parties and to plan them together in a group. That way every child within that group gets the party they want and every mother knows she has a team of supporters she can turn to.'

'And all for a very modest annual payment.'

'Well, it was a real brainwave of yours to ask Carly and

Ricardo to get involved, and Julia and Silas. With the charity funding Ricardo and Silas give us, and the young people from Ricardo's orphanages who we help to train as nursery and ancillary workers, we're not just providing parties for children but we're providing education and work as well.'

'Like I said you are a very clever woman,' Marcus repeated.

'I was certainly clever enough to fall in love with you.' Lucy agreed.